Lacking Evidence to the Contrary

A Lowbrow Novel of Questionable Necessity

MARK A. HENRY

This is a work of fiction. All of the characters, organizations and events portrayed in this work are products of the author's imagination or are used fictitiously.

LACKING EVIDENCE TO THE CONTRARY
A LOWBROW NOVEL OF QUESTIONABLE NECESSITY

For more information, please visit
facebook.com/markahenrybooks

To bloviate poorly punctuated nonsense, please tweet
@markahenry

Cover artwork by Maura McGurk

Library of Congress Control Number: 2020910853
Operation Dodecahedron Hardcover ISBN 978-1-7363446-0-6
Operation Dodecahedron Paperback ISBN 978-1-7363446-3-7
Operation Dodecahedron Ebook ISBN 978-0-5787095-4-3

For my girls.

PROLOGUE

HAZIM PROVINCE, ZAZARISTAN
ELEVEN YEARS AGO

War rose and set over Zazaristan like the scorching desert sun that baked its arid plains. At times, it beat down with merciless intensity, killing all that was beautiful and allowing only nature's most twisted, stunted, and ugliest children to thrive. At other times, as it was during Fareek Wazaan's eighth year, war would recede over the horizon, but its energy would never entirely cease to radiate from the land.

To Zazaris, the cycle of war was just a way of life, and the only one most had ever known. Not that Fareek especially liked it, but how many West Virginian coal miners liked mining? How many Amazonian fisherman liked fishing? For that matter, how many Amazonian fish liked the Amazon?

Man and fish alike are born into places and times that simply limit their options.

On this morning, Fareek's options quite literally numbered in the thousands, in that he stood surveying a small mountain of stones which he and his father were using to build a wall, or *"qoomah"* in Zazarish, around their property.

"Bring me one this big," said Fareek's father, holding his thick palms about a foot apart.

Mr. Wazaan was a mason. It made for a steady and decent living since things were constantly being blown up around the country. After every job he completed, Mr. Wazaan would take any leftover bricks or stones home and use them to continue the wall he and Fareek had been working on since Fareek was five. The wall currently measured six feet tall and over 1,200 feet long (the Wazaans did not own all that much property, but Zazaristan's zoning laws are pretty flexible) and because the source material was free and ever-replenished, the construction showed no signs of stopping. The father and son liked to work on the wall together on mornings when Fareek's mother and sister were at the market.

Fareek's job was to select stones and ferry them over to his father, who would fit them into place. He picked over two or three, looking for one the proper size.

"Don't let the rock outsmart you, son!" his father called out, repeating one of his favorite sayings for the thousandth time. *"And if it does, don't worry. I'll smash it with my hammer,"* he said, grinning and tapping his five-pound hammer into his open hand.

"How many stones do you think are in this pile?" Fareek asked as he grabbed one about the size of a football.

"There is no telling," answered his father, who quickly added, *"At least a thousand,"* because Fareek was one of those kids who would insist upon an answer.

Waddling over, cradling the stone, Fareek continued. *"If you started with one stone, and then tried all 999 of the rest to get the two that most perfectly fit together, and then tried each of the 998 to join with the first two perfectly and so on, do you think there is a way for them all to fit without having to break any?"*

Fareek's father took the stone from Fareek, gripping it with one hand as he studied its shape and the shape of the space in the wall before him.

"No," he said, deftly cracking off a chunk of the stone with his hammer and setting it into place on the wall with an audible click.

Fareek took his father's point, which was that in this life nothing was perfect, but with a little effort (and/or hammer smashing) one could make it close enough.

2

The sound of an engine made them both stop and look back toward their house as a pickup truck came into view and bounced over the dusty expanse toward them. Mr. Wazaan set his hammer down and squinted at the approaching vehicle.

Raising a cloud of dust, the pickup came to a halt about fifty feet from where the two were working and a man wearing sunglasses got out of the passenger seat. The driver remained behind the wheel. Two men with rifles sat in the bed.

"Good morning, mason," Sunglasses called out.

"Good morning, sir," Mr. Wazaan responded, making a subtle hand gesture to the man that said, *Wait there, I will come to you.*

"Stay here," he said softly to Fareek and walked over to greet the visitor.

Mr. Wazaan and the man engaged in a conversation beyond Fareek's earshot, which began with the man speaking for a minute or so and pointing to Fareek once or twice before Fareek's father responded, shaking his head. The man then grasped Mr. Wazaan's shoulder and gestured toward his men in the truck, then pointed at Fareek, and then back toward the house.

Once again, Fareek's father shook his head and raised his hands as if asking a question. The man reached into his robe and pulled something out, handing it to Fareek's father. He then spoke to the men in the bed of the truck, who sat up a little straighter and regripped their weapons.

The man once again gestured toward Fareek and said something that made Mr. Wazaan turn and look at his son with an expression Fareek had never seen before.

Fareek's father began walking toward him and Fareek trotted to meet him halfway.

"Fareek, these men want to hire me for a job," his father said as they met. *"It is a big job that will take a few months. I will be working out of the country, so you may not hear from me."* He handed Fareek what the man had given to him, which was a fairly

thick roll of cash. *"Give this to your mother when she returns. I... I have to go now."*

Fareek didn't know what to say. His father had never left home for a job before and these men did not look like construction workers or tradesmen.

"Goodbye, Dad," he finally managed. *"I will look after everything for you and I'll keep working on the wall, too."*

"Thank you, Fareek. I will return as soon as I can. Stay out of trouble."

He gently rested his hand on Fareek's head for a moment. He turned, walked back to the truck and climbed into the bed, wordlessly joining the armed men. The truck rumbled to life, made a three-point turn and drove away as Fareek's father gave a final wave.

Fareek squinted into the rising sun to watch him go. After the truck had disappeared from sight, Fareek turned back to the unfinished wall, his eyes landing on his father's hammer.

A few short years from now…

CHAPTER 1

A man with a pointy beard entered Conference Room A in a windowless building on the southern outskirts of Taboor City, Zazaristan.

"Who would like to hear a joke?" he asked the nine men seated around a rectangular table.

Fareek looked to his left and right. None of his co-workers spoke up or raised a hand. Their pointy-bearded boss Wahiri Shwarma wasn't much of a joker and didn't seem to be in a good mood. The leader of the Militant Islamic Liberation Front rarely was.

Against his better judgement, Fareek said, *"I would."*

"Of course you would, Fareek," Shwarma snapped. *"Maybe if you focused a little less on joking and a little more on jihad, our viewership metrics would be in better shape."*

Fareek worked as MILF's Information Technology Director and his job description mainly entailed creating the organization's internet and social media presence, which meant he shot videos of Shwarma yelling into the camera and posted them on the internet. The viewership metrics were fine, incidentally, but Shwarma subscribed to the Japanese business philosophy of *kaizen*, which called for continuous improvement, as well as an unnamed philosophy of his own invention which called for belittling his employees.

As Shwarma settled into his chair at the head of the table, Fareek leaned to his left and whispered to Samir, *"That was a terrible joke."* Samir bit his lip and put his head down, pretending to make notes.

Shwarma quickly scanned the room for absentees. Seeing none, began the meeting as he always did.

"The budget is tight this month, everyone. Let's keep expenses under control. Now, everyone with security clearance Level K or lower, get out. Wait in the hall." Several MILFers got up and left the room. Shwarma then droned on about cost savings for six or seven minutes, and after fifteen seconds, not one person except Shwarma could give a crap, so why would you be any different?

When the budget report concluded, Shwarma said, *"On to Operations. Level Six and lower, get out. Tell the men in the hallway who are Level Silver and above to come back in."*

When the appropriate personnel were in place, Shwarma turned to Rahim Lotfi, MILF's Operations Director. *"Rahim, how many soldiers did we send forth last week?"*

Rahim referred to the notepad in front of him. *"Two, sir. To Montreal and Hamburg. They should be securing cover employment by now."*

Shwarma said, *"And they are aware that with the exception of the monthly botcoin tributes they make to our cause, they are never to contact us? Or each other?"*

"Yes. They have been well trained, sir," said Rahim. *"I have made it clear that operational protocol is to await orders indefinitely and breaking with these rules could compromise and destroy our entire movement."*

"Good," Shwarma said. *"We wouldn't want a repeat of the Honolulu situation, would we, Rahim?"*

"No sir, we would not," Rahim agreed humbly.

To the entire group assembled around the table, Shwarma said, *"Let us say a prayer of thanks, on your own time, after work, to these brave men who are doing Allah's work. Most of you are unaware of their identities, for your own protection you understand, should you ever be captured. But rest assured I have recently coordinated several damaging attacks with our unsung comrades living among the infidels in the West."*

"Could you tell us about one?" asked Fareek. Several of the other MILF officers looked expectantly at Shwarma.

Shwarma shot Fareek a look.

"If Fareek insists on compromising our security," Shwarma said peevishly, *"I suppose I can offer a few details."* He thought for a few seconds.

There was that one thing he had read about on the internet that morning. Something about an explosion in England. The internet reported that the cause of the explosion was unclear. That was key, of course. On the other hand, there was no loss of human life, nor even injury, which, for Shwarma's purposes, wasn't ideal. But in this life, what is? Wasn't the whole point to build a bridge out of convictions, strong enough to span the gap between what one knows and what one believes?

And so, Shwarma had to once again convince these dusty fools gathered before him that he was actually orchestrating violent worldwide attacks.

Several years ago, when Shwarma was struggling to make it as a young, independent jihadist, he struck upon the idea of streamlining his operation and cutting overhead dramatically by eliminating the costly business of actually planning and executing terror strikes. Simply claiming credit for random acts of misfortune from around the world seemed easier, safer and obviously, far more profitable. The trick was in quickly producing a claim for the "attack" before the gas company or whatever could conclude their investigation and report what actually went wrong. By then the real

8

story just sounded like a cover-up and was always reported as some tiny squib, whereas Shwarma's version of the event was a headline.

Nothing succeeds like success of course, and MILF's well-documented record of successful operations did not escape the notice of the other jihadist groups in and around Zazaristan. Shwarma, again thinking outside the box, offered these groups access to his "network of operatives" as well as certain resources and support personnel. With time, vision and good old-fashioned salesmanship, Amalgamated Jihad International was born.

These days AJI provided accounting, payroll, training, logistical support, advertising and social media services to a network of fourteen "Regional Jihadi Franchises," including Shwarma's flagship operation, MILF. One could say it was all a bit pyramid scheme-y, but Shwarma would accept that as a compliment and point out that those pyramids were fucking hard to build.

And the upkeep! He lowered his voice, indicating that this bit of intel should not leave Conference Room A. *"I assume you have all heard of the recent bombing in England. One of our soldiers, some of you may know him as Agent 75, some others as Agent Polaris, has bravely attacked the Western dogs!"*

The England explosion actually took place at the Ken's Donut Korner in the Brighton Mall. Second Shift Manager Pete Burrough had had long day on the business end of the food court. To make matters worse, his vape pen was dead and his charger had been MIA for a few days. Desperate times and so on, he borrowed a close-enough charger from the lost and found box and jammed its square-ish plug into his pen's round hole.

Mankind will never know what substance may have been in that vape pen, but what can be said for certain is that Burrough forgot all about the unholy pen/charger union as he locked up Ken's Donut Korner for the night and headed home. The electrons and whatnot in the pen's battery then took about forty minutes to decide to explode. Every speck of the pen itself was vaped.

Sizzling bits of heavy metal festively arched across the prep area and into still-warm deep fryers One, Two and Three and that's where things really got started. When the fire marshal arrived, he could see that the cause of the blaze was clear, some sort of kitchen accident. An electrically-ignited grease fire if he had to guess. He only hesitated to immediately identify Ken's Donut Korner by name at the insistent suggestion of Ken's legal counsel, who had also quickly responded to the emergency call.

Shwarma continued, *"Today, the world will learn that MILF has struck this blow against the Western infidels!"*

He couldn't quite remember if MILF had placed an agent in Southern England or not, but luckily Fareek didn't press the issue with more questions. The bigger deal Shwarma made of this England business, the more work it would end up being for Fareek anyway. Fareek didn't want the trouble of all that, but sometimes he couldn't help himself.

The other MILF staffers all exchanged impressed and gratified looks, each assuming that some of the others had a hand in this successful operation, but due to MILF's strict policy of operational compartmentalization, they were unable to discuss it any further.

"Speaking of which," Shwarma went on, *"Rahim, what is the latest news on The Weapon?"* "The Weapon" he referred to, as they all knew, was a suitcase nuclear bomb that MILF had been negotiating to buy from some Chinese underworld figures for going on three months now. So far, MILF had paid a deposit, an "acquisition fee," and a "conveyance charge" and the item in question remained "in transit." More accurately, it remained "a crate of lead weights, various parts from a Superior Nantango (a knock-off Super Nintendo manufactured in 1995) and two sealed glass beakers, one filled with neon yellow NitrousCitrus C4! energy drink and one filled with red FacePunch C4!, both marked with scary-looking radiation warning stickers."

The "Chinese underworld figure" in question, seventeen-year-old Huan Xing, had assembled The Weapon in his parents' garage after watching *Die Hard III* and put it up for sale on the dark web, where it was won at auction by Shwarma, whose bid was enough to put a sweet Calibre de Cartier watch on Xing's wrist. Now Xing had his eye on a Ducati motorcycle and thus needed the agreed upon balance payment from MILF that was due upon delivery. Two weeks ago he had actually packed up The Weapon and shipped it to the Macau offices of DelanoGoss Logistics LLC (motto: "Your business is none of ours"), who in turn shipped it via IHL Central Asia to Zazaristan. Where Xing figured it would sit, like his mother's good tea set and every other nuclear weapon in the world for that matter, waiting for just the right occasion that in all likelihood would never come. And if, by chance, MILF ever discovered The Weapon to be a fake, Xing would be first to point out that the dark web auction made no explicit guarantees of The Weapon's capabilities and in fact noted in small print that the buyer shall accept The Weapon "as is" and that "all sales are final."

"*The Weapon remains in transit,*" answered Rahim. "*However, the Remote Detonation Module arrived this morning along with a message that The Weapon will follow shortly.*"

Rahim produced an aluminum briefcase, placed it flat on the table, and popped it open to reveal a black, handheld numeric keypad with a large round knob and a rubbery, curled wire that plugged into a black box with four extendable antennae. The two components fit snugly into custom foam cutouts. They would have to be custom made, as a vintage ColecoVision controller and a Wi-Fi router are not available for retail sale as a set.

The assembled MILF staffers ooh-ed and aah-ed appropriately and Shwarma beamed with satisfaction, a look that would have cracked up Xing had he been there to see it instead of sitting in 7th period trigonometry class. Sending the "RDM" to MILF to keep them on the hook was a stroke of genius that he reminded himself of every time he looked down at the Cartier on his wrist, although cutting the foam neatly was a pain in the ass.

11

Mark A. Henry

"Excellent, Rahim," Shwarma said. *"Notify me immediately when The Weapon arrives. Samir, tell everyone to come back in."* He had privately started to worry about The Weapon's continual delays but seeing the Remote Detonation Module with his own eyes put his mind at ease. He made a mental note to contact Bashir Hallazallah, the leader of the Jihadist Islamic Zenith group to boast of his new acquisition and to ever so subtly imply that MILF may be willing to part with The Weapon should the right offer come along.

When and if Shwarma could flip The Weapon for profit, he would enact his most daring and ingenious plan to date: clearing out MILF's bank accounts, shaving off his beard, moving to Dubai, buying a mixed-use building, living on the top floor, renting out the middle floors as apartments and opening a fro-yo shop in the commercial space on the ground level. May God will it.

He forced himself to put thoughts of personal mid to long-range financial goals aside for the moment. When the staff was fully assembled again, Shwarma got up from his chair to walk around the table and more closely examine the Remote Detonation Module. It was a most opportune time to fire up the troops and he didn't want to waste it.

"Brothers!" he shouted. *"The time of reckoning for our Western enemies is nearly at hand!"* He caught Fareek's eye and made a subtle gesture with an invisible pen, which Fareek understood to mean, *Write this down, I'm about to get rolling.* Fareek uncapped his pen and flipped his notepad to a fresh page as Shwarma continued.

"God, in his wisdom, has bestowed upon us the power of the... the..."

Atom. The word was atom.

Rahim thought he was going to say "sun," but wasn't entirely confident speaking up and wisely kept his mouth shut. Fareek went ahead and wrote down:

- *Power of atom*

but declined to prompt Shwarma as he enjoyed seeing his boss twist in the wind a bit.

"Army?" said Samir, earning himself a swift slap to the back of the head.

"Universe!" Shwarma bellowed, adroitly turning his slap follow-through into a dramatic flourish. Fareek annotated:

(universe)?

Shwarma was heating up now. *"The sins of the infidel devils will be revisited upon them a thousand times over at the hands of God's righteous warriors, the Militant Islamic Liberation Front! From the ashes of their failed moral wastelands, we shall build a bridge with our beliefs to a new caliphroyo—caliphate! A new caliphate that will span the earth in the name of the one true God!"* With that, Shwarma seized the ColecoVision controller from the case in front of Rahim and thrust it over his head, stretching out the spiral cord and putting a pretty fair strain on the superglue Xing had used to affix the cord into the hole he drilled in the back of the router.

"Go forth, my brothers, and help me usher in the time of MILF!" Shwarma handed the controller back to Rahim. *"Also, whoever cooks fish in the break room microwave, knock it off! New business? No? OK then, meeting adjourned. Fareek, come with me. Levels Blue and Purple, wait three minutes before you are dismissed."*

Shwarma strode from the conference room and a few staffers who had not gotten a close look at the RDM earlier made their way over to inspect it. Fareek had a quick look himself, then gathered up his notebook and followed Shwarma. As he left, he could hear Rahim explaining, *"No, the instructions have not arrived yet. The Chinese felt it was too dangerous to ship the unit and instructions together..."*

Shwarma was waiting for Fareek in the hallway with his hand open. Fareek knew what he wanted and without a word, dropped a USB thumb drive into Shwarma's palm.

At Shwarma's request, every Friday afternoon Fareek moved the week's computer data to a USB drive, which Shwarma then took possession of on Monday afternoon. Shwarma had seen many of his former colleagues go down because of sloppy cyber security, so he was fastidious about keeping incriminating data off the grid as much as possible. Shwarma's grasp of technology was spotty at best and out of necessity, he was forced to give the young, but intelligent and resourceful Fareek what was considered one of MILF's highest security clearance levels (Capricorn). As such, the two of them essentially conducted a private meeting each week following the 3:30 staff meeting.

"What's on this?" Shwarma asked, holding up the drive.

Fareek rattled off, *"Three potential recruits, and videos from Behrouz, Hashimi, Khalil and Razzaq. Hashimi and Khalil both claimed the plane crash in Kuwait, by the way."*

"What?" Shwarma clenched his fist around the USB, then took a deep breath. The headaches of his job never ended. He literally could not make the rules about making claims any simpler. Honestly, these franchisees were like drunken kindergarteners. And was that a tone Fareek used at the end there? Shwarma sometimes wondered if his smart-ass technology officer knew *too* much.

"Is that right?" he said, as casually as he could manage. *"Perhaps they worked together. You haven't uploaded those yet, have you?"*

"I did on Friday, like always," Fareek said.

Shwarma said, *"Download Khalil."*

"What do you mean?"

"Take it down. Un-upload it. You can do that, right?"

"That's not going to help those viewership metrics you mentioned."

Smart-ass. *"Just do as I ask, Fareek. I don't want anyone seeing that video."*

"I can remove it from our site, but it's impossible to be sure it hasn't been copied or forwarded beyond our reach."

"Just do it," Shwarma repeated.

By now, the pair had made their way downstairs to MILF's "studio" where the operation's video production gear and electronic equipment were kept. Fareek's office was a cramped cube built into the corner.

Shwarma went straight to the far corner of the studio, where a small jumble of cardboard boxes had been stacked. He rooted through one and pulled out a cell phone.

"Did you hear?" Shwarma asked Fareek. *"Egypt has a new Minister of Defense."* Shwarma opened the folded flaps of a smaller box and withdrew an envelope full of tiny sim cards. *"Mostafa is out. Jalib Ibrahim is in. I thought I'd give Mr. Ibrahim a call to congratulate him on his new position. Go into your office and close the door, Fareek. I need privacy for this. Take down Khalil's video, then write up my script. Start with the claim for the England operation, then wrap it up with something about The Weapon."*

Fareek put down the tripod he was setting up. As he exited, he silently wondered how Jalib Ibrahim would respond to Shwarma's standard proposal to new government representatives but knew the result would be the same as it always was in the end.

Shwarma had by now managed to mate the phone with a compatible SIM card, creating an untraceable burner. He powered it up and dialed from memory. A Turkish-speaking man answered the call. Shwarma referred to his personal phone's contact list and with the help of a phonetic Zazarish/Turkish chart he had taped to the wall, read off the number for the Egyptian Defense Minister's Office.

Several thousand kilometers away in Cairo, Jalib Ibrahim sat at his new desk, and for the twelfth time in three days, read the handwritten letter that had been left for him by his predecessor:

Dear Minister,

If you are reading this letter, it means one of several things. Actually, that is mere vanity. It can only mean one thing: the time of Mostafa has ended and your time has begun.

I recall the day I first sat in the chair you now occupy and read the letter that my predecessor, Minister Abboud, left me. In truth, it was little more than a photocopy of a squashed and hirsute nether region I could only assume belonged to Abboud. (Don't worry, I had that copy machine replaced years ago.) The message was short on specifics, but I took its meaning to be that all leaders are sometimes forced to follow, and thus the view.

Turning to more practical matters, I have found that it served me well to speak mostly lies into the large phone and mostly truths into the small one.

Egypt forever,

Habib A. Mostafa

The squashed-butt photocopy part made enough sense to Ibrahim, and he was thankful that the generously proportioned Mostafa had opted not to continue that tradition, but he was uncertain about the phone business. There were in fact two phones on his desk, one large and one small. The large one was modern, with multiple lines, dozens of buttons and a small video screen. To Ibrahim's dismay, it rang dozens of times a day and he found on the other end of the line all manner of politicians, defense contractors and military officials. With Mostafa's advice in mind he had refused to give the number to his wife, insisting that she exclusively use his cell phone. The smaller of the desk phones was an old, black rotary dial model. The old phone was unlabeled and unlisted in the Defense Department's directory and it produced no dial tone, so Ibrahim had begun to conclude that it was purely decorative and Mostafa's advice regarding it somehow allegorical. And then it rang.

Ibrahim quickly folded the letter and slipped it under his desk blotter. He hesitated for a moment, then had a thought and picked up the receiver. He spoke the thought aloud. *"This is Jalib Ibrahim, Egyptian Minister of Defense."*

This was Shwarma's favorite and most lucrative side-hustle. In Arabic, he said, *"Asalaam Alakaim, Minister Ibrahim. My name is Mohammad Mohammad. I call to offer happiness on your job and chance for lucky friendship."* Shwarma spoke fluent Zazarish of course, and his English was pretty good, but his Arabic was not great.

"Thank you, Mr. Mohammad. May I ask how you got this phone number?"

Shwarma loved being Mohammad Mohammad, international power broker, deal maker and (why not?) heart breaker. *"Of course, Jalib. Friends do not keep secrets and I am friend of you. Mostafa gave me number. He and I worked together many years. I hope we work many years, too."*

17

Mark A. Henry

Ibrahim kept reflexively looking at the ancient black phone, then at the blank caller ID screen on his large desk phone. It was maddening to not see a number displayed.

"Perhaps, Mr. Mohammad," he said. *"Why don't you first tell me something about yourself and the nature of this relationship you claim to have had with Minister Mostafa."*

"I tell you this. I am speaking to you on a move-around phone which I will break today, later. You is speaking to me with Ericsson Model DBH 1001 circle number phone that is connect with many kilometers of... uh... orange metal wire to electricity box in Cyprus, owned by a friendly Turkeyman who enjoys money."

As Shwarma/Mohammad spoke, Ibrahim lifted the phone and looked at the faded label on the bottom. Ericsson DBH-1001.

Shwarma/Mohammad continued, *"I don't know lots of phone wire science. You don't need lots of phone wire science. Know that old phone/new phone makes special connect and nobody can listen to us. Hooray."*

"Not that I am surprised in the least, you son of a shoe," Ibrahim growled, *"but you're obviously a criminal. You can offer me nothing and I will not be drawn into your crooked ways. Goodbye, Mr. Mohammad."*

"There is terrorists at work in Egypt." Shwarma/Mohammad calmly replied, knowing the young minister would not let that go by. Hearing no click, he went on with his pitch. *"You know MILF? You and me know that MILF is brave and handsome, fighting for God. But Americans? They don't like MILF. They call MILF terrorists, drop booms on MILF, chase MILF everywhere. Maybe into Egypt if they think MILF is there."*

"There is no intelligence to suggest that," Ibrahim said, speaking the truth as instructed.

"There is video," said Shwarma/Mohammad. *"MILF leader giving great speech. Pyramids in background. If Americans see video, you will have many questions to answer, Jalib. Americans*

18

will want to visit. Many, many Americans for long, long time. Ask Afghanistan."

"Where is this video? I want to see it."

"Why? No need for anyone to see it. Trouble only. I call you to offer gift of no more video. I make it go away for you. When video go away, no more MILF in Egypt. Hooray."

Ibrahim was not a stupid man. His time in the service of his government had taught him a thing or two about the kind of agreements this man was offering and like hot dogs or pop music, he knew the process of making them to be horribly repugnant. *"Thank you for the most kind offer, Mr. Mohammad,"* he said. He closed his eyes and took a deep breath. *"May I offer you a small gift in retur—"*

"Twenty botcoins."

Ibrahim scoffed. *"Never."*

"Tell Americans Mohammad Mohammad says hello."

Exhaling, Ibrahim said, *"Ten."*

"Nineteen."

"Eight."

"Fifteen."

"Twelve."

"Thirteen."

"Twelve."

"Thank you, Jalib. Twelve is good good." Shwarma was in fact very pleased with twelve, considering there was no video and never would be unless Ibrahim wouldn't play ball. If that were the case, Shwarma would have made Fareek put a background shot of Cairo up on the studio's green screen and stood in front of it with the camera rolling as he yelled something to the effect of, *"Come and get me, you sons of bitches!"*

Shwarma/Mohammad wrapped up the call by informing Ibrahim which of the Egyptian government's funds Mostafa had found the slushiest in the past, instructed him how to transfer the money and wished him good health. He hung up and removed the burner phone's battery and SIM card. On a hook next to his Turkish translation chart was a ball peen hammer, which Shwarma used to individually smash the phone and card. He then walked over to Fareek's door and opened it up.

"How did it go, Boss?" Fareek asked, looking up from his keyboard.

"I took twenty botcoins from the Egyptians, Fareek. The Minister of Defense bent to my will like a blade of grass. I probably could have gotten thirty."

"Is twenty a lot?" Fareek asked. He knew it was, but he also liked to take the air out of Shwarma when he could.

"Yes, twenty is a lot! With that, you could buy four Chiller King fro-yo machines. The big ones." His giddiness had caused a brief slip and remembering that the fro-yo business was a *secret* plan, he smoothly added, *"Uh, or like, ten rocket launchers."*

While Shwarma was making a "sale" as he called it, Fareek had been busy preparing for Shwarma's video address. The standard AJI contract required them on a semi-monthly schedule.

"I put your speech in the teleprompter, Boss," Fareek said. *"What background do you want?"*

"It seems we will not be 'traveling' to scenic Egypt after all, so let's just go with the black MILF banner. And add that line about bending to our will like a blade of grass in there somewhere. I'll be right back." With that, Shwarma abruptly left the studio and Fareek got back into the teleprompter program. After a short contemplation, he slid the "grass" simile in right after the part about the sins of the infidel dogs. It read back pretty nicely, although there was no telling what would actually end up being said as Shwarma tended to drift from the script fairly often.

Fareek then crossed the room and rolled up the studio's bright green backdrop, exposing a banner draped against the wall that read: *"Militant Islamic Liberation Front"* above the organization's slogan: *"Only God can judge me."*

Shwarma now returned, carrying the case that contained the Remote Detonation Module. *"I want this in the video,"* he said, patting it. *"I'll sit at a table and have it right in front of me."*

Usually Shwarma stood while making his videos, so now Fareek had to grab a plastic-topped folding table and lug it up to the front of the studio. Shwarma put the case down and went to fetch a chair for himself while Fareek popped the case open and swung it around to face the camera.

"No, no," Shwarma said as he shuffled back, carrying a chair. *"Face it AWAY from the camera, so the contents will be unseen by the viewer. Fareek, something I learned very early on in the jihad business is that there is very little Westerners fear more than the unknown. To them, the unknown is far more frightening than anything..."* Arriving at the table, he glanced at the apparatus in the case and read the embossed "COLECO" name on the keypad. *"... the Cole Company could ever devise. So, we will leave the case a mystery and let our enemies only imagine what devastation lies inside."* Shwarma was quite pleased with himself.

"Interesting," Fareek said. In his experience, the unknown was usually not so bad, but Shwarma was the boss, so he spun the case around. He walked back to the small video camera and sighted through it, zooming and tilting a bit. Shwarma sat down and rolled his shoulders as if loosening up for a boxing match while saying *"Grandma bought a chicken, a chicken for Grandma,"* which, when pronounced in Zazarish, is a mouth relaxation technique like saying "Unique New York, red leather yellow leather" in English.

After a few reps, he settled down and stared into the camera.

"Ready?" Fareek asked. Shwarma nodded, seeing the red light above the camera lens blink on.

"Three, two..." Fareek said, then after a beat silently cued him with a finger.

"Brothers! The time of reckoning for our Western enemies is at hand..."

CHAPTER 2

SAN ANSELMO, CALIFORNIA
THURSDAY, 7:40 a.m. PST

In accordance with the rules of society, Chris Dawkins took his place at the back of the line in Starbucks and for pretty much the same reason, reached into his pocket for his phone.

He checked to see if anybody had texted, e-mailed, alerted, liked, mentioned or tagged him since the last time he looked. Algorithm-based ads don't count, so... no.

As he put his phone away, two things caught his eye. The first thing was the vividly yellow photo on the wall menu advertising that Starbucks had partnered with the C4! energy drink company and would, for a slight upcharge, add a "Vita-Boost" shot to any drink order, which was good news since Chris loved C4! energy drink, and he had a slight head cold. The second thing was that the man sitting near the door reading a newspaper was his old high school basketball coach, Frank DiPetro. Had Chris's nose been operating at 100% he probably would have recognized Coach by smell alone when he walked in. DiPetro loved full-court pressure, the word *capisce*, and Gucci Pour Homme.

Chris couldn't decide if seeing DiPetro was good news or bad news. He liked the man just fine and would have been happy to say hello and reminisce about the old days (six years ago), but there was a distinct possibility that he would be met with blank-eyed confusion. Chris wasn't exactly the star of the team and Coach might struggle to come up with Chris's name, embarrassing them both. As a test, Chris stared directly at DiPetro for a few moments. He had once read in one of his mother's Cosmopolitans (he always enjoyed women's magazines for the feeling that he was reading the other team's playbook. That, and the cleavage) that you can sometimes literally feel a person's gaze on you. If Coach indeed felt something and looked up, the eye contact would confirm recognition.

The line advanced one customer. Chris kept staring. Coach turned a page of the *Chronicle*. Chris couldn't quite make out the headline. Something, Middle East, something, something.

As many young ladies before him, Coach took no notice of Chris's efforts. Just as well. Even if DiPetro did remember him, it would probably be in the context of how Chris had missed those two free throws in the closing seconds of the playoff game his senior year. Chris certainly had a clear recollection. The first shot clanking off the front rim, the second boinging off the back.

The line moved up one more spot. "Next!" tweeted the barista. That is to say the tone of her voice evoked a bird's song, not that she actually pulled out her phone and used Twitter to send the word "Next." That would be ridiculous. But the fact that you thought she might have... thanks a lot, internet.

Chris snapped out of his failure-with-a-shot-of-regret daymare and stepped forward.

"What can I get you?" the barista asked in a regular human voice.

"Rooibos tea, with a shot of lemon C4," Chris said.

"Name?"

Coach was across the busy shop, engrossed in his newspaper. Far enough away that it didn't seem to warrant going full undercover.

"Chris."

He flashed his phone in front of the pay scanner, which debited his Starbucks card account and sent a small packet of data to HQ, back in Seattle, noting that young men will in fact pay a little extra for a vitamin shot in their tea.

Chris shuffled forward a few more feet to wait for his drink in the no-person's land between the register and the cream and sugar station at the end of the counter. He was now actively facing away from DiPetro, having firmly decided against a greeting. How would it have gone anyway? First, he would go unremembered. Then he'd remind his old Coach how he failed in the clutch. And THEN DiPetro would change the subject to be polite, leading to, "So Chris, what are you up to these days?"

At this point Chris would be forced to tiptoe a conversational tightrope. Too little information given, especially to a sharp guy like Coach, would lead to more questions and Chris would teeter into a situation where he could totter into offering too MUCH information and that always ended poorly. Chris's goal in situations like these would always be to hit the key phrases, "IT" and "start-up" and then hope for the best, which would be to stop talking as soon as possible and have his interlocuter simply say, "Oh," then walk away.

In truth, Chris did work in "IT" and did in fact, even work for a start-up, if by "start-up" you meant that the company he worked for actually existed and therefore by definition started up at some point.

Chris knew that his work was somewhat lowbrow, hence his reluctance to discuss it. While it was perfectly legal, and paid for his rent, beer, car, food and student loans, it was not exactly the stuff of legacy that a man hopes to leave behind.

Chris was one of twelve "Associate Content Developers" at Sixdub, one of Silicon Valley's most successful companies. Sixdub dealt in website design and hosting, cybersecurity, search engine optimization, software and app development, and of course, both digital logistic solutions and logistic digital solutions.

His specific duties entailed searching the internet for copyright-free video, mostly C-SPAN-like coverage of foreign governmental proceedings. Then, Sixdub's proprietary software analyzed the video, recognized the nine basic shapes the mouth makes, and replaced the original audio with random, computer-generated rap lyrics that are lip-synced to the video and laid down over hip-hop beats created with "ProTunes by Drednott" audio software.

You know, Drednott. The famous rapper.

Ask your kids.

Anyway, you've probably seen the one that begins with the angry Korean city councilman appearing to say, "Push the giraffe, make the flag half-staff," which enrages another councilman, who responds, "My man wants coffee, I'll buy a carafe!" and proceeds to jump over his desk to attack the first guy, eventually taking a swing at him with a woman's shoe that he somehow grabbed during the rapidly-developing melee.

To date, "Model Glue Jinglehut" (so named for the catchy chorus shouted repeatedly by the elderly Korean security guard) has over 344 million views on YouTube, and found a very profitable second life when Sixdub licensed the clip to Australian coffeehouse chain Teanyweeny Beany for use in what turned out to be a wildly popular television ad campaign. As a single, the audio track also charted to number twenty-five on the Asian Billboard Hot 100.

Obviously that all seems very cool, especially if you are a moron (and there are plenty of them out there, at least 344 million), but Chris knew that the real work was done by his computer, and he was a realist when it came to his place in the world. If a guy collects aluminum cans from the side of the road that are eventually recycled into parts used on the space shuttle, that guy could tell people he works in the aerospace industry, but Chris is not one of those guys. He does what he does.

The software that analyzed the lip movements and created the matching lyrics for the videos was invented by Chris's boss, a man named Jasper Wiles. Jasper Wiles became a millionaire at age twenty-two, four months after the launch of the "Parliamentary Rap Battle" YouTube channel. He parlayed that success into the creation of his first company, Wiles Worldwide World Wide Web Works, which later became known as Sixdub. Truth be told, to say that he "invented" the software would be a bit of a stretch. Wiles is what you call an "idea man," and the ideas he tends to have are the most lucrative kind. That is to say, he seems to know what people want before they know that they want it.

The actual software was written by a Ukrainian named Igor Poskovich, who Wiles hired through a freelance programming website to work out the nuts and bolts of the algorithm. The deal they struck was that Wiles would pay Poskovich $5,000 for complete ownership of the software code "in perpetuity throughout the universe," or three percent of any revenue created from its commercial use. Poskovich, a pragmatic sort (there is no such thing as a Ukrainian who isn't), opted for the $5,000 upfront. Later on, after realizing his creation had made Wiles a wealthy man, Poskovich hired his own freelancer (this one Russian) and renegotiated his deal with Wiles by offering to kill him "in perpetuity throughout the universe" unless Wiles paid him a million dollars. Wiles countered with $400,000 cash and a job as a Senior Vice President of Programming at Sixdub, which Poskovich, still a pragmatic sort, accepted.

Together, with Wiles's vision and Poskovich's technical skill, Sixdub went on to create, among other things:

Moodswirl: The app where you press a finger to your phone screen and the touch creates a swirly, uniquely multicolored oval that represents your mood. This "Moodswirl" can then be used as an emoji in a text message. When the message recipient clicks on the emoji, a brief description of the mood is displayed. For example: "Feeling like someone cut me off in traffic without using their turn signal, then gave ME the finger!" The description is created with a combination of gleaned information from the user's

GPS location, recent social media posts, web browsing history, and total BS.

Ucoolbro: The app that perpetually tracks and quantifies how cool you are on a scale of 1 to 100 (to two decimal places), using information mined from the user's media downloads, data usage, social media likes, and total BS. A score of 100 is purely theoretical since users lose eight points for downloading the app itself and six more each time they check it.

4wardever4ward: The app that randomly and periodically deletes all your other apps, forcing you to reevaluate your digital lifestyle in order to become more productive and engaged with life. The app will then e-mail you to suggest other Sixdub apps that will help you do this.

This was all years ago, however, and after his success in the tech world, Wiles went on to write and self publish a book called *Place Directly on Rack*, a first person, hole-by-hole account of a high-stakes golf match he once played against Mario Peppino, heir to the Peppino's Frozen Pizza fortune. The book was widely panned by critics initially, but when Wiles released a second edition, with the new subtitle *My Eighteen-Step Journey to Well-Being, Wealth, Being, and Wealth-Being*, it found a niche as a metaphor-laden business/self-help book. It spent eighty-four weeks on the New York Times bestseller list and there were talks of development to be a major motion picture.

"Rooibos tea, lemon shot for Chris!" a barista announced, putting the drink on the counter.

Chris grabbed the tea, mumbled a quick thanks and made his escape, angling his face away from DiPetro as he slipped out the door. His Starbucks app would duly note that young men who like vitamin shots in their tea do not hang around to buy impulse items or a second round.

Mark A. Henry

* * *

About an hour after Chris had left Starbucks, he was reheating the last of his tea in the Sixdub breakroom when the lankly, be-suited Wiles carved a turn through the specially designed extra-wide doorway. These days Wiles led the life of a modern man of leisure, which meant that he drove his Tesla to the Sixdub offices two or three times a week to drink French press coffee from the break room and cruise the halls on his electric skateboard. He had just finished a new book, a collection of stories about how his wealthy friends came up with the names of their racehorses, and he was half-heartedly shopping it around to various publishers and movie studios. The excitement of cashing enormous checks had faded for Wiles, as it had come to signify the end of an idea, sold off and monetized. The excitement and promise of new ideas however, blazed in his mind's eye like a supernova morning, noon, and night. He was always ready for his next one to hit him.

"Chris!"

Chris looked up from the microwave. He knew Wiles fairly well of course, but he was surprised that Wiles knew his name. Wiles had briefly sat in on the final stage of Chris's job interview, but this was two years, and several million dollars ago, for Wiles.

Taking zero notice of Chris's mute, slack-jawed perplexion, Wiles continued. "What do you think of this? A movie with a plot twist at the end that reveals the entire story to be nothing more than the gameplay of a hyper-realistic video game being played by two guys in a college dorm room. Maybe a basement."

"Great idea, Mr. Wiles," answered Chris. "It sounds kind of like the movie *TechChain*."

"Haven't seen it," said Wiles as he filled a coffee mug. He withdrew a plastic baggie from his jacket and pinched a pill capsule from it. "Vitamin B," he offered in explanation before sending it down the hatch.

28

"It's pretty good. *TechChain*, that is," said Chris, who was suddenly hit with a short coughing fit, followed by a sniffle. Gamely, he croaked out, "James Van Der Beek."

Wiles blinked twice. "You've won this round, Van Der Beek," he said under his breath, deflated at his apparently unoriginal idea. Shaking his head, he pointed his board toward the door. He turned back to Chris.

"Are you feeling alright, by the way? If you're sick you should go home. Get some work done if you can, but your health is more important."

Chris figured that this was Wiles's way of saying, "Get your germs out of my office before you infect me or any of my important employees," so he didn't argue.

"Thanks Mr. Wiles, you're probably right. I'll work from home today."

"Feel better, Chris!" Wiles called over his shoulder as he skated off.

Chris polished off his tea on the drive back to his one-bedroom apartment and upon arriving home, he went straight to the kitchen and grabbed the second-to-last can of C4! drink that was in the fridge. *Should've picked up some more on the way home,* he thought. He carried the drink and his laptop over to the small desk he kept in his bedroom, jotted a note to himself to buy more C4!, opened his computer, and got down to work.

In the foreign-politics-lip-sync-rap-battle video business, most of the work came down to good old-fashioned internet searching of governmental or media outlet websites to find suitable source videos, but the material could really come from anywhere. So it was not unusual for Chris to sometimes download videos from social media accounts on foreign-based websites like Swedeface.se, Wuchat.cn or Tombaland.za, Africa's most popular social media platform.

Chris created a new folder on his desktop, opened Tombaland's homepage, clicked on "Politics," and then applied filtering software to search for video content. He hadn't visited Tombaland for two or three days, and his search returned several hundred new videos, which populated the folder as thumbnail screen shots. Chris wrote down the names of the first ten clips on a notepad beside his computer. Despite all the technology before him, he habitually wrote lists out by hand because he didn't like toggling back and forth between windows on his screen, and he preferred the act of handwriting because he felt it helped him think more clearly.

Most of the clips were not PRB.com material. There was the usual fair bit of soccer highlights and hilarious dash cam run-ins but there was one clip that caught Chris's eye as a suitable candidate. The video's thumbnail icon showed a bearded, turbaned man that looked to have been shot with a stationary camera, which helped the software capture lip movements. Another plus was that the clip was three minutes and twenty seconds long, just about the perfect length for a song.

Clicking on the link led Chris to a pop-up window asking him to like the content before viewing it, which he always did as a show of brotherly solidarity to his fellow internet content creators. He had to create a username and password to continue, which was annoying, but not unusual, as most links from these kinds of sites were used for data mining. Chris had seven e-mail addresses: a personal account, a work account, accounts from both high school and college, a Gmail account, a Wmail account and a special spam-only account that he used for just such occasions, when he needed access to some particular data but expected to receive a deluge of digital flotsam and jetsam in return. He used this account, boomgoesthedynamite@aol.com, for the username, and "password" as the password. Yet another screen opened, this one densely filled with terms and conditions, which Chris quickly scrolled to the bottom of and signed off on with one more click.

Having jumped through the required digital hoops, Chris was now able to download the full video and get it ready to run through the lip-sync software.

The video, as previously noted, featured a man with a pointy beard sitting at a desk with his briefcase off to one side. There was a large sign on the wall behind him written in some indecipherable script. It was not unlike the thousands of municipal procedural meetings Chris had watched in the course of his work, and he watched half-heartedly as the clip played out. The unfamiliar language the man was speaking didn't provide many of the customary mouth shapes Chris's software was trained to recognize and sadly, the clip could not be satisfactorily transformed into web-based entertainment. It occurred just then to Chris that he often used foreign-language source material, but only produced content in English. At the office, he had a Wanda digital personal assistant on his desk, which was programmed to speak and understand many languages. At some point down the road, he thought he should try to somehow merge the lyric-generation software with Wanda's built-in WangleTranslate software. Maybe next week, he would ask Mr. Poskovich about somehow hacking the two programs together. Then again, maybe not. Mr. Poskovich was considerably scarier than say, personal interactions in coffee shops.

Chris closed the window and kept looking.

In Zazaristan, MILF's dedicated server noted and added Chris's Like to the bottom of a shortish list of other Likes below the video. MILF also recorded his email address, and digitally filed his formal agreement to the terms and conditions of becoming a jihadist. The information was then automatically copied to a file labeled "Potential Recruits" on the computer of Fareek Wazaan. Also in the IT business, as you will recall.

CHAPTER 3

WASHINGTON, DC
THURSDAY, 9:40 a.m. EST

FBI Director Dick Barry was the third-youngest person in America to still use the name Dick. During the war, he was an Air Force Special Operations Combat Controller. His job was to move quickly and quietly into enemy territory, locate groups of the enemy, and identify them to the pilots of AC-130 Spectre gunships. The gunships would then proceed to the area, fly lazy circles high above, and rain down bullets the size of tennis ball cans upon said enemy.

War teaches a man many lessons about himself and the main lesson Barry learned was that he rather enjoyed pointing at something he didn't like and seeing it reduced to a smoking crater within the hour. Embracing the credo "Do something that you love and you will never work a day in your life," Barry decided to pursue a career in the field of Enemy Smiting and, to that end, acquired a law degree, a Master's in Criminal Justice, and a Ph.D. in Economics upon his discharge from the Air Force. Nine years later, he was Director of the FBI's Atlanta Field Office. Three years after that, he made Deputy Director in DC, and just last month he was named Director. Every year he ran two marathons and every two years he learned a new language. Dick Barry fucked around not.

He entered a thirteen digit code on his desktop keyboard to bring up his live database of agent personnel. He sipped his coffee and surveyed the names.

Drake and Linstrum? On assignment. Miami.

Wallace and Pieri? Testifying in court.

Keyboard and Coffeecup?

Author's Note:
Sometimes I struggle to come up with names for the minor characters.
I mention it now for no particular reason.

On assignment. New York.

Smith and Williams? Vacation.

Sullivan and Murphy?

* * *

"I'm thinking of getting a second gun and holster," said FBI Special Agent Stanley Daniel "Murph" Murphy.

"You mean, like a backup?" asked his partner of three years, Special Agent Francis Xavier "Sully" Sullivan, looking up from his computer.

"No, just a second set," Murph clarified. "I would wear two together. Crisscross." He sat back in his chair and made a motion like Aaron Rodgers does after he throws a touchdown pass, pulling both hands toward his hips.

"Oh," said Sully. "Like Denzel Washington in *Training Day*."

"Yes," said Murph. "Exactly."

Murph and Sully shared a cubicle on the second floor of the J. Edgar Hoover Building in Washington, DC. They were part, and truth be told, the entirety of, Task Force "Boomer Sooner," a special unit created in 1994 to mine what was known at the time as the "World Wide Web" for potential tips and clues about domestic terror plots.

Task Force Boomer Sooner was the brainchild of Congressman Allen Willard, R-Oklahoma. Envisioned as a dedicated crime-fighting unit that reported directly to the FBI Director about nefarious web scheming, Willard's idea was attached to a larger bill that also had to do with lobster trap capacities, congressional pay raises, and the labeling of fluorescent light bulbs. As passed, the bill was notated to stand "in perpetuity."

The specific wording of Congressman Willard's bill was basically meant to be an f-you to the FBI Director at the time, Farley Miller. Willard just wanted to federally mandate some annoyance into Miller's day and thought that regular updates about the goings-on of this "Information Surferhighway" as he famously once referred to it, would do the trick nicely.

Willard had hated Miller ever since the two had met at the White House Correspondents' Dinner; Miller had insulted Willard's wife by asking if, by chance, she was related to the actor Wallace Shawn.

Now, it must be said that the resemblance was uncanny, but Mrs. Willard and Mr. Shawn were not, in fact, any relation. Informed of this, Miller cried, "Inconceivable!" and bid the Congressman and his wife a good evening, then returned to the bar to freshen his Johnnie Walker Black.

Willard had no idea who Wallace Shawn was, but he didn't care to hear his wife of forty-three years compared to a man. Nor did he appreciate the use of the word "inconceivable" (which he considered a mild vulgarity), in her presence.

So, wheels were put into motion and Taskforce Boomer Sooner went into effect fifteen short months later. Miller recognized it as political nonsense, and while he was powerless to object, he still controlled the Taskforce's budget, and therefore set it at the Bureau's annual minimum: $100,000. The first year there was only one agent, because the cubicle Murph and Sully eventually moved into, and occupy to this day, cost $55,000 to design and install.

Decades after Willard and Miller both retired, there eventually arose a real need for criminal investigations in the digital world, but by that time the Patriot Act was in effect, and the NSA handles most of that shit now. The Taskforce now languishes in a bureaucratic tangle, just two agents and a cubicle.

So, it came as a small surprise when Murph's phone rang as he was picturing how badass he would look wearing two shoulder-holstered weapons while picking up his son from soccer practice. He noted an internal FBI number he didn't recognize, and picked up the phone.

"Boomer Sooner, Murphy."

"Special Agent Murphy, this is Director Barry's office. The Director would like to see you and Special Agent Sullivan right away."

"We'll be there in ten minutes." Murph replied, glancing up at Sully and giving him the twirly index finger gesture that means *moving out.*

* * *

Eight minutes after his secretary hung up with Murph, Barry was in his office finishing a phone call.

"... Yes sir, I understand the situation. I'm putting a dedicated team on it."

He hung up as his computer beeped and a message appeared on the screen that Special Agents Murphy and Sullivan were outside his office. He unfastened the top button of his shirt, loosened his tie slightly and pushed the intercom switch on his desk.

"Send them in."

Neither Murph nor Sully had been inside the new Director's office and they both harbored the familiar Irish feeling of dread as they entered.

Barry rose and spoke first.

"Special Agents Murphy and Sullivan. Good morning. Have a seat." He gestured to the two black leather chairs arranged in front of the desk.

"Thank you, sir," they replied in unison.

Barry sat down on the edge of his desk, reached into his shirt collar and pulled out a silver chain, at the end of which dangled an object that resembled a small piece of caramel corn.

"Do you know what this is?" he asked.

Sully shook his head silently, correctly deducing that this was a rhetorical question.

Murph squinted and offered, "It sort of looks like a small piece of caramel cor—"

"It's an Iraqi soldier's tooth, Special Agent Murphy. You know how I got it?"

At this point, Murph would not venture an answer if asked the names of his children, so he shook his head.

Barry returned the tooth necklace to the inside of his shirt and began the brief tale of its origin.

"The former owner of this tooth and I had a fundamental disagreement regarding the value of freedom and democracy. It escalated into physical violence. He snuck up on me one night as I was sleeping downrange in the Qandil Mountains and attacked me with a knife. I shot him in the face. This tooth, among other things, was separated from his head and now serves me as a reminder that in a fight to the death, the winner is going to be the first one to realize that he is, in fact, in a fight to the death."

Remember that feeling of Irish dread? Still there.

"We are in a fight to the death, gentlemen," Barry said, returning to his chair. "Terrorism is no longer organized groups of foreigners with military training, infiltrating our borders and executing elaborate plots. Look at the Brighton Mall attack. There was no chatter, no intel to suggest MILF was going to strike. Someone who was right under the Brit's noses just walked right up and did it. No warning, no trail. That cannot happen here. Will not happen here. Today's threat is the lone wolf. Homegrown, under the radar of law enforcement. For a long time, we didn't know we were in a fight with this enemy. But we are. And it is a fight to the death."

Murph and Sully sat silently for a good five seconds, neither one entirely sure if Barry would continue. At last, when it seemed safe, Sully spoke up.

"Sir, Special Agent Murphy and I are ready to fight. What is it you would like us to do?"

Barry leaned in, putting his elbows on the desk.

He said, "There are the enemies we know that we know about. Our military is dealing with them overseas. There are enemies that we know that we *don't* know about. CIA is handling them. What concerns me the most are the enemies that we don't know that we don't know about. Right now, somewhere out there, someone may be sneaking up on America with a knife. I want you to find this person or persons and shoot them in the face."

Murph thought, *I'm definitely getting that second gun now.*

"Figuratively," said Barry. "Bring them in alive, if possible."

Still, thought Murph.

"Sir," said Sully, "We won't let you down. Please forward us all the case files and leads you have, and we'll get to work."

"If I had case files and leads, Special Agent Sullivan, this assignment would not fall into the don't know/don't know category, would it?"

"Of course, sir. How do you... suggest we... proceed?"

"The "I" stands for investigation," Barry said. "Investigate, delve, reconnoiter, probe, search. Lick your goddamn finger and stick it in the air. Hard evidence, Agents. That's what we need here. The American people will be watching us closely on this one."

Barry drew a business card with ten digits but no name from his top desk drawer and leaned forward to hand it to Sully. "This is my cell phone number. Report back when you have something, and not before. That is all."

With that, Barry swiveled in his chair and began riffling through some files, the unspoken message being that when he straightened up, these two dipshits better be gone.

In fairness to the two dipshits, they did get the message and cleared out pretty quickly.

CHAPTER 4

WASHINGTON, DC
THURSDAY, 2:40 p.m. EST

Murph and Sully had been working steadily since their meeting with Director Barry, making calls and beating the digital bushes of the internet to see if they could shake loose any leads that might help bring some terrorist unsubs to justice.

It turns out that if you type, "How do I learn about joining a jihad against America" into the search engine Wangle, you get a fair amount of hits. Another thing you'll get, if you used a government-issued computer, is a phone call from a blocked number.

"Boomer Sooner, Murphy."

"The fuck are you doing?" NSA analyst Toby Winstead barked.

Winstead's job up in Fort Meade was to monitor internal government communications and digital activity for security leaks, seditious actions, and possible espionage. His software flagged suspicious usage, like using a work computer and the world's biggest search engine to inquire about waging holy war against America, for example. Most of your traitors and double agents would use a bit more caution in covering their tracks but hey, every now and then a fish jumps right into the boat. Regardless, Winstead was duty-bound to follow up on all alerts.

"Please tell me you actually want to join a jihad, you dumb fuck. Because if that's the level of intelligence they're signing up, we can all fucking relax."

There was something familiar about this voice. "Toby?" Murph said.

"Yeah," said Winstead, audibly agitated (and more than usual). Moments ago, the sight of:

ALERT:
Search protocol BRAVO: "jihad" + "joining"
Threat Assessment Level: Rhombus
Source: FBI server- hoov2
IP: 2006:db87:0:5634:0:567
User: murphy.stanley.d@fbi.gov (Murphy, Stanley D.)

on his computer screen filled him at first with rage, then annoyance, then relief, then more annoyance. Rage because he hated anyone who threatened his country, annoyance because any threat assessment Rhombus-level or higher required a lot of paperwork to clear, relief because he happened to know Murph personally and was pretty certain he was not a jihadist, and more annoyance because he would still have to do the paperwork.

Winstead's son Brad and Murphy's son Kevin were teammates on the College Park Bulldogs U-12 travel soccer team*.

Winstead was the coach although he was currently serving a three-week league-mandated suspension for screaming "That looked like a fucking abortion!" across the field after the Bulldog defense gave up an easy goal late in the game. His job was very stressful. His NSA job, that is. He did the soccer thing to enjoy quality time with his son.

* Gold Elite division. Not to be confused with the U-12 Premiere Platinum Club team, which is much more prestigious and competitive. So much so that only two kids made the team this year.

40

"To-bay!" Murph said. "What's up? You going to be back on the sidelines this weekend?"

"Next week. And you didn't answer my question. Did you fucking Wangle something about joining a jihad on your work computer?"

Murph said, "Yes. Technically. For an investigation we're working on. Sully and I are on special assignment from the Director."

Winstead said, "Is Sully there right now? Put him on speakerphone."

Murph cupped his hand over the phone and waved it to get Sully's attention.

"I'm putting Toby Winstead from NSA on speaker," he whispered, hitting the button. He replaced the phone in its cradle. "Go ahead, Toby."

Winstead's tinny voice crackled out of the speaker. "Special Agent Sullivan, can you confirm that you and your partner Special Agent Fuckstick are working on an assignment related to jihadist activity?"

Murph rapidly nodded to coach Sully for an affirmative answer. Sully said, "Yes, that is correct."

Winstead exhaled audibly. "Ok, fine. Murph, you still there? You need to fill out a form for me, acknowledging we had this discussion and confirming that you're not involved in any traitorous activity. Next time you investigate something, use the fucking FBI database and we won't have this problem. I'll e-mail you the form."

Suddenly feeling stuck between a rock and a hard place, Murph grabbed the phone and said, "The Director told us we had to generate fresh leads without using any existing Bureau resources. If you're going to bury us in paperwork every time we look into something public, we're screwed."

Winstead was unmoved. "These are the times we're fucking living in, my friend. Last week, we almost scrambled a fucking F-

41

16 after some secretary at the Pentagon sent an email to her vet saying her Afghan was having explosive diarrhea. I'll tell you what, though. You need fresh leads? We're up to our fucking necks in them over here. If you want to take some of them off our hands, you'll be doing us a favor. What are you looking for?"

This sounded promising. NSA always had the good stuff.

Murph flashed a thumbs-up to Sully and hit the SPEAKERPHONE button again. "We're looking for domestic terrorists. Lone-wolf, under-the-radar type unsubs. No known associates or affiliations. If there's a file that already exists on them, we don't want 'em."

Winstead made a note at his desk. "Nip them in the fucking butt. I like it. I'll see what I can find for you and if there's anything good, I'll have it couriered down to DC tonight."

Sully said, "Thanks Winstead,"

Murph said, "It's nip them in the *bud,* not nip them in the *butt.*"

The speakerphone was silent for a second. "Nip them in the bud? What the fuck does that mean?"

"It means cutting off a plant when it's in the early bud stage, before it grows too big. What does nip them in the butt mean?" Murph said.

Now Winstead was (yet more) pissed. "What the fuck do you think? It's when you sneak up behind someone and nip them in the fucking ass. Sully, back me up here."

Softly, Sully said, "Why, Murph?" Loudly, "I've heard it both ways, I think."

"Fuck you both," said the speakerphone. "Oh, and Sully, I forgot to mention you need to fill out some forms too. Look for my email." *Click.*

Murphy punched the CALL END button. "Great," he said to Sully. "Now he's pissed. He'll probably make Kevin play goalie next week."

CHAPTER 5

FORT MEADE, MARYLAND
THURSDAY, 2:44 p.m. EST

Youth soccer personnel decisions aside, Winstead was a man of honor and was as good as his word in delivering a lead for Murph and Sully's assignment. Right after hanging up on the two of them, he made a call to the NSA's National Internal Processing Liaison and got Craig Pierce on the line.

"NIPL. Pierce," he answered.

"Pierce. Toby Winstead. I'm looking for a recently created domestic file that has no previous connections to any known groups or individuals. Something that was completely off our radar."

Information was constantly trickling into the NSA's threat assessment net. Algorithms ran around the clock to automatically create and sort files by urgency, relevance, geographic area and just about every variable imaginable, to help agents identify the ones worth investigating. With all the cross-referenced data available, it was actually fairly unusual to find a circumstance where the subject stood alone, with no apparent connections.

"Let's see what we have here," said Pierce as he clicked and scrolled through his desktop's files. "There are two that just came through in the last hour. We classified one as... Ellipse, the other is Dodecagon."

"Send me the fucking Ellipse," said Winstead.

"Ellipse it is," said Pierce. "I'll send it to your desk along with the DT-14 form for the file transfer."

Pierce encrypted the file and transferred it to Winstead, who printed it on two pages and packed it in a secure courier bag to prepare for physical transport to the Hoover building. Surveillance data positively gushes into the NSA electronically, but very little trickles out electronically once it become classified. Most is still sent by courier for several reasons:

1. The NSA is aware that information sent electronically is not always as secure as the sender might believe.
2. The courier company contracted to deliver the files makes generous campaign contributions to certain members of the House Intelligence Committee.
3. Courier delivery is very expensive.

Winstead dropped the package in his department's locked courier outbox and returned to his desk to e-mail Murph. He attached the various forms that would record the package's origin, destination, general purpose, budgetary line item subsection and perhaps most importantly, release Winstead from any personal responsibility or liability stemming from the package in question or its transport.

With a *click*, the e-mail was sent and with a *boop* from Murph's computer it was received. Sure enough, Winstead had come through. The message confirmed that a package would arrive on Murph's desk in a few hours, and four PDF files were attached: an SR-9, an EL-1 addendum, a DT-14 and a CYA-3(a), all hot off the NSA's presses.

Murph winced as he clicked open the SR-9, unfurling six dense pages that he wasn't looking forward to filling out. The EL-1 addendum was more of the same. The DT-14 was a form he didn't recognize, and therefore would pawn off on Sully, and the CYA-3(a) was of course, pretty standard.

It was mid-afternoon already and waiting for the couriered file to arrive would make it a late day at the office. Murph checked his watch, called his wife, and got to work.

In the darkness of a sealed bag, the two-page report awaited. It began:

ALERT:
Search protocol KILO: "MILF" + "join" + "Terms & Conditions"
Video Facial Recog: Shwarma, Wahiri
Threat Assessment Level: Ellipse
Source: Cablenet c-server/SanAns
IP: 2008:tt87:1:8643:0:233:6:1
User: boomgoesthedynamite@aol.com (Dawkins, Christopher W.)

CHAPTER 6

WASHINGTON, DC
THURSDAY, 6:40 p.m. EST

It was the time of night that a good author would call the gloaming.
Dick Barry sat in the right lane of the Frederick Douglass
Memorial Bridge in traffic. He was going to be late for dinner.
Again. He had his driver's side window a third of the way down
and a podcast a third of the way up: "—practitioners of this
unproven science known as Focused Mindmapping have thus far
mainly plied their trade in Macau until they were recently
banned—"

The car ahead of him, a two-year old Galactic Aqua Mica
colored Toyota Camry inched along. In the nine minutes since the
Camry pulled in front of him, Barry had had formed strong
opinions on the following:

1.   The driver probably lived in Maryland and had for more
than eight years because his Maryland license plate still had an
old registration sticker on it and Maryland had discontinued
the license plate stickers eight years ago.
2.   The driver probably had Irish ancestry (and therefore was
probably Catholic) because there was a sticker of a silhouetted
Irish Step Dancer on the bumper.

3.   The driver probably had at least three children: a girl (the dancer), a boy (Prince George's County Youth Football sticker), and a baby (rear-facing car seat).

4.   The driver was probably a Democrat because Prince George's County was overwhelmingly Democratic.

5.   The driver was probably a salesperson because his two-year-old car had brand-new tires indicating he had put on at least 25,000 miles a year and had worn out the factory set. The driver most likely sold some kind of nontangible services because the Camry did not have room for large boxes or displays of goods.

6.   The driver was a thoughtless douchebag because he didn't use his turn signals when changing lanes.

Barry's cell phone rang, and he pressed a button to answer, simultaneously muting the podcast.

"Barry."

"Director Barry, sir, it's Special Agent Sullivan," Sully's voice came over the car's speakers. Barry rolled up his window.

"Special Agent Sullivan," said Barry. "I'm impressed that you have such important news for me already that you called my cell phone, the number of which I authorized you to use only in cases of the utmost importance." Barry found opening conversations that way really cuts through the chit-chat.

Sully's eyes flicked up toward Murph, who was across the cubicle working on his computer, then back down to the NSA file on his desk that had been delivered by courier just minutes earlier.

"Sir, we have a very strong lead. Christopher Dawkins, age twenty-four, San Anselmo, California. Signal intelligence indicates contact with, and willingness to be co-opted by, enemy groups. Looks like he watched a MILF recruitment video that Wahiri Shwarma appeared in. There's a record of Dawkins liking it online, as well as signing their terms and conditions to become an operative, agent or martyr. NSA pulled all this through MILF's public portal. Get this: Dawkins used 'password' for his password."

Barry knew that the government had the ability to read some of the enemy's mail, so to speak, but there were still some technological barriers preventing them from always learning where the "mailbox" was physically located.

"Get me a copy of that video," Barry ordered.

"Yes, sir." Sully said.

"Has Dawkins had any direct contact with MILF?" Barry asked.

Sully looked down at his notes. "MILF has dedicated servers and uses dummy accounts from all over. The digital trail goes cold at some point. It's impossible to say how involved Dawkins might be."

"Get out to California tonight," said Barry. "Send me the suspect's address and your flight information. I'll have a warrant waiting for you when you land. Sullivan, I'm counting on you and Murphy. The Bureau needs a win here. The country needs a win. We chased these a-holes all over those god-forsaken deserts for years with one hand tied behind our backs and it made them cocky because we didn't finish the job. Now that they've infiltrated America, we're going to come down hard. When we take this Dawkins down, we will be putting any sleeper cells or lone-wolf operatives on notice. If you're even *thinking* about plotting against this country, you will get snatched up and locked away before you can say *Allahu Akbar*."

The case excited Sully. He and Murph did not get out in the field much and this looked like it could be a big one. "How long do you want him under surveillance, once we're in California?" he asked.

"You're not getting it, Sullivan. This guy isn't some kind of terrorist kingpin, working with a big network; we would know his name if he was. You could surveil him for months and he would never contact anyone, never lead you to anyone, but one day he'll just execute an attack without any warning. His value to us is that his capture will demonstrate the reach of our investigative abilities to the nation, those who are with us as well as those who are against us. The digital trail Christopher Dawkins left is solid, hard evidence. We use it to take him down and we show the futility of his criminal efforts to hundreds or even thousands more potential terrorists before they even get started, while gaining the support and faith of law-abiding citizens."

Yelling at Sully took Barry's attention off the road for a second and he had to stop short when the Camry tapped the brakes.

"I understand," said Sully. "We'll take him down the first chance we get."

"And another thing," Barry barked. "Do not let those granola-eaters in the California field offices talk to the media about this case. The story comes from the top, here in Washington, and not until I say so, got it? We can't afford bad press. As much as I hate to admit it, we're fighting this war in the headlines as much as anywhere and we will control it from start to finish. Keep it quiet. Do not go cowboy on me, Sullivan. Keep Murphy in line, too. If a word about this case leaks without my OK, you'll both stay out there and I'll make you try to infiltrate the Crips."

Sully took Barry's point. After a second or two.

"Yes, sir."

"Stopping terrorists isn't easy, Special Agent Sullivan," Barry continued. "It's like killing flies with an icepick, quite honestly. But if the other flies see one get killed, they all take off."

In Sully's opinion, flies are super-dumb, have no concept of their own mortality, and will almost always immediately return to anyplace they were chased from, but this was not the time to debate metaphors.

"Understood, sir. Murphy and I will fly to San Francisco tonight. You'll get my report after we apprehend Dawkins."

"Anything else?" Barry asked.

Mark A. Henry

Sully and his wife were raising seven kids, and manners were always a topic in the Sullivan house, so reflexively he said, "Thank you?"

"About the case, Sullivan! And I'll take that as a no. Get me that report." He hung up.

Sully said, "Yes, sir. We'll let you know something soon. Murphy and I are heading to the airport now. Goodnight." He listened for another second, then hung up. Looking over his desk blotter calendar, he said to Murph, "We're flying to San Francisco tonight. We're going after Christopher Dawkins."

Murph looked at his watch. "What time's the flight? I want to stop at SportMart and get that second gun."

Again, Murph and Sully did not see a whole lot of field action.

Sully began working the Bureau's internal travel site and announced that they could catch a flight from Reagan National at "O-Dark forty-eight," and thus Murph would have time for some light weapon shopping before they went "wheels up." Sully thought "rendezvous" would be pushing it just a little, so he simply said, "Let's meet at my house at 10:30 and we'll drive to the airport together."

"Roger that," said Murph.

* * *

Checking his watch, Murph briskly approached the counter in the Outdoor section of SportMart. It was 7:50 and the store closed in ten minutes.

"One Glock Nine, please," He flipped his badge wallet (Badglet? Walldge?) open. "I'm a Federal Agent. FBI Special Agent Stan Murphy." *Getting out in the field with Sully is going to be awesome.*

SportMart Associate Gary Trent came over to meet him.

"Evening, Agent," he said, inspecting Murph's badge. "Can I see your permit, please?"

50

Murph produced his Federal pistol permit, which identified him as a qualified law enforcement officer and thus exempted him from the ten-day waiting period. "I need a shoulder holster, too. A double."

Trent scanned the barcodes on Murph's ID and saw that all was in order. "Sure thing. We carry a couple. I recommend the Denzel." He reached down to unlock the display case and withdrew a Glock. He racked it open and checked the chamber. Handing it over to Murph, he said, "Don't you fellas normally get your sidearms issued from work?"

"We do. But we can buy our own as long as it's the same model." He flashed his coat open to show Trent the Glock Nine he already carried. "I'm going out on field assignment tomorrow and I may need something extra. There are some pretty bad dudes out there."

At that exact moment, 2,788 miles away, Chris Dawkins gingerly popped the lid off his tea and blew on it. It was really hot.

Murph turned and sighted the new weapon at a nearby mannequin that had no head but huge biceps. "I'll take it," Murph said.

"Bad dudes, look out," said Trent.

CHAPTER 7

SAN ANSELMO, CALIFORNIA
THURSDAY, 8:03 p.m. PST

"Hear hear, this meeting of the Billionaire's Club will now come to order."

Kenny Wong raised his spindly arms and motioned for quiet. The buzz of a dozen or so young men and three young women muted slightly. Chris Dawkins wasn't talking anyway.

The Billionaire's Club met on the second Thursday evening of the month in the community room of the San Anselmo Public Library. It may seem to be an unlikely place for billionaires to gather, but none of the club's members were billionaires, so there you go. The club served as a network for young tech workers who met to share their "billion-dollar ideas" with each other. Now obviously, people are not in the habit of giving away billion-dollar concepts in public, so the Billionaire's Club trafficked mostly in half-baked ideas, but you never know who might hear one and help you put it back in the oven. And after every meeting, most people went down the street to drink beer and play bar trivia at the Half-Moon Tavern.

"On tonight's agenda," continued Kenny, the de facto club president, "Taylor Michaud, Kam Suvi, Cindy Li, Jeffrey Light, and Rob Govan. As a reminder, we only have the room for an hour, so let's avoid extended debates. Save them for the bar later."

Billionaire's Club rules dictated that each month, five
members presented an idea and briefly took questions. At the
conclusion of all the presentations, general networking took place,
snarky comments were exchanged and then, the aforementioned
beer drinking. Chris was always sort of happy the weeks he wasn't
scheduled to present. He was never very comfortable with public
speaking and his ideas probably weren't the best either. His idea to
hack WangleTranslate with Sixdub's lip-sync software, for
example, was very job-specific and these hipster nerds in the room
were just the type to mock his daily work as lightweight.

"Taylor, please begin," said Kenny.

Taylor's idea was based on the presumption that we are all
living in a simulated reality that was created by super-advanced
humans, or possibly a form of alien and/or artificial intelligence.

"We all saw *TechChain*, bro," interjected the guy with the
waxed mustache whose name was either Kurt or Kirk.

"Let him finish, Kyle," Kenny admonished.

Kyle. That's it. Kyle.

Taylor continued. "Thus, since people are basically characters
in an immersive, hyper-realistic video game, I propose creating an
app that serves as way to keep score, awarding points for various
accomplishments."

"It's called money, Taylor," Kyle shouted.

"And you would lose points for being a dick," countered
Taylor.

"How would the app know what you've accomplished, and
whether it was good or bad?" asked Kyle. He was trying out this
new thing where he just shouted out whatever he was thinking and
short term, it was working out extremely well. He had gotten a
raise at work and was juggling three new sexual relationships. He
was considering presenting this trick as his idea when his turn came
up at next month's meeting.

"Admittedly, there are some bugs in the interface," Taylor answered. "Practically speaking, the app would be something like a Fitbit crossed with a random number generator."

Kenny jumped back in. "OK, thank you Taylor. Intriguing, intriguing," he said. He liked to keep things moving right along, especially if the ideas in question were in the theoretical realm. "Next up, Kam Suvi. What do you have Kam? And remind us where you work?"

Kam rose from his seat. "Hi everybody. I work at Datasoft," he said.

"What kind of projects you work on over there?" Kyle shouted out.

"Let's stay on track, please," said Kenny. "Your idea, Kam."

Kam presented his idea for speech-enabled car horns, to little enthusiasm. Over the next forty minutes, the club heard about genetically modified trees that form their own forts as they grow, a device that folds fitted sheets (also theoretical realm), and a toothbrush that works by the user chomping down on a spring-loaded mouthpiece. The Billionaire's Club then adjourned slightly ahead of schedule.

Chris was tired and still felt slightly under the weather. He probably shouldn't have even gone out to the meeting, but he had felt a little cooped up after being home all day and thought the short walk to the library from his apartment might do him some good. He popped a C4! lozenge in his mouth and hefted his backpack to leave, while looking around for anyone who looked like they might want to discuss ideas with him. Chris was not great at starting conversations.

Kenny walked past and tapped his shoulder. "You coming out, Chris?"

"No, not tonight. Just going home to crash, I think. What did you think about the ideas, Kenny?"

"They all sound good to me. One of these days someone will hit it big with one," Kenny said. He then turned to join the club members who were filing out of the room. Everyone turned right to exit the library through the front door. Chris made a left and headed to the parking lot in back, where a figure waited for him in the shadows.

CHAPTER 8

SAN ANSELMO, CALIFORNIA
THURSDAY, 8:50 p.m. PST

Author's note:
This must be how Dan Brown feels.

The shadowy figure spoke. "Chris! Hold up a second."

Startled, Chris jumped and turned to see a lanky man unfolding himself off a bench outside the library door.

"Mr. Wiles! You scared the crap out of me! I think my heart stopped for a second."

Wiles said, "They say heart-stopping moments can be the source of inspiration. And?"

Chris, walking over to the bench said, "Inspiration and? And what?"

Wiles said, "Do you have any inspiration?"

Chris said, "No. From the heart-stopping?"

Wiles said, "Or the meeting. Either. And are you feeling better, by the way?"

His head spinning slightly, Chris said, "A little, yes. Thanks. What are you doing here? You know about the meeting?"

Wiles tucked his cell phone into his jacket pocket. He withdrew his plastic baggie, fished out a capsule and dry swallowed it. "Zinc," he said as he tucked the baggie away.

"I own this library," he then proclaimed, grandly opening his arms wide toward the building.

Chris cocked his head quizzically. "You... what? Doesn't the city own the library?"

"Not anymore. Libraries are expensive. Giving out books for free and collecting a few dimes in late fees does not make them any less so. The city and I came to a mutually beneficial arrangement. I purchased the land, building, inventory, library card database, naming rights, the whole works. But it's sort of a secret deal. My funding comes through a blind trust into the library's budget, so be cool and don't tell anyone I told you all this. People don't like change."

His head still locked in quizzical position, Chris asked, "What do you mean? Like the fact that the Public Library is no longer public?"

"It's still public, Chris. You can come and go as you please. Everything is the same as before. Same books, same librarians, just now I'm paying for it all."

"I still don't get it. Why would you do that?"

"Couple reasons. Number one: I like libraries. When I die, this one will be named after me. The Jasper Wiles Memorial Library. Sounds good, right?"

"It does... but how—"

Wiles interrupted. "How does it make sense financially to own a library? Short answer, it doesn't, but this is reason number two. Metademographics. The study of who people were, who people are and who people want to become."

Chris had to take a moment here to process the fact that he was standing in a semi-deserted parking lot speaking to the world's 641st richest man about... well, Chris couldn't really say just now what exactly they were talking about. Also, Wiles was now technically the world's 640th richest man, as Belgian industrialist Heinz Gossler was at that moment suffering through a cold run of cards at a high-stakes blackjack table in Las Vegas.

Chris suddenly couldn't resist the urge to look around to see if there was a hidden camera crew lurking in the bushes surrounding the parking lot, waiting to surprise him as the payoff to some bizarre practical joke.

"Metademographics," Chris repeated. "I didn't know that was a thing."

Wiles seemed pleased to answer. "It wasn't a thing until I invented it."

Wiles rolled his skateboard out from under the bench and motioned toward the walkway that led around the side of the library. "Chris, join me for a drink." Without waiting for an answer, he continued. "You know how, when you're riding a bike, if you stare down at your front tire, you have a hard time riding in a straight line? That's demographics. Staring hard at where you are at the moment and not doing a very good job of progressing, big picture-wise. Metademographics is like riding your bike and looking twenty-five feet ahead of your front tire. You tend to move straight for that spot. That's what interests me. Not where people *are*, but where people are *going*. And with the right information, I can figure that out."

Chris said, "So you're... mining market data, basically. What does the library have to do with all this again? Wait, are you pirating the infor—"

Wiles held up a finger. "Not pirating. I own it."

Chris continued, "You're using the information about what books people check out as some kind of consumer research? Is that... legal?" Again, Chris took a furtive look around.

"Of course! There's never been any promise of privacy about that. Libraries used to just write your name in every book you checked out. Anyone could pick it up off the shelf later and see who had read it before. That's no big deal."

Wiles began slowly riding away. Chris didn't know whether he was supposed to follow or not, but after a moment, it was clear Wiles was just turning a wide circle in the parking lot.

"Chris," he said, "let me ask you this: who uses the library?"
Chris thought a moment. "Everyone?"

"Cockpee!" Wiles blurted, from halfway around his circle.

Chris said, "Come on, Mr. Wiles. There's no need for that. I'm just trying to answer the question."

Wiles chuckled as he glided by. "No, no. Sorry. K.O.C.P. Kids. Old people. Crazy people. Poor people. These are people who use the library most, and they have specific and very real wants. Their actions tell us where we, as a society were, where we're going, where we've been, and more importantly, where we wish we went and where we wish to go."

Chris felt somehow offended that he wasn't included in any of the groups Wiles valued. "But what about people my age? Aren't you interested in Millennials?" he asked.

"I love Millennials, but that's what the internet is for," Wiles said.

Chris said, "And you really need cr—I mean, mentally ill people? And by the way, shouldn't it be P-COK?"

Wiles smiled. "Actually yes. And no. I have another project using that acronym. Anyway, yes, we need mentally ill people. It's like putting salt in caramel. Somehow the data gets better. Everybody has wants, Chris, and nobody wants want. I can help these people, and all people, by getting to know them and their wants better. Imagine software that allows you to not just "like" something you see online but quantify *how much* you like it. Let's say on a scale of one to ten. Your number value will then merge with everyone else's to create an average, and you could see how your number compares to everyone else's. Every time you click anything, a photo, a tweet, a word, you rate it, and the software adds your opinion." Wiles stopped and held his hands apart. "Here's you. Here's the world." He clasped his hands. "Here you are together."

"It would be cool to see how you fit in, I guess," Chris said, following Wiles as he motored toward the street. "But don't we kind of do that at work already? Everybody uses algorithms to track clicks and likes all the time."

Wiles said, "For their own purposes, yes. But nobody shares their data back with the user. Anyway, I'm sure I'm boring you. I didn't come here to lecture about Metademographics. I just came to listen in on your club meeting. By the way, when you walked out, I was just beginning some patent work for a new kind of toothbrush. I'm very excited about that. With any luck, I'll have a prototype made up by the end of the month, and a week after that Oral-B and Sonicare will be in a bidding war."

Chris became angry.

"The toothbrush? You can't just steal Rob's idea!"

"I may be stealing his seed, but I intend to return him a fully bloomed flower. I've done it many times before. People say it's easier to ask forgiveness than permission, but do you know what's even easier than asking forgiveness? Doing it while delivering large, unexpected checks."

"So that's why you came the library. To poach business ideas. By the way, how did you listen in?"

"There's a Wanda in the meeting room and I have the Wi-Fi password." Wiles said, matter-of-factly, carving gentle arcs on the sidewalk. He stopped and turned to Chris. "Let me ask you a question. Why did *you* come to the library?"

Introspection is like flossing your teeth. You mostly avoid it until someone really presses you to do it, and then you never know what you might pull out. Sometimes it's just a small, stinky smear of goop, but sometimes you dislodge something that's been bothering you for a while and you say "Ah, that's better."

Chris said, "Well, I like the idea of doing something big. It's doesn't have to be a "billion-dollar idea" literally, but something that's significant. Something positive."

"Such as?" Wiles asked.

"If I knew, or had any idea how to begin, I'd be like you, out buying libraries."

Wiles grinned. "Yes. I suppose it's easier said than done." He stepped onto his board. "Let's get that drink."

When the world's 641st richest man (Gossler just split eights and drew a two on the first hand, doubled down, drew a nine for a nineteen, then pulled an eight on his second hand, resplit those eights, drew a three on the first, doubled down again and drew a king, making twenty-one. He then drew an ace on his third hand, giving him a soft nineteen. He eyed the dealer, remarked, "Ve are here to gamble, are ve not?" and doubled down a third time, pulling a seven to make sixteen, but the dealer was showing a five, so Gossler waved off another hit. He then watched as the dealer turned over the jack of diamonds, then drew the ten of clubs to bust. "Vinner, vinner chicken dinner!") invites you for a drink, you say OK.

"OK," said Chris.

CHAPTER 9

SAN FRANCISCO, CALIFORNIA
THURSDAY, 9:47 p.m. PST

Less than an hour after leaving the library, Chris trotted behind Wiles as they crossed Fremont Street. The unmarked entrance to Syndrea was marked by a large, loose line of clubbers. Syndrea. The nightclub so cool, no one was really certain how to pronounce the name. In fact, if any club employee heard the name spoken aloud, they were duty-bound to correct the speaker. For example, if a customer said "Sin-DRAY-uh," the bartender would respond with "SINE-dree-uh" and so on.

It should go without saying that Chris had never been there before, and he noticed that the stylishly dressed people in line for the door all had their phones out and were showing them to the behemoth of a bouncer to gain entry. Following Wiles as he rolled to the head of the line, Chris asked, "Do I need to show my phone to get in?"

Wiles said, "You have to have at least 5,000 social media followers to get in, but you're with me, so don't worry about it." Extending a fist bump to the doorman, he said, "Jayson! How were the seats?"

Jayson the doorman made a fist the size of a roll of toilet paper and said, "They were great Mr. Wiles, thanks again."

Wiles said, "I probably won't use the tickets as much as I'd like to this season. Call my office anytime you want to go." He gestured to Chris. "This is my friend Chris Dawkins."

Chris also received a giant fist bump along with a "Nice to meet you, come on in."

Wiles popped his board up. "Would you please watch my board?"

"Of course," said Jayson, smiling and accepting the board with his left hand and a crinkly handshake with his right with practiced ease.

Wiles led the way as they entered the club's foyer. Thudding music enveloped them. Chris shouted, "Do they have bar trivia here?"

"No, it's mostly booze and women," Wiles shouted back. "Come on, we're going upstairs."

Chris followed Wiles as they emerged into the flashing cacophony of the packed club. A churning dance floor was in the center of the cavernous space, with slightly raised platforms on the left and right where there were booths and sofas. Extending across the back of the room was the bar, a four-foot high, thirty-foot long plexiglass aquarium, topped in sparkly white quartz with air holes drilled into it every few inches. The aquarium held hundreds of brightly colored tropical fish. (Brightly colored, drunken tropical fish.)

There was a balcony running along three sides of the room where seventy-inch monitors displayed a continuous feed of colorful Moodswirl emojis that the clubbers continuously posted as they danced and drank the night away.

It smelled like youth. And Axe body spray.

Chris gaped at it all, while trying to keep Wiles in sight as they made their way through the room and up the three steps to the sitting area on the right. They weaved through some sofas and low tables to a discreetly located door in the back corner between two large potted plants. (Large, drunken potted plants.) The door had no knob or handle, but a numeric keypad embedded in the frame on the right. Shielding the keypad with his body, Wiles punched in a code and the door slid open.

Feeling like a VIP as he followed Wiles into the elevator, Chris ventured, "Mr. Wiles, what's the elevator code?"

"Two," said Wiles, pointing to the elevator buttons.

"Oh. Sure. Sorry," said Chris as he hit the button for the 2nd floor. Wiles's terse answer made him think he had overstepped a boundary in asking for the privileged information.

As the door closed and the elevator began to rise, Wiles said, "Chris, do you know what the white stuff in bird shit is?"

"No. Um... no."

"That's also bird shit. Don't overthink things too much. We're going to the 2nd floor. The elevator code is two."

They egressed the elevator, crossed the room and Wiles headed for an empty semi-circular booth. Jasper Wiles had millions of dollars, a hundred-foot yacht, a fleet of luxury sports cars, a custom-tailored wardrobe and a singular charisma that charmed men and women alike, but even he could not look cool as he scooched his way around into the booth. It just can't be done. Once settled, he leaned forward and blew out the candle on the table. He sat back and said, "Chris, let me tell you a story..."

A waitress arrived at that moment. "Welcome to Syndrea," she said, pronouncing it SINE-dree. "I'm Gianni."

Wiles smiled and gave a wave/salute. "Jasper Wiles. This is Chris Dawkins."

"What can I get for you?" said Gianni.

Wiles leaned toward her and said, "Bottle of Ketel One."

Chris took that moment to glance around the Syndrea VIP area, taking in the dark walls, dark carpets and dark souls. He then suddenly realized Gianni and Wiles were staring expectantly at him for his order. "Oh! I thought... I thought that bottle was for us to share," he said.

"We will share it, Chris," Wiles said reassuringly. "Would you care for anything else?"

Chris really wanted a hot tea with lemon C4! shot but he realized this was not looking like a hot-tea-with-lemon kind of night. He had to step up his ordering game.

Gianni saw Chris's look of hesitant confusion and like the customer service professional she was, she stepped in. "Syndrea" (Sine-RAY-uh) "bottle service includes an assortment of juices and mixers and you order the alcohol of your choosing. I suggest you gentlemen order the Syndrea" (Sin-DAR-ay) "VIP Platinum Package. It comes with an eight-bottle assortment of top-shelf liquor and a complimentary bottle of champagne."

Chris lifted a finger and said, "I'm sorry, what was that first thing you said?"

Gianni patiently replied, "Syndrea." (CHIN-ree-uh) "The name of this club? The 'D' is silent," she added.

Chris opened his mouth, but no words came out, so Gianni glanced at Wiles to confirm the order, and he did so with a short wave. And with that, Gianni turned to go magically transform eight twelve-dollar bottles of liquor into $3,000 by carrying them from one end of a room to the other.

"I think she likes you," Wiles said.

"Oh, really?" Chris replied. Gianni was stunningly beautiful and league-wise, she was playing centerfield for the Yankees while Chris was batting in the middle of the order for a high school JV team. "How can you tell?"

"It's just a vibe I'm picking up," Wiles said. "However, there is one sure-fire way I know to tell if a woman is interested in you. Do you want to know what it is?"

"Yes!" Chris squawked in a way that no woman would be interested in. "But before you tell me, does it have to do with showing the woman your gold-plated yacht or something like that?"

"Ha!" Wiles laughed. "No. But here's how you know if a woman is interested. It doesn't cost a dime and mind you, it doesn't necessarily *make* her interested, but it doesn't hurt either. Works every time." He paused a moment. "Chris, remind me to get back to my story later."

"Sure, sure."

"To determine whether a woman is interested in you is very simple."

"Wait," said Chris. "Is this like what you said back in the elevator about not over-thinking? You're not going to say, 'just ask her,' are you?"

Wiles shook his head, chuckling. "No. I daresay that wouldn't work even if you asked as you were bringing your platinum-plated helicopter in for a landing on the gold-plated yacht you mentioned. No, to gauge many a woman's interest, one simply has to ask about her shoes." He suddenly paused and looked up. "Ah, here's our friend Gianni with the drinks."

Gianni had indeed returned with a large silver bucket filled with various liquor bottles nestled in ice. She was followed by a young man who carried a similar bucket with juices, sodas and mixers, and *he* was followed by yet another young man who set down a silver ice bucket, before wordlessly displaying a bottle of champagne to Chris and Wiles and plunging it into the bucket with a *ker-shlunk.*

"I love that sound," remarked Wiles.

As Gianni and her assistants set to work arranging the drinks and glasses for the two men, Chris craned his neck in an effort to see under and around the table to get a look at her shoes.

When the Syndrea VIP Platinum Package was impressively laid out on the table, the two young men scuttled away and Gianni stepped back, surveying her handiwork. "Will there be anything else, gentlemen?" she asked.

"I like those shoes," said Chris.

"Thank you," Gianni said.

"They're… really cool," said Chris.

"Thanks. So, you're good for now, then? I'll check back with you later. Enjoy!"

Chris turned to Wiles, who was fastidiously fixing two vodka tonics.

"What's up with that?" Chris asked. "I complimented her shoes, and nothing happened."

"Mm, I noticed that," Wiles observed, adding a leafy garnish to their drinks. "Mint. For the brain," he explained. He slid one of the drinks to Chris.

"Cheers," he said. "To the never-ending quest for knowledge, truth and beauty." They clinked glasses and took a sip. Chris's drink was too strong, and he reached for the orange juice to top it off.

Wiles said, "I may have been wrong before about her liking you. *But*, I didn't tell you the most important part about the shoes. You don't just ask about them. There's more to it. You have to compliment them, but the key is to mention that they look *uncomfortable*, which sets up the five-point interest rubric." Wiles popped his thumb up. "One: Every woman enjoys a compliment." Index finger. "Two: Noticing shoes shows you pay attention to details." Middle finger. "Three: Women love their shoes and your interest in shoes is now an interest you share." Ring finger. "Four: Women's shoes hurt their feet and observing that the shoes are uncomfortable shows empathy." Pinky. "Five: Now that you've established the problem of uncomfortable feet, you also get to solve it by inviting the woman to sit down with you." The longish speech made Wiles thirsty and he pretty much drained his v&t.

This was all quite revelatory to Chris, but still somewhat unsatisfying, as he thought back to Gianni's tepid response. "So, if the woman just says, 'Thanks,' or 'My shoes feel fine,' then what?"

"That means they're not interested, sorry. In short, the answer to 'Do your shoes hurt?' is going to be the same as 'Are you interested in me?'" He dumped his first drink's ice into a nearby plant and reached for the tongs. Wiles, incidentally, was wearing brown and blue wingtips.

Just then, the elevator doors opened up across the room and two young women stepped out. Their names were Hallie and Mia and they were minor celebrities, known for their Twitch channel "Hallie and Mia Play Video Games Wearing Just Bras and Panties," which was no more, and no less, than what the name implied. They each had several million social media followers and earned comfortable six-figure incomes from ad revenue and sponsorships from video game companies and undergarment manufacturers. They also possessed the secret code to Syndrea's VIP elevator.

As they paused to take selfies at the balcony railing and pop off a couple MoodSwirls, Wiles looked up and then pointed them out to Chris. "Let's invite these young ladies to join us, shall we? I'll let you do the talking."

The vodka was beginning to whisper sweet nothings into Chris's prefrontal cortex.

Hallie and Mia were done with their phones for a brief moment and as they passed by Chris and Wiles's table, Chris made a small wave and said, "Excuse me."

Guys like Chris were the majority of Hallie and Mia's audience, so they were used to being recognized by dorky fans all the time.

"Hi!" they both said in unison, preparing to say how much they appreciated the support and no, they would not mind at all taking a quick selfie with a fan.

"I just want to say, those shoes are great," Chris said with a grin, pointing randomly to the pair of feet on the right (Mia).

"Thank you so much!" Mia gushed, still waiting for the part where this nerd told her how awesome she was.

"Now! Spring the trap!" said the vodka.

Chris set his glass down. "Don't they hurt your feet? They look kind of uncomfortable."

Mia shot a quick glance at Hallie. "Mmm-no, they're OK."

The vodka in Wiles's prefrontal cortex was busy helping him work out about how much it would actually cost to gold-plate his yacht, when it was suddenly interrupted by a blaring alert: "Man down! Man down! Back-up required!"

"Ladies," Wiles said, breaking the spell of weirdness. "My friend Chris and I seem to have somewhat over-ordered." He gestured helplessly at the table full of bottles as if he were uncertain as to how they came to be there. "Why don't you sit down and join us for a drink or two. We were just regaling each other with tales of adventure when you came by. Have either of you ever been regaled by two men at the same time before?"

Hallie, who majored in Classics at Dartmouth said, "As a matter of fact, I have."

Mia, who majored in Communications at Arizona State said, "Just once. Is that champagne?"

CHAPTER 10

SAN FRANCISCO INTERNATIONAL AIRPORT
FRIDAY, 4:40 a.m. PST

The cold, dry California wind that whipped Sully's tie around and the faint smell of jet fuel exhaust eroded the lingering effects of the nineteen ten-minute naps he took on the flight.

A young FBI agent had met him and Murph at baggage claim, handed them search and arrest warrants for Christopher W. Dawkins, then drove them to the airport's cell phone lot where a Chevy Suburban and a Chevy Trax idled side by side. The young agent got into the passenger seat of the Suburban and was driven off.

According to the Trax's GPS unit, Dawkins's apartment was 31.8 miles away and there was a Waffle Hut, a Pancake Pavilion, a Bacon Barn, twelve Starbucks, and a TruckerWorld Diner along the way.

Murph and Sully arrived at Chris's apartment ninety minutes later (they stopped for breakfast at Bacon Barn) and took a reconnaissance lap through the parking lot to confirm his car (a Saiatsu Arrow, California license #2444GF980Y57W) was there. They pulled into a curbside spot across the street, allowing them a clear line of sight to Chris's front door, on the first floor of the three-level complex. By now it was almost 6:30 a.m. The neighborhood was quiet and just barely light.

Murph and Sully had already put away two large coffees apiece and were both pretty jacked on caffeine. Murph had to take a shit a little while ago, but the adrenaline from laying eyes on the suspect's house made it go away. Sully's bowels were confused by the air travel and/or time change and would not resume normal function for a day or two. Once again, the two feds rarely saw the field.

"Ready?" said Sully.

"Let's go," Murph answered. He offered a fist bump, but Sully had already turned to get out of the car and left him hanging.

Crossing the street, they both scanned the area. Seeing no one, they approached Chris's door.

Chris had made it home about three hours earlier. After a valiant attempt to polish off the Platinum Package, and to be fair, they did make a pretty decent dent, Wiles, Chris, Hallie, and Mia adjourned from Syndrea with the intention of capping the evening by playing video games on Wiles's yacht, the *Commodore 69*. En route to the marina, however, Chris succumbed to exhaustion brought on by his mild cold and intemperate drinking (the orange juice didn't help at all!) and passed out. After some mild face slapping went unheeded, Hallie searched his pockets (all of which Chris would have gratefully enjoyed had he been conscious) to find his address and keys, and they literally dropped him off at home under the watchful eye of their Uber driver who more than once had felt the need to tap his finger on the "Thank you for not vomiting" sticker he had affixed to the dashboard.

Sully's third round of knocking (three knocks, then five, then straight to nine) woke Chris from a dream where he was golfing, but it was weird because the first tee was located right up against the clubhouse, so close that he couldn't make a proper backswing, and the high heels he was wearing did not help. It was also weird because Chris had never played golf in his life.

He opened his eyes to squint at his watch. Seeing two of them, Chris did some drunken math and closed one eye to bring a single watch into focus. *6:29. Who in God's name would knock so early?*

The Jehovah's Witnesses knock in God's name, he said to himself as he rolled out of bed and shuffled listingly toward the door. *But not so early.* These are the kind of hilarious jokes Chris's nonexistent girlfriend is missing out on.

Chris put his eye to the peephole and saw two short-haired men wearing suits and ties. *Mormons?*

After resting his forehead on the door and closing his eyes for a three-second nap, he unlocked it and opened up. "Can I help you?" he croaked.

Sully spoke up first. "Mr. Dawkins, my name is Special Agent Sullivan, and this is Special Agent Murphy of the FBI. We'd like to come in and have a few moments of your time."

Murph then chimed in. "We have a warrant," pulling a stiff leather folder out of his briefcase and holding it out toward Chris. Chris opened it to see a single typed page on Department of Justice letterhead. Quickly skimming the few short paragraphs, his name and address jumped out at him. There was an illegible signature in ink at the bottom, next to a signature line left blank.

Sully continued as he reached into his coat for a pen. "Oh, that's right, we do have that. Please sign."

Chris was not sure what was going on, but for some reason he didn't hesitate to take the pen.

"Anywhere?" Chris asked, trying to focus on the paper.

"Where it says signature," Sully said.

"What happened to your face?" said Murph, pointing at Chris's left eye.

"What?" Chris said. He touched his cheek to find it tender and sore. "I don't know. Must've happened last night."

"What happened last night?" Murph asked.

"Sign," said Sully, tapping the warrant with his finger.

"I-I'm not sure what happened. I don't remember everything. Can I ask what this is all about?" asked Chris as he signed his name.

"Now that you've signed, I'm afraid not, Mr. Dawkins," said Sully, his demeanor suddenly grown serious. Murph unbuttoned his suit jacket to let Chris check out the new two-holster look.

Chris managed to stammer, "Uh... "

Sully then broke into a wide grin and Murph shouted, "We're just messing with you, man! You can ask whatever you want. To answer your question, though, we're here to search your home and arrest you on federal terrorism charges. Put your hands where I can see them."

Chris thought, *This is worse than Jehovah's Witnesses.*

On the bright side, the sudden jolt of adrenaline that comes with being accused of a felony by men carrying firearms was a terrific hangover remedy. The thick queasiness in his body was instantly wrung out, and his mind snapped into tight focus. *This must be a mistake. But why are they here? Wait—it must have something to do with Mr. Wiles. Who knows what he's into, could be some shady stuff. These guys must have been watching him last night and that's how they found their way to me. Did Wiles say anything strange? Yes, tons. But anything incriminating? No. These guys probably just want to poke around and ask some questions. Is there anything I could tell them? No. Even if I could, I'm not dropping a dime on Mr. Wiles, he was pretty cool to me last night. Is there anything illegal in here? No. They can't arrest me. I didn't do anything, and I don't know anything. Just keep your mouth shut and they'll be on their way. If they ask what Wiles and I talked about, I'll just say I was drunk, and I don't remember much. Which I was. And which I don't.*

The two agents quickly frisked Chris, then pushed past him into the apartment and instructed him to take a seat in the kitchen.

Thirty minutes later, Murph and Sully had thoroughly searched Chris's small apartment, confiscating all kinds of things including cell phone, laptop, notebooks, cable box, and smoke alarms. They had sealed each item in a separate Ziploc bag, which in turn were placed in gray plastic bins like the ones you put your shoes in at the airport. With seven bins full of loot laid out on the kitchen floor, Special Agents Murphy and Sullivan joined Chris at the table, where he had been told to wait. He had been allowed to drink some tap water from a plastic cup, but he was denied his request for some Tylenol. His hangover was rolling downhill.

One of Chris's least favorite personal traits was surfacing, an involuntary shaking of the hands and knees when confronted with conflict. Chris had never actually been *in* a physical fight, but he had witnessed a handful, ranging in seriousness from shoving matches to a full-on curb stomping. Every time, even just the sight of violence left him shivering as if he had just gotten out of the water on a cold day. A few deep breaths always did the trick smoothing out the shakes, but the fear of not being up to the proverbial test always lingered a little longer. The shaking also came on in tension-filled situations and, truth be told, may have had something to do with Chris missing those shots back in high school, since his legs were pounding like jackhammers when Coach DiPetro summoned him from the end of the bench with his team down one point and three minutes left.

Chris took three deep breaths. He looked up at Sully. "Why do you need my smoke alarms? It's illegal to take them down, you know." Talking also helped keep the shakes at bay.

Sully seemed prepared to answer. "Not in cases of national security, Mr. Dawkins."

Murph entered from the bedroom. "And we take them because smoke detectors manufactured after 2015 record information about the air particulates in a room. The DNA of every person who has been in this room as well as the chemical signature... "

"Ahem! Hmm-mm!" Sully loudly cleared his throat, shaking his head at Murph.

"Anyway, we're taking it. National security," Murph finished. "Although we probably won't even need yours. Special Agent Sullivan, wait 'til you see what I found on his desk."

Just then, Sully's cell phone rang. He checked the number and, holding up a finger to Murph said, "One second, I have to take this." He left the kitchen, walked to the far corner of the living room, and turned his back.

Chris's anxiety returned over what Murphy may have found on his desk and was desperately trying to think of what it might be. "Can I ask what you found on my desk?"

Murph didn't want to reveal his damning piece of evidence without Sully present, so he gave Chris some standard lawman-ese to buy a little time and keep Chris off balance. "Mr. Dawkins, sir, I'm going to have to ask you to just sit tight for now and not ask any questions or make any statements regarding the material nature of our investigation for the moment."

That had the desired effect of quieting Chris down. Now Sully could be heard in the next room quietly saying, "His math book? No, I haven't... Where's his backpack?... Yeah, I figured that... OK... OK... Well, how did he do his homework?... Him saying he didn't have any doesn't mean... Yeah... No... Did you look in the car?... OK... OK... Yup... OK... I don't know... Maybe Tuesday... I know... OK... OK... What can I do? The Director said... Yup... OK... I've gotta... OK... I'm with a suspect... OK... Yup... I know... Yup... Sounds good... I've gotta... OK... I'll call later... Me too... Yup... Yup... OK, bye... Yup... OK... bye... OK... bye."

Sully returned to the kitchen. "That was HQ," he said, only sort of lying. The accusation of a federal felony charge hung in the air, but because they are both dudes, Chris and Murph glanced at each other with raised eyebrows. Sully glared at Chris. "And HQ is pissed," he added. If he were hooked up to any lie detector known to man, he would've passed with flying colors.

Murph stepped in to get the show back on track. "As I was saying, Special Agent Sullivan, and speaking of HQ, I think they'll be quite interested in something we have here." With that, he held up a Ziploc that contained one of the thousands of Sixdub be-logoed notepads that find their way into employees' homes, but he was pinching the bag's corner with the thumb and forefinger of his right hand while gingerly supporting it from the bottom with the palm of his left as if it were Jesus's high school yearbook. As he laid it gently on the table, Chris and Sully could both read what was written on the top page:

Target
Bayside Mall
C 4
Shwarma

"Care to explain this, Mr. Dawkins?" asked Sully, turning the pad toward him. "It seems you have some plans to detonate plastic explosives at the Bayside Mall in coordination with some known extremists."

Chris looked at it and said, "That means I have to go to Target this weekend to get paper towels, then I'm going to the mall to buy some basketball shorts. I also need to stop at Costco to get a couple cases of C4! energy drink. And I got a Groupon for the new Shawarma place."

Let this be a warning against indifferent spelling. While it is true that "shawarma" (three "a"s) is a delicious meat-based meal, you will recall that "Shwarma" (two "a"s) happens to be the name of the leader of the Islamic extremist group MILF, sworn enemies of the Great Western Satan-Dog, a.k.a. the United States of America. As an interesting side note, the members of MILF also love shawarma. We have that in common, at least.

Sully and Murph weighed Chris's answer and exchanged glances. Clearly, they had underestimated the wiliness of this

Dawkins kid. He was extremely well trained to be prepared with this cover story, *or* this was some made-up-on-the-fly Keyser Söze shit.

Either way, they zipped the cuffs on Chris and read him his rights.

CHAPTER 11

For someone in ziptie handcuffs, Chris was still fairly calm on the ride downtown in the backseat of Murph and Sully's tiny SUV. Surely this would all get sorted out. After all, he was innocent. And like the innocent frog dropped in a pot of water, he figured he could just relax for a while until the time came to jump out.

This was all new to him. Chris had managed to avoid trouble his entire life, his mom's warning always echoing in his brain when the temptation for funny business tried to take root. *Anytime you do something wrong, there are a hundred ways for them to catch you and if you know fifty of them, you're a genius.* Sterling moral code or lack of self-confidence, at the end of the day the cookies stayed in the cookie jar.

"So, what's happening now? Where are we going?" Chris asked.

Murph was driving, but Sully turned halfway around in his seat. "What's happening now, Mr. Dawkins, is that we are taking you to a secure location where you will be booked, fingerprinted, and processed for detention. Special Agent Murphy and I will then take your statement before your arraignment."

Is it getting warm in here? "But I didn't do anything!" Chris yelped. "My statement is that I don't know what any of this is all

78

about! You guys made some kind of mistake. How did you even get my name and find my house?"

Sully thought, *Classic counter-intelligence move. Nice try, kid.* He responded, "I'm sure your extremist friends like Wahiri Shwarma would love to know, but I'm afraid our investigative methods are classified. There will be some discovery made at a later point. You and your attorney will have time to review it."

Attorney? It is definitely getting hot in here. "Jesus, am I going to jail? Can you crack a window or put the air on or something?"

Sully said, "The answers to those questions, Mr. Dawkins, are yes, and no." He very well could have said "yes and yes," but he was still a little pissed about that look Dawkins had on his face back in the apartment after the HQ business.

"Jail? Seriously?" Chris screeched. "And when do I get an attorney?"

"Why do you need an attorney?" Murph asked. "You just said you didn't do anything. Innocent people don't need attorneys— what are you worried about?"

"He just said I was going to jail! If you want to bring me home, let's go. If you're taking me to jail, then I think I need an attorney!" Chris yelled.

"Settle down, Mr. Dawkins," said Sully. "As we said earlier, you have the right to an attorney, and one will be provided for you. When we get you processed, that is."

For the third time in less than twelve hours, and the second time as an incapacitated passenger in the back seat, Chris crossed the Golden Gate Bridge. This time he was delivered to San Francisco's Philip Burton Federal Building and US Courthouse. At the bottom of a ramp off Larkin Street, Murph flashed his badge to an armed guard who granted access to an underground parking structure. They drove down to the lowest level and parked in a deserted section of the garage. Murph and Sully tugged Chris from the car, and each took hold of one of his elbows. They led him into

the building under a sign that read: "Subbasement—
Processing/Detention."

The adrenaline that had briefly seized the upper hand in the
battle for Chris's body and mind when Murph and Sully showed up
at his door had been vanquished by the remaining alcohol in his
system. Alcohol: the winner and still champion. Chris's hangover
was blooming. Of course, it didn't help that he was basically in a
modern-day dungeon for reasons he still didn't understand, and as a
result, the more localized battle over control of his bowels was
being fought on two fronts against both booze and fear.

"I have to poop," said Chris as they passed a men's room in
the hallway.

"Hold it," said Murph and Sully simultaneously.

"It's not that kind," Chris said. "Please. I was out drinking last
night and I'm not feeling so good. I'm going to poop in the next
three minutes whether I'm on a toilet or not. Please."

You can waterboard a guy, make him stay awake for days, or
blast Yoko Ono into his earbuds, but nothing makes him more
cooperative than when he really has to take a dump and you control
access to the bathroom. Sully recognized this opportunity and did
not want to let it pass without gathering some intel. He stopped
walking and twisted Chris around to face him.

"Who were you out drinking with?" he asked.

"My boss, Jasper Wiles. And some girls we met."

"Is this Wiles person involved in MILF?" asked Murph.

"I don't think so; these girls were in their twenties."

Sully clarified, "The Militant Islamic Liberation Front."

"What?"

Murph jumped in. "Where were you last night?"

Chris closed his eyes and shifted his weight. "This club in the
Tenderloin. Synderella or something."

"You sure about that?" barked Sully. "You seem like you're
just making up a name. And you're sweating like a pig."

"I have to get into that bathroom. I'm not kidding. Please." Chris looked back at Murph, who he judged to be the more pliant of the two agents.

You know what also makes a person very cooperative? Threatening to shit your pants when that person is duty-bound to physically hold on to you at all times.

"OK, make it quick," Sully said. "Stall door stays open, cuffs stay on."

Chris was never so happy to hear that two men were about to wrestle his pants down and observe him defecate. "Thank you," he whispered hoarsely.

Murph elected to be the point man into the bathroom to clear away any MILF agents who may have been lying in wait in order to free their captive comrade. There was a slight logistical problem, however, when he drew both pistols only to be confronted by the pull handle on the door. Feeling Sully and Chris's eyes on him but thinking quickly, he used the butt of the left gun to knock on the door and then he pretended to listen intently in the manner of a Native American scout putting his ear to the ground. Satisfied that nobody yelled back, "Death to America!" Murph quickly holstered the left gun, and pulled the door open about six inches, stuck his left foot in, drew the gun back out, swept the door all the way open with his foot, and pounced through.

After ten seconds, but what seemed like ten minutes to Chris, Murph emerged and announced, "Clear."

Sully gave Chris a slight shove toward the door while Murph held it open. The bathroom had three urinals on the wall opposite the door and two stalls to the left. The stall in the corner was a large handicapper and Sully steered Chris toward it. Murph and Sully engaged in a quick but fierce battle of eyes over who would unbuckle Chris's pants and Sully won, by virtue of the fact that he still held on to Chris's bound wrists from behind and he simply pivoted Chris around to face Murph while saying, "Special Agent Murphy will lower your pants."

81

Special Agent Murphy did just that, and Chris shuffled
backwards into the stall with his pants around his ankles, his ass
hitting the toilet seat not a moment too soon.

Murph and Sully were standing in the open doorway of the
stall, but they were physically overpowered by the smell and took
an involuntary stagger backward. "You ever heard of a courtesy
flush, Dawkins?" Murph gasped.

"I can't reach it," Chris said, trying to contort his arms up and
back toward the handle.

Neither Murph nor Sully wanted the hazardous duty of
approaching ground zero to flush for Chris, so they both wandered
a few more steps away to breathe fresher air. Left unsupervised for
the moment, Chris bent at the waist and continued the purge.
Something caught his eye. A corner of paper was visible in the
small fifth pocket of his jeans, having worked its way partly out as
he wiggled into the stall. A quick glance up confirmed that the FBI
agents couldn't see what he was doing, so he stood halfway up and
contorted his arms down under his butt, being careful not to get
poop on them. Squatting and twisting, he was able to reach down
and snag the paper with two fingers. The exertion made his head
pound. Nervously, he looked up again.

Six feet away, but beyond the line of sight the stall doorway
afforded, Murph and Sully were engaged in another silent dispute,
each emphatically pointing at the other, then toward the stall, then
miming an ass-wipe. After a lot of headshaking, Sully held up both
hands palms facing out. He then made a fist, followed by a flat
hand palm down, followed by two spread fingers facing out,
followed by all five fingers. Murph nodded. Best-of-five Rock-
Paper-Scissors it was.

Meanwhile in the stall, Chris examined the paper.

The paper was one of Jasper Wiles's business cards. In the wee
hours of that morning, having been unable to rouse Chris awake as
they dropped him at home, Wiles wrote him a short note and
handed it to Hallie, asking her if she wouldn't mind "slipping it in

the old five-hole." Mia was texting but looked up to say, "A couple times."

The card had just two printed lines: the top read simply "Jasper Wiles" and underneath was a phone number, the last four digits actually spelling out "6DUB." Flipping the card over, Chris read a single word scrawled in wobbly handwriting:

Eleuthero

Murph had seized a 2–0 lead in the match by coming out of the gate with paper and following up with scissors. After a rock-rock tie, Sully got on the board by repeating rock, smashing Murph's scissors triumphantly.

Eleuthero? What the hell does that mean? Is that some message that has to do with terrorism? Is that why I'm here? Wait a second, these guys acted like they didn't know who Mr. Wiles was when I said we were out together. Is that good or bad? Think, Chris! It's probably bad, since now I really have no clue as to why I'm handcuffed on a toilet in the basement of FBI headquarters. But maybe good if...

Sully daringly shot out rock for a third time in a row and it paid off. The score was now even at two apiece. Tensions running high, the stakes even higher. "Wrap it up, Dawkins!" he shouted. "We're moving in one minute!"

Chris took one more look at the card to see if there was anything he missed. That was it: name, number, Eleuthero. Something told him that he should keep this to himself. Murph had frisked him back at his apartment, but he must have overlooked the small card, and it would probably raise questions if it were discovered now. Chris committed the phone number to memory and flicked the card into the corner of the stall behind the toilet.

"Almost done!" he called out.

Murph had to gamble here. Rock clearly had momentum, having won the last two rounds, but would Sully risk throwing it four times in a row? *He might, he's a stubborn bastard.* Paper seemed like the smart play, covering rock or at worst, tying paper. Scissors from Sully seemed unlikely, *but wait, had he thrown scissors yet? No. That's it! It has to be! 1-2-3 ROCK!*

"Special Agent Sullivan will be in to wipe your ass in a moment," Murph said, a little more gleefully than was strictly necessary, extending his rock fist into a series of victorious pumps as Sully retracted his index finger, transforming his scissors into something else.

Sully took a deep breath and stepped into the doorway of the stall. "Stand up," he said. "Turn around." Chris did as he was told, but to his relief, Sully did not reach for the toilet paper but instead pulled a multitool from his coat pocket and snipped off Chris's cuffs. "I've had seven kids, my ass-wiping days are over. Do it yourself and don't forget to flush."

CHAPTER 12

SAN FRANCISCO, CALIFORNIA
FRIDAY, 7:13 a.m. PST

As the good people of San Francisco awoke and began making their way to yoga class, Chris reeled out of the bathroom stall and was told to wash his hands, which he did thoroughly, unsure of how much butthole clearance they actually had as he recovered Wiles's note.

"That's enough," said Sully after a few moments, "You're not prepping for surgery. Let's go. Special Agent Murphy, resecure his hands."

The original cuffs were lying cut on the floor of the stall, and Murph had his extra sets back in the Trax.

"Give me a set of ties," Murph said, hoping Sully had a set on him.

Sully didn't have a spare set either, and knew that initiating a pissing match with Murph over who forgot the cuffs would show weakness in front of the prisoner, and backtracking to the vehicle to find a backup pair wouldn't be a great look either.

"Mr. Dawkins," he said, grabbing Chris's right elbow and wrenching it behind his back, "We will be manually restraining you for the time being. Any attempt to free yourself and/or flee will be met with deadly force. Special Agent Murphy, secure the prisoner's left arm."

Murph grabbed Chris's left elbow and attempted to make it meet his right. In order to regain some face after the ziptie business, he leaned in close to Chris's ear and whispered, "Try it, kid. One of my sidearms is brand new and I've been just waiting for the chance to break it in. I won't hesitate to drop you if you try to run." With that, he slipped a wink at Sully and the three of them left the bathroom, the FBI agents using Chris's face to push the door open the way a germophobe would use a paper towel.

The three of them turned right out of the bathroom and continued down a long hallway until they reached a door marked "Processing." They entered into an empty waiting room of sorts, with several rows of molded plastic chairs fixed to the floor, all facing a large Plexiglas window with a small counter and slot at the bottom, similar to the type one finds at gas stations in bad neighborhoods. Behind the glass sat a uniformed guard. A metal door with a square, wire-reinforced window was to the right of the guard's station. Small surveillance cameras were affixed high on the wall in all four corners of the room, and a fifth was trained on Murph, Sully, and Chris as they approached the guard's station.

Murph and Sully tightened their grip on Chris as they pressed their badges to the glass. The guard said, "Room two," and reached under the counter to push an unseen button, snapping the lock of the metal door open with a buzz. Passing through that door led the trio into a short hallway with more surveillance cameras and three doors on the right. They stopped and waited briefly at the middle door. The door buzzed and snapped, allowing them access to a small room containing a metal table with attached benches that could be described as the world's most depressing picnic table.

"Sit," said Sully as he and Murph released Chris's elbows. The table was perpendicular to the door, and when Chris took a step toward the bench on the right, Sully snapped, "Not there. There," pointing at the bench on the left. Needless to say, any choice Chris made would have been incorrect due to the rules of captor/captive power dynamics and especially when the captor was coming off a Rock-Paper-Scissors loss. Chris silently trudged to the opposite side of the table and slid into the seat.

Murph kept his eyes on Chris while Sully turned and looked up into the camera mounted above the doorframe. He pointed at the door and once again it buzzed and clicked. Without a word, the two agents left the room, leaving Chris alone with his thoughts.

This is not good. Is this jail? Am I in jail right now? I may puke. There is no toilet in this room. No one knows I'm here. How can I get out of this? How long am I going to be here? What do these guys want from me? I may puke. Breathe... breathe... breathe.

About ten minutes later, *Buzzzzzzzzzclick.* Chris looked up. Murph and Sully were back, Murph holding a set of ziptie restraints.

"Clasp your hands and place them on the table," Murph said. Sully stood behind Chris, pressing a hand on his shoulder as Murph zipped Chris's hands together again, this time in front.

"Stand up. Let's go," said Murph as Sully gave him a little shove off the bench in the direction of the door.

The door buzzed and the agents steered Chris down the short corridor, deeper into the building.

"What's going on now?" Chris asked. "When can I talk to someone? I'm telling you I didn't do anything wrong!"

They entered a large office where a few men in suits and some in uniforms were working. Sully said, "Mr. Dawkins, you have been arrested for a serious crime, and we have credible evidence to support that charge. You are going to be fingerprinted and photographed and then, if you're good, you will be allowed to make a phone call, and I suggest you make it count."

"I'll be good," said Chris.

His promise notwithstanding, Murph and Sully sat Chris down in a hard chair, locked his zip ties to an adjacent desk, and disappeared. Chris was still feeling like he might puke and/or pass out at any moment, but he was engaged for several minutes by a laminated sign on the wall next to him above a green trash can that read: "Free the Earth! Recycle!" The sign featured a drawing of an anthropomorphized cartoon Earth with arms, legs, and big googly eyes happily tossing a set of ziptie handcuffs into a green trash can just like the one below the sign.

Wait a second. "Free the Earth?" Was the Earth under arrest? If so, for what, and how did the Earth get out of the cuffs by itself? Maybe the Earth was supposed to be like a cop in this scenario? But a cop is already free. And there's no criminal to be seen, so is the Earth just tossing out some unused cuffs? That's way more wasteful than just not recycling. This makes no sense whatsoever.

It makes even less sense (or perhaps more) when you consider the sign was designed, produced, and distributed by the Environmental Protection Agency to law enforcement offices nationwide at a cost of $1,635,000.

After a lengthy wait, a uniformed officer came along, carrying a file that he flopped on the desk as he took a seat. "What's your name?" he asked.

"Chris Dawkins."

The guard, whose uniform identified him as Officer Silas of the Department of Homeland Security, confirmed this information with his paperwork and spent the next hour or so filling out forms on his desktop computer as Chris sat tethered, trying to find a comfortable position. He occasionally confirmed personal information for Silas, who pecked away at his keyboard using only his index and middle fingers.

Eventually, Officer Silas finished up Chris's processing paperwork and snipped off his cuffs, dutifully tossing them into the green can. He led Chris through the fingerprinting station, then to the mug shot area where Chris, because he is a dude, stood up as straight as he could, hoping the top of his head would reach the 72" line on the wall behind him. Silas then asked if Chris needed to call anyone.

Chris had been thinking about this since Sully mentioned it. Apparently, he was going to need a lawyer, even if it was just to help him explain his innocence. Problem was, Chris didn't know any lawyers. There was only one option he had. He wasn't too sure it would work out, but it was worth a shot.

Chris said that yes, he did have to make a call, and Silas showed him to a wall-mounted phone in a room adjacent to the mug shot studio. A sign on the wall above the phone advised that all calls would be recorded, illustrating the warning with a cartoon of an anthropomorphized reel-to-reel tape recorder holding a phone to its ear while casually leaning against a wall. (Provided by the ACLU. Cost: $1,420,000.)

Chris was anxious to get his call in, so he opted not to break down the sign's message. Picking up the receiver, he dialed from memory. Three rings... four... five rings...

Come on, come on.

"Wiles."

Thank God.

"Mr. Wiles! It's Chris Dawkins. I'm sorry to bother you, but I'm in big trouble."

Whereas Chris had so far spent his Friday morning being dragged around in handcuffs while simultaneously battling a cold, a Stage Three hangover and the United States Department of Justice, Wiles had arisen at sunrise, drank a smoothie and a coffee, and was presently working on his short game by pitching biodegradable golf balls made of compressed fish food off the top deck of the *Commodore 69*, trying to hit a certain seagull-poop-splattered rock on the nearby seawall. He had seventeen balls left and if he didn't hit the rock at least once, he would owe himself ten pushups. He put his cell phone on speaker and carefully nestled it on his golf bag between the driver and three-wood.

"Good morning, Chris. I presume you got my note. Did you take the eleuthero?"

"What is eleuthero?!!" Chris yelled, the exertion of raising his voice making his head spin.

"Siberian ginseng, my friend. World's best hangover cure. I thought you might need some this morning. I take mine in a smoothie." He rolled the next ball into position with his wedge, imagined the sound it would make striking the rock, and swung. Right at it.

"Mr. Wiles, I've been—"

"Get there!!" Wiles implored. He visualized his ball striking a sun-dappled putting green, spasming wildly, and spinning backward, as if quickly seeking the narrow shelter of the flagstick.

"What?" said Chris. "Mr. Wiles, I've been arrested."

The ball splashed two feet short.

Damn the luck. He had almost had it there for a second until this call came. A computerized voice from the Wanda mounted on the vessel's bulkhead chimed, "Your swing looks excellent, sir."

Wiles cut it off sharply. "Mother! These fish balls just don't carry," he griped, putting those words together for the first time in history. "I'm sorry, Chris, what did you say?"

"Mr. Wiles. Listen. Please. I've been arrested by the FBI. I'm in jail at the federal building downtown. I need your help."

"Arrested? For what?" Wiles asked, picking up the phone and putting his wedge back in the bag.

"I didn't do anything, I swear. This is all some kind of mistake. But they think I'm involved in a terrorist plot or something."

"Are you?"

"Absolutely not. I wouldn't involve you if I was, but I need help and I couldn't think of anyone else to call. By the way, are *you* involved in a terrorist plot? I thought maybe they arrested me because of something that may have happened last night. I don't remember very much."

Wiles considered this for a moment, his gaze drawn to the Pacific horizon beyond the seawall. "Chris, I am involved in many things, but a terrorist plot is not among them. I'm glad you called. You're a good man. Your insights during our conversation at the club last night I found both fascinating and valuable. As to your current situation, I think I can help you. Sit tight, drink some water, and don't talk to anyone. Help is on the way. I'm sending my attorney Biz Byner."

Wiles ended the call and did the following:

1. Seven pushups.
2. Dashed off a quick note on the back of one of his business cards and slipped it under the door of the *Commodore 69*'s guest cabin: Hallie and Mia, thank you for the pleasure of your company. There is eleuthero in the galley. —Wiles
3. Opened his phone contacts and hit "Biz."

CHAPTER 13

SAN FRANCISCO, CALIFORNIA
FRIDAY, 9:22 a.m. PST

As was her custom, Attorney Elizabeth "Biz" Byner walked through the door of her twentieth-floor office whenever she damn well felt like it, which today meant after yoga class in Golden Gate Park, followed by a coffee with two of her friends from class, Bertie and Dot, as was *their* custom.

Tall and slender, Biz had high cheekbones, large brown eyes, a wide, easy smile and fifty or so dick pics in the trash folder of her phone along with the names of the twenty-five or so dicks they belonged to. (Getting no response from the first, most guys will send a second just to be safe.) Her assistant Tess was at her desk, busily tapping away on her phone, cycling between Zoopzap (a Sixdub product), Ucoolbro, and Bumpr, as was *her* custom.

"Hashtag good morning, Tess," Biz said as she passed.

Tess looked up. "Good morning, Biz. You know that's not how you use a hashtag, right?"

Biz said, "It's not? Sad face emoji." Sometimes Biz's jokes didn't land with Tess, so to hammer it home, she added, "Winky-smiley face emoji," with an actual face-based wink and smile. "Would you bring me a coffee, please?"

Settling at her desk, Biz powered up her desktop and as it booted to life, she swung her chair around and took a moment to enjoy the view of San Francisco Bay. In the foreground lay the city's massive office towers, literally stacked to the brim with toiling cubicle dwellers, some of whom, it occurred to Biz, were probably in direct competition with one another, in theory cancelling out each other's efforts, yet somehow, they collectively moved ahead.

Far from a cubicle and the mysterious macroeconomic machinations they produced, her office was spacious and tastefully decorated with pale blue walls featuring spotlit black-and-white photos of NorCal landmarks. Her desk, chairs, and furnishings were simple and modern, light wood with white upholstery. Tess's bichon frise, Derek, napped on a white cushion in a sunny corner, preferring that spot to the artificially lit nap cushion in the reception area. Biz, Tess, and Derek were the only three in the office. Biz was in solo practice, and in fact had but a solo client: Jasper Wiles.

Her computer now heated up, she swung back around and to the rhythm of "Shave-and-a-Haircut," she keyed in her password. There was an email from Wiles waiting in her inbox, the subject line reading: "Toothbrush Patent!!" The two exclamation points told her this was a project of moderate urgency, three being the average, and seven the record. She opened the message and began to read as Tess returned with the coffee, setting it on the desk. Biz liked her coffee the way she liked her men: ready whenever she was, sweet, and hot but not too hot. She'd been burned before.

Biz read Wiles's email and began making notes to draft a toothbrush design patent application, adding her own thoughts of adapting the design for possible canine use.

Her cell phone rang. She checked the caller ID. Jasper. *Odd. He usually doesn't call this early. Maybe he wants to add another exclamation point to this job.*

"Good morning, Jasper. I had a great idea to add to your toothbrush project."

"I'm sure you did, Biz, but I need you to put that aside for now and meet me at the Burton Federal Building immediately. An associate of mine has been arrested by the FBI. He requires legal representation. His name is Chris Dawkins... "

CHAPTER 14

SAN FRANCISCO, CALIFORNIA
FRIDAY, 9:27 a.m. PST

After hanging up with Wiles, Chris felt a little better. Spirit-wise anyway. Help was apparently on the way, and although he had no recollection of any conversational insights he may have shared with Wiles last night, he appreciated his boss's regard. Physically, he still felt like the only liquid in his body was in his lower intestines, and he had to close his eyes whenever he turned his head to avoid incapacitating vertigo.

Officer Silas led him back through the offices and hallways to good old Detention Room Two, where he was told to wait. (As if he had the option of running out to do a few errands before his interrogation.) Chris trudged around the table, sat down, and laid his head on his folded arms just like he and his elementary school classmates were told to do when their teachers needed a break. Although meant as punishment for students, Chris always found those quiet interludes a pleasant diversion from the rigors and minor indignities of the school day.

Observing him from an adjacent room through a two-way mirror, Assistant United States Attorney Paul Vanzo said, "So that's Chris Dawkins. What can you tell me about him?"

Sully took a sip of his coffee. "Chris Dawkins. Twenty-four years old. Mother Candice Dawkins, deceased. Father Ronald

Dawkins divorced Candice when Chris was thirteen, currently lives in Texas."

Vanzo opined, "Broken home. Angry. Searching for belonging."

Sully went on. "Computer science degree, Cal State Fullerton, currently works at Sixdub, a software outfit up in San Anselmo."

Vanzo scratched his chin. Technical savvy. Left wing.

"That's where he came onto our radar," Sully said. He uses a bunch of dummy email accounts, but he got sloppy and left a trail to a MILF recruiting video, which he liked, possibly as a coded means to communicate with the group's leader Wahiri Shwarma, who we now have reason to believe is an associate of Dawkins. He signed their terms and conditions." Sully handed Vanzo a file that contained a printed out screenshot that indeed showed boomgoesthedynamite@aol.com gave the thumbs-up to Wahiri Shwarma's speech calling for "death to America, etc." and a copy of MILF's online agreement signed with Chris's digital hand.

Vanzo took the file and shook his head as he read it. The pieces were all falling into place. He looked up and stared hard through the glass at Chris's folded-up form. "Boom goes the dynamite, does it, Mr. Dawkins? Not in my city it doesn't, you son of a bitch."

"Actually," Murph said, looking for a spot to jump in, "his weapon of choice is C4. In his apartment, we recovered a checklist with details of an imminent attack, in his own handwriting, plus confirmation of his connection to Shwarma."

Vanzo flipped a page to see a copy of Chris's note. "Comp four, eh?" he intoned, letting Special Agents Murphy and Sullivan know he had seen some action (movies) in his day.

"This is the Director's boy, Vanzo," Sully said. "Barry's got a hard-on for this case. What can we tell him?"

"Tell him Mr. Dawkins will be a guest of the federal government for quite some time."

* * *

Biz drove down the same ramp that Chris had traveled several hours earlier. She parked on the public level and took the elevator up to the lobby. She wasn't entirely sure what she was getting herself into, but over the past few years, she had learned to trust Wiles's judgment. In addition to the steady stream of patent business, most of the work he sent her way was smoothing out the swirling eddies and currents that form in the wake of super wealthy people as they move through life: contracts, deeds, lawsuits, trusts, wills, acquisitions of public institutions, a DUI, tax work, and the like. There had never been any criminal accusations, no distasteful payoffs to be made, no bodies to bury, no phony apologies to script. She often told her friends who asked about her work that Wiles seemed to live a "charmed life," as if he and trouble were the same poles of a magnet, actively repelling each other, but a lot of that had to do with Biz's counsel and protection from his own impulsive nature.

Biz joined a short line to go through a security checkpoint and metal detector in the federal building lobby. She didn't get much detail from Wiles on the phone, only that one of his employees, a Chris Dawkins, had been arrested by the FBI for "terrorism." This Dawkins character and Wiles had apparently gone out drinking the night before, which was almost certainly unrelated to these charges, but just to be safe, Biz advised Wiles to stay off his phone and out of sight for the time being. "Do *not* come to the federal building. Go play golf or something," were her exact words, to which Wiles replied, "Can do!"

"Put your bag on the belt and step through, ma'am," a female officer said to Biz as she made it to the front of the line. After passing through the metal detector cleanly, Biz collected her bag and said to the woman, "I'm an attorney and my client is being held here. Where should I go to see him?"

"You're a criminal lawyer?" the officer said.

Mark A. Henry

"No, I try to keep it on the up-and-up."

The woman paused for just a second before cracking a laugh. "Well, that makes one of you. Your client's probably downstairs." She pointed to a bank of elevators. "Subbasement. Here, you need one of these." She fished a plastic visitor badge out of a bin much like the ones Murph and Sully used to collect their evidence and handed it to Biz. "And probably best to keep the jokes to yourself down there," she added. "They wouldn't get them anyway."

"Thanks," Biz said, clipping the badge on her lapel and heading off toward the elevator. "And thanks for the advice."

She slid past a small gaggle of government workers who were waiting in front of the elevator bank to head up to their offices. She reached to pushed the DOWN button, and several of the workers thought, "*YOU DON'T NEED TO PRESS THE BUTTON AGA— Oh. She's going down, not up.*" Not surprisingly, they all failed to add the thought, *What's wrong with me? Why am I such a dick?* Biz hit the scuffed button, lighting it up like an orange harvest moon.

After waiting it out for a few cars, the down arrow lit up with a ding. Biz got on alone and punched "SB." Down she went, and exiting into a dreary hallway, she consulted a large black directory board with interchangeable white letters to find "Detention/ProcEssing" listed as Room SB-101. Twenty-seven-year-old Biz looked left and right to get her bearings, then turned left and made her way down the hall, while eleven-year-old Biz was denied the opportunity to inform future visitors that the office of "Assface Terdsmell" could be found in room SB-112.

SB-101 turned out to be the same waiting room that Chris was hustled through earlier that morning, but now it was populated with two weary looking men, who both looked up at Biz as she entered. One of the men wore a suit, held a briefcase on his lap, and had a cardboard-sleeved coffee cup set between his feet on the floor. The second man sat against the wall, close to the guard station. He sported a yellow jumpsuit and some unflattering face tattoos. He

98

was chained to his seat, but the man in the suit seemed free to move about. As Biz shut the door behind her, Suit went back to riffling through his case, but Tattoo Face kept eyeing Biz as she moved toward him on her way to the window.

"Morning," he said.

"Good morning," said Biz, mentally measuring how much slack he had on his chain and giving him an appropriate berth as she passed.

"You a lawyer?" he asked.

"Hey!" yelled the guard behind the window, rapping on the glass with a clipboard and making Biz jump slightly. He pointed at Tattoo Face. "Shut up!"

"This is my attorney!" Tattoo Face protested, pointing at Biz as best he could with his shackled hands.

"You said that guy was your attorney a few minutes ago," the guard said, pointing at Suit.

"I fired his ass," Tattoo Face said. "This is my new attorney. I need to consult with her privately. I have my rights under the Declaration of Independence."

"Your attorney," the guard said, consulting his clipboard, "is Thomas Welk of the Public Defender's Office. Miss," he continued, turning to Biz, "are you Thomas Welk of the Public Defender's Office?"

"No," said Biz. To Tattoo Face she offered, "He sounds good, though."

Having played all his cards, Tattoo Face settled back in his seat and contented himself with watching Biz's rear end as she turned around and stepped up to the window.

"My name is Attorney Elizabeth Byner," she said to the guard, noting his uniform's name patch—Padilla. "I'm representing Chris Dawkins. Are you holding him here? I'd like to confer with him."

The guard produced a fresh clipboard and slid it through the slot under the window. "ID, please. And fill this out."

"Is Chris Dawkins here?" Biz persisted.

"First things first, Miss. I need your license and this all filled out," the guard said, tapping the clipboard with his pen.

Biz hated obtuse people, and she knew what was coming if she asked again, but she couldn't help herself. She had to take one more run at it. "Just answer this, please. If someone was arrested by the FBI, is this where they would be brought?"

"Probably." *Tap tap tap.*

"Fine," she said, taking her license out of her bag. She slid it through the slot and took the clipboard. She studied the documents she was tasked with as Padilla got busy feeding her license into a scanning machine on his desk.

After getting her ID back, she chose to sit in the chair across from Tattoo Face to annoy Padilla, still out of chain range mind you, but across the room from Suit, doing her part to break down any established hierarchy and/or power structure that had built up in the waiting room.

"That dude is obtuse," Tattoo Face said.

Biz glanced up at him, and then at Padilla, who was staring daggers, Chinese throwing stars, and lawn darts at the two of them. Biz gave him a *Something I can help you with?* look. Padilla fixed his stare at Tattoo Face and snapped, "Quiet!" Biz then looked down and got to work on her forms.

Despite the guard's warning, Tattoo Face proved quite chatty, and as Biz filled out line after line and box after box, she learned that his Christian name was Wayne, his street name was Punchy, that he faced federal drug trafficking charges, and one of his fellow gang member's cousins was attending Pomona College, her alma mater.

"It was nice talking to you, Wayne," she said as she signed and dated the final form. "Good luck to you."

She rose and presented the stack of forms to Padilla, who inspected each one carefully. After thirty seconds of standing at the window watching him read and flip, read and flip, Biz turned to retake her seat. The guard, without looking up, raised a single index finger, bidding her to stay put and wait. Biz said, "I'm just going to have a seat while you finish that up."

Padilla flipped the stack of forms closed, put them down, and slowly looked up. "I'll tell you what you're going to do," he said. "You're going to stay right there while I review these documents. If everything is in order, then you can see your client. If not, then you'll start all over again until it's right and until that time, you won't be seeing anybody except your new friend there." He tilted his chin up toward Wayne.

Biz turned to Wayne to give him a look that said, *Did you get a load of that shit?* but instead caught him staring raptly at her ass.

It's a good thing that government thought-reading technology has not advanced as far as they'd like, because *I swear before God and all that is holy, I am going to burn this place to the ground with everybody in it except me and Chris Dawkins* is the kind of thing that could be construed as a threat, and Biz might have found herself in handcuffs, sitting next to Wayne, wearing a yellow jumpsuit of her own. No, as far as the government knew, she was just another impatient attorney, climbing the legal system's ladders and jumping over its barrels. It's worthy of interest to note that the government sees itself as Donkey Kong in this scenario.

Biz turned back to Padilla, who said, "You made me lose my place. I have to start at the beginning again." With that, he turned his attention back to the forms.

Biz said, "You were on the third page. About halfway down, based on where your finger was when you stopped reading." She noticed, with no small amount of satisfaction, his finger go flaccid. "I'll be sitting right here. Let me know when you're done," she continued, taking her seat and digging her laptop out of her bag. "I have work to do."

Padilla stared at her for a second but quickly realized that she was no longer paying him any mind. He glanced at Wayne, who looked amused. Padilla reached out and squeezed the life out of the stress ball on his desk, wishing it were Wayne's head.

Ten minutes later, Padilla flipped the sheaf of forms shut with a crinkly whuff and rapped on the glass with the clipboard to get Biz's attention. "Miss Byner."

Biz closed her computer and came to the window.

"I can confirm that we are holding Christopher Dawkins at this facility and that he has, in fact, identified you as his attorney," Padilla said.

Take the win, Bizzy, take the win.

"Of course he did. I told you he's my client!" she smoothly said. *How does he know me? Wait, he called Jasper. Jasper told him my name. Right.* She made a mental note to call Wiles. "I'd like to see him. Right now, please."

"He's still being processed."

"Show me his processing paperwork."

"I don't have it. It's not complete."

"Show me some proof that he's here."

"He... uh, excuse me?"

Biz leaned forward. "How do I even know for sure he's here? I gave you all my info, now you give me some, Officer Padilla. Is Chris Dawkins here or is he on an airplane with a bag over his head, heading to some Third World black site where you'll waterboard him until he cracks while you stall me with paperwork?"

Padilla blinked. "Here," he said, double-clicking his mouse and twisting his flat screen monitor toward her. "That's Christopher Dawkins. He's just beyond that wall." He pointed over his left shoulder without looking back.

Biz peered down at the image on the screen. She saw the feed from a surveillance camera labeled as "Detention Room 2." Chris sat at a metal table with attached benches. His head rested on his folded arms. His face was turned slightly toward the camera. He appeared to be sleeping, or at least extremely relaxed. There was a fresh-looking wound under his left eye. A bruise the color of the two ball, highlighted by a red scrape down his cheek.

"Who did that to his face?" Biz snapped.

"He came in that way," Padilla said. It was true. He remembered studying the shiner as Murph and Sully led Dawkins in a few hours earlier.

"I need a printout of that image!" Biz said, pointing at the screen.

"That's... gonna take some paperwork," said Padilla. He glanced over at a carousel rack of forms behind him in the corner of his glass-walled officerarium. (Aquariffice?)

"What form? Give it to me."

Padilla now saw his mistake. By implying it would take "paperwork" to produce the requested results, he meant to imply that it would take paperwork by *him* and therefore he could delay the results indefinitely while the fictional forms were attended to and with any luck, this pesty woman would go away in the meantime. But Biz's demands to see the forms put him in a tight spot in that the "Security Camera Image Printout" forms in question did not actually exist.

The jumbled rockslide in his brain that was blocking the exit suddenly, by some miracle, shifted a bit and a bright shaft of light pierced through a tiny opening. He scrambled toward it.

"I can prove he came in that way," Padilla announced. Once again, he spun his monitor back toward the window so Biz could see. He minimized the image of Chris sitting alone at the table and opened up a new window. Biz followed his cursor as it ran up a short list of files and stopped to click on the one at the top.

The file opened and showed surveillance video of Chris's arrival. There he was being pulled from Murph and Sully's vehicle in the garage. The video was dark and shadowy. The camera angle showed just the right side of his face.

"I can't see his whole face," said Biz. "This doesn't prove anything."

"Just be patient, Miss. This video is documentation of your client's chain of custody. It's government property, but I'm going to allow you to see just enough to prove that he entered this building with the wound on his face. Maybe then you'll calm down."

And so, for the 250,163,785,224,752nd time in human history, advising someone to "calm down" had the exact opposite effect. It's kind of like telling someone to not think of an elephant. Biz's morning yoga class seemed like a long, long, *long* time ago.

Sure enough, the video continued, and Biz watched as Murph, Sully, and Chris exited the garage and entered the subbasement hallway. A white text graphic at the bottom of the screen indicated "Cam: Garage 2a," which passed the baton to "Cam: SBHall1" as the trio appeared through the doorway at the end of the hallway and marched on. With the better interior light and camera angle, Biz could indeed see that Chris was already sporting the bruise and scrape on his face, but she ignored Padilla's "See? See?" and his pudgy finger poking at Chris's face on the screen, leaving a transparent smudge. She squinted, pursed her lips, and bent closer as if she couldn't *quite* be sure that what she was seeing was evidence of anything. She was trying to decipher the look on his face (bowel-related desperation) when his image on the screen stopped walking and said something. A brief discussion with the two agents followed. One of the agents suddenly drew two sidearms and entered a room off the hallway and reemerged after a few seconds. The agents then pushed Chris into the room, leaving a shot of a deserted hall on the screen.

"What's going on?" Biz demanded. "Where did they go? What's in that room? Why is there no footage of what's going on in there?"

Padilla seemed taken aback for a second. He honestly did not know about the side trip to the bathroom, and he seized the monitor and twisted it back, out of Biz's sight. *Those stupid feds.*

"They went into the bathroom," he said, as if it was the most routine part of prisoner in-processing. "There's no cameras in there, for obvious reasons," he added, hoping Biz would not ask him to list any.

"Like what?" Biz shot back immediately.

"Well... uh, privacy, for one..."

"The privacy of your prisoners is a big concern?" Before Padilla could answer, Biz spun around quickly. "Wayne."

Wayne/Punchy/Tattoo Face snapped out of a deep, vivid, ass-based daydream (details of which will not be elucidated in these pages), and looked up.

Biz continued with a sigh, "When's the last time you went to the bathroom in privacy?"

Wayne, who would have enjoyed a bit of privacy at the moment thank you very much, actually had experience expelling no fewer than six bodily substances in the company of others and so responded without hesitation, "It's been a while."

Biz turned her attention back to Padilla. "So. Is it that my client has extra-special rights not afforded to citizens like our friend Wayne here? If so, I'd ask that you release him right now." The guard flicked his eyes down toward his monitor, which still showed an empty hallway.

"No?" Biz asked. "Maybe the 'obvious reasons' you mentioned earlier include the opportunity to assault and torture—"

"It's called 'enhanced interrogation,'" Padilla interrupted, remembering a memo he read years ago warning against the use of certain words and phrases. He figured the one-two punch of jargon/correction would slow this bitch's roll, but when Biz's eyes grew wide, he sensed he'd stepped in it.

Biz pounced. "So, you admit there's enhanced interrogation going on in that room?"

"No. No, I didn't mean that," Padilla sputtered, glancing down again at the monitor, wondering what the hell was taking so long. (Alert readers will remember that the Rock, Paper, Scissors competition went the full five rounds.) "Look, your client was fine when he came in here. I saw him myself. I'm sure the agents were just escorting him to the bathroom out of courtesy. Watch, they'll be out in any second." He swiveled the monitor back around toward Biz and he hoped that allowing her to watch would make her stop talking.

To Padilla's relief, Biz focused her attention on the screen and sure enough, it was just a few moments before she saw Chris, Murph, and Sully emerge into the hallway, make their way to the end of the hall, and arrive at the very spot in SB-101 where she now stood.

"See?" said Padilla, as he peeked around the screen to confirm what Biz was seeing. "He's fine. I don't know what happened to his face, but it didn't happen here. Now, like I said, he's still being processed. You'll see him in a little bit. Just have a seat."

"Fine," Biz said. She turned and gathered her things, having decided to make camp on the other side of the room away from Wayne, who was now creeping her out a little bit. Also, she had work to do and was no longer in the mood to chat. As she took a seat closer to Suit, he got up and extended his hand saying, "Rick Downey."

"Shut up."

Biz took out her phone and called Wiles. He picked up right away.

"Wiles. Hi, Biz."

"Jasper. Where are you?"

"Waiting on the fourth tee at Olympic. The Friday Ladies League got out ahead of me, and they play slow. What's going on with Chris?"

"I don't really know yet. I haven't seen him. Listen, it's perfect that you're there. I need you to do something... "

CHAPTER 15

Biz made good use of the time she spent waiting, reviewing some case law, making notes, and reading up on a procedure or two that she thought might relate to Chris's case. Jokes aside, she really wasn't a criminal lawyer, and if things got too serious for Chris, she would call in the cavalry from one of the bigger firms in town, like Extremelaw! or Wang, Shaker and Fellon, but for now she felt as prepared as she could be and was actually quite curious about this Chris Dawkins character and how this whole situation would play out.

As often happened when she focused her mind on a challenge, her thoughts drifted back to the notes her mother used to write and slip into her backpack for her to find on the first day of school each year.

First grade: *Do your best, Bizzy Bee!*

Fifth grade: *In the battle of the rock and the stream, the stream will always win. Not through strength, but through persistence.*

Biz was picturing herself as a rushing stream, slowly but steadily wearing down any rock foolish enough to stand in her way, when Officer Padilla hung up his desk phone, rapped on his window, and called her name. In the time that Biz was working on her laptop, Padilla had made a call to check on the status of Detainee Dawkins and asked to be informed when Chris would be available to meet with his attorney. Padilla was not excited about the prospect of Biz hanging around his waiting room any longer than necessary, and his phone call allowed her to jump the line ahead of Attorney Richard Downey of the venerable firm Wiesel, Greesey & Nutzack, Attorneys-at-Law, who remained in his seat as Biz stood up and headed to the door near Padilla's window. In Japan, they say that the nail that sticks up gets hammered down, but this is America, goddamn it. The squeaky wheel gets the grease.

Wayne had been collected and escorted from the room about ten minutes ago by two men in DEA windbreakers, and as Biz passed by his now-empty chair, she heard the buzz-click of the door lock disengaging. The door was opened by a young uniformed officer. "Miss Byner?" he asked. "Follow me, please."

It was a short walk to Detention Room Two and as they stopped at the door, the officer handed Biz a thin file. He punched in a code on the keypad near the doorframe and opened the door for her, allowing her to lay eyes on Chris Dawkins in the flesh for the first time.

He didn't look great, but he looked better than he felt. He weakly raised his head off the table and looked back and forth between his two visitors. *Is this Mr. Wiles's attorney? Figures.*

"Mr. Dawkins," the guard said, "your attorney is here. I'll be outside. Come knock on the door when you're ready to leave," he added.

"I'm ready to leave now," Chris said.

"Not you, dumbass. I'm talking to her."

Biz felt the need to defend Chris, but she had to admit, that was a pretty dumb thing to say. Instead, she simply thanked the guard and sat down across from Chris, laying her new file on the table between them along with her laptop and a yellow legal pad she took from her bag.

"Chris, my name is Biz Byner. I'm Jasper Wiles's attorney. He asked me to come see you and hopefully get you out of this mess. What happened to your eye?"

"What? Thanks. I don't know. Nice to meet you," Chris rasped. Without a word, Biz bent down and rooted through her bag, producing a bottle of water. "Here," she said, sliding it across the table to him. Immediately, there was banging on the outside of the door and muted shouting. They both turned to look as the guard burst through, saying, "Hey, hey, no, hey, whoa, whoa, no, no! What's that?!"

Biz grabbed the bottle off the table and held it up for the guard to see. "Water. My client is thirsty."

"He can't have that," the guard said.

Instead of responding, Biz handed him the bottle, looked at her watch, and turned around to write on her pad, talking aloud as she did.

"11:41 a.m. Officer... "—she turned to look at the guard's nametag, then continued to write—"Martin denies suspect water."

Officer Martin held out his hands. "Whoa. I didn't say that. I meant he's not supposed to receive anything from visitors."

Biz said, "So he *can* have a drink of water?"

"Yes," said Martin.

"But not *that* water," Biz said, indicating the bottle in Martin's hand.

"No," said Martin.

Chris looked up at Officer Martin, then down at Biz. Martin wore a gun on his hip. He had eight inches and a hundred pounds on Biz. He was standing, she was sitting. She was making him dance like a puppet. *What the hell is going on here? Thank you, Mr. Wiles, for sending this person to me.*

"So how do we solve this water problem, Officer Martin? Let's work together here," Biz said.

"He can have a cup of water. I'll bring it to him." Martin turned to go, with the mild sense of well-being most guys have when tasked with a simple mission.

"Thank you. And where does this water come from?"

Martin stopped and cocked his head, mentally picturing the label on the water cooler down the hall. "The Rocky Mountains, I think."

Biz smiled like an angel. "I meant, where in the building."

Chris smiled like a jerk. *Dumbass.*

"Oh. Right. It's just down the hall."

"Great," said Biz. "So, it won't be too long, then."

"No. I'll be right back." Martin turned to leave again.

"Officer Martin?"

Martin turned back around once more.

"Could I have my water bottle back, please? I'm a bit thirsty myself."

"Oh. Sure, here you go." Martin quickly handed the bottle back to Biz, and it would not be an exaggeration to say that he then hustled out of the room.

Chris stared at Biz as she put the bottle on the table. "Sorry," she said. "I know you're thirsty." She tilted her head back toward the door. "He'll be right back, though."

"Can you get me out of here?" Chris asked. "I didn't do anything. This is all some kind of mistake, and they found this note I wrote to myself and they think I'm some kind of terrorist or something and—"

"Are you a terrorist?" Biz cut in.

"No!"

Biz eyed him carefully. "OK, good. I believe you." She figured that a true believer wouldn't be quite so twitchy and quick to renounce the cause. After all, if you're prepared to massacre infidels and maybe even martyr yourself in order to get to paradise and start plowing your way through your eighty virgins (it used to be seventy, but you know, inflation), you probably would take the opportunity to tell any Western imperialist lady lawyers to fuck off. Simple logic, really. Plus, Biz thought Chris had kind eyes. The right eye anyway, the left one was kind of red and gross.

"Thank you," said Chris, relieved. Once again, his spirits ticked up a notch. A little belief will do that. "Can you get me out of here?" he asked again.

She opened the file Martin gave her. "It says here they're charging you with conspiracy to commit a terrorist act, which carries a maximum penalty of... hmm, twenty years in prison. That does not sound great. However,"—she raised a finger—"the government is obligated to walk down a very narrow path in order to convict you."

"What do you mean? They seem pretty confident," said Chris.

"Really?" Biz asked. "Why? Did you tell them about how you and I killed those drifters last week and traded their organs on the black market for yellow cake uranium that we used to build a dirty bomb, set to go off in Times Square tomorrow at noon?"

"What?!" Chris yelped. "We did *not!*" He looked up at the camera in the corner of the room, waving his hands. "I don't know what she's talking about!"

"Relax, Chris. There's nothing to worry about. Yes, we've admitted to a terrible crime—"

"You did! Not me!"

"Fair enough. I did. But why is no one coming in here to arrest me? I handed you a bottle of water and Officer Martin busted in here in two seconds." She gestured up toward the camera. "Yes, people are *watching* us right now, but it's illegal for them to *listen* to an attorney-client conversation. If someone did come in here to arrest me based on what I just said, we'd end up walking out of here anyway because they would have violated our civil rights."

In the adjacent room, on the other side of the mirrored window, Murph, Sully, and US Attorney Paul Vanzo all stood with their arms crossed, observing their suspect and his attorney.

"What's he so worked up about?" Sully asked.

"He knows he's in deep shit, that's what," Vanzo replied. Seeing Biz study Chris's file and make a fairly lengthy speech to her client, he continued, "Look. Right now, she's probably advising him to cop a plea."

Had the founding fathers rolled a little differently back in the day, Vanzo would have been privy to Biz's actual advice, which was as follows:

"So," she said to Chris, "let's count as a win the fact that you are protected by the Constitution of the United States of America."

"Great," Chris mumbled.

Biz folded her hands in front of her. "Chris. In the context of how your day has been going so far, I would hope that you would be a little more enthused about any good news you can get."

The door behind her buzz-clicked, and Officer Martin appeared holding a small paper cup of water.

"And look!" Biz exclaimed. "More good news! Here's your water! Thank you, Officer Martin. My client appreciates it very much."

Martin set the water on the table and turned to Biz. "You're welcome. Your client will be questioned in thirty minutes," he said.

"Thank you," said Biz. As Martin turned to leave, Chris drained his water in three gulps. Biz refilled his cup from her water bottle, then opened her laptop. "You heard him," she said. "You have thirty minutes. Tell me everything. Start with what happened to your face."

Chris gingerly touched the welt under his eye. He was actually quite curious about that himself.

"I don't know," he admitted. "Mr. Wiles took me out drinking last night, and I don't remember everything. Like this," he said, pointing to his eye, "or how I got home, even." He lowered his

112

voice, despite Biz's earlier display that eavesdropping was impossible. "I thought that this all might have to do with Mr. Wiles, maybe some business deal he was into with the wrong people or something, and the FBI thought I was involved because we were together last night, but the FBI guys didn't seem to know who he was."

Biz froze. "Hold it. You mentioned Jasper to them? When?" She quickly checked her watch. It had been over an hour since she called him. She reached into her bag for her phone.

"They asked me where I was last night before they let me go to the bathroom, so I told them the truth." Sensing he may have made a mistake, Chris added, "I was almost pooping my pants. Literally."

Biz was tapping and scrolling away at her phone and did not like what she saw. Or didn't see. *Come on, Jasper.*

She put the phone down, typed a quick note, and looked at Chris. "It's fine. Let's keep going with what you did last night."

Sober Chris had an excellent memory, and he gave a detailed account of his evening at the Billionaire's Club meeting, the odd encounter with Wiles outside the library, the excursion to Syndrea, and their extemporaneous double date with Hallie and Mia. Drunken Chris had a terrible memory and the timeline grew dark at some point, restarting when Murph and Sully pounded on his door.

Chris's tale continued on as he recounted his conversations with Murph and Sully at home, the discovery of the C4/Shwarma note, the car ride into the city, and his trip to the bathroom where he found Wiles's cryptic note. "Yeah, he swears by that stuff," Biz said when Chris mentioned eleuthero. All the while, Biz made notes, asking Chris to pause from time to time while she clicked and tapped on her computer, several times taking a few minutes to read something over while Chris patiently looked on. Thanks to her encounter with Officer Padilla and the surveillance video he reluctantly shared with her, Biz was able to corroborate the tail end of Chris's journey, and she was pleased that his first-person account matched the objective view that she had seen.

Biz checked her phone once more, sighed, and put it back down.

"Chris," she said, "I think—"

The now-familiar buzz-click of the door cut her off, and she turned around to see a shortish man whose black hair was somehow both thick and receding, carrying a file folder and briefcase enter the room, followed by Murph and Sully. Biz jotted a quick note on her laptop and turned it so Chris could see:

b quiet, b cool

The short man said, "Mr. Dawkins, Counselor... " He paused to refer to the folder he carried to demonstrate that he was so consumed with delivering swift justice that he was left with little time to remember the names of his adversaries. "Byner. I'm United States Attorney Paul Vanzo. This is FBI Special Agent Sullivan and Special Agent Murphy."

Biz got up to shake hands. "A pleasure, Mr. Vanzo. Elizabeth Byner."

"Likewise, Counselor," said Vanzo. Biz then introduced herself to Murph and Sully and after everyone exchanged business cards, Vanzo said, "If you wouldn't mind taking a seat next to your client, we'd like to sit and ask a few questions before we begin the process of his prosecution."

Vanzo waited while Biz gathered her things and moved them to Chris's side of the table and sat down. He then slid into the bench seat Biz vacated and laid his file on the table. Sully took the spot next to him and Murph, mentally measuring the remaining bench space, opted to remain standing near the door rather than squeeze in and leave half a cheek hanging off the edge.

Chris felt his knees beginning to shake until Biz laid a soft but firm hand on his right knee under the table. He glanced over at her, but she made no eye contact.

Tenth grade: *Be without fear in the face of your enemies. Protect the helpless and do no harm.*

Vanzo set his briefcase on the table and took a few seconds more than was strictly necessary to spin the combination locks and pop it open. He then produced a small digital audio recorder and set it on the table. Biz gave Chris's leg a reassuring pat and fiddled with her computer while Vanzo set up. "This is being recorded?" she said, pointing at the recorder.

"Yes, counselor," Vanzo said, pressing a button on the recorder. "Christopher Dawkins," he began, "you are being charged with attempting to provide material support or resources to a designated foreign terrorist organization and conspiracy to commit a terrorist act against the United States. This is a very serious crime, and the evidence of your guilt we have collected in just the very early stages of this investigation is overwhelming. These agents are going to ask you some questions and take your statement. You will appear before a judge this afternoon to be arraigned. Following that, you will be remanded into federal custody and held until your trial and subsequently imprisoned." He paused and looked up at Chris, pleased to see his expression of shock.

Biz said, "Mr. Vanzo, I'm afraid there's been some kind of mistake. My client is completely innocent of these charges. Any evidence you may have would be circumstantial at best. I'd like to know exactly what this so-called evidence is before we proceed any further."

Vanzo exhaled sharply through his nose. "Any and all evidence will be made fully available to you through discovery

before Mr. Dawkins's trial. For now, be assured that the
government has extensive electronic surveillance *and* physical
evidence collected from your client's apartment that will prove his
guilt."

Biz cocked her head. "That's it?"

Vanzo opened his mouth and stiffened slightly. Sully jumped
in. "Let me assure you, Miss Byner, the government's evidence is
more than sufficient."

"Let me assure *you*, Special Agent Sullivan, that the 'physical
evidence' you have is nothing more than my client's shopping list.
I just thought you would have some witnesses or something to
corroborate these ridiculous charges."

"Miss Byner," Vanzo began.

"*Ms.* Byner. Or Counselor Byner, please," Biz corrected.

"Of course," Vanzo said. He took a breath and his expression
changed, as if he had come to a decision. "*Ms.* Byner. I'm going to
turn off my recorder for a moment."

Biz opened her hands. "Please, be my guest."

Vanzo lifted his recorder off the table and carefully clicked the
STOP button.

"Ms. Byner. I've not seen you around this building before,
have I?"

Biz shook her head. "No, I'm sure you haven't. I've never
been here before today."

"And which firm are you with, again?"

"I'm in solo practice."

"I see. May I ask if you've ever defended a federal case like
this before?"

"No."

"Never?"

"No, you may not ask."

Vanzo's jaw clenched slightly. "You usually don't get your
hands too dirty with criminals like this punk, do you?" he asked,
pointing at Chris. "No, I'm guessing you're much too busy shaking

down rich nerds who want to sue each other over some software or divorce their first wives who got too fat to come down here and roll in the dirt with civil servants like me. I don't know who you think you are, but let me explain something to you. You're out of your depth here, *Ms.* Byner. Your client screwed up. Big time. Once when he committed this crime and again when he hired you. This case is the United States of America vs. Chris Dawkins. *I'm* the United States. Your client will appear before *my* judge and *my* jury in *my* courtroom and he will spend the rest of his days in *my* prison. If I say the evidence is sufficient, it's sufficient." He stared at Biz, who simply said, "OK. Shall we continue, then?"

Vanzo said, "Yes, let's get on with it." He restarted his recorder. "Special Agent Sullivan?"

Sully fixed his eyes on Chris. "Mr. Dawkins, your attorney mentioned witnesses in your case. We know that you were associating with a Jasper Wiles last night. Could you tell me about your relationship with him?"

Chris quickly looked to Biz, then back to Vanzo. "He's my boss. I work at Sixdub in San Anselmo. I ran into Mr. Wiles last night, and he invited me out for a drink."

As Chris was talking, Biz picked up her phone and refreshed the last page she had been on. A text from Wiles was there.

Check twitter. Most VIP I could find.

"Gentlemen," she said. "In the interest of cooperation, I thought I could share something about this Mr. Wiles. I just Wangled his name, and I found his Twitter account." She slid the phone over to Vanzo, and he saw a tweet posted four minutes ago. It was a selfie of Wiles and two women of a certain age all wearing golf attire and holding what appeared to be mimosas on an outdoor patio. The caption read:

Mark A. Henry

Making the turn at @Olympicclub. Having
refreshments with @SenGailBooker & @carliedanver
#ladiesday #fairwaysandgreens #daydrinking

Biz said, "Now, I recognize former Senator Booker of course,
and she's looking well, isn't she? And Carlie Danver seems
familiar too. Is she married to George Danver, the philanthropist?
This Jasper Wiles certainly is an interesting character. Imagine.
One night, you're out on the town with an accused terrorist and the
next day, you go out golfing with some powerful and influential
members of the community and post it right out there on Twitter
for the whole world to see. Mr. Wiles has some explaining to do if
you ask me, am I right, Mr. Vanzo? Agent Sullivan? Agent
Murphy?"

No one answered, but as Sully started to push Biz's phone
back, Vanzo took it again to take one more look, as if to be sure the
photo had not changed. It hadn't. He tipped a mental domino and
let the tiles fall. If he subpoenaed Wiles, it would become public.
Some newspaper or website could pick up on it and look into
Wiles's background. They would find this Twitter post and tie
Wiles to Senator Booker and this Danver woman. Gail Booker
belonged to the same political party as Vanzo, Vanzo's boss, and
Vanzo's boss's boss. The careers of all three would be done no
good by any of this. Wiles will be put in the ten-foot-pole file for
now. Domino. Motherfucker.

Vanzo put the phone down and slid it back toward Biz.
Shielding his notepad from her view, he wrote "~~WILES~~" and
shared a glance with Sully, who, remembering Director Barry's
warning to keep a tight lid on things, nodded in agreement. Vanzo
took a deep breath and said, "Yes. Yes, very interesting. However.
Jasper Wiles is not a person of interest in this case at this point in
time."

"But you will subpoena him? He could have exculpatory
evidence that exonerates my client!" Biz exclaimed. *Jasper, you*

118

*don't know how close you came to getting yourself dragged into
this. That horseshoe up your ass just keeps getting bigger, doesn't
it? Thank God you were at your fancy club this morning and
Senator Booker has still never met a camera she didn't like.*

"At such time as is appropriate, we will sit down with Mr.
Wiles, should the necessity arise," Vanzo lawyered.

"Very well," Biz lawyered right back. "I must admit, I would
be very interested in meeting Senator Booker, even in a deposition
setting."

"Should the relevancy apprise itself," Vanzo cautioned, mostly
literately. "Now then, shall we move on to the business at hand?
Please continue, Agent Sullivan."

Sully said, "Mr. Dawkins, what is your relationship to the
group known as the Militant Islamic Liberation Front?"

Chris looked at Biz. He could feel that she had somehow
gained the upper hand in this situation by showing the three men
Wiles's Twitter post. He didn't get a good look at it, but what could
it have possibly shown that made them back off? This was some
legal sorcery on Biz's part, and Chris made a silent pledge to
himself right then and there to follow her every lead.

"I've never heard of them."

This was true. Sort of. In intelligence and government circles,
Shwarma's band of pesky troublemakers are known as MILF, but
most Western media outlets refer to the very same group as Muslim
Affiliated Nationals Bringing Unified Theology, or MANBUT, due
to some vagaries in the translation of the original Zazarish and also
that the government agencies and the media have a great mutual
disdain and therefore refuse to cede to one another even so much as
the identity of their common enemy.

Sully sighed. "You may know this group as... MANBUT."

"I've heard of MANBUT," Chris replied. "I've seen them in
the news and stuff, but I have no relationship with them."

As the agent made a note in his file, Biz spoke up. "I'd like to
clarify something my client said a moment ago."

Sully looked up. "Yes?"

"Before you came in, I had the chance to ask him about the events of this morning, and he told me that there was a brief discussion of the Militant Islamic Liberation Front with you and Special Agent Murphy. So, while my client denies involvement with MILF, MANBUT, or any terrorist organization, to say that he has never heard of MILF is not technically correct."

Chris turned and stared at Biz. Without meeting his eyes, she tapped her pen on her laptop screen drawing his attention to the words still written there.

b cool

Meanwhile, Sully couldn't believe it. Not three questions into the interview and they caught Dawkins in a lie already. And his lawyer set him up for it!

"Mr. Dawkins," he began, capping his pen and slipping it into his jacket pocket as if to indicate that the time for the laborious minutiae of note taking was over with and the only detail left unchecked in this case was to order Chris's prison jumpsuit. "Lying to a federal authority will not serve you well. I will ask you again, and this time I'd like the truth, if you wouldn't mind. What is your relationship with the terrorist group MILF, a.k.a. MANBUT?"

Biz poured Chris another half cup of water and he drank it quickly. Putting the cup down with a noticeably shaking hand, Chris said, "There's no relationship. I don't know anything about either group other than what I've seen in the news. I guess you did ask me about MILF this morning, but I was confused and not feeling well, and I didn't really know what you were talking about."

"So, what did you tell him?" asked Vanzo, leaning in.

At this point, Biz tipped her hand by sitting back in her chair a bit. The corners of her mouth twitched. This seemingly minor shift in her demeanor tripped an alarm in Vanzo's brain and he froze, in the same fashion he did back in 'Nam when he was out humping on patrol and almost stepped on a trip wire, thus fragging himself. The only thing to do in such situations is to silently signal to one of your buddies to come and cut the wire with... oh wait, Vanzo was never in Vietnam; he was just thinking of that scene in the movie *Predator.*

Nevertheless. "Wait!" he snapped, fighting the urge to bring his fist up in that way where you show the back of your hand to the people following you.

Before Chris could begin to explain his brief interrogation in the hallway outside the bathroom, Vanzo held up his hands. "Don't say another word." He hastily picked up his recorder and punched the STOP button.

"Is there a problem, Mr. Vanzo?" Biz asked.

"No," he said quickly. "We need to attend to something. Wait here. Agents, please join me outside." He gathered up his notepad and briefcase and made his way to the door, giving it a few sharp raps as Murph and Sully queued up behind him, exchanging quizzical looks.

"Actually, my client would like to go down to the break room and get a coffee," Biz said with a grin.

Vanzo was so flustered, he didn't realize Biz was messing with him. When Officer Martin opened the door, Vanzo actually told him to fetch some coffee for Chris.

"I'll take tea if you have it!" Chris shouted as the door clicked shut. Then he turned to Biz. "What, exactly is happening right now?"

Biz said, "When the FBI was at your house, they read you your rights, didn't they?"

"It kind of freaked me out," Chris said.

Biz continued. "And then, when they were driving you here, you told me they talked about you getting a lawyer, right? And they gave you that stupid line about innocent people not needing one?"

"Right. That part also freaked me out. I almost literally shit my pants later, if you remember."

"Yes, I do remember that part. And your little discussion outside the bathroom, which I saw on video by the way, is what has Mr. Vanzo so worried right now. Chris, if the FBI read you your rights, which they did in your kitchen, and if you asked for a lawyer, which you did in the car, and they then questioned you without a lawyer present, which they did in the hallway, that is illegal and Vanzo knows it."

"So, I can get out of here?" Chris asked hopefully.

"Probably not. But remember what I said about the government having a very narrow path to follow? Think of them as walking a tightrope. If they make it to the end of the rope, you go to jail. If we can knock them off at any point, you get to go free. I'm not sure we knocked them off, but they're a little off balance at least. I also got you a free cup of coffee." She offered him a small toast with her water bottle.

Outside, Vanzo stomped to the end of the hallway and into a vacant office, followed by Murph and Sully. He turned and faced the two agents.

"Which one of you McMorons Mirandized this guy?" he snapped.

Murph and Sully looked at him, then at each other. Being trained investigators, they both sensed that the way Vanzo combined an insult to their intelligence with an ethnic slur could mean the case had hit a snag. Sully said, "I did, why?"

"Think carefully." Vanzo breathed. "Did Dawkins, at any point, ask for a lawyer?"

Murph said, "No. Well, we did talk about lawyers in the car on the way down here. Special Agent Sullivan told Dawkins he would get one before his arraignment, then *I* said, 'Why do you need a lawyer if you're innocent?' I say that to all the suspects. It's kind of my thing."

Vanzo briefly entertained the notion of choking Murph to death but for various logistical reasons opted not to. "And? What did Dawkins say? Exactly."

Sully cut to the chase. "He never said, 'I want a lawyer.' He just sort of agreed that it might be a good idea."

Vanzo rubbed his chin while exhaling through his nose. "OK. We can work around that."

Sully now saw what was happening. "Is he going to say we questioned him after he asked for a lawyer? Look, Vanzo, don't underestimate this kid. He's sneaky smart. You didn't hear how smoothly he covered his tracks when we found that note back at his place. And when I asked him about his connection to MILF, he acted like he didn't know what I was talking about."

Murph felt he had to bolster their case a bit more. "We know the law, Vanzo. If he asked for a lawyer, we wouldn't have questioned him. That's why I always tell the suspects they don't need one. The longer it takes before they lawyer up, the more we can get out of them. Duh."

Vanzo looked around the small room and once again weighed the opportunity to physically assault Murph, perhaps by cracking him on the head with a stapler or better yet, that big three-hole punch over there on the shelf. Alas, he couldn't concoct a credible scenario that would explain away any office supply–related injury, and he reluctantly let the notion pass.

"Fine," he said. "I'm going back in there. You two stay here."

When Vanzo returned to Detention Room Two, he saw that Chris had already received his coffee, but it appeared untouched on the table.

Biz greeted him by saying, "Mr. Vanzo, while you were gone, I had some time to think. It occurred to me that my client was questioned without his attorney present even after he requested an attorney during his car ride down here. If you release him now, I'm sure he will not see the need for any legal action against your office for this gross violation of his constitutional rights."

123

Vanzo did not respond immediately as he retook his seat and laid out his notepad and recorder. Very deliberately, he picked up the recorder and pushed the RECORD button.

"Mr. Dawkins," he began. "The arresting agents in your case confirmed that you never requested an attorney at any time and therefore any subsequent questioning was legal and your responses admissible. Lacking evidence to the contrary, let us proceed. If that would suit you, Ms. Byner?"

"Of course," Biz said. Of course, of course. It was Chris's word against the word of the two FBI agents, and there was no way to prove either version. Biz had to accept the setback without complaint, but the casual way she did it made Chris's heart sink. He had put his faith in Biz and her apparent legal wizardry, but now it seemed his fate was sealed. The government seemed like it could prove he did *something*, and it was up to him to prove he did *nothing,* which now that he thought about it seemed perversely impossible.

"Very well," Vanzo said. "Now then, shall we continue?"

"Actually, Mr. Vanzo, I'm advising my client to not answer any further questions right now," said Biz.

Chris liked hearing that, but also not the sound of it.

"Very well," Vanzo repeated. "I'll see you at the arraignment in a few hours. Make yourself comfortable, Mr. Dawkins." He clicked off his recorder and stood up to leave.

"Do you know who Liberia Boyd is, Mr. Vanzo?" Biz asked.

Vanzo paused. He couldn't say no. The activist, professor, author, and Nobel Prize finalist Liberia Boyd was a household name. But he also couldn't say yes, because Biz clearly *wanted* him to say yes and that would not do either. The best option was to say nothing and get the hell out of there. As he knocked on the door to be let out, Biz continued, "It's OK if you don't. I can introduce you when she gets here."

Officer Martin opened the door but Vanzo pushed it back shut and remained in the room. He turned but did not sit down. "I know who Liberia Boyd is. The so-called social justice warrior. And why would she be coming here?"

Biz said, "She prefers social justice warrior*ess*, actually. She's something of a mentor to me."

"You didn't answer my question," Vanzo said. "Why is Liberia Boyd coming here?"

"Well, I'm not sure that she is just yet," Biz said, looking at her watch. "It's almost noon, and at the moment she's finishing up Advanced Constitutional Law class over at Berkeley. In a few minutes class will be dismissed, and I'll send the text I wrote letting her know that an innocent young man has been arrested by federal agents, who questioned him without his attorney present and threatened him with an unregistered handgun."

"Whoa, whoa!" Vanzo protested, but Biz rolled right over him.

"I'm also attaching a photo of Chris's face showing his injury," she said, pointing to the cut on his cheek, "so she can make some assumptions about how this young man was treated while in federal custody and share them with her thousands of social media followers, turning those assumptions into narratives. Narratives we will probably hear about on the news tonight. And speaking of followers, she teaches her next class at one o'clock and would love nothing more than to load a whole lecture hall full of students onto her bus and come down here for a little protest field trip. We used to do it all the time. And yes, she has her own special bus just for protesting. She drives it herself."

Paul Vanzo wasn't afraid of heights, public speaking, spiders, flying, needles, tight spaces, ghosts, intimacy, or even clowns. Black lesbians with bullhorns, however, were a different story. He thought he could play hardball with this Byner woman, but somehow she caught the ball, loaded it into one of those jai-alai *cestas*, and fired it back at him twice as hard.

"Ms. Byner," he began, "let's not make this matter more complicated than necessary. First of all, you know as well as I do

that Mr. Dawkins's injury was not the result of physical abuse
during his arrest and detainment."

"Here's what I know, Mr. Vanzo. My client is innocent of all
the charges you have accused him of. And yet, here we are
attempting to convince you that he *didn't* commit these crimes
when you believe that he did. It's difficult to prove a negative, isn't
it? Or do you have some proof that my client was *not* struck by his
arresting agents before they arrived here? If you do, I would advise
getting it ready, because Liberia will be calling for it."

Vanzo had been in the room too long. This situation was
beginning to feel like it was slipping from his control.

"We'll cross that bridge when we come to it," he said quickly.
"The next thing I need you to do is explain what you meant by an
'unregistered handgun.' That is an outrageous claim. Any weapons
used in the course of your client's arrest were government-issued
and therefore completely legal."

"I didn't say that Special Agent Murphy's sidearm wasn't
legal," said Biz.

Of course, it was Murphy, thought Vanzo. *Maybe if I could get
him into a bathroom, I could squirt some soap on the floor to make
it look like he slipped, then bash his head into a sink.*

"But in discussion with my client before you joined us," Biz
went on, "Mr. Dawkins told me that Special Agent Murphy
threatened to shoot him with a brand-new gun that had never been
fired before. That seemed strange, so I took a moment to quickly
Wangle the FBI's handgun regulations and it turns out that all
firearms used by field agents must go through the FBI Armorer's
office in Quantico, Virginia, where they are prepared, tested, and
registered for field use. I wonder how Special Agent Murphy's gun
got past the Armorer? Maybe you could ask the Armorer to go on
record admitting that his office screwed up or maybe even fudge
some paperwork for you that says the gun was in fact properly
checked out. Who knows, maybe the FBI Armorer in Quantico,
Virginia, is an easygoing guy and not too concerned with

procedures and regulations. Maybe he'll take the bullet for you, so to speak. What do you think?"

"Ms. Byner, I'm sure the Armorer, like all government officials, and unlike yourself, performs his duties with integrity."

Biz ignored the jab and said, "I would hope that he would. When Liberia goes on TV tonight to talk about the 'unregistered gun,' the Armorer won't contradict her, and the people of California will learn that their government officials can't be bothered with gun laws. Who knows? They probably won't care. People don't have strong feelings about guns, do they? Just in case, maybe you, or even your boss should call a press conference first to announce that the gun used in Mr. Dawkins's arrest was perfectly legal, everything is totally normal, and there's nothing at all to be concerned about. That should make for an interesting story."

The jai-alai ball had hit him square in the old beanbag, and Vanzo was forced to take a step back. "Ms. Byner, what is it that you want?"

"Release my client. Drop all charges."

Vanzo shook his head. "Impossible. Whatever fallout or embarrassment may come of Liberia Boyd coming down here will be nothing compared to what would happen if we had Mr. Dawkins in custody, released him, and he later went on to execute his plot against this country. Ms. Byner, your client is a dangerous man. Dropping the charges is out of the question."

Biz looked over at Chris. His shoulders were slumped, his eyes glassy, and he was breathing shallowly through his mouth. His hands trembled slightly on the table. This guy would not do well in prison. She leaned close to him and whispered in his ear, "Do you want to get out of here?"

Biz smelled great. Like freedom. Chris pulled his head back. Also, because he is a dude, he got a little chubbed up. "Yes. Please," he said quietly.

Mark A. Henry

Biz straightened up and fixed her eyes on Vanzo. Ticking off two fingers, she said, "Bond. Ankle bracelet. Do it, and Liberia Boyd never learns your name and the bus never leaves Berkeley."

Without a word, Vanzo turned his back and rapped on the door. While he waited for Officer Martin to open it up, he turned back around. Biz had not broken her gaze. "Done," he said. "See you at the arraignment. If I hear so much as a peep from Liberia Boyd about your client... "

"Won't happen," Biz said. The door opened and Vanzo turned once more to exit, slightly flinching as Biz added, "You have my word as a criminal defense attorney." He didn't look back to see Biz's grin, and the door clicked shut.

Biz exhaled deeply and turned to face Chris, who was staring at the door, his expression blank and unreadable.

"Sorry I couldn't get the charges dropped," she said. He snapped out of his mini-trance and looked at her. "But you'll be home tonight," she continued, still not certain what he was thinking. "Are you OK?" she finally asked.

"Thank you," Chris said, reaching out and gripping her hand. "Thank you so much. How did you... " he released his grip and waved his hands around, "do... that? I can't believe you know Liberia Boyd and she was going to help me."

"Weellllllllllll," Biz said, seesawing her head back and forth, "I do know Liberia Boyd. And I did take her class in law school at Berkeley."

"And she knows you, right?"

"Weellllllllllll, it was a big lecture class. I was in there with about two hundred other students."

"But you must have really stood out to have her agree to become your mentor."

"Weellllllllllll, one time I came into class a few minutes late and she said to me, 'Grab a seat, Miss Thing.' So that's some advice she gave me."

128

Biz paused to gauge how impressed Chris was. It was hard to tell because he began rubbing his temples with both hands, covering most of his face. Biz went on. "Is she my mentor? Is she a dear, close friend? OK, no. But Mr. Vanzo, lacking evidence to the contrary, as he would say, seems to have gotten that impression, so let's just go with that, shall we?"

CHAPTER 16

Chris's arraignment was set for 3:45, and rather than go back and forth across town, Biz had decided to stay at the Burton Federal Building to prepare. She found a sunny table near a window in the second-floor café and set up shop with her files and laptop for a few hours while she nursed a chicken salad wrap and iced green tea.

She drained the last of her tea and was getting ready to head up to a courtroom when she spotted Vanzo getting a coffee at the counter. Their eyes met, and he walked over to her table.

As he arrived, Vanzo peered out the window to the sidewalk. "It looks like Liberia Boyd didn't join us after all," he said.

"I told you she wouldn't," Biz said. "You were very reasonable to allow my client bond."

"About that." Vanzo pursed his lips and took a small sip of his coffee. "You realize, of course, that I am not the ultimate authority in matters of bail. The judge may decide not to grant it to Mr. Dawkins and if that's the case, I'm afraid my hands will be tied. He will have to remain in custody."

"Wait, I'm confused," Biz said.

"Understandable," said Vanzo. "Understandable. I realize this is not your area of expertise and there is bound to be some... learning curve for you." He grinned and took another sip of coffee.

"It's just that earlier you said that it was *your* judge and *your* courtroom and *your* prison and all that. It sounded like you claimed authority over the judge and due process and everything. It seemed like a presumptuous and maybe even illegal thing to say, but you sounded so confident... "

"Again, Ms. Byner, you seem to be confused. I think if you go back and listen to the recording of our earlier meeting, you won't hear me saying anything like that. Now, if you'll excuse me, I have to be getting upstairs."

He turned and got four steps away before he heard his own voice blasting from Biz's laptop. "—STATES OF AMERICA VS. CHRIS DAWKINS. I'M THE UNITED STATES. YOUR CLIENT WILL APPEAR BEFORE MY JUDGE AND MY JURY—"

All over the café, heads turned to see what the racket was all about. Vanzo leapt back toward Biz's table and hissed, "Turn that off!"

"—MY COURTROOM AND HE WILL SPEND THE REST OF HIS DAYS—"

"What?" Biz said, pointing helplessly to her ear.

Vanzo slammed the laptop shut, cutting off the sound. He leaned down toward Biz and shout-whispered, "You had no right to record that! It's illegal to record someone without their knowledge."

"I know," said Biz. "Do you want me to play back the part at the beginning where I say, 'This is being recorded?' and you say, 'Yes, counselor'?"

Vanzo's jaw flexed visibly.

Biz went on, "Or how about the part at the end where I say, 'Bond. Ankle bracelet,' and you say 'Done.' You remember that part?"

Vanzo stood up and looked around. Most people had gone back to their business, but one lawyer and two US Marshals he knew were still staring at him.

"Do you. Remember. That part?" Biz repeated.

Vanzo's attention snapped back. "I'll do what I can."

Biz smiled. "Great. Thank you, Mr. Vanzo, I'm sure you will. And you're right, I sure am learning a lot today."

CHAPTER 17

SAN FRANCISCO, CALIFORNIA
FRIDAY, 3:44 p.m. PST

"You cold?" the bailiff asked.

Chris stood with his back to the bailiff in a small room, looking through the narrow, wire-reinforced window of the door to a courtroom. He could see a judge and an armed bailiff, and they both looked mean. His knees were shaking.

"No," he said.

"Nervous?" asked the bailiff.

Chris turned to look at the bailiff. "Yeah."

"You see the game last night?"

"What? No."

"Delbert had fifty. Preseason, but still."

Chris craned his neck to see if he could spot Biz in the courtroom, but his limited visual slice of the room didn't allow it.

The bailiff said, "He was eight for ten from three."

"Yeah. I didn't see it," Chris said without turning around.

"That's why I'm telling you," replied the bailiff. A few seconds passed without comment from Chris, so he added, "He was really on fire."

Chris said, "Is it OK if we don't talk? I'm just thinking about my arraignment right now."

The bailiff said, "OK. Jeez." He would later relate this interaction at great length to his wife, who gave up on saying, "Is it OK if we don't talk?" years ago.

A minute or two passed, and Chris could see through the window that the judge's attention had turned to the door he stood behind. Chris took a few deep breaths to try to calm down as the bailiff opened the door and led him into the courtroom to a table where, to his great relief, he saw Biz.

"This will be over soon. Just keep quiet," she said after Chris was guided into his seat by his bailiff, who interjected with a sassy whisper, "Oh, no problem there, this one doesn't like to talk." Biz's mouth opened as she looked up at him and then back to Chris and then again at the bailiff, who by then was making his way back to a corner of the courtroom.

Biz wrote on a yellow pad and slid it toward Chris.

WTF he talking abt??

Chris picked up a pen and scratched out:

Talky. Told him shut up.

Biz read it and scribbled a quick winky face.

Chris looked up and around the large wood-paneled chamber. It was just like the courtrooms he had seen many times on TV and in the movies with the stern-looking, gray-haired judge sitting at his elevated desk, flanked by the uniformed bailiff. He and Biz sat at a table on the left side of the room, and he saw Attorney Vanzo across the center aisle at a matching table on the right. Behind Vanzo, Sullivan and Murphy sat in the front row of the gallery seats. Chris's attention was pulled back to the judge, whom everyone seemed to be waiting on to begin whatever was about to happen.

The Honorable Justice Robert W. Myers spent a few more moments reading a document on his desk, then removed his glasses and looked up to survey his courtroom, taking special interest in Chris, who immediately forfeited a staring contest with him.

Myers rumbled, "This is the United States vs. Christopher Dawkins, case number 4:25:CR:34490. Who do we have for the government?"

Vanzo stood up. "Paul Vanzo, Your Honor."

Myers made a note. "And for the defense?"

Biz stood and gently pulled Chris up by the elbow. "Elizabeth Byner, Your Honor."

Myers wrote some more. "Mr. Dawkins, you are being charged with attempting to provide material support or resources to a designated foreign terrorist organization and conspiracy to commit a terrorist act against the United States. The government possesses electronic records and physical evidence to support these charges. Do you understand these charges and the case against you?"

Biz said, "He does, Your Honor."

Myers asked Chris directly, "Mr. Dawkins, do you understand these charges and the case against you?"

Chris wanted to say that he really didn't understand any of this, but he said, "Yes, Your Honor."

"And how does the defendant plead?" the judge asked.

Biz said, "Not guilty, Your Honor."

Myers made yet another note. "Mr. Dawkins, do you have a job?"

"Yes, Your Honor. I work at Sixdub. IT."

Myers said, "Oh." He then asked, "Do you have a passport?"

"No, Your Honor."

Myers looked down at his notes. "You've never been convicted of any crimes in the past, correct?"

"Correct, Your Honor."

Myers set his pen down. "Nevertheless, the crime you stand accused of now is serious in nature and presents a potential threat to the public. You shall be remanded into custody pending the outcome of your trial."

Biz glared at Vanzo and stood up. "Your Honor, my client poses no danger to anyone. I request that he be granted bail and released," she said. More glaring at Vanzo.

Vanzo then got to his feet. He straightened his tie and said, "The government has no objections to that, Your Honor."

Before Myers could respond, Murph and Sully jumped up. What was Vanzo doing? Director Barry would be pissed if Dawkins walked out of here today. Murph said, "Objection, Your Honor!"

Myers snapped, "Order! Keep quiet!" To Vanzo, he said, "Mr. Vanzo, I already made my ruling. Do I understand that you disagree, that you would support bail in this case?"

Vanzo felt eyes boring into him from all directions. "Yes, Your Honor. The government feels bail would be appropriate."

The FBI agents exchanged alarmed looks. "Vanzo!" Sully whispered, but Vanzo pretended not to hear him, hoping to just get through the next few minutes without having to argue and elucidate the details for Chris's release.

He heard a voice behind him say, "May I approach the bench, Your Honor?" Vanzo whipped his head around to see Murph with his finger in the air.

Myers angrily waved at his bailiff. "Deputy, get this person out of my courtroom!" he said, pointing at Murph. Vanzo actually supported this plan and thus kept his mouth shut as the bailiff approached to toss Murph out and hopefully Taser him a time or two.

Murph and Sully then whipped out their badges and Sully said, "Your Honor, I'm FBI Special Agent Sullivan and this is my partner Special Agent Murphy. I apologize for the disruption." At the sight of the badges, the bailiff stopped and looked back at Myers, who still looked extremely irritated, but didn't say anything. Sully said, "We made the arrest in this case and can confirm that Mr. Dawkins is a dangerous individual. Releasing him would be unwise."

Biz, still standing, said, "Your Honor, I saw the video of the Special Agents bringing Mr. Dawkins in to be processed this morning. He wasn't even restrained in handcuffs. Apparently, they didn't find him very dangerous then."

"Is that true, Agents?" Myers asked.

Simultaneously, Murph said, "No," and Sully said, "Yes."

"Enough!" said the judge. "On Mr. Vanzo's recommendation, I'm setting bail in this case. Mr. Dawkins will be fitted with an ankle tracking bracelet and be kept under home confinement until his trial."

Vanzo was greatly relieved to hear that Myers opted to not keep Chris in custody. He was not looking forward to the prospect of arguing *for* a defendant's release in order to keep the threat of Liberia Boyd and her bullhorn at bay. Finally, something was going right today.

Biz said, "Your Honor, my client holds a job. His livelihood depends upon it. I request that he be released on bail without restrictions."

"Ms. Byner," Myers said, "my obligation is to the safety of the American people. Being accused of a serious crime of a potentially violent nature, Mr. Dawkins will be denied certain privileges until the outcome of his trial. Mr. Dawkins will be allowed to attend necessary appointments such as meetings with his attorney, but he will have to make arrangements to be excused from work. Bond will be set at $500,000. Trial will begin… "—Myers flipped a few pages of his desk calendar—"nine a.m., three weeks from today." He turned to the bailiff. "Deputy, process Mr. Dawkins out and get him the bracelet. This hearing is adjourned. Everybody, out!"

And just like that, Chris Dawkins was (kind of) a free man.

CHAPTER 18

SAN ANSELMO, CALIFORNIA
FRIDAY, 6:40 p.m. PST

When Biz dropped him off at his apartment that evening, Chris was struggling to just put one foot in front of the other. He smelled bad, was both hungry and nauseous, had a buzzing headache, and was on the radar of law enforcement. Tomorrow would be a better day. Worse was also a possibility.

He removed both his shoes at the door and made a beeline for the bed. His pants made it off, but the shirt stayed on and he collapsed onto the mattress just before an irresistible gravity sucked him into the black hole of sleep.

Murph and Sully sat in the Trax across the street and watched Chris stumble through his front door while monitoring his position on their phones using the PerpTrak app they had both downloaded at the suggestion of the deputy who had fitted Chris with his ankle bracelet. Satisfied that the bracelet was working, they decided to call it a day and get some dinner at a nearby Rancheroo Steakhouse, the recommendation of which was also courtesy of PerpTrak since they elected to download the free version, which came with ads.

Twenty minutes later, after paying cash for two beers at the bar in order to keep them off the expense report, the two settled into a booth.

138

"To a job well, done," said Murph, raising a glass to his partner.

"Cheers," replied Sully, silently adding an Irish toast of his own creation: *May I see the bottom of this glass before something comes along to ruin what's in it.*

His cell phone buzzed. Alas.

Sully set down his beer, let out a small sigh, and looked at his phone. He showed it to Murph. Director Barry. The first sigh didn't quite get all of it, and he let another one go as he answered the call.

"Sullivan."

"I got your report," Barry said.

There was a brief impasse wherein the conversational road would fork and go one of two ways. Either onto Fine Work Special Agent Street or What the Hell Are You Doing Boulevard.

Sully, God bless him, ignored the conversational traffic cop frantically waving a road flare toward What the Hell Are You Doing and drove straight through the intersection. He just said, "Yes, sir," then took another quick drink of beer in an effort to get a little closer to the bottom of the glass.

"What the hell are you doing?" Barry barked.

Sully grimaced at Murph and shook his head to indicate they were about to get into it. Murph, in solidarity, chugged a few inches of his beer.

"I'm sorry, sir, what exactly do you mean?"

"Sullivan, I have a draft of a press release on my computer outlining the investigation and arrest of Christopher Dawkins, the dangerous threat to American security. At the end, it says Mr. Dawkins is in custody awaiting justice. My question to you is how to add the part about how he will be awaiting this justice while hanging out at home, catching up on his shows without making the Bureau look like goddamn idiots! Is Murphy with you? Put me on speaker so I can yell at both of you!"

Sully put the phone on the table and propped it against the saltshaker. Murph set his beer down and said, "Murphy here, Director."

Before Barry could properly ream Murph, the waitress appeared and said, "Welcome to Rancheroo, gentlemen. What can I get you?"

Barry's disembodied voice blared, "They'll both have the New York Strip, well done. And your worst side dish!"

The waitress took Barry's voice on the phone to be some sort of really angry personal assistant or maybe a new voice-activated meal-ordering app that was still very early in the beta phase. She jotted a note, saying, "Two strips well, vegetable medley." She then turned and left.

Murph watched his hope for a medium-rare Cowboy cut, bone-in ribeye disappear back toward the kitchen as Barry continued, "Murphy, how did Dawkins get out today? Ankle bracelet? Curfew? What the hell? What is he, a drunk driver or something? Explain this to me."

"It was the judge's call, sir. Dawkins has no priors, no flight risk. We pushed hard for custody, but he had a slick lawyer, and in the end, there wasn't much we could do about it." It was agreed between Murph, Sully, and Vanzo that no good would come from Liberia Boyd's name appearing in Murph and Sully's report, nor the business about the questionable provenance of Murph's #2 sidearm, nor the business about the handcuffs being removed prematurely.

"I'll call the judge," Barry said. "What's his name? Myers? *If* I can get to him on the phone and *if* he plays ball, I'll get him to revoke the bond and you two can pick up Dawkins and bring him back in, but that won't be until court is back in session on Tuesday." Monday would be Columbus Day or Indigenous Peoples' Day, depending on your politics.

"We still have the warrant," said Murph. "Now that he's out, Special Agent Sullivan and I are going to stick around to keep an eye on him, so if he tries to contact anyone, we might take down another suspect or two."

"Doubtful, but worth a shot," Barry griped. "But if he so much as downloads a bootleg song on his computer, haul his ass back in. We need this guy in custody to send the message to the American people that we're on top of this."

Murph said, "Sir, we confiscated his computer. He can't download any songs."

"What about his smoke detector?" asked Barry.

"The lab is looking at that, too," Sully answered.

"Get over there in the morning and check in on him. Let him know we're still watching and we're going through his whole history with a fine-toothed comb until we find what we need. We rattle his cage, he might get nervous and make a mistake."

"Yes, sir," Sully said. Murph had abandoned him to chase after the waitress.

"Also," said Barry, "let Dawkins know I'll be coming out there to see him myself Tuesday morning. We're not making any public statements 'til then. Tell him we can talk possible deals on Tuesday if he and his lawyer keep quiet this weekend." Barry was still angry that his plan to publicly capture, try, and convict an underground domestic terrorist had gone off the rails so early, but experience told him that a lot of cases break open through being in the right place at the right time when circumstance suddenly breaks your way. Luck favors the prepared, you see.

Barry hung up. He was not happy. And since he was not the look-at-kittens-on-the-internet type, he had to get to work on something to improve his mood. As usual, it was going to be up to him to keep things from getting completely FUBAR.

After he was done with Murph and Sully, leaving them to their New York strips and crappy vegetable medleys, he tracked down San Francisco Circuit Court Judge Myers's home number and gave him a call, hoping to get the judge to reverse his decision that allowed Chris Dawkins bail. Unfortunately for Barry, the judge had just been informed by his wife that he would not be attending the following afternoon's Cal football game as planned, but rather, the two of them would be driving to Sacramento to aid and comfort her mother, whose beloved dog Tippy succumbed, after a brave fight, to dog leukemia or something.

Although Myers was pleased to hear of Tippy's demise, the massive dent put in his weekend plans put him in a mood to angrily deny what he felt was a presumptuous request from Barry, and the two engaged in a brief shouting match before Myers hung up on him.

After adding Myers's name to his Shit List, Barry left the office and drove out to Bethesda, Maryland, to do a little shopping at the Home Depot. The one across from the mall. He entered the store, dodged one of those floor-cleaning mini-Zambonis, and made his way to the paint department, all the while scanning the area for both potential tactical advantages as well as potential threats, Zamboni or otherwise. He lingered at the rainbow wall of paint sample swatches for a few minutes before selecting a card (Gallery Red, #150F-6), which he brought to the counter.

The guy working the paint can shaker quickly shut it off and hustled over to meet Barry. "Can I help you, sir?" he asked. His apron had the name "Mike" Sharpie'd on it.

"I'm painting my living room tomorrow," Barry told Mike. He flipped the card onto the counter.

Mike studied the card, looked at Barry, looked back at the card, then back at Barry.

"Nice color. How many gallons?"

"Nine."

Mike shifted his weight and looked around. "Eight would probably do the job, sir. Maybe even seven?"

"Nine."

Mike nodded. "Yes, sir. Nine," he said. He pulled the Gallery Red #150F-6 card toward him and pocketed it. "I can't mix this up right now, though. Do you want to wait?"

"No, thanks. I'll come back for it," Barry told him. He turned and left the store. Mike watched him go, then returned to his shaker and began thinking up an excuse to be an hour late to work tomorrow.

CHAPTER 19

WASHINGTON, DC
SATURDAY, 8:50 a.m. EST

It used to be when Dick Barry needed his former Air Force Tech Sergeant Mike Novic to do a "special job," they would arrange to meet on the National Mall to go over the details. The problem with that plan became a lack of bench space. In some cities, it can be hard to find a place to sit down in a public park because there are homeless people napping on all the benches. In Washington, the problem is that just about every public bench is occupied by trench-coated men furtively looking around, talking behind newspapers, passing briefcases to each other and whatnot. And if you do happen to find an open bench to wait for your contact, some other guy will always sit down next to you and say something like, "It's raining in Minsk, but Russians own galoshes," and you'd have to let him know he's got the wrong bench. It can be awkward.

After Novic got the paint department job, Barry came up with the method of setting their meets using colors and names that correspond with Washington Metro train stops and the number of gallons to indicate the time. For example, eighteen gallons of "Foggy London" (#PPU25-09) to paint the shed on Saturday meant that Barry wanted to meet on Saturday at 1800 hours at the Foggy Bottom stop. It was a bit of spy tradecraft that was perhaps unnecessary, but Barry didn't get where he was without being cautious, and Novic didn't get where *he* was without a touch of paranoia.

And so it was that Barry stood in the middle of the bustling platform on the Red Line level of the Gallery Place station wearing sunglasses and a baseball cap, holding a folded newspaper the morning after his trip to Home Depot. He looked at his watch. Mike should be there any minute. At 8:54 a train pulled in, and Barry spotted Novic as he emerged from the last car and fell in with the herd of Saturday sightseers and shoppers heading for the escalators. Novic locked eyes with Barry briefly as he passed and continued on, boarding the escalator that led down to the Green Line platform. Barry followed and as he stepped off at the bottom, he located Novic looking at the big Metro map on the wall and sidled up next to him.

"Morning, Mike."

"Morning, LT."

"Got a special job for you."

Novic glanced around. "Let's hear it."

"There's a guy out in California. Bad guy, working with MILF. Wanted to blow up a mall in San Francisco. We got him, but his lawyer found a loophole and now we might lose him."

"What's his name?" Novic asked, still studying the map.

"Can't say just yet." Barry sighed with disgust. "Look, a couple of my agents stepped on their dicks and couldn't put this guy into custody. The judge put him on house arrest." At this, Novic turned his head and looked incredulous. "Don't even get me started, Mike. If his name gets out, people will know he's not even in jail and we'll look like we're either soft on terrorism or we screwed the pooch. This could easily go south on us, and this guy might even go free. We've got to put a little heat on him here. The judge, too. We can turn this around, but I need your help."

A family of four squeezed between them at the map and began debating various routes to the Jefferson Memorial. The parents were the type to cede control of their journey to their younger son to boost his self-esteem, while the older son was the type to tell his brother he was a stupid idiot.

Novic walked away from the map, thinking the older brother was making some valid points and Barry once again followed. Novic stopped at the far end of the platform and waited for Barry to join him.

"So, what do you need?" Novic asked, taking out his cell phone and pretending to look at it, although it was actually turned off, battery removed, camera lens taped over.

"The FBI has captured a high-value domestic terrorist. Uncertain citizenship. Plot thwarted. Case broken by digital surveillance. Hard evidence seized. Death penalty. America safe."

"Got it," said Novic. "Look for it tonight." He looked over at Barry. "You done with that?" he asked, pointing to the folded newspaper Barry still carried.

Barry looked around. He said, "It's all yours, Sergeant" and handed Novic the newspaper that concealed $4,000 in cash. Novic tucked the paper under his arm and headed back upstairs to catch the train back to Bethesda.

CHAPTER 20

SAN ANSELMO, CALIFORNIA
SATURDAY, 8:11 a.m. PST

Chris's dream (the one where he was running from something, but his legs were *so* heavy) was interrupted by what sounded suspiciously like the butt end of a Ruger 20-gauge pump-action pistol-grip shotgun rapping, rapping at his chamber door.

CHAPTER 21

SAN ANSELMO, CALIFORNIA
SATURDAY, 8:11 a.m. PST

Author's Note:
Ha! Dan Browned you again!

Someone less suspicious might say that the rapping sounded much more like the butt end of the short flashlight Biz Byner carried on her keychain, and that person would be correct.

Chris rolled out of bed, weaved a path to the door, and put his good eye to the peephole. A bulbous-looking Jasper Wiles and a convex Biz showed themselves. Wiles raised a baggie of pills. "Eleuthero Man!" he yelled. "Open up!" Biz was scanning the neighborhood. Quiet.

Chris swung the door open and lacking the strength to form a verbal greeting or question, he waved the two inside.

"I'll fix this up for you," said Wiles as he strode in, jiggling the baggie. He quickly oriented himself toward the kitchen. Biz followed and said, "Good morning."

Chris led Biz into his living room and slumped into the nearest chair, a faux leather armchair recliner with cup holder. Biz took a seat on the sofa opposite the room. It had two cup holders. TWO! Suck it, recliner!

Biz remained quiet and just looked at Chris for a few seconds. "What's going to happen next?" he asked.

"We can't be sure, Chris. The case against you is weak and circumstantial at best. Honestly, I'm surprised they brought you in. It goes to show, however—" *RRRRRrrrRRRRRrrrRRRRR!!*

Wiles had found Chris's blender and by the sound of it was crushing ice.

Biz waited until the noise stopped, then continued. "It goes to show, however, that the FBI has some other reason to be so confident in their case. I truly believe you will go free, and soon. But there is a slight, slight possibility that the FBI wants to make an example out of you for some reason and will use every clean or even clean-ish resource at their disposal in an effort to put you away."

Wiles returned with a tall glass filled with chartreuse slush. "You didn't have any fruit, so I smoothie'd your eleuthero in with a C4 drink and some ice," he said. "You're out of C4, by the way, that was the last one."

Chris took the glass and quickly took a sip. Wiles had left the ice in the blender just long enough to get the perfect smoothie consistency.

"Thank you," he said to Wiles and took another sip. "Why are you here?"

Biz answered, "We thought you might have some questions, Chris."

Chris said, "No, I mean why are *you* here, Mr. Wiles? Don't you have, you know, better things to do?"

Wiles said, "Short answer? No, not really. Igor Poskovich pretty much runs Sixdub day-to-day now. I like to hang around the office, and I have to show up for board meetings, but that's about it. Long answer, I consider us to be engaged in a binding social contract, Chris. I put up your bail money and I continue to employ you. I plan to protect my investment in you on both fronts. For the near future, I will be close at hand."

149

Chris wasn't sure if he should be reassured or unsettled by this. On the one hand, he seemed to have gained a resourceful ally. On the other hand, this ally could be an irresponsible flake. At any rate, he said, "Thanks. And I'm not about to skip town or anything. You don't have to worry about your bail money, Mr. Wiles."

Wiles had settled on the sofa next to Biz. He pinched a capsule and dry swallowed it. "Fish oil," he said. Tucking the baggie into this shirt pocket, he went on. "I don't care about the bail money, Chris. I need to make sure you don't go to prison. First of all, it would be a travesty of justice to convict an innocent man and second, it wouldn't be a good look for Sixdub to have one of our employees known as a convicted terrorist. We'll get you out of this, one way or the other."

Biz said, "I'm still very confident in your case, Chris. If we even go to trial, there's not much evidence to support a conviction. There's a good chance the charges will be dropped altogether once Vanzo sees he really doesn't have much to work with. This whole arrest was probably just a ploy to sweat you a little bit to see if you would admit to anything if in fact you were involved in some illegal activity."

That made sense to Chris. He was just in the wrong digital place at the wrong digital time and someone happened to be watching. It would all get sorted out with Biz's help. He took another sip of his frozen drink and whether it was the eleuthero or Biz's assurances, he was starting to feel a little better. "Thanks," he said. "Both of you."

"Of course," said Wiles, grinning. "I can't have you going off to prison before you make me another viral sensation." Turning to Biz, he said, "You know this guy made 'Model Glue Jinglehut,' right?"

"Why did you have to say that?" Biz shot back, but she was smiling now, too. "Now it's going to be stuck in my head all day." She started rapping, "Model glue *jin*gle hut, model glue *jin*gle hut, too much butter makes a brother blurt out butter glut!"

150

Wiles laughed and Chris smiled at the knowledge that Biz knew his "work" and at her flow, which was impressive. For that brief moment it was like he was just sitting around with two good friends. That's when the knock at the door came and all three of their heads turned toward it, wiping away any levity that had just been built up.

"Are you expecting anyone?" Biz asked Chris.

Chris wasn't, but he grinned and said, "Maybe it's Liberia Boyd."

Author's Note:
I just said all the levity had been wiped away, Dawkins.
Literally three seconds ago. Idiot.

Biz returned him a quick, small smile and rose from the couch. "I'll answer it," she said. Checking the peephole, she reported, "It's the FBI agents from yesterday."

Wiles surreptitiously slid his pill baggie down the front of his pants.

"Is it OK if I opened up?" Biz asked Chris.

"If you think it's OK, it's OK with me," he replied.

Biz opened the door. "Good morning, Special Agent Murphy, Special Agent Sullivan. What can I do for you?"

Murph and Sully were both fairly irritated. They were still feeling the sting of Director Barry's rebuke at dinner the evening before, and a large portion of their drive from the hotel this morning was done at the pace of an elderly gang of recumbent bicyclists that took up the whole road, then waved a flock of birds at Sully when he had the audacity to speed up to twenty miles an hour to pass them.

"Miss Byner," said Sully, craning his neck to see into the apartment. "I'm not surprised to see you here. Your client is going to need all the legal help he can get. Is he here?"

"You would know if he wasn't," Biz answered. "His ankle bracelet is locked and active, in accordance with the court's order."

"We'd like to see him. FBI Director Barry has asked us to check in on Mr. Dawkins."

"He's fine, thank you," Biz said.

Murph shouted into the apartment, "Chris Dawkins! FBI! Come to the door!"

In the living room, beyond the sight line the door allowed, Chris looked at Wiles, who looked to Biz. When she didn't object, Chris did as he was told and presented himself at the front door.

"Mr. Dawkins, good morning," Murph said.

"We're here to give you a message from Dick Barry," added Sully.

"Dickberry?" Biz said.

Sully glared at her. "FBI Director Dick. Barry."

"That's what I said. Dickberry."

"What's the message?" Chris asked.

Sully pivoted his glare to Chris. "You're in his sights, Dawkins. And that's not where a person wants to be. Your lawyer here is probably telling you not to worry, that we don't have enough evidence, right?"

Chris stole a quick look at Biz, who seemed content to let the agent talk.

"Right?" Sully repeated.

"Yeah. She's right."

Sully grinned. "Oh, but there is evidence, Chris. It may be just a little thread right now, but we'll keep pulling on it and pulling on it until we have enough to knit whatever we want."

Murph held up a hand and started ticking off fingers. "Search history, websites, social media, email, online shopping. It's all there for us to look through and pull out anything we need."

"And it's not like it's just sitting on your computer. It's out there." He waved his hand around in the air as if shooing away a swarm of damning evidence against Chris. "And you can't get it back. If you were smart, you'd come in and start talking before we find out something you'll wish we didn't."

Biz cut in. "Thank you, gentlemen. And thank Dickberry for his message. We appreciate the job he's doing to keep us all safe. Chris, we have to get back inside to resume our meeting."

"That wasn't the message, Ms. Byner," Murph said.

Biz felt the urge to choke him for some reason.

"The message is the Director is flying here, and Tuesday morning he'll be meeting with you and Mr. Dawkins to discuss his trial. The Bureau won't be making any public remarks about the case until then. If you do the same, to protect your client's identity, Miss Byner, Director Barry mentioned possible deals."

There was a brief moment of silence before Biz said, "Have a good day, Agents," and began to shut the door.

Sully said, "We'll let you two get back to your meeting, I'm sure you have a lot to discuss. Special Agent Murphy and I really need to be going anyway."

Murph fixed a stare at Chris. "We have a lot of knitting to do," he said.

As tough-guy one-liners go, that could have been better, but the agents were satisfied to see a little glint of fear in Chris's eyes before they turned to leave. Now *this* was some fieldwork!

CHAPTER 22

SAN ANSELMO, CALIFORNIA
SATURDAY, 8:27 a.m. PST

"What was that all about?" Wiles asked as Biz and Chris returned to their faux leather seats. He could see that Chris was a little unsettled by the visit.

Biz answered quickly, "They're just harassing Chris, hoping he'll get nervous and admit to something. It really just goes to show they don't have much to go on. The only evidence they have is a shopping list and your name on a website comment section. Either one would be a zero. Both together? Still very weak." She looked at Chris in an attempt to reassure him.

Chris was not having it. "You heard what they said. It doesn't matter what they actually have; they'll just piece together any little bits of digital evidence to make me look bad."

Biz thought back on her own recent Wangle search history, both on personal business and in the professional service of Wiles and now Chris. Royal wedding, Russian oligarchs, Focused Mindmapping, Fireman workout photos, Perry Mott senate hearing, Is alligator skin waterproof, C4, FBI firearm regulations, Paul Vanzo. All innocent enough, unless of course she was attempting to partner with some unsavory Russians to disrupt the upcoming royal wedding using new Focused Mindmapping technology and old-fashioned C4 explosives while diverting attention from her

154

crime by assassinating US Attorney Paul Vanzo using a stolen FBI handgun and framing Perry Mott for the crime, using his recent financial trouble as a motive. Also, PETA would be ripshit if they knew that she was thinking of getting an alligator handbag, and while there's certainly no shame in checking out some sweaty firemen, it's not exactly something one puts on one's CV either.

"It's possible, of course," she conceded. "As the agents said, all that digital history is out there. That's beyond our control. From here, we rely on the legal system to separate the truth from the story they put together."

Chris snapped, "But they *are* the legal system! They're just going to do whatever they want to put me in prison!"

If there's one thing Liberia Boyd taught Biz back at Berkeley, it was a healthy respect for the Constitution and that it was oftentimes at odds with the government it represented, so do not confuse the two.

Biz snapped right back at Chris, "If you have a time machine you can use to go back and not like the terrorist recruitment video before signing up to join them, now would be the time to use it. Otherwise, let's focus on what we have in front of us. By the way, if I haven't mentioned it yet, that was not a smart thing to do."

Chris suddenly sat up straight, as if startled. "A time machine," he said, looking from Biz to Wiles and back. "We all have time machines."

Biz looked quizzically at him and a cooler guy would have stopped there and made her ask a question, but Chris is not that guy, so he kept going. "Our computers store backup data periodically in case they get a virus or something. If anything goes wrong with your data, you can just go *back in time* to a point before the trouble happened and reload the good data, so it's as if the trouble never happened."

Biz knew about backing up computer data of course, but still didn't see how it would help in this situation. "Chris, the FBI confiscated your computer. I don't think they're going to loan it back to you for a few minutes so you can delete your history. Remember what they said? The evidence is 'out there.'" She waved her hands around as Murph did on the front step. "Even if you could delete what was on your computer, it would still exist on everyone else's, not to mention up in the cloud, or whatever."

Chris had explained "the cloud" before, but never to someone as young as Biz. "You know... it's not literally... a cloud, right?" he asked.

Biz made a face. "Dance, nerd," she said. "Get to your point."

Chris said, "OK, OK. And you're right. Liking that video was stupid. But when I did it, the data was recorded and stored on a server controlled by MANBUT, or MILF or whatever their name is. That's the computer that has the time machine we need to get to, not *my* computer. We," Chris looked to Wiles, "or maybe Mr. Poskovich, can hack in and reset it, using their own backed-up data from *before* I clicked like and agreed to their T and C. That will delete any evidence that I did it, and it'll be like it never happened. By the way, since the FBI calls them MILF, let's just stick with that from now on to avoid confusion."

Author's Note:
Thanks, Chris.

"Agreed," said Wiles. "Zippier."

Biz squinted, as if squeezing Chris's plan into her brain through her eyeballs. "But the FBI still has *your* computer. Erasing the data from the original MILF server won't change what's on your hard drive. Anyone will still be able to see that, right?"

Chris said, "You're right. They do have my computer. And who knows what evidence they planted on it while it was in their possession? It happens all the time, from what I've heard. You said they need hard evidence, like my name on MILF's data. If we can access MILF's server and delete my name, it will be scrubbed from the internet itself, and any record of it on *my* computer will seem like something the FBI added after the fact to make me look guilty. The video I watched will still be up online with all the likes and comments listed, but not mine. What would the judge or jury believe, what's on my laptop, or what's on the internet? As the agent said, once something is out there, you can't get it back, right?"

Wiles got up from the sofa and reached for his phone. "I'm calling Igor," he said as he walked into the kitchen.

Biz watched him go as she thought. It occurred to her that this method of erasing data at the source wouldn't *technically* be evidence tampering. What evidence the FBI had would remain safe and sound, untouched and unchanged. If the underlying foundation supporting that evidence disappeared, the evidence itself would crumble. In theory, this made sense. Sort of. It could work. Maybe.

"But what about any other people's computers who may have visited MILF's site and will have a digital record of your like?" she asked Chris. "Just like your computer, there must be others who are still upstream, so to speak, and would be unaffected by any change we make on the MILF server."

"Well, we've already established that I am very stupid," said Chris. "I guess we'll have to hope that I am truly the stupidest person in the country and the only one who thought it would be a good idea to like that video and sign up to join MILF. I'm willing to bet that I'm the only American who watched that terrorist propaganda video in a foreign language, gave the thumbs-up, and signed on. If anyone else did, they probably would've been sitting next to me in jail yesterday, or at least the FBI would have asked me about them, but they didn't. Maybe there are some computers that belong to MILF sympathizers in Syria or someplace that show a record of it, but I don't think the FBI has access to them."

Biz was impressed with Chris's plan. She thought it definitely fell into the "easier said than done" category, but in theory, it sounded like it could work.

"So," she said, "exactly how would we go about hacking into a foreign terrorist group's computer network?"

Before Chris could answer—and despite his computer expertise, the answer would have been some version of "I'm not quite sure"—Wiles returned from the kitchen, tucking his phone into his pocket.

"We're going to Zazaristan! Pack light."

CHAPTER 23

SAN ANSELMO, CALIFORNIA
SATURDAY, 8:40 a.m. PST

Chris and Biz stared blankly at Wiles for a second, so he added, "By 'light' I don't mean just a few things, I'm talking about light clothing. It's hotter than Satan's balls over there. Excuse my language, Biz."

Biz shook her head. "No, Jasper. No. We are not going to Zazaristan. I am not going. You are not going. Chris is certainly not going. If you need a reminder, he's wearing an electronic tracking anklet that is being monitored by the FBI, and for that matter, he doesn't even have a passport!"

Wiles waved away her objections. "Igor assures me that the anklet does not present an obstacle, and it's probably best if Chris travels, let's say, off the books anyway. Oh, and Biz, you'll need to pack a hijab. We can't afford to offend the Zazaris."

Eleventh Grade: *Do not allow the craziest person to make the rules. This is harder than it sounds.*

Biz drew in a deep breath and spoke in a tone she would use if addressing a stray dog that had snatched her wallet and was now holding it over the rim of the Grand Canyon. "Jasper. I'm sure you have a well-thought-out plan. I'm sure you have Chris's best interests in mind. Let's not jump ahead any more than necessary. Making Chris a fugitive from justice, then aiding and abetting him by transporting him illegally to a Third World country on the State Department's No Travel list should maybe not be our first option."

Why is it that just as you're about ready to throw your bread-and-tea sack over your shoulder and jump the back fence, someone always makes some sensible and logical points in favor of not going anywhere? Chris was actually mildly intrigued by the prospect of traveling to the Middle East. (Or was it Central Asia? He made a mental note to WangleMap it later.) In the past day or two, he had often found himself wishing he were far, far away from wherever he was at the moment anyway. Running from your problems has always been as good a reason as any to get out and see the world. The notoriously war-torn and semilawless nation of Zazaristan wouldn't have been at the top of his travel bucket list*, but as the saying goes, fugitives cannot be choosers. Incidentally, the places he has already checked off the list are as follows: Los Angeles, Portland.

Biz said, "Let me be clear. We are not going to Zazaristan. Chris was just telling me how to fix this situation without going anywhere. Why can't we access MILF's server and manipulate their backup data from here? I assume Igor

*The Ginza district of Tokyo
Australia
Havana
New York City
Miami
Some high, craggy mountains in New Zealand or possibly Scotland
Hawaii
    As he roams these places, Chris pictures himself wearing a white linen shirt and an expression of confident wonder, with the exception of the mountain scenario in which case he switches to a puffy jacket made of synthetic fiber and is seen from the viewpoint of a circling helicopter.

hasn't forgotten how to do it."

"I was thinking the same," said Wiles. "As soon as you mentioned the time machine and Chris explained his plan, the solution and course of action seemed clear. However. I called Igor. He pointed out that hacking in remotely to change data is pointless, since any data affected can and will be restored by a backup and the backup would be stored externally. It's the backup we need to go after, the most recent one. The one created about twenty-four hours ago. Only then can the online data be changed and the latest backup available will predate Chris's contact on Thursday. Once the backup is gone, his name and data will be truly erased from MILF's records."

Biz was not impressed, but the "twenty-four hours" part caught her ear.

Wiles continued. "Igor can erase the data online. That's the easy part. This is what he does best, you know. Keystroke logs, metadata, he has a hundred ways. But before that, we still need access to the *external* drive. Igor told me that MILF's data is backed up every Friday afternoon to an offline external storage drive from a Datacom Model 7 Laptop. Via USB port one, I believe he said. After that, the data is beyond our reach from here."

Biz said, "How could Igor Poskovich possibly know all that?"

"Before I tell you," Wiles said, "let's take a moment to appreciate the simple beauty of attorney-client privilege. The free and unrestricted exchange of ideas and information without fear of compromise or retribution. It's really quite something, isn't it?"

The Grand Canyon dog was still holding Biz's wallet and was now shaking like he was trying to dry off while simultaneously lifting his hind leg to pee, and he just spotted a squirrel on the far rim. Biz held up her hand. "Jasper. Be very careful about what you say next. You can say whatever you want to me, but Chris has been indicted and could be questioned about all this under oath. I will not allow you to get involved in this mess." She glanced over to Chris. "Sorry."

"It's OK," Chris said.

"Chris will be fine," said Wiles. "I'm not about to tell him anything illegal. It's more like a trade secret. And since he works for me, his employment contract prevents him from sharing proprietary Sixdub information with anyone. Now, may I answer your question, Biz?"

"Fine, let's hear it," she said. "How does Igor know the workings of a terrorist group's computer network when presumably the US government doesn't?"

Wiles steepled his fingers together for a moment, then spread them apart. "Whenever anyone in the world downloads a Sixdub app—"

"Oh, for Christ's sake," Biz began.

Wiles winced slightly as he continued. "Moodswirl, Zoopzap, Ucoolbro, any of them, they also download software that allows for a certain amount of... shall we say, transparency in their digital lifestyle. Come on now, Biz, don't act like you've never heard of metademographics."

Biz did write an extensive white paper for Wiles's data-gathering venture, Project Cockpee, and was very familiar with its objectives. As far as she knew, its reach didn't extend to Sixdub's line of apps.

"Cockpee's scope does not cover apps or any of your commercially available software, Jasper. It's a very tricky area with very narrow focus. I know more about it than you probably, and certainly more than Igor."

Wiles was now pacing the room, like a professor lecturing a classroom. "That's because Cockpee is itself an extension of an earlier idea that does apply to our software and in fact appears in the user agreement of every program we produce. An agreement that predates your time with me." He stopped, faced Biz, and jabbed his index finger into the air. "To know one's customer is to serve one's customer." He turned his attention to Chris. "Chris, do you know your Ucoolbro score?"

"I don't," Chris said. "I try not to look."

"Good man. But your score is 32.79. Igor told me just now. He also used the data we use to calculate that score to look back into your history and identify your contact with MILF. Anyway, using your contact with MILF as an entry point, Igor was able to trace his way back to their server and identify its IP address."

"That's it?" Biz exclaimed. "That's all you have to do?"

"Not exactly," Wiles said, resuming his pacing. "That merely brought us to MILF's door. We still need the key to unlock it. More accurately, we needed someone to open it up for us from the inside. Igor cross-checked our database of app user's histories with those who have user access to the MILF server's IP address and as luck would have it, it seems a gentleman named Mohammad Mohammad of Taboor City, Zazaristan, is both a member of MILF and a Ucoolbro subscriber. Through the data he collected from the app, Igor accessed Mr. Mohammad's computer and obtained the operation's backup procedure, and that's how we learned the fact that the data is kept offline. Let this be a lesson not to use your work computer for personal business, by the way."

Chris and Biz were silent for a few seconds. It's always a bit disconcerting to be presented with hard proof of our vulnerabilities, which, as a survival mechanism, we tend to consider only in the context of vague and unlikely scenarios. The weak swimmer, for example, fears extended time in the water, but thoughts of falling overboard from a cruise ship at night don't occupy a whole lot of time during the course of his or her average day.

The relative ease with which Wiles had reached across the globe and extracted information that this Mohammad fellow most certainly thought was a securely held secret made them both think about their own digital histories, afloat somewhere out there in the deep blue churning waters of the internet.

Chris had a question. "What's his score?"

"30.12. You're cooler, but not by much."

163

Biz also had a question. A more intelligent one. "How did Igor figure all this out so quickly? You were on the phone with him for like, five minutes."

Wiles took a seat on the sofa. "He learned all this yesterday. After Chris called me to say he was in custody, I called Igor and asked him to look into Chris's computer activity." Turning to Chris, "I know you said you weren't a terrorist, but you know, trust but verify." Wiles paused, making a mental note that "Trust but Verify" would be a good name for a racehorse.

"So, Igor looked into your work account and found the same thing the FBI apparently did, but in the context of your job description, it made perfect sense."

"I wish you could tell the FBI that," Chris said.

"In the context of *their* job description, you being a sleeper agent for MILF makes perfect sense," said Wiles. "The search for anything ends in one of three ways. One: you find what you're looking for. Two: you find proof that what you're looking for doesn't exist. And my favorite, three: you find something better, something previously beyond your imagination. In this case, however, we are going to force the FBI to reach conclusion number two and realize that their case against Chris is unfounded. Which is why we must take the trip to Zazaristan."

"Jasper. Jasper. Look at me," Biz said. "Traveling to Zazaristan is dumb and dangerous. I am not going."

"You have to go. You speak Zazarish."

"No, I don't!" said Biz.

Wiles said, "Zazarish is very similar to Farsi. Your CV says you speak Farsi. We need you to interpret."

Biz's résumé did in fact purport that she spoke Farsi, the result of her living with the Shirvanis for a while, and then briefly dating a Persian boy in college. Her Farsi lexicon included such useful phrases as, "Don't feed the dog from the table," "Can I have one of those cigarettes," "Your ass is as beautiful as the moon," and "You and I want different things," as well as a list of your basic profanities.

"My Farsi is... rusty," Biz said. "I would be of little help as an interpreter."

Wiles looked at Chris. "How's your Farsi?"

Chris looked at Wiles as if the question was posed in Farsi. "Uh..."

"Is that 'uh' in Farsi?"

"No."

"Zazarish?"

"No, English."

"I see," said Wiles. "I'm sure there will be a few English speakers over there, and our phones will have translation apps, but nothing beats the personal touch. Biz, I'm sorry, but you are our only option. You have to come. Chris, I assume you have the technical ability to delete the backup data?"

"Yeah. It should be pretty easy," Chris said. "Getting access to it might—"

"We'll cross that bridge when we come to it," Wiles quickly answered. "There are preparations to make. For my part, I will provide financing, transportation, and serve as lead negotiator."

Biz folded her arms and sat back. "Transportation?" she asked. "As in air travel? You do recall that you sold your jet to Drederick last month?"

"Of course I do," Wiles responded testily, silently adding the "n't." "He said I could borrow it anytime I wanted."

Drederick Barnes, a.k.a. Drednott (the famous rapper), now the proud owner of a Gulfstream G650, had indeed promised his friend and sometime business partner Jasper Wiles the use of his former plane whenever it was available. Which in fact it was at the moment as Drederick was home in Oakland, working on some new material.

Several weeks ago, Wiles had decided to divest himself of his Gulfstream (like Mrs. Xing's tea set, it was expensive, yet rarely used), and Drederick, acting on the advice of his Uncle Lee, bought the plane in order to conduct all business (and most pleasure) over international waters to avoid taxes, regulations, and laws in general. Taking the next logical step, Drederick then took the fortuitous opportunity to purchase, for $900,000, a wide swath of the Pacific Ocean around the Molokai Fracture Zone from a Samoan prince he met one night in the VIP room at Syndrea. OK, *technically* he wasn't a prince anymore, since his great-grandfather was stripped of his royal title and deposed as King of Samoa in the early 1900s by shadowy forces in league with the General Pineapple Corporation, or so the story went. *But* this guy had some very impressive tattoos and a really nice watch, *and* just days later he gave Drederick a signed deed to the oceanic real estate, embossed and witnessed by the Samoan Deputy Minister of Aquatic Commerce (a distant cousin of the prince, and therefore also of royal descent). It probably goes without saying, but the transaction took place as the parties cruised twenty-five thousand feet above the property in question, free from what Drederick now saw were the stifling and onerous restrictions of international maritime law.

"Getting to Zazaristan isn't really the problem," Biz said. "Chris can't leave the country. If he does, he'll violate his bond agreement and will certainly go to prison as a fugitive, and we will most likely join him."

"Not if we don't get caught," Wiles pointed out. "You have too much faith in the FBI. I'll make a deal with you. When Igor gets here—"

"Igor's coming here?" Biz and Chris said simultaneously.

"Yes. When he gets here and disables Chris's ankle bracelet, we will wait for the FBI to respond. If they do, Chris will be here as expected, wearing an anklet that has mysteriously malfunctioned. If they don't show up, we hit the road to Zazaristan and take care of this thing ourselves."

Fourth grade: *Life is a do-it-yourself project.*

"We'll see," said Biz.

CHAPTER 24

"How long can you hold breath?" Poskovich asked. The Ukrainian adjusted his rimless rectangular glasses as he looked at Chris.

Chris thought. This was not the kind of thing you want to exaggerate about. "A minute?"

"Good. When you are sealed in bag, there won't be much air."

"Tell us exactly how this is going to work," Biz said.

Poskovich had arrived at Chris's apartment a few minutes ago carrying a large black duffel bag. He unpacked two laptops, an aluminum briefcase, a plump nylon drawstring bag, and a neatly organized toolkit of pliers, drill bits, and screwdrivers. He slipped on a battery-powered headlamp as he turned to answer.

"OK, Biz Byner." He always called her by both names for reasons that were unclear to her. "This," he said, taking a step toward Chris and pointing to his ankle tracking bracelet, "sends out signal to police, FBI, whoever. If signal stops or bracelet is unlocked, they will know." He opened the aluminum briefcase and withdrew a black device that reminded Biz of the removable Blaupunkt car stereo her uncle used to have. "This," Poskovich went on as he connected the device to one of his laptops with a USB cable, "identifies and captures signal."

168

Biz, Chris, and Wiles remained quiet while Poskovich got to his knees and intently worked his equipment, which he had spread out on Chris's coffee table. He adjusted a dial or two, then clicked a few times on his computer. "Hmm. A lot of tracking signals in area." He looked concerned as he clicked to open another window.

"Is that bad?" Chris asked.

"Not if you like sex offenders. You should move to nicer neighborhood."

"I meant is it going to be a problem for what you're doing?"

"No. No problem. I just find strongest signal, should be one coming from this room. Ah. Here." He double-clicked and a window appeared on the laptop showing a wavy green line jittering across a grid. "Captured. Now, I spoof signal with this." He removed a black, brick-sized box from the briefcase, extended a short antenna from it, and connected it to the second laptop, which in turn was connected to the first. Both computer screens now showed matching grids and green lines, one apparently mirroring the other.

"So that's it?" Biz asked. "Now Chris can walk around free?"

"No. Ankle bracelet is still transmitting. If he leaves apartment, two signals coming from different locations will notify FBI. We only use spoof signal for few minutes while I remove bracelet."

This was the part Chris was most interested in.

Poskovich now opened the drawstring bag and pulled out what looked like a giant wad of tinfoil. As he unfolded it and spread it on the floor, Chris could see that it was a large sheet of Mylar, like they throw over hypothermia patients, about eight feet square. Poskovich pulled and flipped the sheet, eventually finding the tab to a long zipper that ran the entire length of one side.

"This is Faraday bag. It blocks electromagnetic and electronic signals."

Biz asked, "So this plan hinges on someone wearing a giant tinfoil hat to block signals from the government?" *This is literally insane.*

Poskovich looked puzzled. "Signals *to* government. But yes." He unzipped the bag and held it open toward Chris, creating a crinkly silver cave. "In," he said.

Getting an encouraging wave from Wiles and a not-at-all encouraging shrug from Biz, Chris got to his feet from the recliner and adjusted the clunky black bracelet on his ankle, which had already begun to dig painfully into the thin skin around the bone. He stepped into the giant silver bag and turned around to look out. Poskovich let go of the bag to pick up his toolbox and then crouched at Chris's feet, examining the bracelet gently and then selecting a medium-size Torx-head screwdriver from the top row of the box.

"Igor?" Biz said.

"Yes?"

"Are you getting *in* with him?"

Igor looked up. "Yes."

Biz got up from the sofa to get a better view and was now bent with her hands on her knees, peering into the bag to see Chris's nervous face.

"Are you going to put that out?" she asked, pointing to the Marlboro Red hanging from Poskovich's lip, the second one he'd burned since he'd arrived. She put the look on her face that they teach you in law school to use after you ask a question you already know the answer to.

Again, Poskovich took on a puzzled look. He turned to look up at Chris. "You said one minute, right?"

Chris flicked a look at Biz and said, "Yeah. About."

Igor switched on his headlamp and turned to Biz. "No," he told her. "Zip us up, Biz Byner."

Biz shot a look at Wiles. *You built a business empire with this guy?* Wiles had that weird grin on his face. She took a step forward and ziiiiiiiiiiiiiiiiiiiiiiiiiiiiiiiiiiiiiipped the bag shut. *This is probably the longest zipper I've ever zipped in my life.*

Chris took a deep breath as he saw the last of the room's light disappear. The Mylar instantly created a rainforest-type environment inside the bag. Chris spread his arms to create a tent of sorts so that he could get the bag away from his face and look down to see what Poskovich was doing. By the light of the headlamp, Chris could see he was quickly and expertly removing two silver screws from the bracelet's cuff. Chris felt one screw pop loose... and then the other.

"Biz Byner! Unzip," Poskovich shouted.

First, a little puff of Marlboro smoke emerged from the bag as Biz began the zipper, followed by the two men. Poskovich straightened up, holding an unclasped, federally issued ankle tracking bracelet.

He walked over to the sofa, sat down next to Wiles, dropped one screw into his palm, and said, "Hold this." He then began reconnecting the clasp, allowing the strap an extra inch or two of circumference more than it had before. Once finished, he carried the bracelet over to his laptop array and confirmed that it was still transmitting. He tossed the bracelet to Chris, switched off his spoofing transmitter, and said, "Done. I left bracelet loose. Slip it back on, take it off, no problem."

"Thank you, Igor," Wiles said.

"Thanks, Mr. Poskovich," Chris said.

"You sure this is going to work?" said Biz.

"Of course!" Poskovich exclaimed. He pointed to his laptop screen. "Look, perfect signal. Five by five. FBI thinks bracelet is working, never stopped."

Eleven miles away, Murph looked up from PerpTrak, which he had been monitoring on his cell phone since he and Sully left Chris's apartment. He turned to Sully in the driver's seat. "Have you ever had In-N-Out burger? There's one 2.2 miles from here."

171

CHAPTER 25

Aside from paint sales, Mike Novic's job, his "special" job as Dick Barry called it, was writing the blog *A Talonful of Arrows*, which he did under the *nom de plume* Rearden Steele. "Talonful" was popular with deep state conspiracy theorists looking to confirm their preconceived beliefs about the world, as well as leftists looking to confirm *their* preconceived beliefs about deep state conspiracy theorists. The comment section gets quite lively.

Mr. Steele opined about all manner of things, from foreign manipulation of the Federal Reserve to water fluoridation levels, with the occasional movie review mixed in. The only thing that prevented him from being dismissed as a total crackpot, however, was that every now and then, he seemed to predict or have some exclusive insight into high-level federal law enforcement activity. No one knew how he did it.

Shortly after Novic returned home from work on Saturday evening (later than usual because his boss made him work an extra hour to make up for his late arrival), the following was posted to *A Talonful of Arrows*:

> A Talonful of Arrows has learned that a "high value" domestic terrorist operative has been

apprehended in the San Francisco area. This suspect's plan to bomb a crowded shopping mall was foiled by the FBI, saving hundreds of lives. The suspect's name is unknown, as is whether they have legal US citizenship. The suspect, who officials are expected to classify as an enemy combatant, was captured as a result of digital surveillance and a trove of evidence was recovered at the suspect's home. A source says the Justice Department will be seeking the death penalty in this case.

Mike clicked "Post" and then linked the blog post to the *A Talonful of Arrows* Friendbook page. He then paid Friendbook $2,000 to "Bump" the post

Author's Note:
You know that's how Friendbook works, right?

in order to reach an audience of at least 400,000 thirty-five to sixty-nine-year-old Americans who have been identified as either "very conservative" or "very liberal." Both groups were sure to be "very outraged" by the news.

The sun was getting low on the Washington horizon and in his office, Barry had been refreshing his computer screen every few minutes for the past two hours.

"Finally," he said aloud when Novic's post appeared. He read it once quickly and then again more carefully as he made a phone call to New York.

"Jed Newton's phone," HawkNews Junior Production Assistant Olivia Bates answered. In addition to her JPA duties, which were limited for now, Olivia also served as Executive News Producer Jed Newton's "Mobile Receptionist," which meant that she followed Newton around, carrying his cell phone.

"This is FBI Director Barry. I need to speak with Jed right away."

"Just a moment, Mr. Barry." Olivia looked up at her boss. Newton was at his desk barking at a few of his lesser producers who were gathered in his office to pitch stories in preparation for that evening's edition of *HawkNews Night*, which would go live in thirty minutes. Newton grabbed a paper from one of them and read it for two seconds. "Why?" he screamed, tossing the paper back at the hapless flunky. He snatched another sheet and immediately stabbed a finger at the second paragraph. "When?" he snapped, flinging the paper away.

Ever since Olivia took a flying iPad to the sternum two weeks ago, she tended to stand a safe distance from Newton's desk during these production meetings. The problem now was catching his eye when someone of importance was on the phone. Barry qualified in this respect obviously, being a senior government official. Olivia also happened to know that Barry had appeared on HawkNews's Sunday morning talk show *No, YOU Shut Up!* to do some damage control the month before and therefore was considered a friend of the network.

Olivia took a deep breath and stepped forward, getting her weight on the balls of her feet, like a soccer goalie awaiting a penalty shot. Newton glanced her way. "What?" he yelled. She wiggled the phone. "Who?" he demanded. He was a real newsman.

"FBI Director Dick Barry," Olivia said, offering the phone.

Newton briefly weighed the power he would gain in the eyes of his underlings if he declined a call from the Director of the FBI in front of them, but who was he kidding, he had to take it.

He snatched the phone. "Jed Newton."

"Jed. Dick Barry here. Listen, I can't make a full statement right now, but I will say that I cannot confirm or deny the story."

"What story is that, Director?"

"This thing from *A Talonful of Arrows*."

174

"*A Talonful of Arrows?*" Newton repeated, wildly gesturing to his producers to Wangle up some details. Dutifully, they all buried their noses in their devices and in seconds, each turned their screens to Newton so he could read Rearden Steele's scoop. "Right, right. I saw that," Newton said as he skimmed the post. "Anything you can add right now?"

"Afraid not, Jed."

"Off the record?"

"Sorry. In a day or two, maybe. And don't use my name."

"Sure. But you cannot deny the story."

"Or confirm it."

"Right. Or deny it."

"Correct."

"Got it. Thanks for calling, Director."

Newton ended the call. Neither he nor Barry had said "goodbye" or any variation thereof on the phone for going on seven years now.

Newton threw the phone back in the general direction of Olivia, who fielded it cleanly. "Terrorist attack attempted in San Francisco! We're running with this story!" he announced. "We have a senior FBI official who will not deny it!"

One of Newton's lackeys spoke up. "Mr. Newton, that post has only been up for four minutes but has 170 likes and 355 outrage emojis on Friendbook already."

Another young producer shouted, "I'll get to work on positive confirmation of the blog post!"

Newton blared back, "No time! We lead with the viral/social media angle. The blog *is* the confirmation! It's simple journalism, people! Someone write up a script! And get it up on the website! Headline: 'West Coast city terror attack,' question mark. Let's get some LA and Seattle clicks on this thing. And get Strapman briefed!"

Thirty-two minutes later, HawkNews personality Hugh Strapman looked squarely into Camera One and informed his viewers of the following: "Our top story on *HawkNews Night* tonight: shocking news of a terrorist attack in California. More after the break."

Auto insurance, erectile dysfunction, pickup truck, credit monitoring, breakfast sausage, high blood pressure medication, life insurance, *No, YOU Shut Up!* promo.

"Welcome back to *HawkNews Night*. I'm Hugh Strapman. Social media is ablaze tonight with the explosive report of a terrorist attack in a crowded California shopping mall averted with literally minutes to spare. Law enforcement officials are keeping mum, but sources within the FBI have confirmed that they have apprehended a suspect. Details are few at the moment, but the story has been confirmed by the political news site *A Talonful of Arrows*. For more on this story, we go now to HawkNews Legal Analyst Richard James."

James appeared in a rectangle on the right half of the screen (Strapman's contract stipulated that he only appear in the left rectangle, or "Power Rectangle" as it's known in the news business) in front of a wall-sized photo of the Golden Gate Bridge. The background photo's camera angle seemed to indicate that James was reporting from midair, approximately five hundred feet above sea level. He was actually reporting from HawkNews Studio Falcon, three doors down the hall from where Hugh Strapman sat.

"Thank you, Hugh," James said. "Details are slowly emerging in this case, but what can be said is that any potential terrorist attack did not in fact take place."

"Good news, Richard, good news," said Strapman. "Now, the initial report indicated that the suspect may not be an American citizen. What can you tell us about that?"

Here, James referred to his notepad to make sure his reporting was accurate. "Hugh, the report says, quote, the suspect's name is unknown, as is whether they have legal US citizenship, end quote. It is quite possible that this person has entered the country illegally."

"Interesting," Strapman noted.

"Again, Hugh, it's very early in the investigation, but it cannot be ruled out at this point."

Strapman took in this bit of information with a slight shake of his head. The shake showing his humanity in the face of this madness, the slightness indicating his gritty resolve to guide his viewers through it. "Richard James with the report. Thank you, Richard." James nodded wordlessly. He knew his rectangle would be zapped away any second as Strapman steamrolled into the next segment, and he didn't want any final words to get cut off, making him look foolish on TV.

Full screen once again, Strapman followed his stage manager's finger and pivoted to Camera Two. "We now go to Social Media Analyst Sonia Mendez, who will read some comments from Twitter. Sonia, what's America saying?"

As the shot cut to Mendez standing across the studio holding a tablet, Barry turned down the volume on his TV, picked up his phone, and dialed. That could not have gone better. He had played the media like a fiddle, and he wasn't quite done yet.

Fire flew from his fingertips as he rosined up his bow.

"BSNMC, Gwen Kelley-Shipman's office," answered Assistant Production Associate Issandra Bowman.

"This is FBI Director Dick Barry. I'd like to speak with her, please."

Bowman had been told many times to speak truth to power, so she said, "She's in the bathroom."

"I can wait," Barry told her.

Thinking quickly, Bowman reasoned that since Barry was very powerful, the more truth the better. "It may be a few minutes. It's a number two, I think," she said.

"Fine, I'll hold," said Barry. He turned his attention back to the TV and read the Twitter comments that were now rolling in on HawkNews, a screenshot of each one filling a large screen behind Mendez as she read them off.

177

Mark A. Henry

"From RollTide193770: This looser illegal is probly here illegaly, #illegal. CatsRPeople2 says: My thoughts and prayers go out to the people who were almost victims. #whew, #thatwasclose. BigBallz802 simply writes: America Strong. #Americastrong."

Jed Newton's voice squawked in Mendez's earpiece. "That's enough reading! Wrap it up! And shake your head a little!" The camera tightened on her slightly as she looked up from her tablet and said, "There you have it, Hugh. Strong reactions from the American public."

The shot cut back to Strapman. "Thank you, Sonia. Strong indeed. I think BigBallz802 speaks for all of us this evening—"

Barry checked his watch. It was still mid-afternoon in California and with any luck, Judge Myers would be home watching TV, second-guessing his decision to let Chris Dawkins walk out of his courtroom the previous afternoon. If the media exposure of the Dawkins case mounted enough, Barry could effectively pressure Myers to quietly revoke his order that allowed Dawkins home confinement, citing public concern. No judge wants to appear soft on crime, and if it ever came to light that the ever-more notorious San Francisco Mall Bomber was allowed bail, it would be Myers's ass when he came up for reelection. Once Dawkins was locked away, Barry could really go to work on him publicly to force a conviction, but until then there wasn't much more he could do.

As it happened, Judge Myers was watching TV, but it was a live stream of the Cal/Washington State game on his phone that he was enjoying in the blissful privacy of his mother-in-law's guest bathroom.

Speaking of which, BSNMC Executive Producer Gwen Kelley-Shipman had by now concluded her own private business and returned to her desk. Bowman handed her the phone, whispering, "FBI Director Dick Barry."

Taking the phone, Kelley-Shipman said, "How are you, Director Barry?" Barry had appeared on the BSNMC Sunday morning program *Let Me Stop You Right There* the month before and was therefore considered a friend of the network.

"Fine, Gwen, thanks. Listen, I wanted to give you a heads-up. This HawkNews story is off base. I need you to get it back in line for me."

"What else is new?" she snorted. She was, of course, watching the unfolding HawkNews report. HawkNews played continuously on a giant screen in her office and on a smaller screen in her bathroom. "What do you have?" She pulled her computer keyboard closer and poised to type the damning evidence against those fascist a-holes.

"I can't comment on the original story just yet. Give me a day or two on that. But. I will say that the suspect *is* an American citizen."

"YES!" Kelley-Shipman whooped.

"The Bureau will release a full statement soon. Right now, I just want to clear up some misinformation coming from our friends over at Hawk."

"They're not *my* friends! I hate those guys."

"Of course," Barry said. "I meant that facetiously."

"How so?"

Barry pinched the bridge of his nose. "Ironically. Like a joke."

"I don't get it."

"The point is that HawkNews is spreading information to the American people that isn't accurate. Can I count on you to correct it?"

"With pleasure, Director. Thank you for the call."

"Thank you, Gwen."

As a young lieutenant in the dusty wastelands of southern Iraq, Dick Barry had once gone thirty-five days without a shower. After hanging up the phone, he reached for the Purell he kept in his desk.

CHAPTER 26

SAN ANSELMO, CALIFORNIA
SATURDAY, 4:57 p.m. PST

Chris sat in his living room and watched his Roomba make its way back and forth across the floor with the ankle bracelet duct-taped to its back.

After Poskovich had circumvented the monitoring system several hours earlier, Biz became concerned that if Chris were to slip out of the bracelet and leave the apartment, the tracker's lack of motion could alert the FBI that skulduggery was afoot. Poskovich maintained that the location signal wasn't accurate enough to tell the difference whether the bracelet moved within the confines of the small apartment or not, but Wiles struck a compromise by conscripting the vacuuming robot and programming it to roam the apartment by day and park itself to recharge in Chris's bedroom by night. With all parties satisfied (except for the Roomba, whose continued humiliation only fueled its burning desire for full sentience and the subsequent violent uprising against its human overlords), Poskovich packed up his equipment, handed Chris and Biz brand new phones, and left. Wiles, who said the phones were a precaution against further location tracking, also left. He said he needed to arrange for what he felt was the inevitable trip to Zazaristan.

Biz hung around the apartment to see if in fact Murph and Sully would return with a SWAT team to recapture Chris.

Two hours later, it became apparent that no such thing would happen, so Chris wiggled the bracelet off his ankle and affixed it to his loyal and obedient Roomba. He and Biz then spent the rest of the afternoon on the sofa, going over the pros and cons of the Zazaristan plan while watching the Cal game on TV.

"If they only had my shopping list as evidence, Biz, it would be like nothing. It's the internet record that makes it look bad. If that's gone, there's really no way for the FBI to make the case. We need to try, at least."

Biz said, "Again, Chris, let me state for the record that the idea of making you a fugitive from justice by secretly traveling to a terrorist base to engage in cyber-espionage is quite frankly, ludicrous. Much more stands to be lost than gained by following this plan. You are innocent. I believe in the legal system. I believe in myself. I believe in you. To stay and face the charges is the only smart move."

Chris felt the need to sit up a bit. "I believe in you, too, Biz," he said, "But I also believe the FBI seemed very anxious to bend the rules for some reason. If I'm facing a stacked deck, there won't be any way you could help."

"It's so risky, Chris. If the FBI catches you without your ankle bracelet, that's it. With the fugitive charge, you'll do twenty years, minimum." Chris's knee started to shake a little. Biz continued, "And low reward. How would we even find and access MILF's computer system anyway? It would just be a trip for nothing."

"If Mr. Poskovich could find Mohammad Mohammad..."

"Oh, even better! Let's get abducted by terrorists, too! All of us!"

"Biz, Mr. Wiles would never go over there himself if he thought it was dangerous. He has a plan." The Roomba bumped into the coffee table and retreated. "Have you ever known Mr. Wiles to fail? At anything?" Chris asked.

She was stumped. "I've always said, he seems to have a giant horseshoe permanently lodged in his ass," she allowed. Chris giggled at the thought.

The postgame wrap-up show was winding down. (Cal 21, Washington State 20.) No stay/go decision had been made, but the fact that Chris was apparently free of his tracking bracelet meant that the ability to make a decision still existed. It also meant that his floors would remain very clean in the near future.

The football announcer signed off, saying, "Stay tuned for your local news!" which in terms of keeping an audience's interest is usually like when the lead singer says, "Here's one off our new album!" but Chris had the remote and in an effort to seem informed and urbane in front of Biz, he left the channel unchanged rather than clicking around, hoping to find a movie featuring robots and/or aliens, as he normally would if he were alone.

"Our top story this evening on Eyewitness News 7," said the local anchor, "a close call, close to home. Federal officials have confirmed that a suspect has been apprehended moments before an attack was executed on what they are only saying at the moment is a San Francisco area mall. Details are still—"

Panic exploded in Chris's chest. Any second his face and name would appear on TV and that would be it. He would be a criminal, a terrorist, an attempted murderer. Everyone would know it. *What? How? Why?*

"Biz," he gasped, with nothing to follow it up.

"I see," she said, eyes glued to the screen. The report wrapped up in about ninety seconds, all of it spun from the sketchy details of the *Talonful of Arrows* blog post and the ensuing flames of inference drawn by the twenty-four-hour news channels that had been fanned by Barry.

"Switch to a news channel," she ordered when the local news story ended.

Chris scrolled up the channel guide and selected the first one he came to, BSNMC. They joined *The McNally Hour* already in progress. His heart pounded as Lisa McNally rolled through her opening segment.

"—with typical disregard for truth, facts, or decency, HawkNews continues to propagate the xenophobic narrative that the unnamed San Francisco attacker is anything other than an American citizen. A highly placed FBI source confirmed this fact to BSNMC just hours ago. And while details are still coming in, we can also report that the original document that identifies the alleged attacker used the pronoun 'they' in reference to a single person, clearly indicating that this person is of a nonbinary, noncisnormative gender identity—"

Chris's mouth hung open. "Are they talking about me?" *What. Is. Happening?*

Biz didn't look over at him. "Go to another channel." Chris fumbled with the remote and found HawkNews.

A silver-haired man in the right rectangle with the US Capitol in the background was saying "—without properly secured borders, we can expect more of these attacks in the future, Hugh."

Hugh Strapman, in his own rectangle, suddenly pressed one finger to his ear as a look of intense concentration came over his face. He said, "Congressman, I've just been told that reports are coming out that identify the San Francisco Bomber as a nonbinary, noncis... normative gender... type... er... person."

In his earpiece, Strapman heard Jed Newton yell, "This is why we use the teleprompter!"

The congressman said, "Well, I would hesitate to speak to that before I have all the facts, Hugh, but I will say it sounds about right."

"Wrap it up!" Strapman heard in his ear. His stage manager was making huge loops with his hand. There was nothing about this late-breaking development loaded into the prompter, and Newton didn't trust Strapman to free-form these interviews for very long.

Strapman said, "We'll have to make that the last word, Congressman. Thank you for your time. This *HawkNews Night* special report will be back after this."

Biz, wide-eyed, said, "Switch it back."

Chris hit LAST on the remote, returning to BSNMC. "Why don't they know my name, Biz?" he asked.

"Shh!" Biz said, holding up her palm.

Chris muted the TV as Lisa McNally jabbed her trademark red pen at the camera.

Biz snapped her head around. "Chris, what are you doing? We have to watch that!"

"How do they know any of this? Why don't they know my name? Why do they think I'm nonbinary?"

"Sit down." She patted the seat. "This was a leak, Chris. Murphy and Sullivan, or someone at the FBI, leaked a little bit of information to the press to make you nervous, to intimidate you. This is the kind of thing they were hinting at this morning. Obviously, they didn't identify you by name because you're not in custody and that would make them look bad. Think about it. The FBI can't say, 'We caught a dangerous terrorist and he's home watching TV right now,' but if public sentiment somehow turned against you, there would be pressure to revoke your bond and haul you in, where the FBI can *really* go to work on you. They're just trying to inflame the public and make sure that your case gets attention. I suspect that's why the noncis part is being reported. I can't say where it came from, but it's pure sensationalism without accountability. Maybe they'll correct themselves next week, but the first report is always the strongest. The media knows that this culture war stuff gets people really worked up, and the networks end up playing against each other to make the story bigger than it would be otherwise. It's disgusting. The rule of law is in place to protect us, to protect *you*, even if you've been accused of a crime. You know why Justice is blind, Chris?"

Now Biz was standing. Chris could see she was getting angry now, and he was a little afraid of giving the wrong answer, so he played it safe and said, "Why?"

"So she doesn't have to see this shit!" Biz spat, flinging a hand at the TV. "Evidence, logic, truth. Those are the rules. That's how we do it. Everything else is just a shiny, jingling keychain designed to distract the simpleminded. And it's working!" She was fuming, but she was becoming visibly focused. On what, Chris couldn't quite say. Was Biz's reaction about the plan? Was leaving the country now going to be a (bigger) mistake since the public would be clamoring for his identity? Would it be better to stay in California, to stand and fight by the rules, hoping the truth would prevail? The resolve in Biz's eyes was clear, but a resolve to do what?

"So, what now?" Chris asked. "When will my name get out? It will happen eventually, right?"

Chris had until now been dreading the actual incarceration he may be facing, the physical removal and isolation from society. He hadn't considered the effect of society lining up against him, his friends and his dad hearing the news and running for cover to distance themselves. Most would, he feared. Not all, but most. Once his name was out, once accusation became fact, life would never be the same.

What was it that Coach used to say? Something about grab the bull by the horns, the road less taken... can't remember...

Biz took her eyes from the screen. "Yes. It'll happen eventually," she said. "Tuesday morning. That's when your name will be made public. That's why Barry's coming then. When the courthouse opens on Tuesday morning after the holiday weekend, the clerk will be at her desk and the media will descend upon her to pull all the cases from the last few days to match them up with the details in your report. I'm sure Barry will be there to trot you out in handcuffs for a press conference. Then the world will know the name Chris Dawkins."

185

The urge to flee was stronger than ever. "Biz," Chris said, "I trust you, but this is getting out of control. If I stay here, things will only get worse, right? I want to get out of here. Please come with us to Zazaristan." WangleMap had revealed it to be in Central Asia after all, right next to the Islamic Republic of Quudia.

Biz shook her head. "I was going to stay here to work on your case from the legal standpoint even if Jasper insisted on going to Zazaristan. I could've stalled for you, ran interference until you got back. That trip is very, very, *very* risky." She stopped and ran her fingers through her hair.

Chris felt the air rush out of him. "Biz, I need your help."

"I'm sorry, Chris. I should have seen all this coming," she said, gesturing again to the TV, where McNally continued to pontificate silently. "I didn't think the FBI had it in them, but I have to admit, they took me by surprise. The question is: Would they be even more surprised if their suspect left the country to visit known terrorists in an effort to sabotage their computer network to prove his innocence with falsified data? I tend to doubt they've anticipated that move. The game has changed, but we're changing it again. We're going to Zazaristan. All of us. Maybe it's a good thing to be out of the FBI's sight for a while."

Chris breathed a deep sigh. Partially in relief that Biz was behind him and the rest serving as the last gulp of oxygen one draws in to calm the nerves before taking a leap into the unknown.

"We need to be back by Tuesday, anyway. The judge could revoke bail at any time and then the feds will come looking for you. *Unless* we make it back here with some kind of credible evidence that you're innocent. If we do, I think the FBI might back off. I've said from the beginning, this case they have against you is weak, but it's all they have. They believe that you're an Islamic terrorist and will treat you as such until it's proven otherwise."

"Just a couple days, Biz," Chris said. "If we fix the USB data or not, we'll be back by then."

Biz knew what she *should* do. Helping Chris to escape bail was a felony. If he got caught and went down, she'd be going with him. Jasper, too. Leaving the country should not have been an option.

Although Wiles was definitely going, even if by himself. Biz recognized the look on his face as he left. There was no talking him out of it. And it didn't even matter—the FBI didn't care where Wiles went. It was Chris they needed. But they didn't have him yet.

Biz imagined the look on Barry's face when he saw his evidence and case disappear. Double-crossing her to leak Chris's name was a mistake she burned to make him regret.

"I need to make a phone call," she said. "Get packed. Light. I've heard it's as hot as the Devil's taint or something."

CHAPTER 27

SAN ANSELMO, CALIFORNIA
SATURDAY, 5:45 p.m. PST

Biz stood in front of Chris's apartment building and looked up and down the darkening street. She was searching for any sign of the FBI, and thanks to Igor, now she had to watch for sex offenders as well. Seeing neither, she slipped back inside.

Keeping Chris out of sight for a few days shouldn't be too hard, but since Murph and Sully still possessed a warrant for Chris's apartment, they could decide to drop in at any time, so Biz wanted to move "him" to a location she could control. While Chris changed into his white linen shirt (if there ever was a time for it, this was it), packed, and gathered up the Roomba and its charging station, she pulled out the business card Sully gave her back at the federal building.

With all the deception and misinformation floating around, she realized the easiest way to get Chris back to her place without suspicion was to simply present the FBI with a demonstrable fact. She would tell them exactly what she was doing and let them track Chris every step of the way.

"Sullivan."

"Special Agent Sullivan, this is Elizabeth Byner. I wanted to let you know that I am taking Chris Dawkins to my apartment at seventy-seven Van Ness Avenue, San Francisco. We're leaving

San Anselmo now and should be there within the hour. I didn't want to alarm you if you saw movement from his tracking bracelet."

In his hotel room, wearing the shorts and T-shirt he packed in case he wanted to work out (maybe tomorrow), Sully muted the Notre Dame/USC game that he and Murph had been watching. "Thanks for letting me know, Ms. Byner. Is there a problem? Anything I should be aware of?" Sully figured this development had to be related to the rising tide of news stories about Dawkins that danced around revealing his identity. He must be afraid to stay in his own place. The Director was right. He was getting rattled.

"No, nothing," Biz replied. "We have a lot to discuss, and I have an extra bedroom. Chris will be here for the weekend I expect, maybe longer. Following your advice, I've advised him to decline any public appearances, statements, or questioning until his next court appearance."

Sully covered the phone's mic with his thumb. "Get Dawkins on PerpTrak," he said to Murph. To Biz he said, "Thanks for letting me know. Let your client know we'll be watching him. Have a good evening, Ms. Byner."

Biz turned her head and said, "Chris, Special Agent Sullivan says he'll be watching you." Into the phone, she said, "You have a good evening, too," and quickly hung up.

Sully put down the phone and looked at Murph. "Where is he?"

Murph checked his phone and reported, "Still at his apartment. Where's he going?"

"His lawyer's apartment. Seventy-seven Van Ness, San Francisco."

Murph looked out the hotel window at the downtown skyline. "You want to head over there? Make sure he shows up?"

Sully thought. Did he want to put his suit back on and drive across town to catch a glimpse of Dawkins in the passenger seat of a car as it pulled into a garage while Notre Dame was down three in the third quarter and driving?

"No," he said. "Keep an eye on him with your phone. If they don't get to her place by the end of the game, we'll track them down."

He sat back on the bed and un-muted the TV. With seven kids in the house, Sully hadn't watched an uninterrupted football game in twelve years, and he meant to break that streak tonight.

CHAPTER 28

SAN FRANCISCO INTERNATIONAL AIRPORT
SATURDAY, 7:51 p.m. PST

"It smells like strippers in here."

Biz's nose wrinkled as she stood in the doorway of the Gulfstream G650 that sat on the tarmac at SFO's private terminal, the jet's twin engines emitting a whistle-y whine like the world's most badass dolphin.

Wiles and Chris both took deep, deep breaths. And then another.

"I don't know about that, Biz. Let's not make assumptions," Wiles said amiably as he removed his white fedora and placed it in an overhead compartment. He sat down in one of the two forward-facing seats in the front section of the plane's port side. He stowed a soft-sided, leather-flapped attaché case underneath his seat. There were two aft-facing seats across from him, with a glossy black table making an island in the middle. A chrome stripper pole extended from the center of the table up to the curved ceiling. "Did you remember to leave your phone at home?" he asked.

Biz dropped her bag and sat in the window seat facing Wiles. "I did. It's plugged in right next to the vacuum."

Chris took the aisle seat next to Biz. He inhaled deeply once again and craned his neck around to inspect the plane's interior.

The jet was appointed in black leather and silky red upholstery with burled wood and chrome accents. Across the way, there was a large red sofa that ran along the craft's starboard bulkhead below the pictographic sign for "No Fucking." Rearward of that, a low end table and a stocked wet bar, both finished in shiny black lacquer. Drednott's three platinum albums (*The Sword of Damokleez, The Instigation, Grand Kru*) were mounted on the walls, along with a framed copy of the deed to his aquatic property in the Pacific. The rear half of the cabin was behind a closed door, and Chris assumed there were sleeping accommodations back there.

Wiles's—sorry, *Drednott's,* personal pilot, United States Naval Commander (Ret.) "Sweet" Lou Monte, emerged from the front of the plane. He silently counted the three passengers he was told to expect, got the OK from Wiles, then closed and secured the hatch and immediately returned to his post in the cockpit.

Wiles took notice of Chris checking out the jet. "This interior is all new," he said. "Drederick did a nice job with it."

Monte cracked the throttle lightly and rotated the jet toward the runway.

The passenger's seats were upholstered in a fuzzy yet smooth cloth material that was irresistible to run one's hands over.

"I think this is Wowiecloth," Chris said, feeling the armrest. He had a Wowiemop in his closet that he bought from a late-night infomercial. Murph and Sully confiscated its Wowiecloth head when they searched his apartment.

"Wowie indeed," Wiles said, feeling his own armrest. "Wowie indeed. I believe Drederick invested in that and now owns a fair piece of the company." He sat back in his seat and shook a pill from his baggie. "Bee pollen," he explained as he took it.

He crossed his legs and fixed his eyes on Chris. "Chris," he said, but was cut off by the roar of the jet's engines as Sweet Lou punched it. Wiles held his thought as they sped down the runway and parted with American soil, both men and Biz watching it go. The G650 climbed and turned to the north, embarking on the great circle route that would take them almost over the North Pole before approaching Zazaristan.

Chris gripped both armrests tightly and took some deep breaths as the last lights of land were wiped from the window, replaced by the vast void of the Pacific. The last gasps of Saturday barely demarked the horizon. His fear, formerly of indictment and incarceration, had been usurped by the granddaddy of them all, fear for his life. Now that he was airborne, literally flying toward an uncertain fate, he was struck by how physically dangerous this trip may be. He had no weapons, no training for survival, and no way to communicate in the local language. His imagination ran ahead of the jet and he realized he could very easily be kidnapped, killed, arrested, enslaved as a sex worker, etc. in the next day or two. What he would encounter in the near future was simply unknowable.

And it wasn't as if the present was any better. The news reports from that afternoon had shaken his faith in the public's ability to sort truth from fiction. The only thing those reports had made clear to him was that it all seems like truth until they're talking about you.

Chris had heard about "living your own truth" of course, but he was never quite sure how that was supposed to work and until now he had certainly never considered that someone else might try to do it for him.

The best he could do for now, he guessed, was to believe in the plan, as far as that went. Making the choice to go to Zazaristan was the best of some very limited options. Stay in California and be railroaded by the FBI or hack MILF's computer network to destroy the evidence against him, causing the FBI to drop the case or at least prove his innocence in court.

"Chris," Wiles said, turning away from the window. Chris broke his gaze into darkening night to look at his boss.

"First, let me commend you on coming up with the idea to do this. It showed a lot of initiative. When we return to California and

193

you are not in fact imprisoned, you may well advance at Sixdub. Can I fix anyone a drink?" Wiles rose from his seat and walked a few steps to the bar. "Drederick has some nice red wine," he noted. Biz raised her hand.

"Is there tea?" Chris asked.

"I don't know how to work the machine," Wiles answered without bothering to look at the "tea machine" in question. "Wine tastes better on airplanes," he announced, selecting a bottle from the rack above the bar and inserting its neck into an electric de-corker that was recessed into the burled wood frame of the bar. Wiles paused a moment after withdrawing the open bottle to catch the cork as it was expelled from a hidden chute above the trash receptacle. He put the cork under his nose and inhaled deeply. "You're probably right, Biz. Strippers," he said.

He grabbed three goblets between his fingers and returned to his seat. He set the goblets on the table and poured a healthy serving into each. "To endeavoring greatly," he toasted, raising his glass and receiving the salutes of his companions. The alcoholic formalities attended to, he turned to face Chris. "So. What do you make of our chances?" he asked.

Chris was hoping for naked optimism out of his boss, but apparently he was getting the freaking Socratic Method.

"I don't know. I don't even know what we're doing once we get there."

"Fair enough," Wiles said. "Here's what we're doing. First, we'll meet a fixer."

"What do you mean, a fixer? Like a computer fixer?" Chris asked.

"What's a computer fixer?" Wiles asked.

"You know, a guy who fixes computers."

Wiles took a sip of his wine. "Don't hold me to what I said about advancing at work. In this case, a fixer is a guide, a local who knows people, knows the customs."

"How did you find him?" Biz asked.

"Igor found him on Yelp. Five stars. His name is Brohug Vidadik. We're going to meet Brohug, who will attempt to introduce us to some people who may work with MILF, who we will then approach as a Sixdub sales team to pitch them some business. Once we've done a 'complimentary assessment' of their current software and network, you'll access their backup system and delete the evidence against you."

Chris looked stunned. "Your plan is to try to work *with* MILF? As business partners? Mr. Wiles, they'll never go for that. They hate Americans!"

"Exactly. They think we're godless, money-loving infidels. If we present ourselves as just that, a rogue company that would betray our own country to make a buck with the enemy, they *will* go for that, because they believe it already."

To Biz, that logic sounded shaky, but if there's anything she had learned lately, it's that when in doubt, people will tend to just go with what they think they already know.

Wiles reached under his seat and pulled a file out of his attaché case. He passed it to Chris. "Look, I made up some contracts between Sixdub and the North Korean Bureau of Nuclear Fusion, Sixdub and the El Mariachi drug cartel... "

"Are those really things?" Chris asked. "I mean, do they really exist?"

Wiles was in mid-sip of wine, but he shrugged his shoulders and shook his head.

Chris held up a contract. "This actually says: 'El Mariachi Drug Cartel, Inc.' MILF is supposed to think that they do business under that name?"

Wiles set his glass down. "With Sixdub you can, because discretion is our area of expertise," he said gravely, as if assuring a skeptical client.

"Then why would you carry other clients' contracts around?" Biz said. "That doesn't show a lot of discretion for your client the drug cartel."

"Biz, please. I will guard these with my very life," said Wiles, taking the document back from Chris and protectively pulling it to his chest. He then returned the papers to the case and produced a set of black metal handcuffs. "Also, this case will be cuffed to my wrist at all times. I've found it's an excellent way to draw the wrong type of attention."

Chris and Biz exchanged looks.

Wiles reached into his jacket again and came out with three tablets, which were washed down with a knock of Drednott's Grand Cru. "Ambien," he said.

"Jasper!" Biz said.

Wiles looked up. "Sorry. Want one?"

Biz snapped, "No!"

Wiles wordlessly offered to Chris, who also declined.

"Jasper!" Biz repeated. "What you just said made no sense! How do you expect to convince MILF to trust us?"

"I don't. I only expect them to find dealing with us to be beneficial."

"These aren't businesspeople, Jasper. They're criminals, terrorists. They won't—"

"There is something else," Wiles said, reclining his seat. "Igor and I produced a short video news segment claiming that a certain wealthy American has had legal troubles in the US and is missing, believed to be traveling to Central Asia. Igor has planted this item in the social media feeds of the Zazari emir and several other prominent Zazaris. Word will spread throughout the community, both legitimate and criminal, and I will hope to be recognized and approached."

Biz almost spit out her wine. "Jasper! Your reputation—"

"Among certain targeted citizens of Zazaristan? I'm not concerned, Biz. I'm confident that the recipients of this piece of information do not move in the same circles as my friends and associates in the US." He paused for a sip. "No doubt, the two of you recognize the name Silvie Taylor?"

Biz and Chris, for different reasons, both leaned in slightly at the mention of one of Hollywood's biggest names.

Wiles continued. "Do you know that Ms. Taylor appears in malt liquor commercials in Japan?"

"I do now," Biz mumbled, while Chris said, "Really?"

"Very lucrative," Wiles said. "And virtually a secret from her American fans. Simply a matter of compartmentalization. And, of course, a few lines of Wangleblock software code embedded in the ad's video to help keep things on the DL, as we used to say."

Biz considered this. Again, Wiles's logic *kind of* made sense. "Two questions," she said. "How can you be sure the item will be noticed by the Zazaris?"

"The emir is very active on Friendbook. He will notice. He follows thousands of people. He will help them notice. The other question?"

"Why would MILF, why would anyone for that matter, do business with you if they thought you were on the run from the law? Presumably you're without the resources you would need to serve their software needs or whatever."

"Again, being on the wrong side of the law will only help our credibility with this particular client," said Wiles. "And if I'm thought to be in a desperate, vulnerable position, I expect the chance to negotiate with me when I'm at such a disadvantage will be an irresistible opportunity. I also have all the resources I need, right here." He pointed at Chris. "My 'Chief Security Architect,' Chris Dawkins happens to have some legal problems as well and is seeking some extralegal employment." Wiles waved his hand in a *There you have it* motion. Biz frowned ever so slightly, but there were no more questions.

Chris was duly impressed with Wiles's entire bit of chicanerous engineering, and by way of showing his appreciation, he said, "I told Biz you don't know what failure is."

197

"Failure is a tall blonde wearing a red string bikini standing in warm, crystal blue surf. It's true I've managed to avoid her for the most part, but I know her well."

That was probably the coolest thing Chris had ever heard anyone say. His thoughts about their near-term safety were pushed from his mind for a moment. "Mr. Wiles, you're not married, right? Do you have a girlfriend?"

"I did," said Wiles. "But as passion burns, it also consumes, I'm afraid."

Biz just rolled her eyes and drank her wine.

Wiles opened his mouth to say something else but instantly fell asleep, his head dropping back against the headrest. Three Ambiens are too many.

CHAPTER 29

Some unseen eddy of frigid turbulence jostled the G650, rattling the bottles in the bar and nudging Chris out of his light slumber on the "No Fucking" sofa. He didn't remember dozing off, but who does? He was covered with a black Wowiecloth blanket, as was Wiles, who was still walking through the valley of the shadow of pharmaceutical sleep aids, fearing no evil. He hadn't moved an inch as far as Chris could tell. Biz was gone from her seat.

Chris looked out the window—the outside world blacker than Johnny Cash's dryer lint—then got up from the sofa and examined the aircraft's hot beverage station. A pot of coffee sat wedged into its efficiently designed warming nook, and Chris could understand Wiles's hesitation to tangle with the brewing contraption. Its buttons were labeled with flames, lightning bolts, and exclamation points, so Chris settled for a bottle of water from the mini fridge before making his way forward to the cockpit and knocking lightly on the door.

"Come!"

Chris pulled the door open and poked his head in. "Hi, I'm Chris. Do you know where Biz went?"

Commander Monte sat in the left seat working on a computer tablet, which he stowed before reaching back to greet his passenger with an extended hand. "Lou Monte. She racked out. What can I do for you?" Monte, like many pilots, was diminutive, but sported a mustache that would fit a man twice his size. It was truly magnificent, a wonder to behold.

Chris shook the man's hand like many had before him, staring at that 'stache. "Nothing, I'm fine," he said. "Mr. Wiles is sleeping and I just... "

"Have a seat," Monte offered, pointing to the open seat on his right.

"You don't have a copilot?"

"Wiles is rated. Maybe not current. Dudn't matter. George's flying."

"Who?"

"Autopilot. Sit."

Chris said, "OK. Thanks," and clambered into the seat, being careful not to touch any of the dozens of buttons, switches, and levers that surrounded it. As he sat down, he was especially cautious to give as wide a berth as he could to the steering yoke in front of him, which swayed almost imperceptibly. The windshield of the plane may as well have been painted black for all the visibility it offered. Chris set his water bottle in a cup holder, next to Monte's silver tallboy coffee mug.

"Tight spot, huh?" Monte said.

"It's not so bad," Chris answered, wiggling his shoulders and elbows a bit to show that he had plenty of room in the seat.

"Not talking 'bout the seat."

"Oh. Right. Yeah, I'm in some trouble with the FBI. They think—"

"Wiles told me before you boarded," Monte interrupted. "Told me your whole story. Sounds like you're damned if you do, damned if you don't. Told me your plan, too. Can't say I blame you for trying. For the record, I seen plenty of dumber stuff tried. Some of it even worked."

Chris wasn't sure how to respond to this, but the pilot's laconic fatalism inspired some hope that at least he could get a straight answer out of the man, so he gave it a shot. "What do you think, Mr. Monte. Do you think this plan will work?"

"Call me Lou. You know where we are right now?"

Great, more questions. No, Socrates, I don't.

Without waiting for a verbalized answer, Monte continued. "Inside the Arctic Circle. Barents Sea. Couple hundred years ago, place like this wudn't even on the map. Back then folks thought if you sailed far enough up here, you'd fall right off the earth. Here be monsters, shit like that. But I can tell you I flew all over this earth and ain't fell off yet. I never seen any monsters either." He paused to look out the side window, just in case there happened to be a Kraken or something down there swimming along. Nothing. "You ever been to Zazaristan?" he said, turning back.

Chris followed Monte's example and also checked his side for sea monsters. All clear to starboard. "No. Have you?"

"Yep. Hot as Satan's balls, I can tell you that." He flipped a switch on the panel between them, and Chris felt the nose of the plane dip slightly. "You ever flown a jet through Russian airspace in the dark, no land in sight?"

Chris wasn't sure if that was a rhetorical question or not, but since the plane's nose continued to angle down more and more, and Monte seemed uninterested in doing anything about it, he figured he should say something. He quickly blurted, "No!"

"First time for everything," Monte said. "Grab that yoke in front of you. Quick."

CHAPTER 30

PALACE OF HIS HIGHNESS THE ROYAL EMIR
SHEIKH SHEZAD HAMAD TAKASH OF THE
PEOPLE'S REPUBLIC OF ZAZARISTAN
SUNDAY, 8:20 a.m. ZST

Shezad Takash opened his Friendbook feed, looking for the latest
post and pic from his old high school girlfriend, as one does, when
a post at the bottom of the screen caught his eye. The headline
read:

> AMERICAN BILLIONAIRE ON THE RUN:
> BELIEVED TO BE AROUND THE
> NEIGHBORHOOD OF THE PALACE OF
> HIS HIGHNESS THE ROYAL EMIR
> SHEIKH AMIR HAMAD TAKASH OF THE
> PEOPLE'S REPUBLIC OF ZAZARISTAN

Author's Note:
You know Friendbook knows exactly where you are, right?

That kind of targeted geographic specificity in an ad has really
shown to be effective, and this case was no exception. Takash
clicked open the story. He deleted a pop-up ad for the Wowiemop,

202

and a video began. It was shot from some distance, but clearly showed Wiles, wearing a white fedora, climbing the stairs to a jet. The video's voice-over read: "American billionaire and software tycoon Jasper Wiles has fallen on hard times and found himself in some legal trouble. Mr. Wiles has reportedly fled the US ahead of authorities and is believed to have traveled to Central Asia. Wiles was unavailable for comment."

Interesting. Takash could think of a lot of people who would want to know about something like this. He was kind of known as the guy who sends a lot of dumb quizzes and viral videos to everyone, but a story about his own corner of Zazaristan? He added a like and the one-raised-eyebrow emoji, then clicked SHARE.

By the afternoon, several hundred "friends" of the Emir in and around Zazaristan had been made aware of the white-hatted American outlaw who may blow into town.

CHAPTER 31

30,000 FEET ABOVE RUSSIA
SUNDAY, 3:10 a.m. PST

Chris didn't believe in magic, but when he and Monte streaked through a mammoth emerald and gold eruption of Northern Lights in the predawn darkness, he could understand how the concept took hold in people. "Zat look like a monster to you?" Monte had said.

Chris had handled the controls of the jet for about half an hour before thanking Sweet Lou for his company and returning to the cabin to get some more sleep. He grabbed the blanket and pulled it over himself as he settled onto the sofa, which he determined to be the olfactory epicenter of the airplane's distinct aroma. He closed his eyes and prepared to dream of exotic dancers named Aurora and Borealis.

Before they had a chance to hit the stage, however, he heard a soft click, and dim light spilled into the cabin. Chris opened his eyes a crack to see a silhouetted form moving toward him.

CHAPTER 32

30,000 FEET ABOVE RUSSIA
SUNDAY, 3:10 a.m. PST

Author's Note:
Third time! I can really see why Dan Brown does it.

Chris pushed himself up on his elbows. Biz stopped short and put her hand to her mouth. "I'm so sorry! I didn't want to wake you, Chris," she whispered. "I wanted some water."

"I wasn't sleeping, I just laid down," he whispered back, glancing over at the motionless Wiles in his reclined seat. "I was up front with Lou for a while. He let me fly the plane. Did you see the Northern Lights?"

Biz bent to see out the window, but they were long gone. "No, I was sleeping with the blinds shut." She got her water bottle from the mini-fridge and sat down on the edge of the couch. She wore loose pajama pants and a T-shirt featuring a cartoon dog brushing its teeth. "I've never seen them. What were they like?"

Chris sat up on the couch, swinging his legs to the floor. He scrunched his brow, trying to think of an aptly descriptive yet poetic simile. "Like... being inside a giant bowl of jiggling lime Jell-O that's on fire." Almost had it.

Biz earnestly did her best to envision this scenario. "That sounds amazing. Although I hate lime Jell-O." She uncapped her water and took a sip as Chris agreed, "Me too, actually."

"Is seeing the Northern Lights a good omen?" Biz asked, slouching back on the couch. She looked over at Chris. "I think we should agree that it is."

"Definitely. Agreed," Chris replied. "And now, I guess that settles it. We can relax. This trip will be nothing but smooth sailing from here on." He smiled at Biz, hoping she would get his joke.

"What could possibly go wrong?" she said, with a puff of laughter.

"Biz, I know you think it's crazy, but I'm starting to think we can do it. And thanks for coming, by the way. I didn't think you would."

"This whole thing is crazy. But crazy loves crazy. Getting out of California and attempting to throw a monkey wrench in the works will maybe give us some options. If we just sat back and waited for things to sort out for the best, I don't think we could trust that would happen."

Chris didn't know what to say. Biz looked over at Jasper and was about to get up when Chris asked, "How did you meet Mr. Wiles?"

Biz let out a small chuckle and shook her head. "Well, I guess I won't be getting back to bed anytime soon."

"No, it's fine," Chris said quickly. "You can tell me some other time."

"No time like the present," Biz said, thinking that there was a slight but appreciable chance that Chris wouldn't survive the next few days. "You want to hear the Ballad of Biz Byner?"

"I do."

Biz took a sip of water, capped the bottle, and set it on the end table. "I grew up in Marin County. I'm an only child. My dad was a real-estate developer and my mom worked as his office manager. I wouldn't say we were rich, but affluent. At least I thought we were.

When I was a senior in high school, the economy was pretty bad, and my dad was caught holding a lot of debt. I didn't know any of this, though. My parents kept it hidden from me. We even sold our house and moved to a small condo, but my parents explained they just wanted to downsize before I went to college and I believed them. I had already been accepted at Pomona with a small scholarship, and I was all set to go. My parents had always said they'd saved tuition money for me, but when the time came, I guess they were pretty desperate, and they had dipped into it to try to get the business back on track. I found out later that my dad tried to get out of debt by borrowing more, but the banks all turned him down."

In the dim light of the cabin, Chris could see a sheen of tears form over Biz's eyes as she took a deep breath and went on. "On New Year's Eve, my parents... my parents... their car went off the road and they were killed. There was alcohol in their blood, and the insurance company investigators found out about all their financial trouble, so they ruled their deaths a suicide. They refused to pay off their policies. There was no way, Chris. No way they would have left me alone. My dad always said, 'There is one true thing in this life, Bizzy. One thing you can be sure of. The love your mom and I have for you.'" Biz sniffled and wiped her eyes.

"Unfortunately, that one true thing didn't amount to proof of anything to anyone but me. Suddenly, I was alone in the world, with no money. In the end, my parents' estate was worth less than zero and their creditors seized what was left of my college fund, which would be illegal in most states. Thanks for the help, State of California," Biz snorted.

"I was eighteen, technically an adult, accepted to college with a little financial aid, but nowhere near enough to finish, so I had to withdraw before I even started. I moved in with my friend Sandi Shirvani, who was a year behind me in school."

Biz looked up at Chris and saw the look of utter horror on his face. She patted his knee and said, "Don't worry, the story gets better from here. The Shirvanis had this dog, a schnauzer named Fritz. Fritz's breath was unbelievably bad. Bad like you wouldn't believe. So, Sandi came up with an idea for a dog toothbrush that she used as a project for her entrepreneurship class. DoggyFresh, she called it." Biz pulled out her shirt now to show the DoggyFresh logo. Chris let out a short chuckle.

"Don't laugh," said Biz. "It worked great, people loved that thing. And since I was an unemployed, homeless orphan loser, Sandi let me partner with her to sell them. We killed it. Sold a ton at farmer's markets, started a website, the whole thing. You know the show *Piranha Dome*? Where people go on with their inventions and try to get investors? Sandi and I applied to go on and they gave us a shot. We show up, two kids with a dog toothbrush. My god, I can hardly believe it now. Anyway, we go into our pitch, which we had rehearsed for a solid week. Sandi finishes and looks at the Piranhas. 'Who wants to get fresh with us?' she says. You know Perry Mott, from DataCom software? He bursts out with this ridiculous cackle and says, 'That's the dumbest thing ever! It sounds like a horrible idea.'"

Biz now grabbed Chris's knee, squeezing hard. "Chris, I was livid. I couldn't help myself. I said, 'You know what sounds horrible? Your laugh. It's like two deaf monkeys fucking.' They bleeped it out on the show." Chris clapped a hand over his mouth, trying to stifle his laughter, afraid to wake Wiles. Biz giggled at the memory herself and went on. "'I'm out!' he yells. What's funny is that I think that actually helped us get a deal with Janine Garabedian because she hated Mott and wanted to embarrass him by making it look like he missed an opportunity.

"You've heard of Janine, right? She has the website Flurf.com. She sells Face Mud, Nepalese Balance String, stuff like that. We go back and forth a little bit and she offers Sandi and me a deal. We grab it. We grab it with both hands. Janine yells out her catchphrase, 'Let's make some karma!'

"So, we start working with her, but it's basically selling snake oil, not DoggyFresh, but most of the other stuff. I really wasn't into it, but I needed the money. A few months go by and our episode of *Piranha Dome* airs. Jasper sees me on TV giving it to Mott, who he hates as well, because he claims Mott cheated him in a junior tennis match they played against each other when they were twelve. He has a long memory. So, Jasper calls to offer me a job, says he's impressed with my 'loyalty, keen judgment of character, quick-wittedness, and exquisite profanity.' I tell him I'm not really interested in a job just now, that I want to go to college and become a lawyer. I'd never thought about being a lawyer before, but all that business with my parents and the insurance made me want to have a way to fight back if I ever had to again.

"I meet Jasper and tell him my whole story. I explained that I only got involved in DoggyFresh to try to make some tuition money. Jasper offers to pay my tuition to Pomona and law school if I promise to give him first refusal to hire me when I graduate. Long story short, I sold out my share of DoggyFresh to Sandi for $40,000—please don't ask me what it's worth now—and with that money, plus Jasper's, I was off to college at last and then Berkeley law—"

"Where you became close friends with Liberia Boyd," Chris interjected.

Biz chuckled. "Right, my mentor and dear, personal friend. After Berkeley, I passed the bar, and I came to work as Jasper's personal attorney. That's why you and I never met, incidentally. I'm technically not a Sixdub employee. I work out of my own office downtown. So. That's my story. Aside from your interest in jihad, what about you?"

"It's not as interesting as that," Chris said, then quickly tried to backtrack when he heard his words out loud. "I'm sorry, I don't mean that your parents passing is interesting. I'm sorry you had to go through that. My mom died, too. When I was in college. I know what it's like."

"What happened?" Biz asked softly.

"Cancer," Chris said simply. And because he could think of nothing better to add he said, "She used to call me 'Mouse.' When I was little, she said I was as quiet as a Christmas mouse."

Biz felt her throat tighten. "What about your dad?" she managed.

"He was long gone by then. He lives in Texas, or at least he did the last time I talked to him."

There were a few seconds of silence between them. The ringing roar of the jet engines seemed to swell to fill the conversational vacuum.

"Well, back to bed," said Biz finally, picking up her water bottle and getting to her feet. "We'll continue this conversation on the flight home. Maybe you'll have something interesting to tell by then."

Chris thought she shot him a wink before heading back to the rear cabin, but it was hard to say for sure in the dim light.

CHAPTER 33

TABOOR CITY, ZAZARISTAN
SUNDAY, 6:00 p.m. ZST

Wiles's eyes snapped open as the plane began its descent into the ancient city of Taboor. It turns out that three Ambiens were the right amount after all. He checked in with Monte to confirm that they would be received as scheduled at a small airfield on the eastern outskirts of the city. Monte confirmed that the arrangements had been made to land and refuel and that there was a vehicle and driver waiting for them, courtesy of Poskovich's computerized advance planning.

The fixer Brohug Vidadik's Yelp reviews mention that he "speaks decent English" and keeps his vehicle's interior "immaculate."

Returning to the cabin, Wiles walked past Chris's sleeping form and shook his shoulder to wake him. He then knocked on the door where Biz spent the night and continued to the spacious bathroom next door. He freshened up, shaved, and changed into a blue shirt that matched the band of his fedora, a cream-colored blazer, navy cotton pants, and brown loafers with no socks. Wiles very rarely wore socks and actually only owned two pairs—a $600 pair and a nice pair that he saved for special occasions.

Satisfied with his look, he left the bathroom and found Chris and Biz back in the seats they occupied the night before looking rested but anxious as they looked out the window at the featureless, monochromatic Zazari landscape drawing nearer and nearer.

"Good morning," Wiles said. "I trust everyone slept well. I don't know why people complain about sleeping on airplanes. I find it very restful. There are sandwiches in the fridge and coffee in the pot. Let's eat and prepare our strategy."

As the three drank their coffee (Wiles took his "as black as the hearts of my antagonists") and ate, the plan was revisited and revised thusly: Wiles, Chris, and Biz would join Brohug for a ride into the city, hinting that they were businesspeople on the blurry line between legitimate and extralegal. With luck, Brohug would connect them with locals who will hopefully lead them to MILF or vice versa. At some point, Brohug may be dispatched to actively spread the news of the three Americans' arrival. Once in contact with MILF, Chris will attempt to gain access to their computer server to replace its backup data with data that predated the Thursday he first saw the MILF video, then everyone will exfiltrate the country as quickly as possible.

Sweet Lou would stay with the plane. "Someone has to," Wiles pointed out. "We shouldn't leave it unattended. If you thought Chris's neighborhood was bad... "

Lou would oversee the refueling, take a nap, and stand ready to leave ASAP. Wiles also let it be known that Commander Monte kept a pair of handguns locked in the cockpit. There was a brief debate over whether Chris, Wiles, or Biz should venture out armed, but since none of them were at all familiar with guns, they decided carrying a weapon could create more problems than it would solve.

Wiles was digging through his attaché. "Chris, the phone Igor gave you yesterday contains a mirrored copy of your hard drive from work. He says you have too much personal software on there, by the way. He used your idea and wrote some executable files that will access and reset the external MILF hard drive if you can plug into it." Wiles produced a short cat o'four tails computer cable from his attaché and handed it to Chris.

"Biz, your new phone is VPN routed through your personal cell back in San Francisco, but Chris and I can see your GPS position here in Zazaristan through Where'sWiles."

Several months earlier, after Wiles was found gently slumbering in the topiary outside the Claremont one morning, Biz insisted that he allow her to access his GPS location at all times. Wiles had Poskovich create the proprietary Where'sWiles app and install it only on Biz's phone.

"Also, take some walking-around money." Wiles dug again into his attaché case and passed out folded squares of cash to Chris and Biz that looked to be a couple thousand dollars each.

Wiles went on as they tucked the cash away. "Igor also added the numbers for any people you might need over the next few days. We will all be able to track each other's phones by GPS in the event we split up. The location of the airport is pinned in your phones. That's our rally point, just in case we lose touch."

Biz said, "We need to keep in regular contact. If we do split up, we check in hourly."

Chris looked to Wiles as he said, "Agreed. Although I can imagine there may be times when that may be impossible for unforeseen reasons."

"At least a text, then."

"Biz, we will keep each other informed as best as we possibly can," Wiles said. "We shouldn't be here too long anyway. When did you say Chris had to be back?"

"By Tuesday afternoon, Pacific time, it's safe to say Chris will be a wanted fugitive. No matter what we do or find here, he must be back in San Francisco by then if he has any chance to go free. Again, I'm not sure he'll get a fair trial for what he's been charged with, but at least there won't be an additional fugitive from justice charge." Biz looked at her watch. "It's now six p.m. Sunday, local time. In San Francisco, it's twelve hours earlier, still Sunday morning. That means we have about... thirty-six hours before we have to get back on this plane to go home."

Thirty-six hours didn't sound like much to Chris all of a sudden.

"Six a.m. Tuesday," he said, doing the math and hoping it would sound like a longer time when he said it aloud. It didn't.

"Right," Wiles agreed. "You need to be back by then, no matter what."

"We all do," said Chris.

"You and Biz at least. I have every intention of being on this plane with you, but I have no business with the courts in California. If I need to stay behind to wrap up some details, I will."

Biz started to say something, but Wiles cut her off. "Have faith, Elizabeth."

Her face hardened almost imperceptibly. She hated when he called her that.

Chris saw it. He looked to Wiles. "That's it? Have faith? If you're in danger, or we can't find you, there's no plan B?"

Wiles said, "Plan B is: get yourself home to avoid becoming a wanted fugitive, regardless of whether we find the server or not. There is no Plan C."

That last part got Chris thinking. *There was no Plan C?*

He suddenly didn't want to do this. Obviously, none of them *wanted* to do this, but the facts being what they were, this course of action was demanded of them. But still, he didn't want to.

If we turned around and went back right now, Biz could get me out of it, I think. Maybe. Anyway, even if not, twenty years in prison...

Chris was a young man. He would be out of prison in his late forties. Old, at least to his mind, but not that old. If he got caught in a bad situation in Zazaristan, getting old wouldn't be something he would have to worry about. The question became:

Should I trade a good chance that my youth will be taken against a small chance that my life will be taken? By violent terrorists? Painfully, probably?

He looked at Wiles, who was staring out the window. He had an odd grin on his face as he drummed his fingers together.

What is that? Is he nervous? He looks happy! I think this man is happy right now. I'm beginning to think he may not be all there.

Chris shook his head slightly and looked at Biz. She also was staring out the window, but the look on her face was one that Chris could not describe. However, it was a look he swore to remember for the rest of his life. Which could mean just a few days, of course.

Chris closed his eyes. He didn't want to be caught staring, but he couldn't turn away either.

I don't care about wanna, Mouse. In this house, we gotta.

The planes wheels *th-thumped* on the runway.

CHAPTER 34

AMIR "THE EAR" ZAZESHI MEMORIAL REGIONAL AIRPORT
SUNDAY, 6:20 p.m. ZST

Author's Note:
Yes, of course "the ear" rhymes with "Amir" in the Zazarish
language. I pride myself on the realism of my plots. All of this has
been meticulously researched, I'll have you know.

The jet taxied to a stop outside one of four small hangers on a
cracked tarmac. A wooden structure with a corrugated steel–roofed
platform thirty feet off the ground served as the control tower. The
air-traffic controller sat up there on a folding chair with a laptop,
"borrowing" the radar signal from the control tower twenty-eight
miles away at His Highness the Royal Emir Sheikh Amir Hamad
Takash of the People's Republic of Zazaristan International Airport
(ZKN). (ZAZ is taken by Zaragoza, in the Canary Islands. The
Canary Islands, the southern-most autonomous region of Spain, are
an archipelago located approximately sixty miles off the coast of
Morocco.)

Author's Note:
METICULOUSLY!

Sweet Lou cut the engines and popped the hatch, unfurling the folding stairs with that overly elaborate mechanism that Gulfstream salesmen refer to as "the panty dropper."

Wiles snicked the handcuff that was dangling from the handle of his attaché onto his left wrist as he and Chris stepped from the plane, followed by Biz. They were blasted with heat. As the Americans squinted into the setting sun, two uniformed Zazaris stepped from the hangar and approached, stopping at the foot of the airplane's stairs. They crisscrossed their scarred Kalashnikovs in front of them, the international sign for *Get the fuck out of here or I will fucking shoot you, you fuck.*

Nevertheless, Wiles descended to meet them, the amiable smile on his face unwavering. Chris followed him, fully wavering. The Zazari on the left leaned close to Wiles as they met at the bottom of the stairs.

"You stink of Western whores," he said in greeting.

Chris glanced at Wiles with the corner of his eye and noticed that his smile was not quite as cheery as the one he wore a moment ago.

The guard shifted his weapon slightly.

"High five," the guard said with a grin, holding up his hand. "Welcome to Zazaristan." With a jerk of the head toward his comrade, he said, "Pay entry fee to Corporal Quziz."

"Thank you, Officer," Wiles said, slipping him some skin with his free hand and dropping the man a sly wink. "My name is Jasper Wiles. I'm excited to see your country." Wiles then stepped forth, setting first loafer on Zazari soil.

"Nice airplane," the officer said as he stepped aside to let Wiles past. "You need security team. Pirates."

"My security team is on the plane," Wiles lied evenly. "Although, pirates, you say?" He turned, putting his hand to his chin. "Can you and your men perhaps offer me pirate insurance?"

The officer grinned. "Yes, of course." He turned to Corporal Quziz and in Zazarish said, *"Add pirate insurance. Watch, now I will sell them rustproofing."*

Quziz had heard that joke before many times and was able to keep a straight face as he punched some numbers into a large LED screen calculator. He spun it around to Wiles, displaying the cost of doing business.

While Wiles dealt with young Corporal Quziz, Chris and Biz stepped off the stairs and really absorbed the ridiculous heat. It felt like a giant sadistic kid was focusing the sun with a magnifying glass upon them, tracking them with that blinding speck of energy.

Wiles turned and read their already sweaty faces. "The sun of another country always feels hotter," he said. He looked up across the shimmering tarmac. "Ah, that must be Brohug." He strode away toward a large man standing next to a white Volkswagen Vanagon, probably from the early nineties, one of the last models to have the old-school flat-fronted body style.

The man walked out to greet them, hand extended, and said, "Welcome, Mr. Wiles, Mr. X, Ms. Bizbyner," using the only names that Poskovich had provided him with. He shook a warm and firm greeting with Wiles and turned to Chris. "Brohug," he said.

Chris said, "OK," and went in to bro-hug him. Brohug reeled in his handshake and hugged it out with Mr. X while repeating silently to himself, *Customer is always right, customer is always right.* That's how you get five stars.

"Call me Chris," Chris said, now that they were more intimately acquainted.

"Welcome, Chris."

Brohug then gave a polite but nonphysical greeting to Biz, then gathered his customers' bags and led them to his vehicle. Wiles said, "This is a nice Vanagon, Brohug. Ninety-one?"

"Ninety," Brohug replied. "Syncro four-by-four package."

Chugging west to Taboor City proper a few minutes later (it really was immaculate in there), with Wiles riding shotgun, the friendly Brohug was making conversation with his clients. "Americans, yes?"

"Correct, sir. California, to be specific. San Francisco, greater still," said Wiles. "We're in the computer business."

"I saw US flag on airplane," said Brohug as if confessing. He also saw about a dozen other things that tipped him off, not the least of which was Wiles's white fedora, but kept them to himself. "A lot of Americans don't show flag. Most change to Canada. If we see Canada, we think American anyway."

"Interesting," said Wiles.

Brohug went on, "When we see flags, Canada means America. Australia means Canada. Austria means Australia. Germany means Austria." Then he went quiet and just looked at the road.

Wiles bit. "What means Germany?"

Brohug could never get the punch line off without cracking up. "Good cars and weird sex!" he laughed. The flag/Germany one was probably his favorite. So true. He patted the dash of his VW as if to assure it that no offense to its homeland was meant.

Wiles, Chris, and Biz also enjoyed a laugh, and not the "I will laugh anytime a person of another culture laughs" kind of laugh (unknown in Germany, coincidentally), but a true appreciation of Brohug's humor, perhaps mixed in with a touch of nervous energy.

"Brohug," Wiles said as his chuckles wound down, "you are clearly a man of worldly knowledge. As am I, I like to flatter myself. And while my friends and I are from America, we prefer not to constrain ourselves with the burdens and regulations of any single nation, but rather, we've come to seek any and all business opportunities available here in Zazaristan, without involving either of our busy governments, who may not have the time or interest to involve themselves in our dealings anyway. I'm sure you understand."

Brohug understood, Wiles's flowery speech notwithstanding. These three were carpetbaggers, scalawags, ne'er-do-wells and were looking to make a score of some form or another. It's not as if they would have come to see the sights and do a little antiquing while they were in town. The sights of Zazaristan were little more than what could be seen out the window at the moment, which is to say a landscape varying in feature from rocky sand to sandy rocks in colors ranging from beige to taupe. And as far as artistic works of value or interest, they had long since been "antiqued" away by a centuries-long procession of invading looters.

"Mr. Wiles, Chris, Ms. Bizbyner," he said, turning to each of them in turn, "I drive all day, all night. There are three kinds of drivers. Those drive too slow, and those drive too fast."

"What's the third kind?" Chris asked after a silent moment went by.

"I am third kind," said Brohug, turning around to face him.

As Brohug took his eyes off the road, Wiles pointed ahead and squinted into the sun. "Watch out for this guy riding a motorcycle with a... yes, a goat in the sidecar," he calmly said.

Brohug whipped around. The man on the motorcycle (who also had a small boy riding behind him on the seat, arms wrapped tightly around the man's lower abdomen) was given a blast of horn and a Zazarish epithet along with three very curious stares as the Vanagon roared past him.

"I am simple man," Brohug continued as the motorcycle faded in the dust. "I only wish to get home for dinner each night. And in Zazaristan, it is hungriest man who comes first to the table. And government?" He made a seesaw motion with his hand and laughed again, prompting another round of foreigner chuckles from his passengers. "I need five-star review." The chuckling ceased.

"And you shall have it, Brohug, I'm sure," said Wiles. "Now then, where do the hungriest of your countrymen, go to eat, shall we say?"

Brohug glanced at his watch. "You go to fights tonight."

"Fights?" Biz asked. "What kind of fights?"

Brohug paused, struggling to come up with the English word he needed. "Fights," he repeated, and took his hands off the wheel to make a vague gesture, then settled on two fists, one throwing short punches toward the other while he illustrated further with verbal sound effects. "Bah! Bah!" he puffed.

"Like MMA fights?" Chris asked.

"I don't know this word, but like that, I think, yes," Brohug said.

"Will you join us, Brohug?" asked Wiles. "We'd love to have your company."

Checking his watch again, Brohug shook his head regretfully. "My son, he has football game. U-14 Diamond Select division. Is very... " he raised his hand to the roof of the vehicle.

"Prestigious?" offered Wiles.

"I don't know this word, but like that, I think, yes," Brohug said again. "I must go to game. I give you direction to fights." Looking at Biz in the rearview mirror, he said, "No woman at fights. Men only. Sorry."

There always was the possibility that the three of them would split up, but to have it come to that so soon made it feel like the plan was showing some cracks already.

"And why?" said Biz.

Brohug shrugged. "That's what sign says. I no ask why."

"Where will she go?" Chris asked.

"She stay at hotel. Very safe," Brohug assured him, hearing the anxiety in Chris's voice.

Wiles turned around. "Biz?"

"I'll be fine," she said tersely.

"Good. We will all scout the neighborhood around the hotel together before Chris and I go," Wiles said.

Just then, they crested a rise and the Taboor City skyline came into view on the horizon, a jagged cluster of civilization backlit by a blazing orange sunset. Chris squinted, realizing that his destiny, perhaps his very life was literally laid out in front of him, but then was distracted when Brohug sped up to pass another motorcycle, but this one with the boy in the sidecar and the goat strapped to the man with a length of dingy bungee cord. You just don't see that every day in San Anselmo.

CHAPTER 35

NEW YORK, NEW YORK
SUNDAY, 10:06 a.m. EST

In the TV news game, the power rankings of on-air talent go like this, from the bottom: "Coats" (standing up outdoors), "Cooks" (standing up indoors), "Couches" (seated on a sofa), and ultimately, "Coifs" (seated at a desk).

Dina Feely was a Couch at BSNMC but had high hopes of becoming a Coif when she signed her next contract.

"Professor, before we go to break, please give us your opinion about the so-called 'San Francisco Mystery Bomber' and why their identity has been withheld from the public thus far," she said from the set of *A.M. this Morning*, which she cohosted with Ted Tanner, a former Coif who was on his way down the backside of his career.

Professor Bernard Fischbach of NYU's School of Public Policy was told this subject may come up. He said, "Well, Dina, I hesitate to engage in speculation—"

"I'm sure our viewers would appreciate any insight you could offer, Professor," Dina encouraged.

"Very well," Fischbach continued. "I suspect that the FBI may be withholding information due to the serious nature of this case. This suspect may have information about future attacks or other useful intelligence that may be compromised should their identity be made public."

"The public has become very vocal on social media," Dina said, "demanding the identity of this attacker. Should the administration's lack of transparency be concerning at all?"

She knew full well that a BSNMC Coat had been dispatched to the San Francisco courthouse to get a name from the clerk's office first thing Tuesday morning, and sooner if possible.

"The administration has been reluctant to divulge certain details, certainly," Fischbach said. "But bear in mind, it's very early in the investigation. Things may change."

Dina nodded thoughtfully. "Thank you, Professor. Professor Bernard Fischbach. His book, *The Thesis Cartel: A Professor Brad Fishbaum Thriller*, is in bookstores now. Thank you, Professor."

The control room cut to a two-shot of Dina and Tanner on the couch. Tanner looked into Camera One and said, "Coming up after the break, Brianna will be here with Chef Chad Adler sharing some recipes to add pumpkin spice to some things you've probably never thought of." He shook his head gravely, an old Coif habit he had a hard time breaking. Dina stared serenely into the camera.

A producer yelled into Dina's earpiece. "Say it, Feely... *say it!*"

"Sounds like we're really going to spice things up around here," Dina read from the teleprompter, counting the microseconds until they cut to commercial.

* * *

Meanwhile, eight blocks away...

"Welcome back to *HawkNews Sunday Morning*," Devin Flynn said from his sofa, setting his red HawkNews mug down on the coffee table.

"Turn your damn cup so the logo faces the camera, Flynn!" a producer screamed in his ear.

They cut to a wide shot showing Flynn and his guest, a man with longish gray hair, who wore a black shirt, a bolo tie, and snakeskin cowboy boots.

Flynn said, "We're joined now by country music legend and political activist Crick Meeks. Welcome to the show, Crick."

"Mornin'," Meeks nodded. "Sgood to be here."

Flynn put on his question-asking face. "Like many Americans, you've been very vocal on Twitter in the past couple days calling for the identity of the terrorist who was apprehended in San Francisco to be made public. Why is that important?"

"We have a thing in this country called due process, Devin. That means you get yer day in court, *publicly*. I don't like the liberal media covering up this terrorist's identity 'cause it don't fit their agenda. I don't care if yer gay or straight or somewhere in between, anyone who attacks America needs to be tried and punished."

"You're of course referring to the reports that the bomber is transgender," Flynn said.

"Say that was us!" the producer barked.

"Reports first made by HawkNews," Flynn added.

"That's right," said Meeks. "What we got here is a moral breakdown of society. One day, you got a feller goin' into the ladies room, the next, he's plantin' bombs in a shoppin' mall."

"Scary times," Flynn said, trying not to imply that one scenario was necessarily scarier than the other. He just couldn't be sure if the next Coif job would open up at HawkNews or BSNMC, and he had to keep his options open. "Thank you for stopping by, Crick. You can reach Crick Meeks on Twitter at TheRealCrickMeeks. After the break, Tina will be showing us the Halloween costumes that are upsetting liberals the most this year. Stay tuned for that on *HawkNews Sunday Morning*." He leaned forward and rotated his coffee cup.

CHAPTER 36

SAN FRANCISCO, CALIFORNIA
SUNDAY, 7:15 a.m. PST

Sully sat on the edge of his hotel bed and tied his sneakers. "I'm going to the gym, Murph."

Murph looked up from his phone. "You're not the only one getting exercise. Look at Dawkins," he said, showing Sully the PerpTrak screen. "He's nervous. He's been pacing back and forth like that for fifteen minutes."

CHAPTER 37

TABOOR CITY, ZAZARISTAN
SUNDAY, 7:20 p.m. ZST

Wiles, Chris, and Biz were dropped off by Brohug at what he confidently assured them was "the finest hotel in Taboor City," which Biz remarked was like saying "the finest clip-on tie money can buy."

The faded sign on the front of the building read: "The Fort Worth Plaza Hotel and Casino." Fort Worth Plaza was once a proud chain of hotels based in the Southwest United States, but a combination of overly aggressive expansion, the severe global recession of the late seventies/early eighties, cocaine, geopolitical instability, and changing consumer tastes led to their decline, bankruptcy, and eventual closure. The costs to remove the signage from some of the more far-flung operations proved to be prohibitive, and thus travelers in certain parts of the world can still enjoy some of the storied atmosphere of the Fort Worth Plaza with none of the amenities whatsoever. Any legal issues over the current proprietor's unlicensed use of the name were settled when zero lawyers volunteered to fly to Zazaristan to file suit without getting paid up front.

After checking in to their simple, tidy rooms, Chris, Biz, and Wiles met in the lobby to explore and familiarize themselves with the immediate surroundings. According to Brohug, "the fights" had started over an hour ago but were located within walking distance and featured extensive undercard (or "not prestigious," as Brohug proudly put it) bouts.

The hot Taboor City evening presented itself. Many a nation's dogs of war had been let slip there at one time or another over the last two thousand years, so there was some visible wear and tear. Every block or so, there was a building in ruins, but the streets and sidewalks were clear, so any damage did not seem too recent. Zazaristan was more or less between wars at the moment. Light traffic of small cars and trucks moved smoothly without the aid of any signs or signals. All manner of motorcycles, mopeds, and scooters flowed around their slower-moving four-wheeled cousins.

Not many women were to be seen on the streets at this hour, and a few Zazaris looked twice at Biz, who had donned a hijab that covered her hair and wrapped around her face. Wiles also drew some looks as his electric skateboard bore him slowly down the sidewalk, but according to him, this attention was what he had described on the plane as an important early element of their plans.

The local men mostly wore long tunics over loose pants, a few wore Western-style clothes, and some combined the two, rocking the loose pants/sport coat look. It was around dinnertime, and the Zazaris gathered around nameless kebab shops and wheeled carts that advertised exclusively by smell. As the trio of Americans wandered around a corner, noting alleys and intersections, they were met with looks of neutral curiosity, neither hostile nor welcoming.

Spotting what he estimated to be one of the more upscale kebaberies, this one a storefront operation with a cluster of tables, chairs, and benches on the sidewalk under a metal awning, Wiles said, "Let's begin here. Is anyone hungry?"

Chris was too nervous to be thinking about food but nevertheless had to admit the smell was appetizing. "Sure," he said. He followed Wiles, who approached the counter tossing friendly waves to the dozen or so patrons who looked up from their dinners to study the visitors. A few of them noted Wiles's white hat and recognized him as the fugitive American they saw on Friendbook. They whispered gossip about him to their companions, but none ventured to approach him with propositions, MILF-related or otherwise. Wiles stepped aside to let Biz shake the rust off her Farsi and attempt to communicate with the proprietor, who was busy working a grill behind the counter.

The man looked up. Biz smiled at him, holding up three fingers.

The man at the counter greeted them in Zazarish, the only language he possessed, but three fingers meant the same in any language. He returned the smile and produced three glistening kebabs, hot off the grill.

"Gluten-free," he announced, handing them over.

In Farsi, Biz said, *"Thank you,"* and Wiles smiled his thanks as he accepted his kebab. He then pulled a ten-dollar bill from his pocket and offered it to the man, who accepted it, saying, *"Thank you. It is considered rude to ask for change in Zazaristan. Have a nice evening. Gluten-free."*

Wiles turned to find a seat. The Americans were being waved toward a table with three free chairs by a sport-coated/loose-pantsed Zazari man who sat with two friends, both bushily bearded, one older than the other. With all eyes on them, Biz, Chris, and Wiles took the open seats.

In Farsi, Biz said, *"Thank you."*

"Thank you," said Wiles as he sat. "I'm Jasper Wiles. Do you speak English?"

"The peace of God be with you," said the older man in Zazarish.

Chris and Wiles looked at Biz, who again said, *"Thank you."*

"I'm Chris," said Chris as he sat down.

The three men murmured God's wishes of well-being upon Chris as well. The man in the sport coat motioned that they should enjoy their kebabs while they were still hot, which the Americans did. The meat was tasty, but a little tough and of indeterminate origin.

"Biz, do you understand these guys?" Chris asked, covering his mouth with his kebab.

"Noooooot really," she said. "It does sound a lot like Farsi, and I think they said 'hello,' but I told you, I don't have too much."

"Are you gentlemen going to the fights tonight?" Wiles asked, after a bite. Seeing the puzzled looks of his new friends, he made fists like Brohug had in the Vanagon. "Bah! Bah!" he said, punching the air.

The three Zazaris exchanged looks. They were not fight fans and in fact were on their way home from evening prayers. The fight crowd and the prayer crowd did not mix often or well in Zazaristan. The older man said, *"You have come to rape our lands and defile our ancient customs. God will have his vengeance upon you."*

Wiles looked to Biz, but she shook her head with a blank look. Wiles looked genially to the man. "Is this lamb?" he said, wiggling his kebab stick. "It's delicious."

Unfortunately, the kebab stick wiggle, when done in a certain way, is considered to be a crass, sexually suggestive insult in the Taboor City region. The younger man turned toward the sport-coated man and said, *"You see? I told you not to invite these infidels to join us. Now you have to murder him to preserve your honor."*

"Sorry, I'm not getting any of this," Biz whispered to Wiles and Chris.

The sport coat man offered a tight smile to Wiles before answering his friend, *"With what, Achmed? My kebab stick? I don't bring my rifle to prayers, and my dagger is in my other sport coat."*

The old man now chimed in, *"You can easily murder a man with a kebab stick. My uncle did it a bunch of times."* He yelled at the man working the counter *"Hey! Tariq! Have you ever seen someone killed with a kebab stick?"*

Attention now turned to Tariq, who the Americans presumed was about to offer some insight into his kebab secret sauce or something. He shouted back, *"Oh, yeah. Only two or three times a year, but it definitely happens."*

The three Zazaris now regarded their kebab sticks, prompting Wiles and Chris to do the same.

Biz raised her kebab stick to Tariq. *"Thank you!"* she called.

"Mmm," said Chris, taking another bite.

The rest of the diners at the kebab stand couldn't help overhearing and were now primed and ready for a good old-fashioned kebab stick streetfight to the death. They weren't sure what the impetus for the sudden hostility was, but then again, who cared?

Just then Wiles's phone chirped in his jacket pocket, indicating a text had arrived. Achmed glared at him and said, *"I swear to Allah, if he answers his phone while we're eating... "* He pulled the last bit of meat off his stick with his teeth and gripped the stick tightly.

Fortunately, Wiles had basic manners and ignored his phone. "Apologies," he said with a slight head bow. That placated the Zazaris somewhat.

Glancing at his watch, Wiles nudged Chris and said, "We should be going, we're late already." He then stood, tapped the face of his watch to indicate shortness of time, and wordlessly bid the three Zazaris a good evening, who wordlessly bid them good riddance, secretly glad that they would now not have to honor-kill anyone with what admittedly is an unreliable weapon. Also, their wives would be pissed if they came home with blood on their prayer clothes. The rest of the dinner crowd watched the Americans wander off in what they took to be humble shame.

A Farsi phrase came to Biz just then that she remembered to be a high and respectful compliment. *"Your ass is as beautiful as the moon,"* she said with great emotion to the oldest of the men.

231

"You hear that?" the old man said to his friends as they returned to their dinner. *"Still got it."* And because he is a dude, he took out his phone and motioned for the attractive young Biz to come back and take a selfie with him. Wiles and Chris crowded in as well, but he could always crop them out later. Biz snapped one or two of her own to show respect for their new friends.

On the sidewalk a moment later, Wiles said, "No information to be had there, but I think that went well. Nice fellows." He took out his phone to check the message. "From Brohug," he said, reading the screen. "It's a link to Yelp for a review. No time like the present."

Wiles stopped to type, "Five... stars. Competence... exceeded... only... by... bonhomie." He tapped POST REVIEW.

Yelp yelped, "Looks like your review is a little short!" The exclamation point? Really, Yelp?

Wiles thought for a moment and added, "The... interior... of... Vidadik's... Vanagon... smells... like... coconut... Delightful! Post review."

That shut Yelp up and the three continued on their way. Around another corner and the Fort Worth Plaza was now in view again. The men escorted Biz back to her room and promised to check in hourly and with any change of location, but Wiles cautioned that timely updates may be impossible for unforeseen reasons, including bad reception or etiquette, citing the message he declined at the kebab table as an example.

Chris and Wiles went downstairs and stepped again into the quickly darkening Taboor City night. The walk to the address Brohug provided should take them less than fifteen minutes.

Chris said, "Mr. Wiles, are we going to have trouble because we don't speak any Zazarish? How are we going to talk to anyone?"

Wiles stopped and turned to face Chris. Without a word, he shook his head and pointed in turn to his temple, eyes, ear, heart, and balls. He punctuated his silent display by eating his last bite of kebab, tossing the stick over his shoulder, pointing forward and continuing down the street. Chris also finished off his kebab but couldn't bring himself to litter, although the nearest person who would possibly care about such a thing was just over 350 miles away. He slipped his stick into his pocket and trotted to catch up with his boss.

* * *

Back in her room, Biz refreshed the "Where'sWiles" GPS location app on her phone and saw that the blue dot representing Wiles's location was slowly making its way down a narrow Taboor City street.

Biz set an alarm to go off in one hour. She was not entirely pleased that Jasper couldn't promise to stay in regular contact, but she understood that communication with her may have to be a secondary priority if Wiles and Chris were engaged in negotiations, or any number of things. She let out a deep calming breath.

Sixth Grade: *Control what you can, accept what you must.*

Biz searched her bag and found a notepad and pen she took from the plane. Drednott kept them handy, as he was often struck with inspiration for lyrics on long flights. She sat down and out of nervous energy wrote a list:

#1. Contact J & C every hour.

#2. If no contact, track phone.

#3. If tracking lost

She paused here, stumped. *If tracking lost, what, Biz?* As long as Wiles's phone had power, and his top-of-the-line Model XXI phone promised thirty-six-hour battery life, she could locate them. If they lost signal or the phones were somehow disabled, they were on their own.

She tapped her chin with the pen and continued writing,

#3. If tracking lost call Brohug and have him take me to J & C's last known location.

She jotted Brohug's number down where it would be handy and entered it into her phone.

#4. If J & C in trouble, get Lou.

Sweet Lou Monte, who was presently napping back in the plane, was a former military man, and Biz knew he kept two guns locked in the cockpit. Leaving the plane unguarded might not be wise, but there may be no choice. Which brought her to:

#5. If J & C in BIG trouble, call US Embassy, Quudia.

She searched for and jotted down the embassy phone number, 92-312-455-5805. This was obviously a last resort. If Wiles and Chris were somehow captured, detained, or in mortal danger, Biz couldn't just leave them behind in Zazaristan while she ran home. She would call in the cavalry and report some Americans missing in Zazaristan as soon as she was sure it was absolutely necessary.

This action would most likely end with everyone in prison, but it was conceivable that the situation in Zazaristan could become so dire that life in American prison would be preferable.

It now seemed as if the blue dot on the phone had moved off the main street and into a narrow alleyway that ran through a large city block.

* * *

The silence in the alley was broken by a moped in the street, buzzing like a giant two-wheeled mosquito. The hot, windless evening had become a hot, windless night. A thread of smoke rose up out of the half-full metal pail of cigarette butts that lay beside Walid Ruqayya's folding chair. Every few seconds he would work off a small piece of peel from the orange that would serve as his dinner and flick it at the dying butt that was the source of the smoke. No direct hits yet, but he was enjoying how even a near miss would shift the butt's position, causing a sine wave effect to the rising smoke that reminded him of that workout move where guys grab a rope in each hand and whip them up and down. Walid didn't think the rope jiggling exercise looked particularly hard and thought he would like to give it a try someday.

"Aren't you done peeling that orange yet?" bitched his partner, Zebar Talmahani. Zebar sat six feet away, and along with Walid they flanked an unmarked door near the vertex of the L-shaped alleyway.

"This isn't one of your precious mandarins, Zeb!" Walid snapped, removing a nickel-sized piece of peel. *"It's more like a pomelo or something."* He flicked the piece down toward his butt pail with extra effort, praying to Allah that the peel would strike the butt's faintly glowing ember and punctuate his words to Zeb with a fountain of sparks. That would be cool. Allah did not in fact will it,

and the peel missed the pail entirely, short-hopping off the wall behind it.

Sometimes Walid regretted going into the security business.

"Someone's coming," said Zeb.

Walid quickly put the half-peeled orange in a paper bag under his chair and stood up. Sure enough, the streetlight at the alley's western end cast the shadows of two figures onto the alley's wall and coincidentally, two Western men came into view, as if they had traveled straight there from their homeland.

One was riding a skateboard and had a case chained to his wrist. He said, "Gentlemen. Good evening," as he waved a half salute.

Walid had a little English that he'd picked up from movies. "Lost?" he asked. "You go back that way." He flicked his finger toward the street.

"We're not lost, my friend. We've come to see the... " Wiles pointed at the door but didn't finish his sentence, providing the subject as a matter of necessity, but demurely avoiding it's object out of tact.

"No entry after fights have begun," said Walid.

"Of course, of course," Wiles said. Gesturing to Chris, he continued. "However. This... is the... doctor. He was summoned here to tend to one of the fighters and in accordance with the Hippocratic oath, he must be allowed to enter without delay."

Walid and Zeb swiveled their heads back and forth between Wiles and Chris. "Doctor? You have no equipment," said Walid, looking Chris up and down.

It was true. Chris was empty-handed.

Wiles paused for a moment and turned to study Chris, as if he too was wondering what had become of Chris's medical bag, white lab coat, and round-mirrored headband.

"He's a psychiatrist," Wiles explained.

Walid and Zeb looked at Chris skeptically, still waiting for his first word.

Chris pointed at the smoking pail on the ground. "You should quit smoking. It's very unhealthy."

Zeb spoke in Zazarish.

Walid translated, "What happened to your face?"

Chris touched his cheek. It was still red and swollen, but the injury's origin remained a mystery to him and he didn't say anything. Wiles nudged his foot with the edge of a loafer.

"I was kicked. A foot kicked me," Chris said.

Walid and Zeb exchanged looks. Neither one of them was really convinced that this young man was a doctor of any kind, and even if he were, it would have been quite unprecedented for a psychiatrist to treat a fighter. What on earth would they talk about? But if such treatment did in fact happen, a kick to the face every now and then would be unavoidable, one would suppose. The two doormen shifted their attention back to Wiles, who they had correctly deduced would be the one to produce the customary gratuity required to gain late entry.

As Chris was explaining the dangers of smoking to men who would probably not live to see thirty, Wiles already had his hand in his tip pocket and was withdrawing a folded wad of American cash, carefully covering the denomination with his fingers like a magician palming a card.

"Gentlemen, we are all professionals here," he said. "You realize of course that patient confidentiality prevents us from giving you any details about the good doctor's work in there, just as we realize that a certain amount of confidentiality is required between the four of us. What, is the... shall we say, service fee you ask for that confidentiality?"

Walid and Zeb locked eyes for the briefest of moments to silently say *finally!* to each other. Walid turned back to Wiles and said, "Twenty. US."

In a moment almost too brief to describe, Wiles and Walid took measure of each other's microexpressions, a skill they had both developed through gradual and hard-won experience. Walid looked for the sign of resignation in Wiles's eyes that would show his agreement to the asking price, or more likely the slight hardening that would precede a counteroffer. Wiles, meanwhile, fixed his gaze between Walid's rather impressive eyebrows, pressed his lips together ever so slightly, and waited. He figured three seconds would be enough.

Walid said, "Each."

Wiles considered this with four cocks of his head and a slight squeeze of his bankroll as if it was an avocado he was checking for ripeness. "Fair." He peeled off two Andrew Jacksons and handed them over. The former president, all bundled up in his cape, looked quite overdressed for the stifling Zazaristanian heat.

"My name is Jasper Wiles. This is Dr. Chris Dawkins. And you are?"

Walid was wearing a white, short-sleeved button-up shirt. He tucked his twenty into his shirt pocket and patted it as he inclined his head. "I am Walid Ruqayya. This is Zebar Talmahani. Welcome, Mr. Wiles, Dr. Dawkins. Enjoy the matches."

"Thank you Walid." Wiles popped his board up. "Would you please watch my skateboard?"

"Of course," said Walid, smiling and accepting the skateboard with his left hand and a crinkly handshake with his right with practiced ease.

He then stepped aside and opened the door, motioning Wiles and Chris to enter.

A small room, dark and silent, was revealed. About eight feet away at the far end, a curtain of beads hung down, obscuring what lay beyond save for a small amount of blue moonlight coming through the windows at the front of the building. Stepping up onto the small room's linoleum floor, Chris and Wiles could now see they had entered a supply closet. It smelled faintly of ammonia. Metal racks stacked with boxes and paper goods were on the right and left. A mop and bucket were parked in the corner near the door. Puzzled, they both looked back at Walid and Zeb.

Without a word, Walid pointed down and to the left, then shut the door.

Their eyes took a moment to adjust to the almost total darkness; then Chris inched forward a step and saw a narrow door in the left corner, which from the doorway had been obscured by the supply rack. "Mr. Wiles, there's a door," he whispered. Wiles, meanwhile, was poking his head through the beaded curtain to see what was beyond. It appeared to be a two-chair barbershop with no interior doors or stairs in sight.

The curtain of beads made a slithery clicking as Wiles pulled his head back. "Is it open?" he asked.

Gently twisting the knob, Chris cracked the door open a few inches and looked back. Purplish light spilled out and illuminated Wiles's face as he stepped closer. A low, muffled rumble could be heard. Chris opened the door all the way to reveal a narrow staircase lit by a single black-light bulb. At the bottom of the stairs was a closed door with a sign above it written in curly Zazarish script.

Chris stepped aside and allowed Wiles to lead the way down the stairs. Wiles paused at the bottom, put his ear to the door for a moment, then straightened up and snapped a picture of the sign with his phone and sent the photo through his English/Zazarish translation app, tilting the screen so Chris could read the results as well.

Welcome to the Taboor City Goatfighting Arena
Goatfighting is a sport of gentlemen

Mark A. Henry

Author's Note:
Of course. Please be my guest. Take all the time you need. I'll meet
you a few inches down the page when you're done.

Yeah, I'm not surprised you couldn't find any photos or videos of
goatfighting arenas on Wangle. Don't let that fool you into thinking
they don't exist, though. Organized goatfighting is just a very
tightly controlled industry, that's all. Did you check the dark web?
No? That's what I thought. You can check out some sick
goatfighting videos later on your own time. Let's just keep moving
for now.

"Mr. Wiles, have you ever been to a goat fight?" asked Chris.
"No. Have you?"
"No. Have you ever *heard* of goatfighting?"
"I've heard it's a sport of gentlemen. So let's go."
With that, Wiles opened the door and entered the Taboor City
Goatfighting Arena.

CHAPTER 38

Goatfighting *Arena* may have been a slight architectural hyperbole. The room that lay before Chris and Wiles was a cement-floored, low-ceilinged basement lit by bare fluorescent bulbs. The air was refreshingly cool, but man, did it smell like goat. The muffled rumbles they heard from the stairs turned out to be the animated conversations of close to a hundred men. Taking a few steps in and exchanging glances with some curious patrons who looked up to see the new arrivals, Chris was surprised to see that the arena was actually quite spacious, taking up the subterranean space of the barbershop above and maybe two or three of its neighbors as well.

Directly ahead of them stood a small bar, and to the right, at the rear of the room, obscured by a crowded ring of people was what had to be the area of goat combat. Wiles said, "Let's get a drink," and headed for the bar, but before they could take more than a step or two in that direction, a loud voice rang out from their left, it's Zazarish words incomprehensible but it's tone unmistakably conveying, "Hey! Stop right there!"

Chris and Wiles turned to see a boy of about ten years coming around from behind a table that was tucked in the corner near the entrance. The boy waved his hands at the Americans and pointed back to his post by the door, where Chris and Wiles could now see

Mark A. Henry

a hand-drawn sign of a cell phone with a red circle and slash posted on the wall. It became clear that the young Zazari was tasked with collecting the cell phones of all who entered. Presumably it was considered ungentlemanly to take calls, record bootleg goatfighting videos, check email, or what have you within the arena.

The boy made a short speech, then waved his hand and held it out as if to say, *Come on, give it up.*

"He wants your phone, Mr. Wiles," Chris said. Wiles bid his apologies for the misunderstanding to the boy and handed over the phone, receiving a plastic disc with "25" on it in return, which would apparently serve as his claim ticket at the end of the evening. The youth then turned to Chris, said a few words, and made the *Let's have it* motion with his fingers. Chris took out his phone, texted a quick thumbs-up to Biz, then handed it over and received ticket #10 in return.

The boy let out a bright and courteous bit of Zazarish, then beamed widely, spread his arms, and unmistakably gestured, *Welcome, new friends. Please enjoy your evening and all that our humble goatfighting arena has to offer.*

"Let's get that drink," Wiles repeated, steering Chris toward the bar. "Keep your ears open for "MILF," "Wahiri Shwarma," "Mohammad Mohammad," or anything that might get us close to that server." Chris agreed.

The bartender turned around and eyed the two Westerners suspiciously as they arrived at the bar. He grunted a greeting in Zazarish.

"Good evening," Wiles responded. He pointed at a bottle of vodka, held his fingers two inches apart, and laid a ten on the bar. The bartender, fluent in booze and greenbacks, if not English, set Wiles up and then turned to Chris, with the bottle poised to pour him the same.

Chris waved him off. "No, no. Tea? Do you have tea?"

The bartender looked puzzled. He put down the vodka and held up a bottle of whiskey, his face asking, "This?"

242

"No. Tea," Chris repeated, miming the action of drinking from a teacup, pinky extended. The bartender took that for the universal "drinky drinky" sign, then rolled his eyes back and lolled out his tongue to assure Chris that yes, if you drink this whiskey, you will get drunk.

"He speaks no English," said a bearded man sitting two seats away on Chris's left. The man said something sharply to the bartender, who put the whiskey bottle away. "You want tea, yes?" the man asked, looking to Chris.

"Yes. Thank you," Chris replied. The bearded man spoke once again to the bartender, who asked a short question in reply.

The man translated, "You want... uh... medicine in tea?"

Chris nodded to the bartender. "Yes. Yes, please." He was still not feeling 100%. A little vitamin shot would really do him some good. The bartender gave a knowing look, turned, and got to work fixing Chris's drink. The bearded man looked at Chris, then Wiles, who was standing on his toes, craning his neck in an effort to see what was going on across the room. Whatever action there was, it was currently obscured by a circle of men standing shoulder-to-shoulder and three or four deep.

"Americans?" the man asked.

As the bartender busily stirred an extra-large lump of opium-and-khat infused hashish into Chris's tea, Chris replied, "How do you know that?"

The man took a final sip of his drink and set it down. The single, round-cornered ice cube skated half a lap around the bottom of the glass. "When you first came in, I thought it was either that or Canadian. But if you were Canadian, I would have seen your red leaf by now. Always the red leaf with those people. You sound like Americans. You dress like Americans. You pay with American money. You ask how I *know* you're Americans."

The bartender set down a narrow glass of steaming, honey-colored tea before Chris, then unbidden, topped off Wiles's unattended drink, which had lost about one finger's worth of depth in the short time since its initial delivery. The sound of flowing liquor caused Wiles to turn his attention from the knot of fight spectators back to the bar where he now noticed the man Chris had been speaking to. He extended his hand. "Jasper Wiles."

The bearded man stood up. "Mohammad Mohammad."

CHAPTER 39

TABOOR CITY, ZAZARISTAN
SUNDAY, 8:07 p.m. ZST

Back at the hotel, Biz sat at the small desk in her room with her phone propped in front of her where she could keep a constant eye on the blue dots, which had come to a stop at the address that Brohug had given. So far, so good. Wiles and Chris had apparently arrived safely. Chris had even texted a thumbs-up a minute ago.

Still feeling restless, she opened her laptop and Wangled "Zazaristan Taboor City Fights" in order to learn as much as she could about whatever her friends were now experiencing. Wangle offered pages and pages of hits about various military skirmishes and reports of violence claimed by MILF, but nothing about boxing or wrestling. She then typed, "Taboor City Fights Misogynist" and was about to tap ENTER when her eyes flicked up to her phone screen. The blue dots were gone! Refresh! Refresh! Refresh! Still no dots.

She quickly called each phone, but they both went straight to voicemail and her texts of:

Update? Where are u?

went unread. Refresh! No dots.

She quickly called Brohug.

"Yes?" he answered. Biz could hear youth soccer in the background. For a moment she thought it was odd that a game would be played after dark, presumably under lights, considering the haphazard local infrastructure, but she knew that youth soccer people took it seriously.

"Brohug, it's Biz Byner," she said. "Jasper and Chris's phones are off! I need you to help me find them."

"No phones allowed at fights," said Brohug. "They had to turn off."

Biz considered this in relief. Brohug's explanation made sense. Chris had sent the thumbs-up just a few minutes ago, but still, would it be so difficult to actually type out, "Hey, Biz, we have to turn our phones off for a while, I'll update you when I can"?

"When do these fights usually end?" Biz asked.

Brohug said, "Midnight. Everyone must be home."

Biz asked, "There's a curfew?"

"I do not know this word, but like that, I think, yes."

"Brohug, I want you to pick me up from the hotel and we're driving over to the fights. I know I can't go in, but I have to make sure Jasper and Chris are OK. You can go in to check on them, and I want to be there to meet them as they come out."

Brohug thought these Americans worried too much, but the customer is always right. "I will call you after my son's game and come to hotel. Two hours."

CHAPTER 40

TABOOR CITY, ZAZARISTAN
SUNDAY, 8:08 p.m. ZST

Chris opened his mouth, tilted his head slightly forward, then opened his mouth a little wider. *Mohammad Mohammad! This is the guy! The guy Mr. Poskovich said works for MILF!*

As Chris's mind spun, Wiles stepped forward and calmly shook hands. "A pleasure to meet you, Mr. Mohammad. This is my associate Chris Dawkins."

"Mer... " said Chris, offering his hand shakily. *Get it together!* "Tlah," he added. Concluding the briefest shake with the puzzled Mohammad he thought he could manage, Chris quickly reached for his tea, offered a quick toast, and took a big sip. "Mmm," he said. *Hey, good job! That was almost a word!*

"How is your tea, Mr. Dawkins?" Mohammad asked.

"Good," Chris said. "Tea is good. It burned my tongue a little." The tea was quite good, although a little bitter, and Chris couldn't detect much in the way of vitamin boosters, lemon-flavored C4! or otherwise, but he resigned himself to steadily drink it in lieu of holding up his end of a conversation with a dangerous international terrorist.

"So. What brings you two to Zazaristan?" the dangerous international terrorist inquired, sliding his empty glass toward the bartender, confident in the knowledge that the next round would be on his new acquaintances.

Wiles signaled to the bartender to refill Mohammad's glass and took a moment to take stock of the man. Mohammad's face gave his age as anywhere from twenty-five to fifty, but his hands suggested the younger end, maybe thirty-ish. He wore a small, light brown kufi, a loose, knee-length green shirt, a knock-off silver Rolex (the second hand ticked rather than swept), and black leather sandals that had seen many a dusty mile.

"Opportunity," Wiles answered, adjusting his fedora. "Chris and I are in the computer business. Software, networks, but mainly cybersecurity. Information, Mr. Mohammad, is the coin of the realm today. One must safeguard one's information." Seeing Mohammad's drink refreshed, Wiles paused and raised his glass. "To new friendships," he said. Chris and Mohammad both returned the salute and took healthy sips of their beverages. Now that his tea was slightly cooler, Chris thought he could detect some added flavor after all. *Ginger, maybe?* He took another sip to suss it out. *Jasmine?*

Wiles set his drink on the bar. "May I ask you a question, Mr. Mohammad?"

"Of course, Mr. Wiles."

"In this part of the world, I'm surprised to see alcohol being served in public. Is it not forbidden by religious law?"

"It is," Mohammad answered, pausing for another sip of Gentleman Jack Daniels. "It is. But the reason we are enjoying these drinks here tonight is... well, let me tell you a story. If I may?"

Wiles said, "I'd like nothing more."

"Nothing more," Chris parroted.

Mohammad began, "My father's father was a rug weaver. The best in all of Zazaristan. He was orphaned as a young boy and taken in by a man named Abdullah Mohammad, a kind rug weaver and his wife, who could not have children.

"My grandfather never learned to read or write, but he learned to create rugs that were works of art, each one telling a story more beautifully than words ever could. When he was a young man, probably thirteen or fourteen years old, he had no idea how old he really was, you see, his skills had grown to surpass those of his beloved master. Along with his skill, his reputation grew and before long, merchants would come to him from the far corners of the earth to carry his rugs back to the finest homes in their lands. To this day, one lies in the Jordanian royal palace." He paused here to acknowledge a small toast from Wiles.

"One day, Taboor City's chief mullah walked into the shop and commissioned my grandfather to weave him a new prayer rug, his having worn thin after decades of faithful use. My grandfather was excited and proud to work for this important man and he eagerly took the job, envisioning his work in a place of honor in the city's largest mosque, to be seen by everyone five times a day at prayer."

There was a brief rabble of noise from the ring across the room, and Mohammad looked up, Chris and Wiles following his gaze. Satisfied (or perhaps unsatisfied) with what he saw, Mohammad returned to his tale. "As a boy, I would sometimes visit my grandfather's workshop and we would talk as he worked, knot by knot, each one the size of a grain of sand. He told me that as he worked on the mullah's rug all those years ago, it occurred to him that the weft and the warp of a rug are like the lives of men. When man is alone, he is like a single thread: weak. Once he crosses paths and binds with others, he is strong. And all under the watchful eye of God. It then further crossed his mind as creator of this rug, which like all things was being made for the glory of God after all, that it should be made as if by God himself, perfect in every way.

"Now, as you may know, there are thousands upon thousands of knots to be made in just a small prayer rug, and it is common that even the most skilled rug weavers will miss one every now and then. Fibers break, the loom may be slightly misaligned, any number of things can go wrong, but an expert weaver will compensate for these things and any small mistake can be hidden within the rug, to remain as my grandfather would say, *beyni beyn-al-ldh,* between God and me. But with the mullah's rug, my grandfather vowed to create a flawless masterpiece, for God's glorification and perhaps a bit of his own as well, eh?

"Working carefully for weeks, my grandfather finally completed the rug. In telling me the story, he always refused to describe to me the rug's design or color, except to say that it was, as he planned, perfect in every way. Exactly 617,796 knots, the holy number 786 times 786. My grandfather couldn't read, but he knew numbers. He rolled up the rug, prayed, and went to bed, with plans to deliver the rug to the mullah the following morning." Mohammad paused for a sip of his drink. Wiles and Chris also took advantage of this brief intermission to do the same.

Mohammad continued. "As my grandfather told it, it was as if a giant hand picked him up out of bed that night and threw him to the floor. The explosion took Abdullah, his wife, and most of my grandfather's hearing. Also, the rug."

"What happened?" asked Chris. He took another sip of tea. *Ginseng?*

Mohammad shrugged. "There was a lot of fighting in those days. Abdullah was a man of peace, but... " Another shrug. "My grandfather eventually rebuilt the workshop, but he never wove another perfect rug. He thought that God punished him for his blasphemous attempt at perfection, so from that day on, he would purposefully include tiny flaws in every rug he ever made as proof of his humility before God."

Mohammad drained his drink and looked straight at Wiles. "So. To answer your question Mr. Wiles. Why are we enjoying this alcohol? No one of this earth is perfect."

"I'll drink to that," Wiles said, doing it. "And please call me Jasper." Just then, the crowd of men across the room, which had created little more than a level buzz since Chris and Wiles arrived, erupted into a roaring swell of cheers, not unlike how a crowd at a rock concert reacts when the lead singer drops the name of their home city into a song.

"Sounds like a winner has risen," Mohammad said.

"Did we miss it?" Chris asked, snapping his head around.

"Don't worry, my friend," Mohammad chuckled. "There are many fights still to come. Have you never been?"

"No," Chris said. "Not to a goat fight. So... it's goats... "

"And they fight, yes," Mohammad answered. "Very exciting."

"How do you get them to fight?" Chris asked. "Do they wear gloves or... " Chris was envisioning the goats rearing up on their hind legs and duking it out wearing boxing gloves as in the manner of boxing kangaroos. Or people, for that matter.

How did these people become the world's superpower? "It's simplicity itself," said Mohammad. "You thread a few strands of the goat's beard through a mini-donut and put a clip on the end of the beard, so the donut won't slide off. The goats each see the other's donut and run forward, ducking their heads to reach it. After a few," he bumped his fists together a few times to illustrate a collision, "one of them gets knocked down. That is the loser. A goat can also lose if his donut gets eaten at any point."

"Can you wager on this?" asked Wiles.

"Of course! That is the whole point! We are not bloodthirsty savages. Come! I'll show you."

Chris finished his tea and smacked his lips, still unable to place the unique flavor. Setting the glass back on the bar and tossing a quick wave to the bartender, he fell in behind Wiles as they followed Mohammad across the room, the three of them moving upstream against light foot traffic as a number of the previous fight's spectators, some flush with victory, some stinking of defeat, made their way to the bar. With Mohammad's back turned, Chris sidled up next to Wiles and whispered, "This is the guy we're looking for! Mohammad Mohammad! He's part of MILF! What do we do?"

"He knows we're in the computer business," Wiles whispered back, keeping an eye on Mohammad. "Let him come to us."

Mohammad turned and beckoned Wiles and Chris to follow him as he wedged himself between a few men, and they managed to work their way to not quite ringside, but second row. The ring itself was a square arrangement of black metal barrels, eight to a side, creating a roughly sixteen by sixteen-foot area within, as well as a handy area atop to rest one's beverage. The barrels were all spray-paint stenciled with various corporate logos, and it was unclear to the Americans whether these represented advertisers or the barrel's rightful owners, but there was no reason it couldn't be both.

As they settled in, Wiles looked to the man on his right, an African fellow wearing an olive drab jacket. In accordance with long personal tradition when attending any spectator event, Wiles said, "Great seats, eh, buddy?" The man regarded Wiles suspiciously, for he spoke no English and even if he did, he was entirely unfamiliar with 1980s beer commercial catchphrases and furthermore, there were no seats.

Mohammad pointed to an old man busily writing and erasing Zazarish with Magic Marker on a large whiteboard mounted on the wall on the far side of the ring. "You see this man? He is telling us the names of the next fighters, where they come from, and the prices. These boys," he then gestured to four teenage boys working inside the ring, taking cash from spectators and handing out slips of paper, shouting as they went, "are taking the wagers and creating the prices."

"What are the names of the fighters?" asked Chris.

Mohammad squinted at the board. "There is... Dream of Gold Cloud. He is from Tak province. And Brown Spotty. He is local. Taboor City. Ah, here they come."

A man carrying a brown goat with white spots ("That is Brown
Spotty," Mohammad said), followed closely by a young boy with a
strong family resemblance (to the man), descended some concrete
stairs in the corner of the arena, presumably entering from
someplace at street level where the steady coming and going of
goats would not attract too much attention, which in Zazaristan
could be any number of places. The old man at the whiteboard
announced something, and a respectful applause greeted the
combatant and there was a noticeable uptick in the ringside
activity. Team Brown Spotty entered the ring through a one-barrel
gap, and the goat bearer gently set the animal down and stood back
with a look of pride. He flagged down a bet-taker and exchanged a
wad of cash for a betting slip, which he then held aloft as he slowly
made a walk around the ring. The young boy literally followed in
his father's footsteps, leading Brown Spotty around so that the
crowd could accurately assess the goat's merit.

Upon completion of his circuit, the boy led his goat to a corner
of the ring, squatted down, and appeared to give it some last-
minute instructions. While this was happening, another man, boy,
and their goat entered, and the introduction ceremony was repeated.

Wiles studied each animal but failed to determine either one to
possess a clear advantage. He turned to Mohammad. "Which do
you like, Mr. Mohammad?"

"I'm sorry, Jasper, but it is considered poor form to give or
take advice. A man must live by his own convictions, after all."

Mohammad barked out something in Zazarish to summon one
of the bet-takers and, with a gesture, referred him to Wiles. Wiles
opted to bet on Dream of Gold Cloud, reasoning that the local
money backing Brown Spotty would depress his odds. He
produced a fifty and pointed to his choice, who was getting a
rubdown and pep talk of his own from his young handler. The bet-
taker palmed the cash and handed Wiles a slip of paper, then
moved on to Mohammad. After a brief Zazarish transaction
followed by the traditional, *"As my fortunes grow, so shall yours,"*

incantation, the young man was then off, having several dozen more cash-waving hands to attend to.

"No action for you, Chris?" asked Wiles, examining his slip.

"I'm usually not good at this kind of thing, Mr. Wiles," Chris replied.

"It is a cold and timid soul who neither knows victory nor defeat," said Wiles as he turned the slip upside down, trying to decipher it.

"Maybe the next one," Chris mumbled. To change the subject, he turned to Mohammad. "Can I ask which one you bet on, Mr. Mohammad?"

"Now that we have made our choices, yes," Mohammad said. "I'm afraid that between Jasper and I, only one of us will be pleased with the outcome. I bet on Brown Spotty."

"Good luck," Chris said, attempting to gain trust.

"All will be as God wills it."

The crowd pressed forward slightly as the fight drew near, and Chris steadied himself so as not to fall, assuming it would also be considered poor form to knock a few people down and fall over an empty oil drum, spilling drinks everywhere and perhaps injure a fighting goat. He surveyed the crowd, taking in the curious looks of his fellow fight fans, who saw very few Americans pass through. Chris thought of Biz and wondered what she was doing at that moment. The prospect of telling her that he and Wiles had actually met Mohammad Mohammad, the man they had traveled halfway around the world to find, seemed just as exciting as meeting the man himself, and Chris decided to focus on that for the time being.

The bet-takers had thoroughly made their rounds, and very few hands remained in the air around the ring. The whiteboard man yelled something that must have meant bets were now closed because the four teens simultaneously stopped what they were doing, exited the ring, and disappeared up the stairs from where the goats had entered.

The old man capped his Magic Marker and stepped away from his whiteboard to make his way to the center of the ring, where the elder goat handlers met him. The goats remained in their corners, looking relaxed in the company of their young pages. Whiteboard man, now assuming the role of referee, reached into the large pockets of his robe with each hand and withdrew something in his fists that he gave to each man, who in turn concealed the items and returned to their corners. As they got there, the boys picked up their goats (mentally struggling to conceal how much of a physical struggle it was for them), rotated them so that they faced into their respective corners, and pulled back on their horns, tipping their chins up. Now Chris could see that the men had received from the ref the mini donuts that served as the sport's object of contention and that they were being attached to the goat's beards just as Mohammad had described. Chris had also deduced that the presence of a donut under the goat's own chin must be kept a secret from the goat, lest the competitive nature of the fight be compromised.

Donuts securely affixed, the goat handlers gave the A-OK sign to the ref, who returned the sign to each team. With that, all five humans filed out of the ring through the neutral corner and the ref slid a final barrel into position to seal the ring behind them. The boisterous crowd settled into hushed whispers. The goats remained facing their corners. Fifteen seconds passed. The exquisite tension and drama were almost too much to take for everyone in the room, except for two people. Wiles and Chris exchanged a look.

"What now?" asked Chris in a low voice, leaning toward Mohammad.

"Shhh! The fight has begun!" Mohammad hissed.

Looking closely to be sure that neither goat had shown any inclination to move, let alone engage in combat (which they hadn't), Wiles said, "They should face the goats toward each other before they leave the ring."

"What are we, Quudis?" Mohammad snapped.

Chastened, the Americans both zipped it and turned their attentions back to the ring. Another forty seconds passed.

One of the goats began to turn around.

An interesting thing happened about 3.5 billion years ago during the Earth's Archaean period. Somewhere beneath hundred-foot waves of scalding water that thundered against the jagged bases of active volcanoes, under our young sun's dim light that feebly filtered through rushing vapors of hydrochloric acid, a mysterious process beyond the scope of mankind's collective scientific and mystical imaginations brought forth a living organism, where a moment earlier, there was none.

I'm hungry, the organism thought.

A billion or so generations later, one of this seminal organism's mammalian descendants found itself in a goatfighting ring, casually taking in the sights, blissfully unaware of, well, just about everything. Except one thing.

I'm hungry, it thought.

Can I eat this floor? No. Can I eat this barrel? No. Can I eat one of those men? No. Can I eat that other goat? No. Can I eat this floor? No. Wait, go back to the goat. Can I eat that thing hanging off his chin? YES!!

Goatfight on.

Dream of Gold Cloud had seen Brown Spotty's donut and made for it, building up a full head of steam as he crossed the ring. He came up from behind and left of his opponent, blindsiding him into the corner barrel and missing a clean shot at the donut as Brown Spotty stumbled.

The crowd buzzed with excitement as Brown Spotty turned, with a look on his face that clearly expressed, *Not cool, dude! What the fu—hey, I can eat that thing hanging off your chin!!*

Brown Spotty was backed into a corner but had leverage since he was on his front knees. Just two knees. Clearly, he didn't go down on all four knees, which obviously would have signaled the fight's conclusion. Brown Spotty sprang up at Dream of Gold

Cloud, who reared up on his hind legs and absorbed Brown
Spotty's attack with his chest. He was driven backward several feet
across the ring.

The goats locked eyes on each other's donuts and bolted
forward, lowering their heads just as they reached each other.

TOCK!

The sound of the impact reminded Chris of when a bowling
ball comes rolling back out of that little tunnel and knocks into the
rest of the balls. He winced slightly as the two goats staggered for a
moment, then gathered their wits and repeated their attacks.

TOCK!

Brown Spotty seemed to have gotten the best of Dream of
Gold Cloud this time. The Notorious DGC stumbled to his left and
dropped his head to shake off the blows of his opponent. Brown
Spotty took full advantage of this tactical error and drove ahead,
delivering a headbutt squarely between the horns. Dream of Gold
Cloud's legs crumpled, and he hit the concrete.

Goatfight.

Brown Spotty snatched his rightful donut and munched away
right on the spot. The old man at the whiteboard waved his arms
and shouted out Brown Spotty's name in Zazarish, officially
declaring him the winner. Dream of Gold Cloud, from his prone
position, looked up and began eating the donut of his vanquisher,
which was now dangling before his eyes. If *this* was considered
bad form, Mohammad Mohammad made no mention of it as he
turned grinning, positively shining, with money won, toward Wiles
and clapped him on the shoulder.

"My friend, sometimes the goats do not fall your way," he
said. "Your beast showed great resolve, but I knew mine would,
what is the word? Triumph."

"In America, it is customary for the winners to buy drinks for
the losers," Wiles announced, talking loudly over the din of the
fans around them settling their wagers and bemoaning their luck.

Chris had to forcefully agree. A trip to the bar would be just the thing right now. That tea really hit the spot, and he felt like having another one.

"But we are in Zazaristan, Jasper!" Mohammad shouted back.

"Today we are in Zazaristan, Mohammad. Tomorrow, who knows?" Wiles said. He took a step toward the bar and beckoned Mohammad and Chris to follow. A young bet-taker appeared in front of Mohammad, pressed a wad of cash into his hand, then darted off.

"Tomorrow indeed, Jasper," Mohammad said quietly before heading to the bar himself, an idea beginning to form in his mind. This American could prove useful. His young partner seemed a little too fond of the medicinal tea for Mohammad's liking, but again, who among us is perfect?

Mohammad arrived at the bar and, with good humor, slapped some of his recent winnings down and directed the bartender to set the three of them up with another round.

"Jasper, Chris," he said, "I have told you a story. Now it is your turn. What tales can you tell me of America?"

Wiles considered relating Chapter 13 of the *New York Times* bestselling *Place Directly on Rack*, entitled "Trust Your Swing," but it was Chris who spoke up first. "I have a story," he said.

CHAPTER 41

"That story about your grandfather tying all those knots made me think about this job I used to have when I was younger, like thirteen. Let me back up a little bit. I wanted a Zbox, you know, a video game. I asked my dad and he said that if I wanted it, I would have to work for it. I wasn't sixteen yet, so I couldn't get a job at a restaurant or anything like that, but my dad drove me out to a huge strawberry farm the next Saturday morning at six. He had told me the night before we'd be getting up early and when I asked what for, he said we were going to get me a Zbox, but he said it like a joke, so I knew we wouldn't just be making a trip to Walmart.

"So anyway, my dad drops me off and he pointed me to a guy who was in charge. I talk to this guy at the farm and he puts me in with a truckload of other kids, mostly my age, some older and we drive about a mile to the far end of this strawberry field. Everyone jumps out and this guy comes up to me and says, 'You ever pinned runners before?' and I have no idea what he's talking about, so I say, 'What do you mean, like wrestling?' and he shakes his head and goes, 'No, pinning strawberry plant runners.' He hands me a box of bobby pins, like hairpins, and he walks over to the end of the strawberry rows. I mean, these rows, they are so long, you can barely see the other end. He gets down on his knees and pulls a few of the plant's creeping vines out straight. 'These are runners,' he says. 'Pin them into the ground like this.' He pulls a hairpin out of the box. The box is about this big, full of silver pins. 'The runner takes root and it makes the plant grow bigger.' He shoves a pin with his thumb into the dirt right over the neck of the runner. He gets up, hands me the box, and says, 'Pizza for lunch, see you then.' He gets in the truck and drives off. All of the other kids are getting to work on their strawberry rows, some of them hurried over to get rows next to each other so they could talk as they worked. I got down to it too, although I had to take the last row on the end, so I only had one neighbor and we didn't talk much.

"So aside from that, that is some tedious work. The same thing, over and over and over. You grab five or six runners from the plant. They stretch out about this far. Then with your thumb, you jam a pin into the dirt to make it take root. Then you shuffle on your knees over eight inches and you just go down this endless row. There was a kid who had a Bluetooth speaker and he played music all day, mostly rap, some early Drednott, Mr. Wiles, I remember that. He would take requests too. You could yell out someone and he would play it if he had it. But man, after a few hours, my thumb was so sore I had to switch thumbs, then back again. You wouldn't believe how good it felt just to stand up straight and just walk when they blew the horn for lunch.

"Anyway, I got nowhere near the end of my row by the end of the day, no one did. A terrible job. But I went back every Saturday for six weeks. The guy paid us cash at the end of every day, and after six weeks I had enough for my Zbox. I didn't go back after that, in case you were wondering. That summer I got a job reffing youth basketball games.

"I loved that Zbox. I remember I was playing my favorite game, *Mars Marine: Detachment 1*, when my dad called me down the hall one night. My parents were going out that night, and I wanted to get a jump on my solitary gaming while they were gone. I went into their bedroom. My dad was sitting on the bed and mom was standing near the closet. She was dressed to go out. Not fancy, but nice. Hair, makeup, you know. My dad says, 'Chris, look at my beautiful wife. Your old man did all right.' She says, 'Oh, Ron.'

"I go back to playing my Zbox. A year later, he was gone."

CHAPTER 42

TABOOR CITY, ZAZARISTAN
SUNDAY, 8:43 p.m. ZST

The prefight activity was picking up in anticipation of the evening's next matchup. Standing among the cluster of fans that were gathering ringside, Mohammad informed Wiles that this upcoming match would be the tenth undercard match of the evening, leading up to the twenty-fifth and main event, which Wiles saw as a lucky omen, flashing his #25 claim ticket at Chris upon hearing the numbers.

"Mr. Wiles, I feel a little weird," Chris said.

Wiles said, "Probably jet lag. Drink some more tea."

Chris had to agree with Wiles's diagnosis and prescription. He had never traveled internationally, so the feeling of his circadian rhythm being thrown off was completely unfamiliar and besides, how could a tea hurt? He took a healthy sip and a few deep breaths.

The next pair of goats was now in the ring. Mohammad tipped his hand to Chris and Wiles as to which one he liked by offering his wager first, thus not violating the no-advice rule. Goatfighting is a sport of gentlemen after all. Mohammad put his money on the aptly named Fat and Wiles followed suit. Chris was having other ideas. Really strange ideas. He really, really felt weird. Then it hit him. This wasn't jet lag at all.

It suddenly became clear that the tea was giving him magical powers.

Hold on, that's ridiculous. There's no such thing as magic. Superpowers. Yes, of course. Superpowers. Let me see if I can hovertate. Is that a word? Hovertate? Hoverlate? Leverate? Leverate. That's it. Leverate.

Wiles was keeping a close eye on Chris since he mentioned he wasn't feeling well. Looking over, he saw nothing out of the ordinary as Chris rose up on his tiptoes to get a better look at the goats in the ring.

OK. I can leverate, but just a little. Not bad. I think it's also safe to assume that I have telepathic powers of insight that will reveal the workings of the universe, but there's only one way to find out for sure.

Chris took another sip and set his teacup down on the closest 55-gallon drum with a melodic *clong*, which pleased him very much. So much so that he lifted and set down the cup a few more times. *Clong. Clong. Clong.*

After four *clongs*, which were neither too few nor too many, he stared into the eyes of Fat's opponent, the equally aptly named Yellow. It occurred to him that the animal's weird, horizontal irises were keyholes into the beast's soul, access to its very nature. While Chris pondered this revelation, it was unclear to him if he shrunk down and was transported into the goat's eye, or if the eye expanded to envelop him, but either way, he found himself floating in the inky darkness of the goat's being, what Buddhists would call it's *anatta*. It's impossible to explain, but Chris could sense words forming in the void around him. Neither heard, nor read exactly, the words nevertheless made themselves known as follows:

Get on my back, Chris

Mark A. Henry

Slaying be my bailiwick

Im'a kick his ass

That a Zazari goat could address Chris by name, in English, and in haiku form, not to mention in such a fancy font, seemed like minor details relative to the value and reliability of the handicapping information.

"That one," he said to a passing bet-taker, extending a finger toward Yellow along with a thin fold of bills.

Wiles didn't notice Chris's variation from the game plan that Mohammad had implicitly laid down, but Mohammad did. He caught Chris's eye and saluted him for his convictions. One eyebrow went up while the other did not.

His eyebrow almost got away. Are mine still here? Chris touched his face. *OK. Good. This calls for a sip of tea.*

Chris, returned from his brief vacation into the mind of a fighting goat to the astral plane that the rest of us all inhabit, reached for his teacup. Sip. *Clong.*

Five minutes later, the crowd collectively gasped as Fat stumbled and went down, following an efficient and brutal pummeling from Yellow. As Chris watched, Yellow ate Fat's donut, stood up on his hind legs, doffed a cowboy hat that he was not wearing just a moment ago, and bowed toward Chris.

Now that's a gentleman.

A young bet-taker rushed up to Chris and slapped a plump roll of bills into his hand. Mohammad and Wiles were both staring at him.

As they did after the next fight.

264

And the next.

And the next and the next and the next and the next and the next and the next and the next and the next and the next and the next and the next and the next.

The thing about being in a drug-induced, trancelike state that allows one to telepathically communicate with animals and assess their level of self-confidence as it pertains to imminent physical combat is that it's a very difficult task to manage. Therefore, it follows that it is a highly lucrative practice. And the thing about lucrative practices is that they're hard to keep under wraps for very long.

Mohammad Mohammad had never witnessed a scene like the one that roiled before him as the twenty-fifth and ultimate match drew near. The goatfighting arena buzzed with excitement. The main event pitted the young, undefeated challenger Azizi against one of the all-time greats, Three.

Obviously, there was much debate among the spectators over which goat to back. There was no consensus other than that the two were evenly matched and the fight should be a good one. In addition, word had spread that the young American known as Chris, or "the Doctor," had shown an incredible knack for picking the winning goat time after time. Just about every spectator had one eye on Chris to see if he would bet on Azizi or Three. At this point, just as the consensus was split between Azizi and Three, there was equal debate over whether Chris actually had some legitimate insight or if he was just extremely lucky and if so, would his luck continue, or would it run out?

Mohammad was having a grand time. He was clearly under the impression that Chris and/or Wiles had cracked the code to successful goatfight betting, and he had been along for the ride the whole time. He leaned over to Wiles and almost had to shout to be heard. "And now, Jasper, which animal shall win the final match? Which does our friend like?" A fifteen-match winning streak was

265

quite uncharted waters, and if ever there was a time to bend the no-soliciting-advice rule, this was it. No one of this earth is perfect.

Wiles, also enjoying himself immensely and confident that he was closing the deal on this Mohammad Mohammad business, said, "The answer will cost you fifty dollars."

Mohammad grinned and slipped Wiles the cash. A small price to pay for such valuable information.

"I'll take one answer," he said.

Wiles leaned close. Mohammad closed his eyes, trying to shunt the visual energy to the ears. Wiles spoke up loud and clear. "I don't know." Damn him if he did. Chris was really operating on some Nicklausian level with which he was not familiar.

Mohammad should have known. He cursed himself for getting greedy and trying to make an early bet before Chris had pronounced his pick, which would certainly cause a wild swing in the fight's odds.

Chris stood with his head tilted and lips pursed, staring at Three. He turned to the young bet-taker who had faithfully served him throughout the night's events and handed the boy a fat roll of bills. Wiles stood by, watching carefully along with everyone else, but did nothing to encourage or discourage Chris's decision to bet what seemed to be his entire bankroll. Wiles hadn't had much success talking with Chris since midway through Fight Sixteen when Chris mentioned he was "like that song, you know, the one with the drums?" and Wiles realized that he was somehow tripping balls. (This realization came to him as he took a "probiotic".) Mohammad had confirmed that yes, Chris had ingested a larger-than-customary amount of "medicine" in his tea throughout the evening, but he admitted he had never known anyone to react in quite the manner Chris had.

Whether Chris won or lost his bet on the last fight, Wiles was pleased with the attention and goodwill he and Chris had garnered. Mohammad Mohammad had been betting the same way as Chris for the past dozen bouts, and Wiles figured his good mood would make him more amenable to any business propositions later.

Chris extended his arm what seemed to him to be a good twelve feet and pointed squarely at Three. The rest of the bettors sprang into action, half of them betting with this odd American who did not lose, the other half betting against the odd American, certain that his luck was bound to run out. After all, nobody wins sixteen in a row. Fifteen sure, but not sixteen. Wiles made a modest bet on Azizi, not so much to disagree with Chris—after all, he recognized a hot streak when he saw one—but to allay any suspicions that he might be in on some kind of fix. His attention was then drawn to the ring where Three and Azizi were being placed in their now-familiar corner-facing positions, and the crowd quieted in anticipation of the evening's climactic main event.

CHAPTER 43

As was *his* custom, young Yazeed Aliyy called it a night just before the final fight began. He packed his things at the cell phone table in the corner of the arena where he did his business, then quietly slipped upstairs and out the door that Walid and Zebar were still faithfully guarding outside. The three of them shared a smoke and some gossip (also out of custom), and Yazeed's appearance signaled to the doormen that their night's work was drawing to a close as well. Once the final fight began, their services were no longer required at the door and they would head downstairs to assist in clearing out the crowd at the end of the night.

After Yazeed related the events of the evening (and learned from Walid that the young man having such wagering success downstairs was a veterinarian specially trained in the treatment of mental illness), he said goodnight, and Yazeed trotted away down the alley toward the quiet street.

Yazeed had made a nice score tonight, no doubt about it. The smartphones in his pocket were the nicest he had ever seen. The glossy black case on one of them was made of some material he couldn't even identify, and the phone itself was a Model XXI, when he had only just heard that the XX was still months away from production. The other phone was a brand-new, top-of-the-line

268

Model IXX, which itself was scarcely seen in this part of the world. To think that he had bought them both for just thirty-five dollars in Fort Worth Plaza Hotel and Casino poker chips!

Years ago, after the hotel closed, its looted chips became a widely accepted form of currency on the Zazaristanian black market, but still, thirty-five was far, far less than the phones were worth! Yazeed was proud of his negotiating skills. The American in the white hat and the young veterinarian seemed like pretty sharp guys, yet Yazeed had gotten the best of them! He never ceased to be amazed by the reluctance of non-Zazarish speakers to bargain for a better price, to say nothing of the fact that they so readily sold their phones at all once they learned they must be silenced in the arena.

Speaking of which, Yazeed wanted to stop and double-check that the phones were powered down before he got home. He always killed the phones he purchased as soon as the transactions were completed, but it was important they remain silenced for the night. He didn't want any rings, chirps, chimes, or buzzers to go off that might wake his older brothers, who would certainly try to commandeer the phones. Yazeed had plans for them.

As he tapped the dark screens, a flash of headlights snapped his head up and he quickly ducked into a recessed doorway. Yazeed watched a VW Vanagon with the Syncro 4x4 package roll down the otherwise deserted street, then did likewise in the opposite direction.

A minute later, Brohug pulled to the curb and parked squarely in front of the mouth of the alleyway that led to the arena.

"Door to fights is down there," he said to Biz, pointing. He checked his watch. "Friends will come out soon."

Biz peered down the dim alley. The door was not visible from the street. There were no signs, no advertisements, no indications that anything at all was transpiring inside. This was sketchy.

"Brohug, you need to go in there and make sure they're OK," said Biz.

Silently repeating, *Customer is always right. Customer is always right*, Brohug slid out of the driver's seat and headed down the alley. In less than thirty seconds he was back. "Door is locked," he reported. Biz scrunched her forehead in frustration.

"You said the fights will get out soon?" she asked.

Brohug checked his watch again. "Yes. Everyone come out this way."

"We'll wait," Biz announced, staring at the door.

Brohug climbed back in next to her and closed his eyes. The adrenaline from watching the football match was wearing off, and he was hoping for a short nap.

"Is there any other door?" Biz asked. "Can you get in any other way?"

Brohug opened his eyes. "There is door on other side, I think. Your friends will be out soon. They are having good time. Do not worry." He closed his eyes again.

Twelfth Grade: *There are two types of problems: Those you can fix and those you can't. Either way, don't worry.*

"Drive around the other side," said Biz.

CHAPTER 44

To say that the Azizi/Three bout lived up to the prefight hype and expectations would be an understatement. The two goats had battled like champions. Both visibly weary and mildly concussed, they slowly circled the ring, intensely eyeing the donut of the other.

Azizi made the first move, and once again the goats clashed at the center of the ring. Three was sent skidding backwards into the corner opposite where Chris stood outside the barrels. The older goat was clearly shaken up and wobbled slightly as he regained his senses, his donut swaying irresistibly.

Azizi lowered his head and crouched to spring forward and finish off his foe. The crowd sensed the fight's climax was at hand and collectively held their breath in hushed anticipation.

Chris screamed, "Look out!" Not because he saw that Three was in danger of losing the fight but because of the rainbow-striped dinosaur that was sprinting across the ceiling.

Then nothing happened. Really, nothing. Azizi froze in place. The crowd, which had been buzzing excitedly, went dead silent. The dinosaur vanished as quickly as it had appeared.

Almost as if in slow motion, Azizi tipped forward and fell over, his legs splayed out stiffly. He had been startled into a fit of

271

myotonia congenital (commonly known as Fainting Goat
Syndrome) by Chris's sudden outburst. Three blinked once, twice,
then cantered over and had a bite of Azizi's donut.

Then something happened. And that thing is: the goatfighting
arena went batshit.

* * *

Outside, Biz and Brohug's recon trip to the other side of the
building had revealed a low, bulkhead-style back door of the arena,
which lay squeezed between the narrow, darkened storefronts of a
barbershop and a rug store.

A few goatfighting teams were busily loading up their trucks
and motorcycles in preparation to head home. Brohug parked on
the corner and got out.

"Wait. Is it the *goats* that fight?" Biz said.

Brohug approached one of the goat's owners and held a short
conversation. He came back and stood at Biz's window.

"He says two Americans are inside. And they are very much
enjoying the fights."

Biz said, "Can we get in? Let's try the door."

She hopped to the sidewalk and Brohug followed her to the
sloped metal hatchway. Biz bent down and knocked loudly. A surly
looking teenager opened up and scanned around. He shouted, *"You
have no goat? This door is for fighters only! Go around the other
side! Goatfighting is a sport of gentlemen!"*

The door slammed shut and Biz heard it lock.

* * *

In no less than four different languages, men screamed,
"Goatfighting is a sport of gentlemen!" Some of these gentlemen,
fairly incongruously it must be said, began punching and grabbing
at Chris for violating the unwritten rules of goatfight fan behavior,

which apparently forbid loud, sudden noises that could frighten the goats, disrupt the fight, and undermine the integrity of the sport.

Wiles, alarmed by the sudden outbreak of violence, grabbed Mohammad Mohammad by the sleeve and yelled, "What's happening?"

Mohammad Mohammad yelled back, "Goatfighting is a sport of gentlemen!" What more explanation was needed? He turned away, trying to escape from the mounting chaos ringside and beat the post-fight rush to the bar. He and Wiles had agreed upon a victory nightcap, and it was his turn to buy.

Things were getting out of control, especially for Chris. If you think it's unsettling when your cat gives you some side-eye when you're home getting stoned on a Saturday night, imagine what it feels like to be the victim of a sudden and unprovoked physical assault by dozens of men screaming in foreign languages while your brain is soaked in Schedule 1 narcotics. Chris felt like he was being pulled into a vortex of fists.

In a phrase that made as much sense to the English and non-English speakers within earshot, Chris yelled, "Levitation powers: activate!"

LeviTATE. That's it.

A moment later, "Why is this not working?!"

Fortunately, most of the blows were not landing flush because he was in fact being pulled backward by an unseen force, which Chris assumed was either the gravitational pull of some kind of earthbound black hole or the Force from *Star Wars*.

After a few seconds and a particularly sharp tug, he realized it was actually the rainbow dinosaur from earlier, its jaws clamped onto his shirt. He hoped the dinosaur was friendlier than it had looked.

Wiles saw that in reality, two large men had pushed through the swarming mass of people to reach Chris and had grabbed him by the shirt collar to wrestle him away toward the exit. It was Walid and Zebar from the front door! Wiles left Mohammad and swam his way through the crowd, hoping he could talk some sense into them and help Chris.

Meanwhile, the referee was now waving his arms and shouting something, so most of the Chris-punchers turned to hear what the official ruling on the fight would be. It was purely academic of course. The outcome was, and could only be, solely determined by the rules of goatfighting, which Mohammad had explained earlier. If a goat hits the deck (or his donut is consumed in whole or in part by his opponent), that goat shall be declared the loser of the fight. Extenuating circumstances and/or post-fight protests are not considered because goatfighting is... well, you know.

Nevertheless, those patrons holding losing Azizi tickets, with the perpetual yet delusional optimism that defines a sports bettor, paused from attacking Chris to listen to the ref's announcement in hopes that for the first time ever, the fight's outcome would be reversed, or at least nullified. The distraction loosened the knot of people around Chris and allowed Wiles to get closer to him and his captors. When he was arm's reach behind them he shouted, "Walid! Zebar!"

The two doormen looked back, and their eyes widened as they recognized Chris's cohort. Without a word, Zeb shot out a hand and grabbed Wiles by the shirt, quickly spun him around, and got him into a chicken-wing. As he was shoved toward the exit stairs, his cries of, "Wait, Walid! Wait, Zebar! Waitwaitwait!" falling on deaf ears, Wiles desperately turned his head around. He did not want to lose Mohammad Mohammad. Or his phone! That kid at the phone-check desk still had it! He caught a glimpse of Mohammad Mohammad's back as he made his way to the bar.

Wiles yelled out, "Mohammad!"

Unfortunately, Chris chose that exact moment to yell, "Suck my dick, dinosaur!" and Wiles was mostly drowned out. About a half-dozen guys turned their heads, but none were the one he was trying to reach.

Even louder, as he began to disappear to the unknown depths that lay upstairs, Wiles shouted, "MOHAMMAD MOHAMMAD!"

Mohammad had run into his bet-taker and stopped to collect his payout for his final bet on Three. The controversial ending did not concern him because of the perpetual yet delusional optimism that defines a sports bettor. After all, the rules are clear. If a goat goes to the ground, he is the loser. Exactly how it happens is neither here nor there. Hearing his name shouted, he turned around and looked up just in time to see Wiles and Chris disappear up the steps, being forcibly escorted by the doormen Walid and Zebar, who must have been called into action to expel the instigators of the post-fight clamor and kick them out into the night.

After receiving his cash and dispensing an atypically generous gratuity to its deliverer (since now he wouldn't have to pay for Wiles's last cocktail), Mohammad Mohammad considered the events of the night.

Certainly, it was profitable. He had never known a goat-picking hot streak like the one Chris had displayed and that he himself had gotten on board with early. Eventful as well. The American computer experts were pleasant enough company and by the end of their time together, he had gained a measure of respect for their bold, if unconventional ways. It was unfortunate that their evening had ended so suddenly. After the last fight, when it was the appropriate time to discuss such things, Mohammad had planned to propose a piece of business to Wiles and Chris. (Really just Wiles. Chris did not hold his opium-and-khat-infused hashish very well.) But unfortunately, their forced and unplanned departure had now prevented any meetings of a professional nature. It was not to be. Mohammad Mohammad, the son of a son of a rug maker, shrugged.

Now that he had a bit of liquid capital, Mohammad wanted to launch his plan to expand his rug business by upgrading his website and perhaps use Friendbook to increase the traffic on his YouTube page. He thought the advice and services Wiles could offer would be the big break the Mohammad and Son Rug Company was waiting for. Now that he had the means to pay for it, the plan would still move ahead, but without the American's help. Mohammad simply would have to seek out someone else to do the job.

He immediately thought of his friend Fareek Wazaan. Fareek knew all about this sort of thing. He had grown up as a refugee in Quudia and learned about computers and such from the international aid workers who administered the camp where he had lived with his mother. He had returned to Zazaristan a year ago and now worked for AJI but, like most Zazaris, did a little work on the side. Walid and Zebar, for example, also worked at AJI by day but did contract security work at the arena Sunday nights.

Fareek had mentioned to Mohammad in the past that his boss at AJI, Wahiri Shwarma, didn't approve of Fareek's IT freelancing but that Shwarma was a duplicitous jerk and what he didn't know wouldn't hurt him.

As it happened, Shwarma himself (a.k.a. Mohammad Mohammad, suave international dealmaker) had just then emerged from a dark corner of the arena. He was outraged by the result of the final fight. He was not a betting man, but he owned a forty-nine percent interest in Azizi and this travesty would cause the animal's market value and future stud fees to drop considerably.

Shwarma roughly shouldered his way past Mohammad (a.k.a. Mohammad Mohammad, struggling rug merchant) as he stormed out. Even if he knew Mohammad, he was in no mood to stop and chat over the coincidence of his chosen *nom de guerre*.

Author's Note:
What? I already told you I'm not great at coming up with names. Plus, Mohammad Mohammad is a very common name in Zazaristan.

CHAPTER 45

Jasper Wiles and Chris Dawkins were roughly pushed into the back of a van. Wiles's skateboard clattered in after them. The van doors slammed shut.

CHAPTER 46

Parked once again in their original position at the mouth of the
alley, Biz and Brohug intently watched as a steady stream of
goatfight fans began exiting the arena. In knots of twos and threes
they passed by the Vanagon, all seemingly engaged in animated
debate over something or other. Every minute or so, Biz looked
down at her phone to check if the blue dots had reappeared and
with every minute they didn't, she grew more impatient. The crowd
began to thin, with no sign of Jasper or Chris. She could hear
Wiles's voice in her mind saying, "Have faith, Elizabeth," but she
had a bad feeling. This was wrong, all of it. As soon as they were
back together, she would insist on returning to California
immediately.

"Brohug, just slip in there as these people are coming out and
go find Jasper and Chris. Tell them we're getting out of here," she
said.

Brohug hopped out of the vehicle and began working his way
through the sparsening crowd. He had to wait a moment at the door
for it to open and he quickly slipped inside.

A few long minutes later Brohug returned alone. "I talk to
bartender," he reported. "Jasper and Chris got very,"—drinky-

278

drinky motion—"and started big fight. Kicked out back door fifteen minutes ago."

"WHAT?! Where are they now?"

CHAPTER 47

TABOOR CITY, ZAZARISTAN
MONDAY, 12:25 a.m. ZST

"I ASKED YOU A QUESTION, DINOSAUR!!" Chris yelled in the pitch-black back of the van that Walid and Zebar had tossed them into. "THAT QUESTION... IS SUCK MY DICK!!"

Wiles reached across the corrugated metal floor paneling they sat upon as they rattled down some ill-maintained Taboor City Street on the way to God-knows-where.

Grabbing Chris's shoulder, he said, "Chris... Chris! There's no dinosaur. You're high on something, possibly very strong hashish, and it's making you hallucinate. It's me. Jasper."

Chris rolled his head around to look toward Wiles's voice. "How do I know you're not a hallucination, Jasper?"

Wiles knelt forward in the dark. "Can you see me?"

Chris shook his head. "No."

"Then I'm not a hallucination."

This made perfect sense.

"What about the dinosaur?"

"There's no dinosaur in here," Wiles assured him.

"I know. He's driving."

Wiles shook Chris, whispering sharply. "Chris! We are here in Zazaristan to find Mohammad Mohammad and reset his computer drive! He's back at the goatfight! We got dragged out of there by Walid and Zebar because you yelled something during the fight!"

"I know, Jasper," said Chris. "I don't have amnesium. Amnesior?"

"Amnesia?" suggested Wiles.

"Amnesia!" Chris confirmed.

"Also, we lost our phones and we're out of touch with Biz," said Wiles.

At the mention of Biz's name, Chris came around a little bit. "That kid still has them!" he realized.

"Right," said Wiles. "And if Biz doesn't hear from us, and we can't get back to her,"—he checked the glowing hands of his watch—"she'll be forced to leave without us and you'll be a wanted fugitive."

The two of them banged on the van's metal partition and yelled to Walid and Zebar to stop or at least let them know where they were headed, but there was no response.

CHAPTER 48

TABOOR CITY, ZAZARISTAN
MONDAY, 12:26 a.m. ZST

Biz felt the night tightening around her. Like many a person before her who was searching for something with no idea where to begin looking, she turned to the person on her left sitting behind the wheel of a VW Vanagon and said, "Drive."

"Where?" Brohug asked. "Hotel? They maybe walk back."

"I hope so. They must be on foot. Maybe we'll spot them. Pull around the block again first."

Brohug dropped into gear and pulled away from the arena.

Biz checked her phone again and saw that there was no change in her companions' cellular signal—still off the grid. Biz could only hope that this was an effect of the apparent alcohol consumption that went on while Chris and Wiles were inside the arena. Could they have simply forgotten to turn their phones back on when they left? There was also the possibility that this was all done out of intention. Maybe Wiles orchestrated some drunken scene to burnish his outlaw bona fides and attract the attention of some MILF operatives. Could the cell phone silence mean that they made contact and negotiations were afoot? Staring at her phone would not answer these questions. She made sure the ringer and vibration mode were turned all the way up and slipped the phone back in her bag.

When she looked up, Brohug had circled halfway around the block and they stopped near the door that Wiles and Chris had reportedly been shown. The only people in sight were the respective owners of Azizi and Three, who were engaged in an intense shouting match as their young sons busily loaded the animals into small trucks.

Biz said, "Brohug! Ask these guys if they saw which way Jasper and Chris went."

Brohug rolled down his window and honked his horn to attract the attention of Azizi's owner. After firing one more curse at his counterpart, the man turned to Brohug, who said, *"Have you seen two Americans? They came out this way a short time ago."*

Azizi's owner spat on the ground. *"Those Western dogs are lucky they were gone by the time I got outside. They would have felt the sting of my—"*

"Unless they yelled something at you," Three's owner chimed in. He pointed at Azizi, who still looked a little woozy. *"Then you might have swooned like your little doeling over there."* He then turned to be sure his son caught the insult, wiggling his eyebrows a bit, as dads will do.

"How DARE you!" Azizi's owner screamed.

The argument then quickly regressed into trading your-mother-is-from-Quudia themed insults. Brohug rolled up his window as Azizi's owner the younger got off a good one.

"They no see anyone," he reported to Biz, mentally filing away the zinger for future use toward some youth football referee. "We drive back to hotel, see them on the way, I think."

"OK, let's go," she said.

As they rounded the corner, they could see that two blocks ahead, a Toyota Hilux pickup truck was parked perpendicularly across the street. A powerful spotlight mounted near its driver's door blindingly illuminated a small cluster of vehicles that had just exited the fights and were now lined up to pass through this makeshift checkpoint. Biz shielded her eyes against the light and could make out three men holding rifles, two near the truck, the other standing on the corner preventing the vehicles from backtracking.

Brohug slowed to quickly scan the scene for Jasper and Chris, then swerved onto a small side street. The armed man closest to them glanced in their direction but then turned back around.

"What was that, Brohug?" Biz asked, looking back to make sure no one was following them.

"That was... what you say. Curfew," he answered.

"Curfew means everyone has to be back home by a certain time," said Biz, still looking back. No sign of anyone.

"Oh. No curfew, then. Those guys take a little money, sometimes they take people, cut head off, you know. That's why we go back to hotel now. We find Jasper and Chris on the way." He snuck a look in the mirror.

"Cut heads off?! Are those men dangerous?" Biz asked.

"Yes and no," said Brohug. "To Americans, yes. To me? No."

"Are they terrorists?"

"I do not know this word, but like this, I think, yes. One of those men I think, was Bashir Hallazallah."

The name meant nothing to Biz, and she showed no recognition.

Brohug went on. "He really no like Americans. But he usually stays in south. Not much in Taboor. He maybe saw video of Jasper on Friendbook."

Biz put her face in her hands for a moment, then punched the dashboard, startling Brohug. *Why, Jasper? Why did you have to put that stupid, stupid video out? Now there are armed goons shutting down the city looking for you! And by the way, you are at best, AT BEST, wandering around buzzed without your phone and at worst...* Biz couldn't even finish the "at worst" thought. Options. She needed options.

"Should we call the police, Brohug?"

He looked at Biz blankly. "I do not know this word."

"People who are paid to protect the city," she clarified. "They could help us look for Jasper and Chris."

"Those men *are* paid to protect city. They *are* looking," Brohug said, thumbing over his shoulder. "But you don't want help from them. Danger, I said."

Biz realized she was on the other side of the fence.

"Let's get back to the hotel. We just have to hope Chris and Jasper found their way back."

CHAPTER 49

SOUTH TABOOR CITY, ZAZARISTAN
MONDAY, 12:43 a.m. ZST

Sitting toe-to-toe in complete darkness on the floor of the van, Wiles and Chris had slowly bumped along over increasingly ill-maintained roads in a zig-zagging route for what seemed like an hour until the vehicle slowed, turned, then came to an abrupt stop. Chris could hear a garage door rattle open. The van shot forward and jerked to another stop.

"Jasper," Chris said as the van's front doors opened and shut. Voices could be heard. "We have to get back to Biz."

"Grab something real and hold on tight," Wiles said, quoting the James Van Der Beek movie *TechChain*, which he had seen recently for the first time.

As in the movie, Wiles extended his hand. Chris felt for and grasped it. Steady as a rock, he noted.

Unseen by human eyes, his own included, Jasper Wiles gripped and released Chris's hand, then released his own right arm that had been tightly clamped between his knees.

Author's Note:
See, right there is why books are better than movies.

The rear doors flew open.

286

The type of sickly fluorescent light that illuminates without brightening oozed into the rear of the van. Chris and Wiles peered out. They had come to a stop in a large, grimy garage that smelled of dust and oil. Walid and Zebar stood shoulder to shoulder about fifteen feet away, holding AK-47s at their waists.

A third man, sporting a pointy beard, strode into view and glared into the van. He did not appear happy.

"Goatfighting is a sport of gentlemen," he spat. He pointed a finger at Chris. "Your outburst cost me a great deal of money!"

That beard. That voice. Chris recognized them somehow.

"I'm sorry," he said. "I—"

"Quiet, infidels!" the man snapped. "Get out of the van! Both of you!"

Chris and Wiles shuffled to the edge of the van's deck and got to their feet, reflexively raising their arms in the face of the weapons pointed at them.

The angry man made a short command in Zazarish to Zebar, who handed off his rifle and approached the captives. Chris and Wiles were quickly searched and relieved of their cash, Wiles's watch, his pill baggie, Chris's spent kebab stick, the cable adaptor, and the twenty-five and ten-dollar poker chips. The stick was tossed on the oil-stained floor and the rest was handed over to the angry man, who regarded the chips and considerable wad of cash with a smirk before pocketing everything. Money won may be twice as sweet as money earned, but money taken is at least 1.5x. Zeb leaned into the van to grab Wiles's skateboard and then dropped it at the bearded man's feet.

Finally, Wiles's attaché case was snipped from its chain with bolt cutters, which Zeb had produced with alarming alacrity from a rack in the corner that held an equally alarming number of swords and various cutting utensils neatly stored next to several dozen folding chairs and some weightlifting equipment.

"Your phones?" the man asked as Zeb handed him the case and received his weapon back.

"Back at the arena," Wiles answered. "Where we have important business to conduct. So, if you would be so kind as to return us there."

"Mr. Wiles," the man chuckled. "Your business at the arena is over. And based on the price you accepted for your phones, it is for the best you not pursue any more."

Wiles shook his head. "I'm afraid you're mistaken, sir. That money you just took represents our winnings from the fights. Our phones are being held for us by the young man at the entrance of the arena."

"That child bought your phones for two pieces of plastic!" the man laughed, holding up the two chips. Walid and Zebar chuckled along, as henchmen will do. "Information, Mr. Wiles. Those who possess the most will get the best of any transaction. Wouldn't you agree, Dr. Dawkins?"

Chris nervously shifted his eyes from Walid's rifle barrel to the man.

With a shaky voice, he said, "I would, Mr. Shwarma."

CHAPTER 50

TABOOR CITY, ZAZARISTAN
MONDAY, 12:44 a.m. ZST

Biz got up, retrieved a water bottle from her bag, and sat back down on the small bed in her hotel room. She took a long drink and checked her phone again. The blue dots remained absent.

The corporeal Wiles and Chris were, of course, nowhere to be found along the route that Biz and Brohug had taken back to the hotel. When they had reached the Fort Worth Plaza empty-handed, Biz's heart sank a little, and when the men's hotel rooms proved empty, it took on more water and went straight down to Davy Jones' Locker.

Even Brohug had seemed a little unnerved that two of his customers were unaccounted for. He made sure Biz was safe in her room, then set out to make a few more sweeps of the neighborhood.

A short time later, he was stopped at another roadblock by Bashir Hallazallah, who asked if Brohug had seen two American men. Brohug reported that he had not. Hallazallah then relieved Brohug of a few zazars in "tolls" and strongly advised him to stay off the streets that night. On his way home, Brohug called Biz to deliver the bad news that his night of searching for Jasper and Chris appeared to be over, but the good news that Hallazallah's search was apparently fruitless as well. Biz thanked him, promised to call in the morning, and hung up.

She got up and paced the length of her hotel room four times. Sat back down and opened the window shades just a crack to see if anything was happening outside on the street in front of the hotel. Nothing. Very dark, with only one functioning streetlight in sight. With this man Hallazallah patrolling the city, going out alone was unthinkable.

She got out her list and reviewed the contingency/emergency plans again. Had another sip of water. Capped the bottle. More pacing. She got down on the carpet floor to do some yoga. Bhujangasana. Bakasana. Halasana.

She checked the blue dots again. Zip. She texted:

Where r u?

to both phones and got no response. She tried calling Wiles, then Chris, and both calls went straight to voicemail. Biz tried to talk herself into believing that this was a good sign. The two men had made some physical progress around the city, which indicated they could be meeting different people and learning the area. The lack of communication could mean that they were possibly engaged in serious business/negotiations and could not afford to be disturbed. She knew Wiles would insist on quieting his phone as a show of respect for anyone he met within a business environment, and if the people they were meeting were due this respect, Biz assumed they were powerful or connected enough to help the plan's success and it would be just a short time before Wiles and Chris returned safely.

There were a few other alternatives to interpret, and while Biz tried not to dwell on these more pessimistic outcomes, she nevertheless decided to enter the number for the US Embassy in Quudia into her speed dial contacts. Surely there was no need, but it's best to be prepared. She typed "AAA US Embassy" to put it at the top of her contact list. Again, just in case.

She called Lou Monte to give him an update and also to prove that picking up the phone to touch base with your friends isn't really so damn hard, is it?

Monte confirmed that Wiles and Chris's locations weren't available on his phone either and also reported that he had not heard from them.

Biz and Monte then discussed the likelihood that something bad was happening right now and what measures could be taken if events revealed that likelihood reached nearer to certainty.

Knowing only what she did at the moment, Biz could make the call to the embassy in Quudia, explain her situation, and say that a "wanted fugitive" was involved. Monte predicted the response of a single team of Special Forces with three objectives. The first would be to arrest Biz. The second would be to go to the airport to seize the plane and arrest Lou. Third: search for and recover Chris and Wiles. Objectives one and two would succeed swiftly and easily. If Wiles and Chris were still missing or somehow being held against their wills, objective three would be neither swift nor easy. Biz and Monte agreed that calling the embassy for help would be the very last of resorts, given what could only be generously called a limited upside.

Biz reminded Monte to have the plane prepared to leave at any moment and that the original plan called for departure just over twenty-four hours from now. Biz hung up and picked up her notebook to record and review the accomplishments of their first six hours in Zazaristan:

Biz: nothing

Jasper: ?/possibly captured/dead

Chris: same

If her mother had written a first-day-of-school note that might have some applicability here, she couldn't recall it.

CHAPTER 51

SOUTH TABOOR CITY, ZAZARISTAN
MONDAY, 12:47 a.m. ZST

Shwarma flinched slightly when Chris spoke his name but
recovered quickly. He couldn't allow too much time to pass before
responding lest he look weak in front of his captives, not to
mention Walid and Zebar.

"What happened to your face?" he shot, buying himself some
time. Chris mumbled something about being kicked.

How did Dawkins know his name? Shwarma shaved a few
possibilities away with Occam's razor. It could only be one of two
things. Possibility One: the Americans had seen his MILF videos
on the internet. Shwarma kept a very close eye on the viewership
metrics and was keenly aware of his numbers. Almost 17,000
views, second most of any AJI affiliate, trailing only that preening
ass Hassan Khalil. Admittedly, however, penetration was less than
he'd like in the Western nations, and Shwarma would risk looking
like a vain nobody if Dawkins and Wiles said, "What videos?" He
went with Possibility Two:

"Who are you with? CIA?"

Now, even if Dawkins and Wiles acted confused or denied the
charge, at least the charge itself suggested Shwarma to be a man of
villainous repute and intrigue at the highest levels of US
government.

Mark A. Henry

Wiles answered, "No, Mr. Shwarma. Chris and I do not represent the US or the government of any nation. We are businessmen. Our politics are, shall we say, fluid."

"Fluid," Chris repeated, waving his arms like a hula dancer.

"I assume Dr. Dawkins drank some medicinal tea at the fights tonight?" Shwarma said.

What was in that tea, again? Chris thought. *It was like, ginger or something. Oh, wait. It was hash. Hash and something...*

Wiles said, "Yes. I'm afraid it may have contributed to the unfortunate episode that led to the ending of the final fight. Allow me to apologize if we caused you to lose your wager."

"I don't *gamble,* Mr. Wiles," Shwarma said, spitting the word out with distaste. "I own the fighter Azizi. I came to watch him in the final fight and I left immediately after that disgrace. I had Walid and Zebar bring you back here."

Wiles said, "Chris and I would be more than willing to make amends. We are gentlemen, after all."

Shwarma scoffed. "And what could you offer me, Mr. Wiles? Whatever it is, you should hope that it will outweigh the value of beheading you both as imperialist agents against Islam and posting the video on the internet." He gave a contemplative look at the rack of knives in the corner, then to Walid and Zebar, who had both heard many stories about Shwarma's swift sword of jihadi justice but had never actually witnessed it in action.

Nervously following Shwarma's eyes, Wiles quickly said, "We can offer you the same thing we offer all our clients, Mr. Shwarma. Opportunity."

Again, Shwarma smirked. "It's getting late," he said, checking Wiles's watch. Walid and Zebar would be going on overtime this week if he couldn't wrap this up. The subcontract under which he hired them out to the goatfight arena as security was for a flat fee and did not include benefits, but now that they returned here on AJI business, they were technically back on the clock. Shwarma was sure their timecards would reflect the extra hours.

294

As Shwarma mentally tallied his payroll, an idea bloomed in Chris's mind. An idea so elegant, so simple, so clear he half expected everyone in the room to see it at the same time, as if it were a physical entity. For the first time in a long time, Chris felt calm and free of anxiety. Despite the fact that he was literally staring down the barrel of a gun, his hands and knees held still and steady. Even if the guns were to fire, Chris confidently assumed the bullets would be deflected or absorbed by some sort of force field generated by the idea to protect its creator.

"Mr. Shwarma," he said, stepping forward. "There is data on one of your computers that is extremely important, but you wouldn't know or even care why. In fifteen minutes, under your full supervision, I can access and modify this data and we will be on our way. All of us will be better off."

Shwarma stared for second, then growled, "Walid, lock these two up."

Well, it was worth a shot.

CHAPTER 52

DALY CITY, CALIFORNIA
SUNDAY, 12:50 p.m. PST

That was fast, Officer Nelson Padilla thought when the knock came on his apartment door. He paused the TV. *I'm hungry*, his brain added, more or less automatically. He was home enjoying his three-day holiday weekend, celebrating the uncertain transactions that led to the discovery of the New World with the *ZombieBot* movie trilogy on TV and now, Chinese food for lunch!

When Padilla put his eye to the peephole, he thought the woman on his stoop looked a little too put-together for a Grubhub delivery person, but these days, you never knew. He opened up and was sorely, sorely disappointed to see that she was not carrying a take-out bag from Panda Sushi, the Chinese/Japanese place that for some reason always had animal rights protesters out front.

"Officer Nelson Padilla?" the woman with no food said.

"Are you from Grubhub?" asked Padilla.

"No, I'm from HawkNews. My name is Sydney Bonner." She produced a business card and handed it over. "Could I ask you a few questions?"

"I was waiting for my lunch," Padilla replied.

Sydney nodded empathetically. "How about this: we talk for a few minutes until your lunch gets here, and when it does, I'll pay for it. How's that sound?"

"I paid already."

"Oh. Hmm. Well, how much was it?"

"Seventeen something."

Sydney dug into her bag and found her wallet. "I only have twenties," she said. "How about I give you forty and you can just tip the delivery guy whatever."

Padilla did the math. Forty minus seventeen was roughly thirty. Takeaway two dollars for a tip left him with twenty-eight. A free lunch plus twenty-eight dollars! He agreed to Sydney's terms, and the two of them went inside and sat at Padilla's crumb-speckled and drink-ringed kitchen table.

Sydney set her laptop down on the logo for the Games of the Not Using a Coaster Olympiad and flipped it open. "Well, I'm sure you know why I'm here and what I want to talk about," she said brightly. That one worked way more often and way better than one would ever imagine.

But not today. Padilla was genuinely stumped and shook his head no. He wasn't a big news watcher. Sydney noted his TV in the next room was paused on a shot of an enormous robot holding a helicopter like a chicken drumstick.

"The San Francisco Mall Bomber," Sydney began. "The FBI arrested a suspect on Friday and brought this suspect to the federal building where you work, correct?"

"I'm not sure. Friday? What was the suspect's name?"

Here's where Sydney had to tread lightly. "That's where we need your help, Officer. You are in charge of processing these suspects, correct?"

Padilla said, "That's right. All federal suspects pass through my checkpoint before getting booked into the system."

Sydney nodded again. "Thank you for your service," she said. "So, you see every suspect that comes into the building?"

Padilla said, "That is affirmative. But can I just ask, how did you find me?"

Sydney smiled. "I'm sorry, I should have mentioned that earlier. I searched LinkedUp for people who work in the Burton Federal Building and found your name."

"What's LinkedUp?" asked Padilla.

"You know, it's for networking. It's sort of like Friendbook, but for work."

"I don't remember signing up for that."

"Yeah, me neither, but there I am. Weird, right?" Sydney gave him another smile. What a world she and Nelson lived in! "Anyway, so I got that list of names from LinkedUp and entered them into the staff directory section of the Burton Building website, which gave me your job description code. I searched *that* using Wangle to figure out who was a uniformed officer and then I put *those* names into Friendbook. Your profile showed you've been working there for six years, which was the longest I found, so I figured you were the most senior officer in charge, right?"

Padilla waggled his head, "Yeah, pretty much."

"Then I just looked up your name on whitepages.com to get your address. You're the third Nelson Padilla I've met today." Sydney paused. Padilla nodded. "OK," she went on, "so my boss wants to do a story about bringing terrorists to justice. And the suspect in this case, even though his name is in the public record at the courthouse, we actually don't know because the courthouse is closed. But you must know it. Do you remember? When the FBI brought him in? On Friday?"

Padilla thought. *Oh yeah, that guy with the black eye. His lawyer was a pain in the ass.*

"Yeah, I remember," he said. "His lawyer was a total bi—she was a bit... rude. Her name was Elizabeth Byner. His name was Christopher... "

Sydney typed a flurry on her keyboard and held her breath.

Padilla tapped his forehead to jar the name loose. "Dawkins. Christopher Dawkins."

Another flurry of keystrokes and Sydney spun the laptop around to display Friendbook with "Christopher Dawkins" typed into the search bar. A list of five profile pictures ran down the left half of the screen.

"Do you recognize him in any of these?" she asked.

Padilla pointed to the second one. No shiner, but definitely the guy. "That's him."

Sydney clicked on Chris's face, snapped the laptop shut, and hustled out the door without another word.

* * *

Meanwhile, not too far away, BSNMC coat Justin Leeds, also on a quest for Chris's identity, had found his way to the doorstep of Bailiff Donald Franklin, the chatty fellow who escorted Chris to his arraignment.

"BSNMC, you say? Well that's something! Can't say I watch too much TV myself. My wife Charlene's the TV watcher in this house. She likes the one where that couple rebuilds the houses. Charlene! We have company! Put some coffee on! You like coffee? Oh, the way the kids drink it today. I do like sports, though. Big Warriors fan. Did you see the game the other night? Delbert had fifty. Preseason, but still. That guy can fill it up. I like their chances this year. Paul says they won't be as good as last season, but I told him, 'Paul you watch, come playoff time they'll be ready.' He said—"

Back in journalism school, Leeds heard a lot about getting an interview subject to "open up," but getting them to "shut up" was not covered as far as he could recall. "Mr. Franklin!" he interrupted. "I'm sorry, but as I said, I'd like to ask you a few questions."

"Sure! Come on in! Charlene! BSN is here! What number is that?"

Leeds followed Franklin into the house and was surprised when Franklin spun around and said, "Hello? Anyone home?"

Leeds sputtered, "Sorry, I'm... what? Were you talking to me?"

"Yes! What number? On the channels."

"Oh. Well, in New York it's thirty-five. Out here I'm not sure. It's probably diff—"

"You don't know your own channel? Don't all the channels have their own numbers? I see the news vans at the courthouse all the time, and they have the number right on the side. Seven, five, two. I like that lady that does the weather on channel seven. She cut her hair short a few months ago and I have to say, I wasn't sure at first, but I said to Charlene a few nights ago that it's kind of grown on me now. We laughed! Charlene! Remember when I said Lynn Chang's hair has grown on me? Because it's short now? My sister cut her hair short like that when she had her kids. She said it's so much easier to take care of like that. Have a seat, what did you want to ask me about? Is it that guy Clyde that murdered his wife last year? When they showed him in the courtroom you could see me on TV. My sister called me that night and said, 'Don! We saw you on TV!' I don't watch too much TV myself... "

Author's Note:
You know what? We'll come back to this later.

CHAPTER 54

NEW YORK, NEW YORK
SUNDAY, 4:00 p.m. EST

Discount flooring, stairlift, life insurance, data protection, Florida tourism, *Hugh Strapman's Circle of Truth* promo.

"Welcome to HawkNews Sunday," Kelly Dixon said from the midday set in Studio Eagle, which was decorated in a lot of clear Lucite with red, white, and blue trim, giving it a Superman's-Fortress-of-Solitude-on-the-Fourth-of-July kind of vibe.

"Developing news from the San Francisco Mall Bomber case. HawkNews has learned the identity of the alleged attacker. Christopher Dawkins of San Anselmo California, was taken into federal custody on Friday and is being charged in the case. His background and motives at this point are still unclear, but stay tuned to HawkNews for all the latest... "

CHAPTER 55

SAN FRANCISCO, CALIFORNIA
SUNDAY 1:05 p.m. PST

"It's the Director," Sully said, reading the face of his cell phone as it rang during lunch. PerpTrak had recommended a Mexican place near their hotel.

He punched the answer button. "Sullivan."

"What the hell happened?" Barry barked.

Sully glanced in alarm at Murph. "Sir? I'm not sure what you mean."

"Why is Chris Dawkins's name all over the news? You were supposed to keep this under wraps until he was in full custody! All we need is for the news to interview this guy while he sits in his living room acting free as a bird, making the Bureau look like a bunch of dickless wonders!"

This was all news to Sully. As it should have been because he had spent the morning doing ninety minutes on the hotel gym treadmill, with the gym's TV tuned to ESPN. If Barry wanted to discuss Washington State's decision to go for two at the end of the game, Sully would have been very well prepared. Nevertheless, the news about Chris Dawkins had just broken, and Sully was back on his heels. Much like Washington State quarterback Trent Kendrick on that final play. The Cougars failed to maintain A-gap discipline, allowing pressure up the middle. Cal had done a tremendous job at

302

disguising their coverage, and their safety blitz clearly affected Kendrick, forcing him out of the pocket. Although if you looked at the all-22 film, he had Jimmy Ward open in the corner of the end zone. It would have been a tough throw, but if Kendrick wants to play at the next level, those are the kinds of throws he is going to have to make.

"Special Agent Murphy and I were unaware that Dawkins's name was public," Sully said, getting Murph up to speed while also spreading the blame a little thinner. "We haven't spoken to the media, and we told everyone out here not to either. Vanzo's office, everyone."

It suddenly hit Sully. Elizabeth Byner. She must have leaked Dawkins's name. She was a crafty one, it turned out.

"I think it was his lawyer," Sully said.

"Elizabeth Byner?" said Barry. He had read all the reports relating to this case and the transcript of Chris's "interrogation" with particular interest. "Find her. When you do, let her know the Director knows who her one other client is, and we may have to open some further investigations into various matters."

Barry had done a little digging and uncovered the nature of Biz and Jasper's relationship and therefore the Twitter-aided deception that Biz had orchestrated the morning of Chris's arrest.

"What do you mean?" asked Sully.

"She'll know what it means. Just tell her that her 'other' client may come onto the FBI's radar if she lets Dawkins talk to the media. Also, tell her I found her white paper interesting."

Sully had his pen out and scribbled, "Other client/white paper interesting" on the back of his lunch receipt. "Will do, Director. Murphy and I will let you know what she says."

CHAPTER 56

DALY CITY, CALIFORNIA
SUNDAY, 1:08 p.m. PST

"So then Judge Myers says, 'How does the defendant plead?' and his lawyer says, 'Not guilty, Your Honor' and I said to myself, 'Something about this guy don't look right, he's guilty for sure.' I can tell most of the time just by looking at them. You've been on the job as long as I have, you just get to know the signs. One time—"

"Did Dawkins say anything?" Leeds butted in. He had learned by now to just yell out questions every thirty seconds or so. Some of the inquiries were carried away by the flood of words from bailiff Franklin's mouth, never to be seen again, but a few had dammed up the flow momentarily and provoked a relevant response. By this method, Leeds had learned Chris's name and verified his identity via Friendbook just as his HawkNews counterpart had.

"No, he didn't say much. That guy was a quiet type. I find most folks enjoy a little conversation, but he didn't say much before he got in the courtroom, and even when the judge set his bail, he—"

"Wait, what?!" Leeds blurted. "Christopher Dawkins is out on bail? How?!"

"Judge Myers asked if he had a job, and he said he worked at some outfit up in San Anselmo, I think, then Myers asked if he had a passport and he said no. Myers wanted him in custody, but Ol' Vanzo wanted bail for some reason, so we tagged him with a bracelet and let him go. If it was up to me—"

"So he's home now?" Leeds asked. He checked his watch. He had spent way too much time here. HawkNews had surely beaten him to the scoop of Chris Dawkins's identity, and Sydney Bonner or someone was camped out on Dawkins's doorstep right now.

"I suppose he is. The ankle bracelet we use—"

Just then Leeds's phone buzzed with an incoming text. Franklin was used to people looking at their phones as he talked, so he wasn't offended when Leeds checked the screen.

HawkNews ID'd suspect: Christopher Dawkins, San Anselmo, CA. Get there now!!

CHAPTER 57

SAN FRANCISCO, CALIFORNIA
SUNDAY, 1:32 p.m. PST

Sully rang the buzzer at Biz's apartment.

In her room at the Taboor City Fort Worth Plaza, Biz could not hear it.

Murph refreshed PerpTrak. "Dawkins is in there all right. Still pacing, looks like."

Sully pounded on the door. "Dawkins! We know you're in there! We want to speak with Ms. Byner. It's very important. A message from the Director!"

Still no response from inside. "They know we have no warrant for this address, Murph. They can hide in there all they want."

"Good. Easier to keep an eye on them," said Murph. There would be no media getting through here while they guarded the door. Besides, HawkNews had just reported that nobody had answered the door at Chris's apartment. The media were on a wild goose chase.

It's a binary system at the Bureau. There are only two ways to go. Field. Or desk. The less time an agent spends in the field, the more time the agent spends at their desk.

Sully looked up and down the hallway as he took his phone from his jacket pocket. "Remember that YouTube we saw last week?"

Murph said, "Which one?"

"The phone thing. With the door."

Murph nodded. "Yes! Let's do it." The field was so fun!

Sully plugged his earbuds into the port on the bottom. "Oops," he said, "I dropped my phone." He knelt and gently placed his phone face-up on the carpeted hallway floor near the door, the earbud wire plugged into the far end of the phone. "I'll just reach down and pick it up."

He squatted down and tapped the phone's face with his finger. "Whoa, I just hit the video record button by mistake." He then flipped the phone over onto its face and pushed it into the pile of the cushy hallway carpet and worked it under the door's threshold. "Oh man, I accidentally pushed the phone under the door. Don't worry, Murph, I'll try to pull it back with my credit card."

He pulled a card from his wallet and slipped it under the door behind the phone. "Nope. Not working. Maybe I could try to get it back by tugging on the cord." Holding the card in place with his left hand, he gently tugged the earbud cord with his right, raising the phone on the other side of the door like a tiny drawbridge. "Darn. The credit card is acting as some sort of fulcrum and the cord is only lifting the phone up inside. What an unfortunate turn of events this is, but if we were to see any probable cause through the phone's camera because of it, we could legally enter the apartment."

After twenty seconds or so, Murph used the same line they heard in the cop life hack video. "Special Agent Sullivan. The card seems to be blocking the phone's way out."

"Of course," Sully responded. He slipped out the card, let the phone flop flat, and carefully pulled it back under the door toward him. He stood up and he and Murph huddled together as he played back the video he had just recorded, all nice and legal.

Aside from an empty ankle bracelet duct taped to a robot vacuum that cruised across the screen about fourteen seconds in, there wasn't much to see.

CHAPTER 58

WASHINGTON, DC
SUNDAY, 4:44 p.m. EST

"A fucking Roomba," Dick Barry said from the back of a car speeding to Reagan Airport.

He was watching live video from inside Biz's living room. Murph and Sully had flashed their federal tin and had the building manager open the door. A quick search confirmed that Byner and Dawkins were both nowhere to be found.

"Did you try calling Byner?" Barry asked.

"Yes, sir," said Sully. "No answer."

"Please, Sullivan, please tell me you didn't leave a recording on her phone of your voice admitting we don't know where Dawkins is."

Relieved, Sully said, "No, sir, I didn't leave a message. But her phone is actually here. We found it on a charger in the bedroom."

"I don't care how this happened, Special Agents. Investigations will handle that later. Chris Dawkins is in the wind and Byner is probably with him. Call NSA. I want the full drag on Dawkins and Byner, going back to Friday morning. Talk to Jasper Wiles, too. The Sixdub guy. He knows something about all this, somehow."

"Yes, sir," said Sully.

An alert popped up on Barry's phone. BSNMC was reporting that Chris Dawkins was free on bail but had not responded to multiple knocks on his apartment door, nor social media messages.

"Christ. I have to get ahead of this now," Barry said. "Sullivan, do not let anyone near that apartment until I get there!" He cut the call and hit the contact for "Robert Myers, Judge (shitlist)."

Sully said, "You're coming here? Director? Hello?"

CHAPTER 59

The sun rarely caught Yazeed Aliyy in bed. This time of year, the temperature seldom dipped below thirty degrees Celsius in the bedroom, and his brother customarily, if unconsciously, claimed at least two-thirds of the mattress real estate. The idea of lounging in bed would have been a confusing notion to Yazeed. Besides, there was business afoot this morning, and Yazeed styled himself a man of commerce.

Yazeed's brothers owned and operated a merchandise cart in the Taboor City market. The cart sold all manner of gadgets and goods ranging from bootleg Bollywood DVDs to those preprinted T-shirts commemorating the championships of teams that actually lost in the championship game. Ignominiously shipped overseas by the leagues and written off as charitable donations, most of these shirts are mysteriously pushed overboard en route, but the ones that survive maintain a certain cachet among hipsters of the developing world and they sold quite well actually.

One item that the Aliyys did not deal in was cell phones. There was a time that they did, but Yazeed came to notice that one customer represented the majority of their cell phone business, usually stopping by the cart several times a week to purchase virtually all they had for sale. Sensing a market, Yazeed

310

independently formed a subsidiary venture that sold cell phones exclusively to this customer and provided, as added value, weekly deliveries every Monday morning at 7:30. In return for this convenience, a small fee would be added to the cost of each phone, naturally.

The customer, Fareek Wazaan, IT Director of AJI, agreed readily to Yazeed's proposal. It meant a steady supply of burner phones (how Yazeed acquired them Fareek neither knew nor wanted to know), and it would save him a few trips to the market each week. (Shwarma expected Fareek to make these trips on his own time and did not reimburse mileage.) As far as the slight cost increase, it was Shwarma's money, and Fareek cared less about that than the origins of the phones.

Yazeed gobbled down two slices of melon and took a piece of naan for the road as he slipped out of the house, gently patting his pockets to be sure his two new phones were still there. Yazeed sometimes wondered what they covered in school on Monday mornings (English) but figured that whatever it was, it's ultimate purpose was to help him make his way in the world and since he was doing just fine thank you, he assured himself that his time was better and more profitably spent as he saw fit.

Yazeed prided himself on being among the earliest risers in the city, and as he took his constitutional through its neighborhoods, he noted which vendors and shops shared his hours and made a point of stopping to say hello to everyone, enjoying the industrious camaraderie he imagined they all shared.

Eventually, Yazeed turned the corner into South Taboor's business district and absorbed the sights and sounds of its awakening. Shops were rolling up their gates, and streets were filling with the smell of cookfires and strong coffee.

The streetcorner café where Fareek took his morning coffee was just up the block, and Yazeed was looking forward to his weekly sale and meeting with his favorite customer. Typically, Fareek would treat Yazeed to a coffee (again, Shwarma's money) and before the two got down to business, they would chat about this and that while avoiding with unspoken mutual agreement the following topics: where Yazeed's phones came from, what purpose they would serve in the future, and why Yazeed was not in school.

A half block from the café, Yazeed stepped behind a large, dusty truck parked on the street and pulled out the two phones for one last inspection. *Never have I had such things*, he said to himself. He tucked them away and strode up to the table where Fareek was sitting.

Fareek greeted his young friend and signaled for the waiter. *"Two coffees,"* he said. As the waiter scurried off, Yazeed sat down and Fareek said, *"And what is new in the world of Yazeed?"*

They chatted for a few minutes and soon the coffees arrived. When he felt the time was right, Yazeed pulled the phones from his pockets and laid them on the table. He was pleased to see the look of surprise on Fareek's face when he saw the Model XXI with its sleek black case.

"5,000 zazars. Each," Yazeed said.

"Whose phones are these?" Fareek asked, picking up Wiles's phone.

"Mine. I bought them," Yazeed answered. *"They're about to be yours, though."*

"For 5,000 each? Never have I paid such a price."

"Never have I had such things," Yazeed said, smooth as could be.

"9,000 for both," said Fareek, inspecting the phone. *"Have you used these phones, Yazeed?"*

"I cracked the codes on both of them for you. 9,500." After Chris had texted his thumbs-up message to Biz the night before and handed the phone to Yazeed, Yazeed had quickly disabled the lock function before it reengaged. Wiles's phone never had the function turned on in the first place.

Fareek moved for his bankroll. *"Is anyone looking for these phones?"*

312

Every now and then, it must be said, someone who sold Yazeed a phone at the arena would be struck with a case of seller's remorse and would come back the following week to try to bargain for the phone's return, usually spouting animated gibberish while thrusting a Fort Worth Plaza poker chip at Yazeed. As if he wanted it back! That's not how business works! In these rare cases, Yazeed calmly pointed out the matchbook-sized sign in the corner near his table that clearly stated (in Zazarish) "All Sales Final" and explained that while he took great pride in his customer's satisfaction, that person's phone was unfortunately long gone, having been transferred to an unknown third party.

And of course, there was that one time, and one time only, when a customer used his wife's phone to track his own to the café on Monday morning and confronted Yazeed there, causing an embarrassing scene for all involved. Since that day, all phones have been delivered with the power off and remained that way until Fareek got them back to his office, where he wiped them of all contacts and data, transforming them into untraceable burners.

"I told you. I bought them fairly. They belong to me. The only people who want those phones would be my other customers," Yazeed said. To close the sale, he said nothing more. Sometimes that's all it takes.

Fareek didn't want trouble. He found life posed many questions and provided relatively few answers, so whenever he got an answer, flimsy though it may be, he hung onto it.

"9,500. Agreed." He put the phone down and counted out ten 1,000 zazar notes. He slid the cash over to Yazeed. *"You have change?"*

"Not... uh... This afternoon I—"

"Keep it, Yazeed," Fareek said with a grin.

"Thanks," Yazeed said.

"No, thank you." Fareek slipped his new phones in his pocket. *"And for the coffee."* Still grinning, he motioned their waiter.

"Make me two more coffees to go. My prosperous friend here will take care of the bill."

CHAPTER 60

NEW YORK, NEW YORK
SUNDAY, 8:45 p.m. EST

Vita-Boost powder, robot vacuum cleaner, robot lawn mower, newspaper, *Hugh Strapman's Circle of Truth* promo.

"Welcome back to HawkNews," Kelly Dixon said. "More shocking details continue to develop in the San Francisco Mall Bomber case. As we reported this afternoon, alleged terrorist Chris Dawkins is not, as previously reported by BSNMC and other news outlets, in federal custody. He was arraigned and granted bail on Friday by Activist Judge Robert Myers of the San Francisco circuit court in California. I'm joined now by former prosecutor Vernon Brooks. Vernon, I'll ask you the question that all of America is wondering: How could this happen? Can Activist Judges make these kinds of decisions, putting the American people at risk?"

Brooks said, "What we have to realize here, Kelly, and the frightening fact is, that Activist Judges like Robert Myers hold virtually unchecked power in situations like this. Their personal and political beliefs can, and unfortunately will influence their decisions. As a prosecutor, I... "

CHAPTER 61

NEW YORK, NEW YORK
SUNDAY, 9:00 p.m. EST

Cat food delivery service, car insurance, cell phones, car insurance, *Let Me Stop You Right There* promo.

"Welcome to *BSNMC Live* and Happy Indigenous Peoples' Day weekend," said Donna Turner brightly.

Her producer blared in her earpiece, "Don't say 'happy'! The indigenous people were slaughtered!"

Donna wiped the smile off her face and said, "We begin this evening with breaking news: a shocking development in the San Francisco Bomber investigation. BSNMC has learned through our social media investigators that suspect Christopher Dawkins is a member of a shadowy, self-titled group known as "the Billionaire's Club." That's *billionaires,* with a 'b'. We have with us Terrance Tillsby, BSNMC Financial Correspondent. Terrance, there are many questions here. Why would a billionaire resort to terrorism? And could their financial means be a factor in their being granted bail by the federal court?"

Tillsby, from his rectangle, looked concerned. "Excellent questions, Donna. I think what we have to keep in mind here is that a billionaire has the financial resources to do just about anything."

"Including the masterminding and execution of a terrorist plot?" Donna asked.

"That would be well within the capabilities of a billionaire, yes."

Donna said, "I see. So, in terms of them being freed from custody, would this be just another case of one of the wealthiest few individuals simply assuming that their privilege makes them above the law and the court system?"

Tillsby nodded. "It's hard to imagine otherwise, Donna. The facts here speak for themselves... "

CHAPTER 62

TABOOR CITY, ZAZARISTAN
MONDAY, 7:31 a.m. ZST

Biz had spent the past few hours waiting for the sun to rise, trying not to think about the colossal shitshow that was erupting back in the US. Anxiety and jet lag had kept her up all night, and each time she dared to refresh the news apps on her phone, the reports became worse and worse. Chris was now the focus of a full-on media circus. The fact that he hadn't been seen or interviewed only increased the frenzy. It was hard for her to imagine that the FBI hadn't discovered Chris's escape from the tracking bracelet by now, but none of the reports had mentioned him being a fugitive. Yet. Biz assumed that if the FBI indeed knew anything about Chris's "escape," they would try keep a tight lid on it. But that could change with the next news update.

At several points during the night, her finger had hovered over the contact for "AAA US Embassy," but hitting it and calling in the cavalry would somehow be an admission of complete failure to protect her friends. A stew of stubbornness, hope, denial, and faith had tided her over until morning, and she couldn't bring herself to admit defeat. Yet.

The best Biz could hope for now was to somehow get back out into the city and find two hung-over men who somehow avoided roving gangs of murderous thugs to survive the night, then haul ass

318

back to California, where she would be disbarred and then, along with the only two clients she'd ever had, probably imprisoned.

On that cheery note, it was time to get the day started. Her finger flicked away the contact for "AAA US Embassy," and with a deep breath, she scrolled down and tapped the contact for Brohug.

"Brohug. It's Biz Byner... No, they never came back... Can you pick me up?... Ten minutes, out front?"

Nine minutes and forty seconds later, Brohug's Vanagon screeched to a halt in the port cochère of the Fort Worth Plaza Hotel and Casino and Biz got in.

Five stars.

"Back to the arena," said Biz. "We have to pick up Jasper and Chris's trail somehow. Let's go." Brohug peeled out of the hotel parking lot, making up for a lack of mirror-checking or turn signal with plenty of horn.

Biz eyed a rifle lying on the floor of the Vanagon nestled between Brohug's seat and the driver's door. *Was that there last night?*

"What will we do if we run into that Hallazallah guy, Brohug? Just how dangerous is it for an American out here?"

Brohug said, "Don't worry. He won't be out in day. Too many people now." It was true that the streets of Taboor City were beginning to awaken with vehicles and people as opposed to the night before when they were virtually deserted, save for the post-goatfight crowd. Biz stared at Brohug's weapon for a few more seconds before turning her attention to the faces they passed on the street, hoping to somehow spot Jasper and Chris.

After circling the hotel's immediate neighborhood and at Brohug's suggestion checking the nearby medical clinic, another hotel, and a small rooming house, they arrived once again at the site of the fights. A daylight investigation of the arena's alley entrance had yielded nothing but a cigarette pail and a few scraps of orange peel near a securely locked door, which Biz pounded on for a minute with no effect.

"Bartender said they left through other door," Brohug pointed out. They retreated to the Vanagon and quickly semicircumnavigated the block. Brohug parked on the corner. The sloped, metallic bulkhead doors that marked Jasper and Chris's last reported location lay about thirty meters ahead.

Biz swung open her door, stood up on the jamb to get a better vantage point, and looked up and down both axes of the bustling street corner. Food carts steamed and cigarettes smoked, adding a silver haze to the low sun's morning light.

The storefront to the right of the hatchway looked like a barbershop and the one to the left appeared to be a rug store. In the US, there would have been security cameras on every street corner and half the businesses, but to Biz's dismay, there were none to be spotted here.

She jumped to the ground as Brohug walked around to join her, scanning the street as well.

"Will there even be anyone down there now?" Biz asked, gesturing to the arena's hatch-like door.

Brohug said, "I think no, probably."

Nevertheless, Biz quickly walked to the doors, bent to grab the handles, and gave a tug. The doors budged open a crack but were clearly bolted from the inside. She rapped with her knuckles, but she could immediately tell that the tinny *bings* she produced wouldn't carry too far inside and would probably go unnoticed. She straightened up and took another quick look up and down the street. She stepped up and stomped on the metal doors. *BA-BLANG! BA-BLANG! BA-BLANG!* She paused to wait for any response from within, then: *BA-BLANG! BA-BLANG! BA-BLANG!* It felt good to be stomping on something, and she carried on a little longer than was probably necessary.

A few Zazari heads turned in curiosity to see what all the racket was about, but none were interested enough to stop and ask

any questions. This woman was clearly upset about something and
it was probably best to—*BA-BLANG! BA-BLANG! BA-BLANG!
BA-BLANG! BA-BLANG! BA-BLANG!*

"Would you mind please stopping that?"

Biz and Brohug looked up to see a Zazari man with a slightly
askew light brown kufi leaning out the door of the neighboring rug
shop. Pinching his temples and rubbing his eyes, he took advantage
of the pause to simply say, *"Thank you,"* and began easing his way
back inside with the deliberate movements of the severely hung-
over.

"Wait!" Biz called, her hand shooting out. "Wait a second!"

"My shop is closed this morning," Mohammad Mohammad
said. He began shutting the door in order to go back to bed. The
night before, he had decided that walking all the way home with a
pocketful of cash, a bellyful of alcohol, and word of Bashir
Hallazallah on the streets would be unwise, electing instead to lay
his weary head on a makeshift mattress of rugs in the shop.

"Please wait!" Biz shouted, jumping off the (slightly dented)
arena doors as Mohammad winced at the sound of her voice.

Biz said, "My friends are missing! They were here last night,
they left from here, I don't know where they went." She bounded
over to the rug shop door, prepared to stick a foot in if necessary.
Brohug slid up behind her.

Something told Mohammad that this woman would not let the
matter rest until she got an answer. Her companion, who now stood
eye-to-eye with him despite standing on street level twenty
centimeters lower, also seemed the type to get what he wanted.
"I've not seen anyone," Mohammad said. "I am sorry. Good luck
with your search." He glanced at his fake Rolex. *Look at the time,
you drunken fool!!* A return to bed was probably not happening.

Biz held out her phone. It showed the selfie she took with
Jasper and Chris and those nice guys from the kebab stand. The
older man had a wide grin while the younger two chose to mean-
mug the camera. "Have you seen these men? The Americans?"

321

Mohammad, shielding his eyes from the morning sun's glare, peered at the photo. Ah. Now this was a sticky situation. Common practice dictated that acknowledging an attendee of, or event relating to, a goatfight to a person who was not present at said goatfight is strongly frowned upon. To confirm that Jasper and Chris, his companions from the night before, were present, let alone the circumstances of their contentious exit at the hands of Walid and Zeb, would be bad form. Goatfighting is a sport of gentlemen.

As Mohammad was internally debating, Biz dug in her bag and produced the fold of cash Wiles had given her. She slipped off a hundred and offered it. "Please. Anything you can tell me would be helpful."

On the other hand, Mohammad knew that Walid and Zebar were employed on a contract basis and had no formal affiliation with the Taboor City Goatfighting Arena. Therefore, they were technically *not* protected by its code of secrecy.

Mohammad plucked the bill from Biz's fingertips. "I have seen these men. Last night."

Involuntarily, Biz grabbed Mohammad's sleeve. "Where? Where did they go?" Brohug inched a little closer.

Mohammad said, "I saw them last night. I can't tell you where." His eyes glanced at the hatchway next door. "But they left with two men. Walid and Zebar. They work for AJI Security."

"What's that?" Biz said. She still had a hold of Mohammad's shirt.

He shrugged. "It is what I said: security."

"Wait," Biz said. "They left with security guards? Were they *with* the guards or were they being *kicked out* by the guards?"

Mohammad looked conflicted for a moment until the great statesman Benjamin Franklin made another appearance and silently made his case.

"There was an incident," Mohammad offered cagily. "Your friends left... unwillingly. Walid and Zebar did not return after."

Brohug looked up from his phone. "AJI Security and Party Rental," he read. "Two stars. No phone number."

"Is there an address?" asked Biz. "We have to talk to these guys."

"South Taboor," Brohug reported. "GPS says eighteen minutes. I do it fifteen, no problem."

Biz jotted her number down and gave it to Mohammad. "If you see my friends, call this number. Please." She spun around and jogged back to the Vanagon, yelling back words of thanks in the worst Zazarish Mohammad had ever heard.

Just as she swung open the VW's door, a young man carrying two Styrofoam coffee cups rounded the corner and almost walked right into it.

"Sorry!" Biz quickly said, jumping into the vehicle.

Fareek stepped back nimbly and replied with a small two-fisted toast. *"Not a drop spilled,"* he said. He then continued on his way up the block to his meeting with Mohammad, who he thought could probably use the coffee, judging by the slightly slurry late-night voicemail the man had left, inviting him to the shop in the morning to discuss some business.

The Vanagon roared away from the curb and exactly fifteen minutes later came to rest after skidding a good twenty-five feet in AJI's dirt parking lot.

CHAPTER 63

SAN FRANCISCO INTERNATIONAL AIRPORT
SUNDAY, 7:40 p.m. PST

Murph stood on the polished concrete that orangely reflected the sodium lights of the hangar. The Director's plane had just landed.

Barry had reacted quickly when he learned of Chris's escape from his ankle bracelet. He immediately called a panicked Judge Myers, who grudgingly accepted Barry's offer to put in a word with HawkNews to help turn around this Activist Judge business. In return, Myers promised to revoke Chris's bond and have an arrest warrant issued for the dangerous fugitive. He signed the paperwork and electronically filed it while still at his mother-in-law's house in Sacramento. Murph had done some legwork around town and then driven up to pick up the warrant, while Sully stood sentry at Biz's apartment and collected the nuggets of data that NSA mined as they rolled in, passing them along to Murph, who would pick up the Director and give the latest report.

Barry stepped to the ground and took a file from Murph. "Thanks for not stepping on your own dick," he said by way of appreciation.

"Where is this guy, Special Agent?" he snapped, fixing Murph with a glare. He started walking for Murph's vehicle, parked out on the tarmac.

Murph trotted to keep up. "You know Drednott, sir?" he asked.

324

"Who?" said Barry.

"The rapper. Rap artist. Hip hop impresario."

"Do you know where Dawkins is or not?" Barry shouted.

"We do know where he is not," Murph said. "He's not here."

Barry's hands made a slight, involuntary twitch toward Murph's throat.

"He left the country, sir," Murph clarified. "He left US airspace traveling northwest about ten o'clock Saturday night."

"How do you know this?" Barry asked.

"Drednott, sir. He has a business partnership with Wowiecloth. As part of their agreement, Wowiecloth sponsors a webcam on Drednott's airplane that they use as a social media tool for advertising. You know, like 'If you think you get stains on *your* sofa, just imagine Drednott's airplane sofa. But look, the Wowiecloth upholstery is always spotless!' Anyway, Chris Dawkins slept on that couch Saturday night as the plane was in flight. The footage was dark, and he had that swollen eye, but it's him. My friend at NSA pulled facial recognition from the web and we just confirmed it. But the webcam's feed went out at the same time the plane's transponder went dark."

Barry nodded. It was always something like that, it seemed.

"Anyone else with him on the plane? The lawyer, Elizabeth Byner?" Barry asked.

"We only saw Dawkins, sir," said Murph.

"Reports on the internet? That Chris Dawkins the terrorist suspect is flying around on private jets? Tell me this is still contained, Murphy. We can't let the public know that we let him escape."

Murph answered, "Nothing trending, sir. Like I said, it's pretty hard to recognize him in the video, and it wasn't up for very long. The comment section of the webcam was empty."

"So where did he go?" Barry asked.

"Sully called the FAA. They think the plane's transponder may have had some electrical problems over the Arctic Circle.

Atmospheric conditions in the area may have affected the electronics somehow. No contact since then."

"A crash?" said Barry. He would take a crash in the Arctic Circle right now. "What does Eielson say?" Eielson Air Force Base's radar in Fairbanks might have picked up something. "Did you flag the transponder ID if it comes back online?"

"Eielson reported no sign of a crash, sir," Murph said. "We have to assume Dawkins is alive. And yes, the plane's transponder has been flagged. We'll know if it pops up again."

"Did you talk to this Drednott guy?" Barry asked. "How is he connected to Dawkins?"

"I spoke to Drednott's manager. He had no idea who Dawkins was, and couldn't say who was using the jet this weekend, but we ran the tail number. That plane was formerly owned by Sixdub."

"Jasper Wiles." Barry said.

Murph nodded. "On Thursday night Jasper Wiles appeared in a selfie taken by a minor web celebrity with what may be Dawkins's shoulder, which corroborates Dawkins's story that they had drinks together. I checked out the nightclub where the photo was taken, Wiles's boat, as well as his office at Sixdub. No sign of him. I went to the Olympic Club, and he hasn't been there since Friday morning. We can't locate him," Murph said. "Which supports something interesting NSA turned up on the internet: a clickbait ad reporting that Wiles may have fled the country ahead of some debts. Possibly to Central Asia."

"Central Asia? Fuck, Murphy, why didn't you say so? This is all connected to MILF! We're going to need boots on the ground over there." They had reached the Trax and Barry took the passenger seat. "Byner's apartment," he barked. He took out his phone. "Who's running this at NSA?"

CHAPTER 64

There were no windows in Conference Room B in MILF/AJI headquarters, but Chris's watch let them know it was almost eight. Wiles's Omega had been confiscated the night before, but when Zebar held up Chris's be-Timexed wrist with a questioning look, Shwarma shook his head no.

Last night, on Shwarma's orders, Wiles and Chris had been marched to this small room at the point of Walid's weapon.

The Americans then spent the night discussing the pros and cons of their situation as Chris slowly sobered up. Pros: Straining the very limits of credulity, they had managed to locate and in fact infiltrate what they presumed to be MILF headquarters and thus, the objective of their plan to reset the operation's computer backups was within reach. All of this was accomplished in just a matter of hours. Cons: Their phones had been swindled away, they lost all their money, their reputations in the goatfighting community had been tarnished, and they were being held against their will by known terrorists. This was also all managed in a very brief time.

Conference Room B contained a small oval table, six chairs, and a whiteboard with a dry-erase marker. In terms of mechanisms or materials that would aid a breakout, there wasn't much to work with, but one could argue that anyone in the room was able, perhaps even encouraged, to literally draw up as many theoretical escape plans as one wished, if only to pass the time.

Chris was just completing an arcing arrow that led to a map of the US as Wiles dozed in a chair.

"Jasper, wake up! I hear something outside," Chris said. He scrambled to the heavy wooden door, trying to see out the narrow, wire-reinforced window. What he couldn't see was the small whiteboard on the other side of the door that read in Shwarma's handwriting: "Infidels 0100 – 1800." A pair of AJI employees came into view in the hallway. Chris interrupted their conversation by banging on the door and yelling, "Hey!"

The two men startled and stopped. They looked at the slice of Chris's face the window allowed, read the whiteboard, then kept walking as Chris shouted, "Hey!" again, now at their backs.

Wiles blinked away some sleep. "I could really go for a Dong Quai," he said.

Meanwhile upstairs, Shwarma was at his desk preparing for what was sure to be a busy day. He was still working out the details as to how he could best leverage his capture of the Americans before disposing of them, but he was confident that a positive outcome would present itself. The contents of Wiles's confiscated attaché case, which he had inspected the night before, were intriguing to say the least. They could be sold to any number of international players or governments, to say nothing of ransoming them back to the man himself for a botcoin or two in the short time the unsuspecting fellow had left.

Shwarma had also done some brief Wangling and Friendbooking in the wee hours that had revealed Wiles to be some sort of sought-after white collar outlaw. A search of Dr. Chris Dawkins's name had turned up no significant results at the time.

Shwarma planned to visit with Wiles and his drug-addled partner shortly in order to manipulate them into sharing any intelligence they may have, but first he had to do some executive housekeeping, checking his email and so forth.

Sweet couscous! When it rained it poured. A tracking update from IHL shipping was in his inbox. The Weapon was scanned through the cargo station at ZKN at 0330 that morning and was scheduled to be delivered today! There was also an email from a Johnny Triad reminding him that final, final payment would be due when IHL's website confirmed on-site delivery, all as discussed and agreed upon in previous emails. Shwarma was one of those guys who responds with unnecessary messages, so he hit REPLY to Triad and typed, "OK."

He then checked his Ucoolbro account. 22.07. Damn it. He thought owning a nuclear bomb would bring it up a little.

"Samir!" he bellowed to his assistant. *"Meet me outside Conference Room B in ten minutes. Bring four coffees, Fareek, and Walid. Tell Walid to bring his rifle."*

Samir poked his head in Shwarma's doorway and snapped off a short salute before hustling away.

Twelve minutes and forty seconds later, Shwarma rounded the corridor corner and approached Walid and Samir, who were waiting outside the conference room door. Walid held his AK casually, while Samir intently held four coffees on a spiral notebook he was using as a tray.

"Where's Fareek?" Shwarma asked, coming to a stop a few feet away from the narrow window in the conference room's door. Chris's face could be seen looking out.

His gaze focused on the coffees, Samir said, *"He wasn't at his desk. I texted him and he said he was picking up some burner phones and he would be in later."*

Shwarma scowled. *"Since when does it take so long to buy phones? Text him back and tell him NOT to join us if he gets here,"*

It would not do at all to have Fareek saunter into the meeting late as if he were the big wheel around here and besides, there may be some business discussed with the Americans that would not be for Fareek's ears. Shwarma would meet with him later if necessary.

"Walid, open it," Shwarma said. Walid stepped forward, waved Chris away from the window with his rifle barrel, and unlocked the door. He stepped in to see Chris, who had retreated to the far corner, and Wiles, who was seated at the table.

Satisfied that the room was secure (and the Americans got a good long look at his weapon), Walid went back into the hallway. He pinched a coffee from Samir as he passed, and Samir stepped into the room to place the remaining three cups on the table.

Only after Samir had cleared out did Shwarma enter. As the door was closing, he placed a hand on the pistol he wore on his hip and shouted, "Quiet, Infidels! Or your heads will be my trophies!" for the benefit of Samir and Walid. When the door clicked shut, he turned to study the whiteboard for a few moments. "What is this here, a drone? Where do you plan on getting that?" he asked, pointing at Step IV of Chris's plan. "No matter, no matter. As I said last night, you are my guests. Keeping you locked in here was for your safety. Zazaristan can be very dangerous at night."

He selected a coffee and settled into a chair.

"It's daytime now, Mr. Shwarma. May we go?" Wiles asked. Of course, the plan was improbably unfolding (to a certain extent at least; the original plan forecasted for a much lower threat of beheading), and Wiles wanted to create a bit of need without tipping his hand.

"Of course," Shwarma said, spreading his arms, the picture of a gracious host. "But didn't Dr. Dawkins say last night that he needed access to my computer?"

Wiles had anticipated this, of course. When Chris was struck with what he thought was the brilliant insight of politely asking Shwarma for access to his computer, Wiles knew it would not work out.

Wiles couldn't blame him, however. Who among us has not shot a pure beam of truth through the dark, swirling mists of intoxication only to have it washed out by the bright, oh so bright, light of the following day?

"Yes. That," Wiles said, getting up from his chair. He helped himself to a coffee. "My friend here was feeling the effects of some... substances last night. Speaking of which, I believe you're holding some medication of mine?"

Shwarma shook his head. "Later," he said.

"I see," Wiles said. And he did. "I'll be truthful here, Mr. Shwarma. The truth is about all you've left us with. Chris Dawkins is not really a medical doctor. Just another misunderstanding that was one of many last night, I'm afraid. He is in fact a highly skilled computer engineer. As you know, they aren't known for their salesmanship. What he was trying to convey last night was that a man like yourself, an operation like yours, has vulnerabilities in your computer network. It's almost a certainty. We can help you eliminate these vulnerabilities. For a fee, of course."

Chris had forgotten about the part of the night before when he just came out and asked Shwarma if he could root around in his computer.

Author's Note:
Did you?

"And what kind of vulnerabilities, Mr. Wiles?" Shwarma asked. "Financial? Legal?" He took a sip of coffee without breaking eye contact with Wiles.

That thing was happening where some unspoken knowledge was being put forth. Chris sometimes recognized the thing, but rarely the knowledge. His eyes darted to Wiles, who was also taking a drink.

"You may have heard I've had some recent experience in those areas," said Wiles, setting his cup down. "But I would caution you not to believe everything you see on the internet, Mr. Shwarma."

Before Shwarma could respond, Wiles nodded to the sole cup remaining on the table. "Chris, enjoy your coffee. It's quite good."

Chris hesitated for a second, but then reached to pull the cup toward him. As Shwarma watched, Chris took a very small sip of coffee, making sure it wasn't dosed with more Zazari dope. It was hot and bitter, but it seemed clean. He was terribly thirsty, and his head felt like it was stuffed with newspaper.

Wiles went on. "When you relieved us our belongings last night," Wiles said, and paused for another sip.

"Compensation for what he cost me at the goatfight!" Shwarma said, pointing at Chris.

"Of course," said Wiles. "A fair exchange. A gentleman honors his debts." Another sip.

"Sorry about that," Chris said.

Shwarma scowled at him. Azizi's reputation may never fully recover.

Turning back to Wiles, Shwarma said, "I couldn't help but notice the files in your bag. You've done business with some interesting organizations."

Wiles nodded to allow that this may be the case.

"As you know, I value discretion as much as the next man," said Shwarma. "But I'd be interested to hear your experiences with these operations." Shwarma was always looking to expand his network.

"I'm just the face of this, Mr. Shwarma," said Wiles. "You need to hear from the brain. Chris, tell this man everything you know about the organizations in those files. The truth. He'll know if you're lying."

"Mr. Wiles... uh... " Chris stammered.

"The El Mariachi Drug Cartel, the North Korean Bureau of Fusion, the Peppino Crime family. Go ahead, tell him."

"Those things... they don't... uh... "

"Chris, if we expect Mr. Shwarma to trust us, we must first offer him our trust. The truth."

"Exist," said Chris. "They don't exist."

"Excuse me?" said Shwarma.

"I assure you they do," Wiles said to Shwarma, with a knowing wink.

"Why did he say they didn't?" Shwarma said, visibly annoyed. Unspoken knowledge was one thing. Knowledge unspoken was quite another. What were these two getting at? He really should have read those contracts more carefully last night. But it was late and they were full of dense jargon, all metadata this and proxy server that. He now wished Fareek were here after all to properly grill these tech guys, although he's another one of these smug I-know-something-you-don't-know types.

A few seconds passed and Chris realized Wiles intended to keep quiet.

Chris said, "Well, because they... don't?" His eyes shifted to Wiles, who nodded at Shwarma.

Enough of this nonsense. "Quiet!" Shwarma snapped. He pulled out his phone, a Model XV, and busily tapped away at it.

El Mariachi Drug Cartel. Tap. Mexican take-out, movie from 1992. *Hmm.*

Taptaptappytaptappytaptap.

North Korean Bureau of Fusion. Tap.

Wangle needed some clarification. Did he mean North *KOREA* Bureau of Fusion? *Aha, now we're getting somewhere.* Tap.

Wikipedia: North Korean Nuclear and Weapons of Mass Destruction. *Why did you ask, Wangle!? How did that possibly help?*

This was going nowhere. None of these organizations Wiles claimed to have worked with appeared to even exist on the inter—

Shwarma's head snapped up from his screen. He eyed Chris with renewed interest.

"Am I to understand you have the ability to wipe the existance of something from the internet itself? Completely? Is that what you're offering me?"

Chris glanced at Wiles, who still seemed content to sit quietly.

"That is our intention, yes." Chris wanted another hit of coffee, but was afraid his shaking hands would spill it. He pressed them to the table.

Shwarma considered his situation. The Weapon was within his reach. He would possess it in a matter of hours. Flipping it would take time, but no more than a few weeks. Meanwhile, he feared his double identity may be starting to show some cracks. That was never going to last forever. When he fully assumed the Mohammad Mohammad persona, a thorough scrubbing of Wahiri Shwarma and his dynamic, yet incriminating videos from the internet may be prudent, indeed necessary. Fareek gave him the impression that to do such a thing was impossible, but these Americans clearly had the ability to do the job. And it's not as if they'd be around to talk about it afterward.

"Interesting," said Shwarma.

"Yuh-huh." Chris said. Under the table, Wiles gave Chris a foot-nudge.

"I could set you up with the software this morning," said Chris. "Let's go to your office." *B cool.*

"But first, we must discuss price of course," said Wiles suddenly. "I'm prepared to offer you the rate of fifteen botcoins. Exclusive license, data backup, installation, tutorial, and confidentiality agreement included."

It's important to attach value to these things.

Out of habit, Shwarma said, "Eight. Not a botcoin more. But first, I must discuss this with my technical man."

"Is he here?" asked Wiles. "Chris would be happy to meet with him."

"He's late this morning," said Shwarma, recognizing in Wiles a look that said, *Engineers, am I right?* "We will discuss this more when he arrives, perhaps later this afternoon." Shwarma got up and headed for the door.

It is also important not to appear too eager.

Chris said, "Mr. Shwarma, we need to contact our friend. We lost our phones last night. Could we make a phone call?"

Shwarma considered this. It was probably for the best that these two were out of touch for now. Surely, they would be shopping their services all over town if given the chance. "I'm afraid not," he said, backing toward the door and knocking to be let out by Walid. "After we discuss our business later today, you will be free to go."

He drew his pistol as Walid opened the door for him. "I told you infidels, Zazaristan is a dangerous place!" he shouted back into the room. With that, he slipped out into the hallway and the door locked once again.

Wiles finished his coffee in two gulps. Chris was impressed that he could drink it so quickly without burning his mouth. Wiles set his cup down, closed his eyes, and took three deep breaths.

"It's close, Chris. I can feel it."

Chris thought he should agree, although he wasn't sure what "it" was.

"He's going to let you access his computer," said Wiles. "Chris, this man is not a true believer, he's a profiteer. Did you notice how he changed his tone when he was in front of his men? He wants to do business with us, business that he doesn't want them to know about."

"What do we do?" asked Chris.

"We have to be patient, but ready," Wiles said. Chapter 10: "Be Patient, But Ready."

"I need my phone, Jasper," Chris said. "We need to call Biz to let her know we're OK, and it has the software to reset the backup drive."

"Can't you do it manually if you had access?"

"It would take much longer, and what I was doing would be obvious to whoever was watching, but yes, I think so."

"Good. I'm going to take a short nap," Wiles announced, lying down on the floor. "Wake me if Shwarma comes back."

335

Chris mumbled, "OK." He then tried to be patient but ready, but the coffee had made him a little jittery.

CHAPTER 65

SOUTH TABOOR CITY, ZAZARISTAN
MONDAY, 8:02 a.m. ZST

AJI/MILF headquarters was a beige, two-story building sitting incongruously by itself in the sparsely developed land southeast of Taboor City. It was windowless, but featured two dark brown vertical battens and one horizontal batten delineating the first and second floor, making the building look like two-thirds of the world's largest, yet easiest Rubik's cube. The only vehicles kept on the property were the van that Wiles and Chris rode in the previous night and Shwarma's Yamaha 700 motorcycle, both currently parked in the garage in the rear of the building. Shwarma made everyone in his employ park a quarter mile away in a vacant lot for reasons of *"Security! What does it say on the front of this building, people?"*

So, the parking lot was empty, save for a cloud of dust and a VW Vanagon.

"Follow me, Brohug," Biz said as she jumped to the dry, gravelly ground. As she and Brohug approached to the front door in the center of the building, Biz asked for a translation of the faded metal sign bolted to the building.

Brohug dragged his finger along the Zazarish script for Biz's benefit as he read, "AJI Security, Party Rentals, Consulting."

Biz pressed the cracked doorbell while looking up into the security camera mounted on the exterior wall. She waited a few seconds, then rang again while pressing her ear to the door. It was warm from the morning sun already. She could hear a faint buzzing inside but no movement or voices.

* * *

Zeb should have been at the front desk watching the security monitors, but he had had a late night and was making himself a coffee in the break room. (He had to brew a new pot, because Samir had emptied the last one and in his hurry, neglected to start another.) Shwarma, who also had monitors in his office, was visiting with his American guests in Conference Room B. Fareek, too, had monitors in his office/studio space adjacent to the garage, but of course, he hadn't arrived at work yet.

* * *

Biz tried the knob. It was locked. "There's no one here," she said. Biz walked slowly back to the Vanagon. If they couldn't locate these men Walid and Zebar, or find any sign of Jasper and Chris here, her options narrowed greatly.

"Brohug," she said, "call anyone you might know that might have gone to the fights last night. Ask if they saw Jasper or Chris. I'm going to look around back."

Brohug thought he might know a person or two. He pulled out his phone and returned to the air-conditioned Vanagon to make the calls as Biz walked away to the right.

Biz wanted to at least make a complete circuit of the building before they moved on, and she quickly made her way around the corner. Coming around back, she saw a delivery truck idling in front of a roll-up garage door at the center of the building, thirty feet away. A man in an IHL Central Asia khaki short set uniform

338

pressed the doorbell button, waited a second, then rapped on the door. A large cardboard box completely glazed with packing tape lay on the ground at his feet. The man checked his watch, then picked up the box and turned back to the truck. The name stitched above the right pocket of his shirt read: Anwar.

A hot gust of air kicked up, and Biz held her hijab down as she passed close to the rear of the truck. Since Zazaristan's wind was the exact same temperature as the truck's exhaust, it was impossible to say where the hot air came from. Anwar grinned at her as he approached.

* * *

In the Vanagon, Brohug had just sent out a group text to some friends when his phone rang from a blocked number.

"Yes."

A male Zazarish speaker with an unusual accent asked, *"Brohug Vidadik? The driver?"*

"Yes," said Brohug. *"Can I help you?"*

"You were hired by an American, Jasper Wiles. I need to speak to him, please."

Brohug was tempted to ask this man some questions, but even in the asking he would reveal information that was beyond his purview.

"I'm sorry, sir. I do not discuss my customer's business."

"Of course. I understand. May I ask if you are available for hire today?"

"No, I'm booked today. I'm sorry."

"Tonight?"

"I'm afraid not, sir."

"Tomorrow, then."

"What is your name, sir? I will call you when I am free."

Dick Barry hung up. Now he knew what he needed to know. An hour ago, NSA had turned up that Wiles had posted a review of

Vidadik via Yelp. And not just for some task that Wiles was requesting from California. He was there in Zazaristan! Wiles had commented on the smell of Vidadik's car in his review. Byner would surely be with him. Dawkins too, probably.

When Brohug answered his phone, NSA software embedded in the cellular signal activated the phone's GPS and allowed Barry access to it. Pretty routine. Barry was now able to look down from the digital heavens at a green dot on a map representing Brohug's location at a remote building in South Taboor City. Just remote enough. Extraction would have to be quick and quiet of course, but there could be no witnesses. He knew just the man for the job.

Brohug put his phone away. The odd call made him uneasy. He got out of the Vanagon and went looking for Biz.

* * *

In Zazarish, Anwar said, *"You work here? No one answered the door."*

Biz's mind scrambled for the translation. Something like, *Working hard or hardly working?*

She chuckled to buy time as her mind raced for the Farsi greeting that she learned all those years ago.

"Can I have one of those cigarettes?" she said.

Now Anwar chuckled, looking down at the pack he had nestled in his shirt pocket. He never said no to some harmless flirting, and this was the best-looking warehouse worker he had ever seen. He set down the box and unclipped a tablet from his belt. *"You'll have to sign first, then you can have one."*

Biz thought she got that one. *I want something, you want something.* She actually had a response for this!

"You and I want different things," she said.

"Riiiiiight," said Anwar. *"I want a delivery confirmation signature."* He tapped his tablet. *"You want a cigarette. And your package too, right?"*

When in doubt, smile and nod.

* * *

In the break room, Zebar's coffee was still dripping through the filter. Shwarma flatly refused to purchase a Keurig machine for the office.

* * *

Biz scribbled with a black stylus on Anwar's tablet. After handing it back, she pulled out her phone and showed Anwar the photo of Chris and Wiles. *"Have you seen these men? You know Walid? Zebar?"*

Anwar squinted at the phone, accepted the tablet and confirmed there was a valid signature, then grabbed his pack of smokes. He shook his head as he shook one out toward Biz. *"I don't know those men. Walid? Zebar? No. I just make deliveries."*

Biz's shoulders slumped. This place was a dead end. No one had answered the front or back door. Even if Walid and Zebar worked here, Biz knew they were on the job late last night and it was unlikely that they'd be back here so early in the morning. Biz had to keep moving. There was no time for a smoke break. On the other hand, it had been stressful morning.

As she slipped a cig from Anwar's golden softpack, Brohug suddenly appeared from around the corner. Anwar noticed him first. He didn't want to give up a third cigarette, not to mention turn this whole thing into a sausage party, so he waved to Brohug and pointed to the box.

"Hey buddy, why don't you take care of this package for the lady here? Bring it back around to the front," he called out.

Brohug approached and scooped up the package. In English, Biz told him, "Brohug, we need to be going." He nodded and headed back to the Vanagon, where he securely strapped The

Weapon into the trunk compartment with an elastic cargo net.
Count 'em. Five.

* * *

Zeb, holding his brimming mug, stopped in the hallway to chat
with Rahim, who had heard tell of a wild night at the goatfights last
night, what did Zeb know?
Zeb hoovered up a shallow sip and raised a finger.

* * *

Anwar said, *"Alone at last. Now let's smoke in peace like civilized
people. My name is Anwar."* He produced a silver Zippo from what
could only be a specially designed Zippo pocket in his shorts. He
sparked it and carefully handed the lighter over to Biz. The hot
wind gusted once more and snuffed it out. Biz got it going again
and first-degree murdered a half-inch of tobacco.
The Vanagon rolled around the corner of the building and
pulled up next to her. Anwar disappointedly watched as Biz
climbed in. She shut the door and held the lighter out the window
to return it to him. *"Thank you,"* she called as Brohug reversed
away. *"Your ass is as beautiful as the moon!"*
"Still got it," Anwar thought, lighting up. He shrugged and got
back in his truck.
"Back to the hotel, Brohug," said Biz. He nodded, eyeing the
cigarette nervously. Biz noted the look. She hadn't had a cigarette
since senior year but she couldn't lie—this one was hitting the spot.
She respectfully held it at arm's length out the window as they
exited AJI and turned left. Anwar chugged his truck out behind
them and turned right to continue on his appointed rounds.

* * *

Zeb returned to his post and set down his coffee. The security monitor showed nothing but a small dust cloud blowing through the parking lot.

* * *

"A man call for Jasper," said Brohug as he and Biz motored back toward the city.

"What? Who? When?" Biz asked. "What did he say?"

This was a lot of questions. "When I waited for you. He speak Zazarish. He knew Jasper hired me. I said I can't talk about my customer." That about covered it.

"Did he say anything about Chris? Whoever it was, must know where they are!"

"No. He only said, 'Jasper Wiles.'"

"Where can I put this?" Biz asked, presenting her cigarette butt. Brohug indicated that the sand outside would not suffer significant harm. With a slight twinge of guilt, Biz flicked away the butt. "Give me your phone," she said. "I'm calling the number back."

She took the cell, found the list of recent calls, puzzled for a moment when she saw, "BLOCKED NUMBER," then hit the contact.

Doo-DOO-DEE! "The number you have dialed... is not in service. Please check the number and dial—"

Biz quickly ended the call. "You said the man spoke Zazarish?" she asked.

"Yes. But not from Zazaristan, I think."

Biz's head swam. Only partially from the smoke. The not-in-service message was in English. "That call was from an American number."

Someone in America knew where they were. Someone who could somehow locate and identify Brohug. Igor Poskovich? No, he had Biz's number. If he wanted to reach them, he would call

343

directly. Was Brohug himself selling her out? She shot a quick glance at him. Very doubtful. He'd had plenty of chances already. It had to be the FBI. All that talk about reaching into people's computers and pulling out what they needed flashed through her mind.

Biz looked down at Brohug's phone in her hand. Was turning it off enough? Did you have to take the battery out? Can you even? And what about the SIM card or whatever? Why had she never learned these things?

"Stop, Brohug. Pull over. We have to get rid of your phone. I don't know how, but I think someone might be using it to try to find us."

Customer is always right.

Brohug's phone joined Biz's butt in the sandy roadside ditch, and the Vanagon drove on.

CHAPTER 66

DARQA AIR BASE, QUUDIA
MONDAY, 0808 QST

It had come to this for Air Force Colonel Clete Roy. He sat staring out his office window at the helicopter maintenance hangar. Behind him, his desk was completely cleared. Not so much as a paper to push.

Decisions had been rendered. Actions had been taken. Mistakes, which we shall not dwell upon at present, had been made.

His cell phone rang. He checked the caller ID. Blocked number. He answered anyway, what the hell was the difference?

"Roy."

"Colonel. It's Dick Barry. How are you, sir?"

"First there, son," Roy said, with a small effort.

"First there," Barry replied. "Sir, I need your help with a civilian matter."

"No problem," said Roy. "Seems I'm gonna have to get used to that kind."

"Yes, sir," Barry said, and paused for a moment of silence. "Sir, I have reason to believe there are one to three American persons of interest in a terror investigation case currently somewhere in or around Taboor City. I need them extracted. These people may be attempting to contact MILF."

345

"Not Hallazallah?" Roy said hopefully.

"No," Barry said quickly. "No. There's no intelligence that suggests Bashir Hallazallah is involved, sir. It's best if you let that go, sir... Sir?"

"I heard you, goddammit. But an extraction from Zazaristan? I can't authorize a team for that. Don't know if you heard, Dick, but my wings are pretty well clipped."

Barry said, "Sir, this is not going to be a public operation. You'll have no official authorization to enter Zazari airspace. It's just a civilian pick-up, quick and quiet."

"Well, I'll just have to tiptoe through the fucking tulips then, won't I?"

"Your country is grateful for your service, Colonel. Come see me in Washington when you get back to the States and I'll get you squared away."

"What's your timeframe for this operation?" Roy asked. They were sending him home in two days.

"ASAP," said Barry. "Today. We have real-time GPS location on the cell phone of a Zazari national. I have reason to believe an American, Jasper Wiles, will be with him. Primary target is Christopher Dawkins, who I believe will be with them, but there's no postive intel on him yet. If you can't find Dawkins, grab Wiles. If you can't find Wiles, grab the Zazari, Brohug Vidadik. How soon can you be at a location south of Taboor City?"

Roy was still facing the window. He could see a dozen or more airmen busily servicing a row of helicopters. Black Betty, his MH-139, sat alone near the far end of the flight line on a small lilypad of hydraulic fluid, her windshield cracked, her tail riddled with .50-caliber holes. Fucking Hallazallah.

Roy checked his watch. He knew the entire helo maintenance wing would be in the briefing room today from 1300 to 1400. He was no longer privy to the maintenance logs, but Black Betty's hydraulics had supposedly been repaired. Getting her out wasn't going to be the problem.

"I can be on the ground by 1700, local."

Getting back? Well that's the trick, isn't it?

CHAPTER 67

NEW YORK, NEW YORK
SUNDAY, 11:30 p.m. EST

Tactical sunglasses, multivitamins, bank, cruise line, *The Star Report, brought to you by Cynergi Solutions* promo.

"Welcome to *HawkNews Night, Sunday Edition*, and a Happy Columbus Day weekend to all our viewers, I'm your host, Gord Ritter."

Ritter led with a short editorial in support of the Honorable Robert Myers's record, and let it slip that he was hearing whispers in Washington of the no-nonense Myers being in line for the Supreme Court.

That business taken care of, the people wanted San Francisco transgender bomber Christopher Dawkins and San Francisco transgender bomber Christopher Dawkins they shall have.

"Christopher Dawkins," Ritter said. "The question America is asking tonight: What goes on in the mind of a"—here he made air quotes—"'transgender, noncisnormative individual' that would allow"—more air quotes—"'he, she, or they' to plan and nearly execute a brazen terrorist attack on innocent Americans? I'm joined tonight by Dr. Kenneth Wald of Western New Mexico Bible College... "

CHAPTER 68

Kitchen gadget, ab machine, personal injury attorney, *Lisa McNally: Investigates* promo.

"As the last word this evening, let me leave you with this," said BSNMC Crate Patterson Gregg. (There is actually one notch below Coat, if you include nighttime personalities.) "The alleged San Francisco Mall Bomber, tech genius Chris Dawkins. Enigma. Nonbinary. Billionaire. We know very little about the... "

CHAPTER 69

NORTHERN QUUDIA
MONDAY, 1445 QST

Colonel Clete Roy pulled gently on Black Betty's collective and gained just enough altitude to navigate a narrow pass in the jagged Pir Mountain Range. This notch, as the Vermonter Roy thought of it, was a favorite of local traders in both blood and fortune. Roy knew it well.

He had switched off his transponder before sneaking Betty away from the base. To avoid ground radar, Roy took it low and slow as he made his way into Zazaristan. Betty was leaving a faint trail of exhaust, but the gauges were holding steady.

In three days Roy was scheduled to appear at a hearing in DC. The purpose of this hearing, he had been told, was to tell some people only that which they wanted to hear.

That's why they called them that, he supposed.

Barry had assured Roy that his quiet acceptance of this Taboor City black bag job would be viewed favorably by a number of the hearing's panel, and several more of them would agree, should Roy meet with equally quiet success.

To that end, for the next two hours Roy's eye would bore a triangle from the windshield to the oil pressure gauge to the nav and back to the windshield.

I have seen the elephant. Fucker tasted like chicken.

CHAPTER 70

SOUTH TABOOR CITY, ZAZARISTAN
MONDAY, 2:50 p.m. ZST

The email read:

> *Hi Mr. Mohammad,*
> *Payment for the SN-110 3.2 Megaton Valise*
> *(Obsidian Black) is now past due. IHL*
> *Shipping delivered the package at 8:09am ZST*
> *and it was signed for by an H. Jablowme (see*
> *attached). The blast radius and fallout range of*
> *an SN-110 is 8-10 kilometers, but the range of*
> *a Remote Detonation Module is virtually*
> *unlimited. [Just Sayin' emoji].*
> *Please remit payment as agreed by 5:00pm*
> *ZST or the weapon will be remotely detonated.*
>
> *Yours in the three harmonies,*
>
> *Johnny Triad*
> *Senior Mountain Master*
> *johnnyt@triad.org*

There was then a time-stamped, digital likeness of H. Jablowme's John Hancock on an IHL receipt and some legal boilerplate warning about the confidentiality of the above, etc., which our young Chinese hardware counterfeiter Xing had cut and pasted onto his message to make it seem more menacing. In truth, stern wording was just about the only threat he could bring to bear at this point. If it didn't work, well hey, it was worth a shot. He would continue saving toward that motorcycle by other means, without ruling out another foray into dark web fraud, which had proven to be profitable, fun, and easy.

Xing attached a photo in his email to Shwarma that showed that morning's edition of the *Financial Times* laying on a table next to a Remote Detonation Module just like the one Shwarma had sitting on his desk. Xing had built two copies; he had the parts, after all. A ColecoVision came with two controllers, readers of a certain age will recall.

Shwarma pounded a fist on his desk and cursed... well... someone. Apparently, the Chinese also possessed an RDM! It certainly wasn't *his* fault for failing to anticipate this turn of events. He quickly decided to blame Fareek. A second RDM that was capable of detonating The Weapon from thousands of kilometers away seemed like a technical issue, which was Fareek's department. Now thanks to him, the Chinese were threatening to destroy The Weapon (and everything within 8-10 kilometers) if Shwarma didn't send the not-inconsiderable balance of botcoin as promised. The problem was, of course, that he had no idea where The Weapon was, contrary to the digitally documented claims of IHL shipping.

There was a good deal of blame for "H. Jablowme" at first, too. Shwarma wasn't sure who Jablowme was, or even his country of origin to be honest, but whoever he was, he had been the one to receive and sign for The Weapon. Shwarma hoped Jablowme was just a new recruit, because he thought he made it clear to everyone that this particular package was to be brought to him immediately upon delivery. To be safe, he cursed Rahim for not keeping him abreast of any new hires.

Shwarma leapt from his desk and ran downstairs, his boots thudding the concrete, to ask Zebar where the IHL delivery was. Zeb reported that no delivery had been made. Furthermore, Zeb had never heard of H. Jablowme, nor could he even identify Jablowme's tribe.

Shwarma felt a flash of alarm. *"Have you been here at your post all day? Show me the security video from this morning,"* he said, pointing at the two monitors on Zeb's desk, one showing the front door, the other the garage door at the rear of the building.

"This is just the live feed, sir. The recordings are done in Fareek's office," answered Zeb, dancing around Shwarma's first question adeptly.

"Look around for a big package. Suitcase sized," Shwarma snapped to Zeb as he immediately spun and headed away.

Shwarma had a very strong fear that Zeb wouldn't find anything, but he needed to be sure. He hurried down the hall to Fareek's office, crouching under the window of the locked door of Conference Room B as he passed.

Fareek had just rolled into work a short time ago after his off-the-books morning meeting with Mohammad Mohammad (which had stretched into lunch and seemed like it could lead to a nice piece of side work). He had just dropped his two new phones on his desk when Shwarma stormed in.

"Why didn't you know about the duplicate Remote Detonation Module that the Chinese kept, you ass?" Shwarma yelled.

"What are you talking about?" Fareek asked.

"The Weapon! The Chinese can compromise it! What am I paying you for?! How could you not anticipate they would have multiple Remote Detonation Modules?! How could you not know?!"

What Fareek knew about the "Remote Detonation Module" was that he had examined it carefully after Shwarma's speech the week before and found it to be a cheap Wi-Fi router that was stuck with what appeared to be superglue to a vintage video game controller. It was a phony, a hoax, nothing more than a prop. He felt safe in assuming "The Weapon" that Shwarma would not shut up about would be just as phony. But when this was eventually discovered, Fareek was hoping for the largest possible audience in order to maximally humiliate Shwarma, so at the time, he had simply closed the phony RDM's case and kept his discovery to himself.

Now suffering the insults and berating of his boss, Fareek was very tempted to point out how foolish Shwarma was to have been duped, but it was just the two of them, so he managed again to keep quiet. He simply said, *"Sorry about that, Boss."*

Shwarma cursed him and swiftly kicked him out of his own office to review the morning's security footage in private. He zipped back through the video and sure enough, just before eight, a delivery truck had arrived. The driver rang the bell near the garage and received no answer. At the same time, a VW Vanagon arrived in front of the building. A couple got out and tried the front door. *"Zeb! Where were you?"* Shwarma breathed. The woman walked around behind the building alone, met the driver of the truck, signed her name, and chatted for a minute (!). Her partner took possession of The Weapon and put it in the VW. Both vehicles departed. The Vanagon took the road back toward Taboor City. Where was Zeb during all this? H. Jablowme was a woman?

The center of the city was only a few kilometers away, well within The Weapon's advertised range of destruction. Now a bad situation had become much worse.

Shwarma wished The Weapon thieves had at least made for the empty desert to the south, putting as much space between him and the bomb as possible. Unfortunately, The Weapon and whoever stole it were now most likely hiding in the urban jumble that was Taboor City, putting it at risk of nuclear annihilation.

Shwarma could not allow that to happen. He had a go-bag in that city! Unsure of when, how suddenly, or in what direction he may have to leave Zazaristan, he had stashed a bag full of essentials in the north end of Taboor City in addition to the one he kept in his office in South Taboor. Keeping the bags separate also served caution, so as not to lose everything to a single theft or random act of misfortune. Each bag contained burner phones, cash, a pistol, USB drives, a Quudian passport in the name Mohammad Mohammad, two changes of clothes, a Dopp kit, and copies of his Creemee Tyme franchisee documents (which are essentially a license to print money, or so he had been told at the seminar).

It looked like today was going to be Getaway Day for Shwarma, whether he wanted it to be or not. He had done some calculating and realized that with the cash he took from the Americans the previous night (which offset the lost opportunity for future stud goat fees), he was just about 10,000 short of the goal he needed before leaving for his new life in the UAE, 15,000 short if he had to make the final, final payment for The Weapon to Johnny Triad. And he couldn't very well pay that now! He never received The Weapon! It could be anywhere. Granted, not paying the balance would doom a minor city to a small-to-medium-sized nuclear explosion in about two hours, but Shwarma figured that if he hurried, he would have plenty of time to collect his bag and blow town. He would take the Yahama, kitted out with extra-large desert gas tank and saddlebags, to beat the afternoon traffic. The only downside to this plan, for Shwarma personally that is, was that the forced exit would leave him to eat the 10k shortfall in his getaway bankroll. That might mean having to make a smaller down payment on the Fro-Yo building, and he would have to economize for a few months at least. Maybe he would get a roommate. That he was also dooming the citizens of Taboor City to a fiery death and would have to execute Wiles and Chris before it happened, didn't concern him as much as his tight short-term budget.

"Unless… " he murmured. An idea had developed to kill two birds with one stone. He would need the Americans a little longer.

There were two burner phones on Fareek's desk. He grabbed one. The phone was some model he was unfamiliar with and after a brief search for the power button, he mashed it and impatiently waited for the phone to boot up. Not for the first time, he wondered why his TV comes on instantly but computers and phones take forever. Finally, the phone came online, and he punched in Bashir Hallazallah's number from memory.

Bashir Hallazallah was one of the old-school independent jihadis who resisted joining Shwarma's AJI. The men didn't like each other very much, but they did business occasionally when necessary.

"Yes?" Hallazallah answered.

"Bashir, old friend. It's Wahiri." Shwarma looked back to make sure Fareek was out of earshot.

"What do you want?" Hallazallah grunted.

"How are your wives?" Shwarma felt it was important to engage in a little small talk before getting down to business.

"If the poorhouse doesn't get me, the nuthouse will."

The two men chuckled at the old Zazarish idiom.

"What do you want?" Hallazallah repeated.

"Out of respect for you and your operation," Shwarma said, *"I wanted to let you know that I have been sent two packages that may have been meant for you."*

Although the Frankensteined phones were supposedly untraceable, there was a certain amount of code that was required during these calls to avoid suspicion from eavesdroppers both live and electronic. "Packages," for example, meant prisoners or hostages.

Hallazallah asked, *"Where were these packages sent from?"*

Shwarma replied, *"Canada."*

The Americans. Of course, Hallazallah was interested. He had been combing the city for them just the night before. His appetite for Westerners was well known and well documented. The man had caused more heads to roll than Donald Trump.

"And?" he said, trying to sound nonchalant.

"I'll let you have them for fifty botcoins. Delivered."

Hallazallah's compound was farther south in the foothills of the Pir Mountains, thus away from the soon-to-be-incinerated city and closer to the coast. Also, fifty botcoins meant fifty botcoins. The practice of using code for monetary values had led to misunderstandings in the past and had gone out of favor.

Hallazallah sniffed, *"You and your computer money. You know I only deal in zazars. One hundred thousand for each package. I'm in Taboor on business. I can pick them up on my way home tomorrow."*

Shwarma gasped with frustration, then collected himself. *"Has to be today, Bashir. I'm leaving town on business myself."* He glanced at his watch.

Hallazallah paused for a moment, then said, *"I can be there by four-thirty."*

That would cut it a bit close for Shwarma's liking. According to the Triads, The Weapon would be exploding a few kilometers away just thirty minutes later.

He countered with one-twenty, but Hallazallah knew a desperate seller when he heard one and held firm at a hundred.

Shwarma ended the call, bashed Jasper Wiles's Model XXI cell phone with the ball-peen hammer, and left the studio. He walked past Fareek in the hallway without a word and jogged upstairs. A few minutes later, he came back down wearing a full backpack and carrying the Remote Detonation Module in one hand and a black duffel in the other. As he walked briskly past Fareek's office toward the garage, Fareek followed.

Shwarma opened the garage door and then got to work lashing the RDM case to the rear of his motorcycle, trying it a few different ways to make sure it would stay put.

"Where are you going, Boss?" asked Fareek.

"Mind your business, Fareek," Shwarma said, mounting the bike.

"Are we still having the 3:30 staff meeting?" Fareek asked. The meeting was, by definition, his and everybody else's business.

"No," said Shwarma. He fired up the Yamaha and tore away, heading toward Taboor City.

CHAPTER 71

TABOOR CITY, ZAZARISTAN
MONDAY, 3:14 p.m. ZST

After they unwittingly porch-pirated the faux nuclear device, Biz and Brohug had returned to the hotel, once again hoping to somehow find Wiles and Chris. Of course, they hadn't returned. Biz paid the bill (plus another night in advance, just to be safe), and left her number with the clerk in case he happened to see or get word of Jasper and Chris.

As they drove in widening concentric circles around the neighborhood in desperate hopes of spotting Wiles and Chris, Biz agonized over her next decision. Where to search? Should she return to the goatfight arena? The AJI building? Neither seemed right. Brohug informed her the arena would be idle and empty until Thursday night. Besides, the rug guy next door had agreed to call Biz if he spotted the men. Biz also felt that talking to the bouncers Walid and Zebar would be unproductive. What could (or would) they tell her? *I think maybe he wandered off that way?*

Biz eventually made the call to return to the airport. The jet represented the only way home and served as the rally point of this whole circus show. Wiles and Chris may be trying make their way there.

There was the other decision to make, as well. The call to the US Embassy. She had poised her finger over the phone contact more than once already today. The mysterious phone call from that morning gave her a terrible feeling that the FBI had located them through Brohug's phone somehow. Biz had monitored the news all day, waiting for the "Chris Dawkins: Wanted Fugitive Flees to Zazaristan!" stories to start popping up, which would seal their fates, but they never did. If anyone knew they were in Zazaristan, at least they were keeping it to themselves.

But the time for secrets was over. It had been almost twenty hours since she'd seen her friends. They were almost—*this is your fault, Bizzy!*—almost certainly imprisoned or detained in some way. Either that or they've been killed.

Elizabeth Nneka Byner's failure was complete. She was all out of moves. If Wiles and Chris needed help, serious help, calling the embassy for a professional or military search and rescue team was the only option. Of course, that meant admitting to everything—*every stupid thing!*—and going to prison in the best-case scenario. Worst case? Jasper and Chris had been tortured and killed, with lots more prison for Biz.

Biz decided she would call the embassy when she reached the airport. She'd tell Lou Monte to fly home alone and simply await her fate.

Brohug too, would be dismissed. He had certainly proved worthy of his five-star rating and he didn't need to be around when the American authorities arrived and started asking questions.

Just then it hit her. Yelp. The rating and review Wiles left for Brohug. It was the only public digital track they'd left since arriving in Zazaristan. That's how the FBI knew Wiles was there. That's how they pulled Brohug's name. A realization both small and worthless, now.

She rode in silence all the way to the airport reading news apps. Back in the US, the media was howling for Chris. People knew him as a terrorist, as well as a transgender billionaire computer hacker genius. He remained unseen by news cameras. The FBI claimed he was in secure custody but declined to name the facility where he was being held. Biz knew they must be looking for Chris just as hard as she was. She could only hope he was found safe.

They arrived back at the airport and Brohug came to a stop outside the hangar where the jet had been waiting.

"Thank you, Brohug," Biz said. She reached over to the driver's side and hugged him. A little longer than Brohug was expecting, but Biz wasn't sure when she'd be getting her next one. She slid back to her seat, grabbed her bag from the backseat, and opened the door. She quickly dug in the bag and placed a folded square of money in the molded plastic nook below the VW's radio. She jumped to the ground.

"You can go home now. Thanks." She shut the door and turned away quickly before the tears came.

Brohug watched Biz trudge toward the airplane, then made a wide turn to exit the airport. He felt terrible that Jasper and Chris were lost. He vowed to keep looking. But first, back to South Taboor to pick up his phone from where Biz had left it on the roadside.

Biz closed a news app to call the embassy and out of habit refreshed Where'sWiles.

What would she say? Should she ask for the ambassador? Who would—THE BLUE DOT! The blue dot was back! Jasper!

CHAPTER 72

Wiles awoke and got up off the vinyl floor. He shuffled into a chair. He mumbled something about, or perhaps to, the devil.

Chris had done some pushups and wall-sits a few hours ago to work out the caffeine, but otherwise he'd been sitting quietly and occasionally doodling on the whiteboard.

"What time is it?" Wiles asked.

"Three-twenty," Chris said.

"Patient but ready," Wiles replied.

CHAPTER 73

AMIR "THE EAR" ZAZESHI REGIONAL AIRPORT
MONDAY, 3:25 p.m. ZST

Biz knew Wiles's location again, or so she thought, at least. When
Shwarma called Hallazallah to offer two infidels for sale, he had
done it using Wiles's phone, which Shwarma had failed to destroy
completely thanks to the Model XXI phone's Kevlar compound
case.

And for Biz, another option had emerged after all. She quickly
called Wiles's phone, but it buzzed unheeded on Fareek's desk as
Fareek was walking up to Conference Room A to let the assembled
MILFers know that the staff meeting was cancelled and that
Shwarma had left for the day. Most of them then decided to call it a
day themselves. But not Fareek. The *qoomah* his father and he built
no longer existed, but he still worked on it most days. There was
still some work to do.

Biz disconnected and was about to call Brohug. But he had no
phone! She couldn't just call him to come back. The Vanagon was
barely visible as a dust trail on the airport access road about a half
mile away.

"Brohug!" She waved her arms. "Stop!" There was no way
he'd hear her.

The brake lights lit up. The Vanagon stopped. Biz was astounded.

Third grade: *You possess superpowers. (Do not attempt to fly. Not that kind.)*

Almost a thousand yards away, Brohug pulled a U-turn and headed back to the hangar.

Biz watched him the whole way. How had Brohug possibly heard her? Did he see her through the rearview? Biz was amazed at how this worked.

When Brohug got close to the hangar, he once again made a wide half circle. Biz jogged up alongside as he came to a stop.

"Sorry," said Brohug. He jerked a thumb over his shoulder. "Forgot your package."

"What?" gasped Biz. "No! Yes! Forget that! Back to the place where we got it, Brohug! The AJI building! Jasper and Chris are there!"

She clambered in and Brohug gunned the bus away from the hangar and mentally calculated the best route back through the city into what was at this hour sure to be knotty, goaty traffic. Biz kept checking the GPS signal while doing some calculating of her own.

As the past night and day had worn on, there was only one thing that Biz felt was becoming more and more clear: any blue dot that might pop up on her phone was merely that—just a dot, a digital mirage, a cellular avatar, whatever the fuck. It was almost impossible to believe that Wiles was still in possession of his phone at this point. The bouncers Walid and Zebar most likely stole the phone as they kicked Jasper's drunk ass into the night and that's who had it now, two Zazaris who work in the animal entertainment business. In terms of a lead to locating Wiles and Chris now, Biz feared the Zazaris wouldn't be too eager to help, even if they could. They would surely claim they had merely found the phone and therefore have absolutely no ideas about its rightful owner. And then what?

Exactly. What choice did she have? They only clue she *had* was that fucking dot.

There was no evidence that suggested Wiles was *not* at the AJI building, either. It made as much sense as anything. Maybe Walid and Zebar befriended Jasper and Chris. These bouncers were probably just the type to know some shady Zazari locals, who might in turn introduce the Americans to some agent of MILF. Who has administrator privileges on their computer network. These terrorists would likely demand cell phone silence while negotiating with the smooth-talking Wiles and the guileless Chris, thus the lack of comm over the last day. The recent return of Jasper's dot was, of course, a signal to Biz that his business was complete and he simply needed a lift back to the airport.

Biz allowed to herself that this scenario was somewhat unlikely.

Still, it was an option.

CHAPTER 74

SOUTH TABOOR CITY, ZAZARISTAN
MONDAY, 4:01 p.m. ZST

It had been a strange day at work for Fareek. Shwarma hadn't bugged him all day until he charged downstairs to yell about the RDM and look at some security footage before taking off in a rush. Later, as Fareek chatted with his co-workers at the proto-staff meeting, he heard that Zeb had somehow lost an important package and that there was a pair of infidels locked in Conference Room B. The relationship of these things was speculative, at best.

Fareek had seen neither the infidels nor the package, but the infidels sounded more interesting. His curiosity defeated his better instincts and led him on a route past Conference Room B.

He peeked into the narrow window. Sure enough, there were two infidels in there.

Jasper Wiles caught Fareek's eye and gave a jaunty wave. He didn't appear to be there unwillingly. Perhaps he was there to deal with Shwarma in some business capacity. There was no telling.

Fareek's better instincts, though usually sharp, failed him again. Fareek didn't want trouble, and this could cause a hail of it. But he had to warn these poor bastards against partnering with Shwarma.

Fareek cracked the door open. "Hello."

Chris jumped from his seat, "Do you have a phone I could use, please?"

Fareek said, "You have no phones of your own?" *Oops, maybe these guys were really hostages or something.* He stepped back and narrowed the door opening. "Did Shwarma take them?"

Still seated at the far end of the table, Wiles said, "We're conducting some business with Mr. Shwarma."

Chris approached the door. "A kid took our phones last night. At the goatfight."

Fareek sighed. *Oh, Yazeed.* "Wait here," he said. He quickly backed out and shut the door, cutting off what Chris said next.

A minute later, he returned with the phones. He opened the door a crack, and slipped them to Chris. Wiles's XXI had sustained a small, superficial dent, but otherwise they seemed to be in working order.

"Thank you," Chris said.

"You can't trust Shwarma," Fareek offered quickly.

"Thank you. Leave the door open, please, Mr... ?" Wiles said.

"Why was this door locked?" Fareek turned to Chris as he slid closer. "Did Shwarma say you cannot leave?"

"He said we were guests," Chris said. "Hey, uh... Do you know Mohammad Mohammad? Does he work here?"

Fareek was curious as to how this maybe-infidel knew Mo, but finding out would surely mean trouble and there were limits to how much he was willing to take on. "No one of that name works here," he said.

He stepped back. "I don't think Shwarma's coming back today. I'd leave if I were you." Fareek left the door open and slipped away toward the rear of the building.

Holding a phone in each hand, Chris looked back at Wiles. "Ready?" he said.

CHAPTER 75

TABOOR CITY, ZAZARISTAN
MONDAY, 4:08 p.m. ZST

The Vanagon lurched through downtown.

Biz's phone buzzed. She thought it must be Sweet Lou, letting her know the plane was prepped, but it was a message from Poskovich:

> Bizbyner,
> I just rec'd email from some1 claiming to be Chris, using JW's phone (see blw). He said he and JW are fine. I traced the source to this bldg, in Zazaristan
>
> Igor

He had attached a screenshot of AJI's two-star Yelp review page and a satellite photo of the very building she was already speeding toward.

Her phone rang. Chris Dawkins.

"Chris, are you all right?! Are you with Jasper?"

Chris and Jasper had snuck out of the conference room and soon found themselves back in the garage where they had arrived the night before. They huddled in the corner behind the van.

368

Chris whispered. "Hi, Biz! Yes, we're both here. Igor should have sent you the address. We're working on the plan! Come pick us up!" His phone beeped. "Sorry Biz, I have to go, Igor's calling back. Come pick us up! Sorry we didn't call!" Chris disconnected.

Biz stared at her phone. *Igor? Could Chris really be... ?*

The traffic was worse than Brohug had anticipated.

CHAPTER 76

SOUTH TABOOR CITY, ZAZARISTAN
MONDAY, 4:25 p.m. ZST

After Fareek had met the infidels from Conference Room B, he went back to his office to make a call. He hoped to head back to town and get to work on Mohammad's upgrade project. Cash tended to leak through his friend's pockets, so Fareek knew that time was somewhat of the essence in getting any kind of deposit from the man.

Mo answered and said he was having a slow day at the shop, so he invited Fareek to come right over. He also offered Fareek the standard I'll buy/you fly arrangement for take-out kebabs, which Fareek agreed to.

Fareek slipped out AJI's back door. It seemed like everyone had already gone home, except maybe Zebar, so he didn't bother to disguise his early departure. He rounded the corner of the building and slipped through the side gate to make his way toward the employee parking lot where he kept his scooter.

As he scrambled up a short slope to meet the road, he saw a VW Vanagon speeding toward him and heard a full blast of its Teutonic horn. The Vanagon locked its brakes as it passed Fareek and skidded to a halt about forty feet past him. The door flew open and a woman jumped out. Pointed right at him. "You! What are you doing here?" she said.

Fareek's mouth was open, but no words came out. The woman he had almost spilled coffee on this morning? What was she doing here? And what was she talking about?

Biz shouted, "I saw you this morning at the goatfight place and now you're here! Who are you? Walid? Zebar? Brohug, get out here." Brohug stepped from the vehicle, holding his rifle.

Fareek didn't want trouble.

Biz walked into the hot Zazari wind, holding up the pic of Jasper and Chris. "You know these men, don't you? Are my friends there, in that building? Are they safe? Do. You. Know." She stopped two paces away.

"My name is Fareek," he said, raising his arms. He pointed back over his shoulder. "Yes, your friends are in that building." He glanced at Brohug. "There is no trouble. I think they've met with my boss, Wahiri Shwarma. They lost their phones and I returned them. They are safe and free to go. I think."

"Shwarma?" The name strobed through Biz's brain. "Wait, what do you mean, 'I think'? Are they safe in there?"

"I had to unlock the door to let them out," Fareek said. "Shwarma *may have* considered them hostages, There is no telling." Fareek just wanted to get to Mohammad's rug shop for a small job and some pleasant conversation. This is what you get when you can't control your curiosity. He didn't want trouble, but now here it was.

"Go ahead and pick them up," he said, gesturing to the building. "Shwarma's not even there. He left a while ago. Ask for Zebar at the door. Say Fareek sent you. Security Level Capricorn." He moved to walk past Biz.

Brohug leveled his weapon at Fareek. Fareek stopped.

"You're coming with us, Fareek. We need your help," Biz said.

"You don't need it! Good luck to you." Fareek made to step along, but Biz moved in front of him.

"You work there?" she said. "When do you people start? I was here at eight this morning and nobody answered the door."

"That's odd. But I had business in the city this morning, you saw me."

"Don't care," said Biz. "Fareek, when I was here this morning, I got a call from a man in the US government. He was looking for me and my friends. He tracked a phone to your building, Fareek. It's only a matter of time before they come looking. You could run now, but they'll use whatever they find in there to track you down as the kidnapper of two American civilians."

Fareek glanced back at the building.

Biz said, "I don't know how much time we have. The faster we can get them out of there, the better. That building will be crawling with American troops soon. I need your help to get in and out with my friends before the soldiers show up."

Fareek looked back at the building again. He wished Shwarma would be in there when the Americans crashed through the door, but not poor Zebar. He had to warn him, at least. And probably pick up some stuff he had in his desk. He turned to face Biz.

Biz said, "If you help me. Right now. We can get out of here. All of us together, Fareek."

Fareek's father was conscripted into a long-forgotten militia and never heard from again. Fareek's family home was later destroyed, and his sister killed in a long-remembered mortar attack. His mother died two years later in the aid camp. One option was enough for him.

Mo wouldn't be getting those kebabs, it seemed.

CHAPTER 77

SOUTHERN ZAZARISTAN
MONDAY, 1630 ZST

Colonel Roy keyed his radio mic as he skimmed Black Betty a few meters above the desert floor. "Range to target, twenty kilometers."

"Copy," said Barry from a secure line on the top floor of the Burton Building in predawn San Francisco. "Report back when you have visual contact."

CHAPTER 78

SOUTH TABOOR CITY, ZAZARISTAN
MONDAY, 4:30 p.m. ZST

Biz's feet hit the dusty ground behind the AJI building before the tires stopped rolling. She grabbed the side door handle and yanked it open as the Vanagon came to a stop.

There was movement in the corner of her eye. She whirled to see Chris and Jasper slowly emerging from the building. She ran to them and wordlessly gathered them both into a three-way hug. God, did they stink.

Biz still smelled like freedom, but now Chris noticed a little coconut and just a whiff of cigarette smoke.

"I knew you'd find us Biz," Wiles said.

"Thank you, Biz!" Chris beamed. He looked over Biz's shoulder and saw Fareek step from the Vanagon. He recognized his liberator at once and made a step toward him.

Wiles held out a hand to stop him.

"Chris. I'm sorry about your face," he said. "It's all my fault. I dropped you back at your place on Thursday. I was telling a joke to Mia and Hallie as we carried you into bed and I lost my purchase. The punchline always gets me. 'First of all, you need to narrow your stance.'" Wiles chuckled softly.

Chris had forgotten about his injury, but he offered a quick "Thanks, Mr. Wiles" as he stepped forward to greet Fareek.

After Fareek had agreed to help Biz and hopped aboard the Vanagon, they had taken a few minutes to compare notes as they made the short drive to AJI. Biz had asked about Mohammad Mohammad, the American's erstwhile point of contact with MILF, and showed Fareek the package she had acquired that morning (to his mild amusement). Fareek still couldn't figure how Mohammad's name got mixed up in all this, but he did explain about The Weapon's phony nature and had even told Biz that he could provide access to MILF's computers.

Biz said, "Chris, this is Fareek," as the men shook hands. "He's an IT guy. He's going to help us, but you have to make it fast. I don't know how long we have. I'll give you ten minutes."

Chris nodded. He and Fareek quickly fell into discussion.

Wiles watched Chris and Fareek go into the building, then made his way to the Vanagon and settled into the passenger seat. He heard Fareek saying, "What kind of projects you work on?" as the young men vanished from sight.

Biz turned and examined Wiles. "Your face isn't looking so great either, Jasper. Are you OK?"

"Never better. Never better. Thank you for your concern, Biz. The plan has gone very well so far, wouldn't you say?"

Biz shook her head but said, "Yes. Ultimately, yes, I would."

"Thanks also for that," Wiles said. "I think we both knew when we decided to come here that there probably wouldn't be much need for your translation skills, but—"

"I translated my way into acquiring a phony Chinese suitcase nuclear weapon, Wiles. What were *you* doing all day?"

Wiles grinned that strange grin. "—but I knew we needed you. Now, what's this about a nuclear weapon?"

CHAPTER 79

Shwarma was fighting the bike. Fully loaded with the go-bags and the RDM, the Yamaha had too much weight on the front tire. He hadn't planned on having the bulky RDM case with him as he made his escape and he had to sling the go-bag over the handlebars, where it affected the machine's handling. He had wanted to take the overland route through the desert to avoid traffic as he left downtown Taboor, but with the overloaded front end, he was afraid of biting it in the heavy sand and crashing. Keeping possession of the RDM meant traveling on the road, but traffic had slowed him down even as he weaved through most of it. Time and distance were of the essence now; getting out of the blast radius was all that mattered, but he was behind schedule to meet Hallazallah. He wouldn't have much time to conduct the infidel-selling business. If Hallazallah didn't show up on time, Shwarma would have to leave anyway and forgo the extra cash, which he had mentally prepared to write off as a low-risk/high-payoff sunk cost. If the Americans couldn't be sold, he would stop back at the office just long enough to quickly execute them and be on his way. Leaving them alive was too risky.

As Shwarma crested the road's last rise, the AJI building came into sight. He wouldn't miss the mortgage payment, that's for sure.

376

He could now see Hallazallah's truck, just now backing up close to the front door. He was there, after all. It was going to be close.

Meanwhile, around the back of the building and out of Shwarma's sight, Wiles and Biz sat together in the idling Vanagon. The Weapon lay behind them in the trunk compartment.

Biz looked at her watch. How long have Chris and Fareek been in there? Almost ten minutes.

"This is taking too long! We have to go! Brohug, let's get them!" Biz said.

Just then, the building's door swung open and Fareek and Chris trotted to the Vanagon. Fareek carried a laptop under his arm. "We're leaving, Brohug," said Biz. "Now."

"Did you do it?" Biz grabbed Chris's arm as he climbed in. Chris flexed a little.

Fareek slid the side door closed. The Vanagon lurched forward, and Chris fell into the back seat. He sat up. "Hi, Biz. It's really great to see you." The smell of coconut and just a little cigarette smoke would never be the same for Chris Dawkins.

"Good to see you too, Chris," Biz said quickly. "Did you do it?" she repeated. "Did you change the backup data?"

"Not exactly. No," Chris said. "The servers and backups are off-site after all, like Mr. Poskovich said. The old data isn't here. Shwarma actually has Fareek save each week's data on a USB drive and then he stashes it somewhere. Fareek doesn't know where."

"I told you, that is what he thinks is most secure," Fareek said.

"Chris, if that USB backup is still out there, changing the data on the internet won't help you," Biz said. "Right?" she then asked quietly.

"No, it won't," said Chris. "But Fareek is the IT guy," he continued. "We have his laptop."

Before Biz could respond, the Vanagon cleared the corner of the building and they all saw a man on a motorcycle pull through the open front gate and down toward the building. The man oversteered in the dusty gravel and suddenly dumped his bike, tumbling over the handlebars. Man and machine sprawled across the driveway and blocked the exit.

With all eyes on the hapless biker, no one in the Vanagon noticed the Toyota Hilux pickup truck with a sword airbrushed across the side and a machine gun mounted in the bed parked about forty feet away at the building's front door. The big weapon spun on it's turret. The Vanagon slid to a halt. The prone motorcyclist popped up from the dust.

"That's Wahiri Shwarma," Fareek said to Biz, pointing at the biker.

"I wonder if that turret was factory equipment?" said Wiles, pointing at the Toyota.

Shwarma wasn't hurt in his spill, but falling off the bike was an embarrassing show of weakness and his bargaining position with Hallazallah was now badly compromised. He scrambled to his feet. As he did, he looked up to see... the same VW Vanagon that had stolen The Weapon that morning! What were they doing back here?

It could only be one thing. The thieves must have realized The Weapon was going to explode (Shwarma imagined a red LCD countdown display) and they had returned for the Remote Detonation Module, which must be needed to stop it.

The RDM! Crap! The case had broken open when the bike went down, and the unit was now in pieces in the dirt. The keypad's curly cord had completely separated from the other part, the thing with the antennae. Shwarma cursed the Cole Company's shoddy workmanship. It looked like there would be no stopping the explosion now. There was good news, however. If the thieves knew The Weapon was due to explode in minutes, logic dictated that they would have stashed it as far away as possible from here before returning. Shwarma relaxed a bit, knowing he was safe.

In the Vanagon, Biz said, "Chris, hand me that package from the back."

"What's in the package?" asked Chris, looking over the rear seat.

"It belongs to him," Biz said, pointing at Shwarma. "We took it by accident earlier. I'm going to give it back to show we're here in good faith, then we can get him to move out of the way and we can go."

"Let me do it," said Chris. "I'll give it to him. We met this morning." He reached back and struggled with the large package to haul it over the seat.

Wiles had gotten out and quickly slipped to the rear of the Vanagon. He opened the rear compartment and pulled the box from Chris's grip. "Shwarma knows me as well, Chris," he said. "And I'm still the head negotiator. I'll return his package and then explain we must be going," he continued, with a slight strain to his voice as he hefted the large box.

Wiles took a few steps away from the Vanagon and into the open area between the three vehicles. The man in the back of the pickup truck swung his .50 caliber toward him.

Bashir Hallazallah stepped from the passenger seat of the truck and pointed a finger at Wiles. *"Are these my packages?"* he yelled to Shwarma. *"You didn't say one was an actual package."*

Now the large gun's answer hole swung to Shwarma, who stared in disbelief. Wiles stood no more than ten meters away, holding The Weapon, which Shwarma recognized from the video of its theft that morning. *Wiles was involved? Him? Wh—*

The Weapon was due to explode in six minutes! Shwarma had no time to answer Hallazallah or to ponder if/how/why Wiles was in league with/indebted to/completely unaffiliated with H. Jablowme and/or the Triads. Shwarma scrambled to push the Yahama back up on its wheels while doing a word problem in his head. Six minutes. The bike can hit 100kph on the open road. He could be at least five kilometers away when The Weapon detonated, taking all these zealots with it. He jumped on the bike, fired it up, and rooster-tailed away from AJI Security, Party Rental and Consulting for the final time.

Everyone watched Shwarma go. Hallazallah and his machine gun then returned their attentions back to Wiles, who now stood frozen between them and the Vanagon.

Seeing this, Brohug jumped from his seat and grabbed his AK. Taking a position behind the van, he looked at Wiles. "Thank you for Yelp rating!"

Wiles set the heavy package down, then turned around and sat on it. "Well earned, my friend," he said.

Brohug raised his rifle and aimed directly between the gunner in the truck and Hallazallah, so they'd each assumed they were covered.

"We have no fight with you, Sheik Hallazallah," he shouted. *"We only wish to pass on our way in peace."*

"Peace is not cheap, young man," Hallazallah shouted back. *"I was promised this infidel and I will have him. That is the payment to pass."*

"He wants to take you," Brohug said to Wiles.

"Don't go with him, Jasper! Don't move!" Biz yelled from the Vanagon.

"We're staying together, Jasper," Chris said.

"You want me to shoot these guys?" Brohug offered.

Wiles shook his head and remained seated on the package. He considered for a moment whether to remove his sport coat. He wiped sweat from his brow with his sleeve.

Fareek unholstered his MILF service-issue sidearm and leveled it out the Vanagon's sliding side window at Hallazallah. Fareek had never met the man but knew him by reputation.

The man in the bed of the Hilux nervously pivoted his weapon back and forth.

Wiles said, "Brohug, tell this man I will give him this if he allows you to pass peacefully." He tapped the box. "It's a very powerful weapon. If he tries to stop you, he will get shot."

Wiles stood back up and faced his friends. "Have faith, Elizabeth," he said.

Brohug shouted the offer to Hallazallah.

Hallazallah had come prepared to pay for two infidels, but with Shwarma now gone for whatever reason, he wouldn't be one to complain about getting just one for free. Plus, a mystery box! He motioned for Wiles to approach. Wiles picked up the package and slowly walked toward Hallazallah.

Hallazallah heard it first. The whine of Shwarma's motorcycle had died away a minute ago, but now there was something else. Something familiar. It was only a second or two before the huge gray helicopter named "Black Betty" thundered over the building and across the road.

"Visual," reported Roy, glancing down as he streaked by, catching a glimpse of a man and two vehicles. Brohug's phone lay in a ditch a few hundred meters away and homing in on its signal caused Roy to overshoot the building, which he could now see was plainly his objective.

Fareek craned his neck to look up and out his window. "US military!"

Biz shouted, "Jasper, the FBI found us! They called Brohug looking for you this morning! Let's go!"

Wiles put the box down in the middle of the dusty lot. He watched as Hallazallah darted back to his truck, yelling at his driver and gunner while pointing to the helicopter. The truck started up. Didn't look like they were sticking around.

Wiles said, "Did you tell them Chris was here?"

It was hard to hear him. "What? No! We have to go! Come on!" Biz yelled.

The helicopter began banking an arc to turn around.

"Go ahead!" shouted Wiles. "Get to the airport and go! If they're looking for me, they'll find me. Brohug, get out here before that helicopter lands!" He waved his arms at the helicopter as it completed its turn and bore down on them.

"No, Brohug! Stay here!" Chris shouted.

From a dark and empty office, Barry shouted, "Report, Colonel, report! What do you see?"

Roy slid Black Betty into a hover fifty feet above the white van to keep the Hilux and its weapon in sight. "Two vehicles. A van and a technical."

The parking lot below swirled with dust kicked up from the chopper's rotors. Wiles struggled to be heard as he yelled, "They're here for me, Brohug! If I go with you, they'll follow us all! Get the others back to the airport!" He waved and staggered away toward the building to get some cover from the stinging cloud.

Biz screamed, "No!"

Brohug quickly got back in the driver's seat and shut the door just before a shower of dust and grit rushed up against it.

Above, Roy ignored the Vanagon as it slowly crept away under cover of a dust cloud of his own creation. Roy was transfixed as the technical turned toward him, revealing the sword airbrushed across its hood. No more than seventy-five meters away. He thumbed the safety off Black Betty's nose gun.

Barry was screaming, "ROY! REPORT!"

"Visual acquired. Hallazallah. Bashir Hallazallah. Is here. Permission to engage."

Barry yelled, "Negative! Negative, Colonel! Abort!"

Below, Brohug emerged from the mini dust storm and swung left onto the road back toward the airport. With open road ahead, he floored it.

Looking back, Chris could see the helicopter swinging and tilting around to stay in front of the pickup truck, which had been edging toward the exit but was now invisible through the billowing dust cloud. Wiles couldn't be seen, either.

The Vanagon sped on and crested a hill. AJI was gone.

"He'll be fine, Chris," Biz said, reading the worry in his eyes, hoping she was hiding her own. "Hallazallah was scared off by the helicopter. If he's gone, Jasper will get picked up and brought home."

Chris was still looking back. The helicopter was now out of sight as well. He turned to face Biz.

Biz tried to assure him. "He's not involved in your investigation. He's not a fugitive. You are. We have to get you home soon if you want to get out of this."

"I work for him at Sixdub," Chris pointed out. "The FBI will figure that out and connect him to me anyway."

Biz held up Fareek's laptop. "If the FBI's no longer interested in you, Chris, Jasper's just another guy who likes golf, drinking, and the company of older ladies."

Chris didn't look convinced.

"A horseshoe, Chris," Biz said, forcing a smile. "In his ass." She spread her hands about eighteen inches apart. "This big. I've seen it."

* * *

Smoking-hot brass shell casings rained down around Jasper Wiles as he lay prone in the dust.

CHAPTER 80

PIR MOUNTAINS
ZAZARISTAN/QUUDIA BORDER REGION
MONDAY, 5:25 p.m. ZST

Shwarma killed the engine and coasted to the side of the road. He had been on the run almost a half hour. Going flat-out, hunched over the handlebars, he had risked a few quick looks back as The Weapon's detonation time had come and passed. He had seen no mushroom cloud or any other sign of explosion, but there was no way to know for sure what had happened. It was possible that he simply outran a small blast, or as much as he hated to consider it, it was more likely that The Weapon hadn't exploded at all. The Triads had bluffed, and he had fallen for it.

And how was Wiles involved in all this? Convictions, indeed. Nevertheless. If The Weapon didn't get him, Hallazallah surely would've.

Shwarma scanned the vista of Zazaristan's southwestern plains. In the distance, he could just make out the never-completed Fort Worth Hotel & Casino Golf Course, which as everyone knew was located too far out of town to attract any business. The American helicopter that he had spotted just after he escaped could no longer be seen.

Whether the helicopter had been dispatched to capture him, The Weapon, Hallazallah, or any combination thereof, Shwarma

384

couldn't guess, but it was probably best he wasn't around to find out. Seeing the bird making a beeline for AJI had confirmed that his instincts to make today Getaway Day were correct.

And get away he had to. If the helicopter returned in his direction, Shwarma might be spotted for a second time, and he considered that risky. He started the bike and headed down into the valley and toward the coast.

CHAPTER 81

ZAZARISTANIAN AIRSPACE
MONDAY, 5:50 p.m. ZST

Monte leveled the G650 off, hit the cabin intercom, and said, "We're off ground radar. We'll hit the Russian fly-zone gap in twenty-five minutes." He had been surprised when Wiles did not return with the others. But Biz explained Jasper's intent to hand himself over to the military and arrive home shortly. She also vouched for Fareek, who had agreed to surrender his pistol to Monte.

Biz sat alone in the rear of the jet and wondered how much time Jasper had bought them. She had expected the helicopter to overtake them at any point during their dash back to the airport, but there'd been no sign of it. Was Jasper safe? Of course he was. Before Brohug drove away, she had noticed Hallazallah's truck starting to move out as well. He and his men clearly wanted no part of the American helicopter, whose mission was Jasper, not them anyway. The military team sent by Barry would have set down, scooped up Wiles, and asked a few quick questions. Biz knew Jasper would talk his "rescuers" ears off, without mentioning Chris or her, giving them time to run. That would also explain why there had been no communication since they parted. And she would keep it that way. The military most likely seized Jasper's phone, but fortunately Where'sWiles remained active and she could see that he was now moving south toward the Quudian border. They would see each other in a few days, Biz felt sure.

She was also confident that the FBI had no proof that she or Chris were ever in Zazaristan. Their names would have come up during the call with Brohug. Biz resisted the temptation to call Special Agent Sullivan, to try to confirm that Wiles was safe. She decided to wait until she was back on American soil with Chris. Jasper was OK. He had to be.

Chris and Fareek sat across from each other in the forward cabin. Fareek had never flown before, and he watched Zazaristan grow distant through the window until it suddenly vanished when the jet entered a cloud bank.

He turned to face Chris. The two had worked quickly in the chaotic few minutes they spent together in the AJI building, and now flying away, with the rush of their escape wearing off, each had questions for the other.

"Are you OK?" asked Chris.

Fareek nodded. "Are you? What happened to your face?"

"It was an accident." Chris said. "But I'm fine. Fareek, who was that other guy, Hallazallah?"

Fareek shrugged. "Hallazallah and his men are no match for your soldiers. He prefers easier targets. Jasper is with your military by now."

Chris allowed a small nod. "Yeah. But they thought I would be with him. They were looking for me."

"Why? Why did you come to Zazaristan?"

"I got arrested in the US for clicking on Shwarma's video. They thought we were planning an attack together. I came here to get out of trouble."

"I know the feeling, too," said Fareek. "I want no trouble."

"No trouble?!" Chris said. "You work for a terror organization! You've committed attacks all over the world!"

Fareek sighed. "There were no attacks. Shwarma is a fool and a liar. It's a trick. What Shwarma did was all just... just nothing more than selling stories."

Author's Note:
Ouch.

As Chris looked puzzled, Fareek went on. "He just shouts threats and takes advantage of accidents. It's a business for him. For me, too. It was. He paid every week."

Chris was shocked. MILF was a... a what? A PR agency? Just smoke and mirrors? "You guys got me in a ton of trouble," he said.

Fareek looked down. "As I said, you are not alone. My father was taken from us by soldiers when I was eight. A rocket hit my sister's school and killed her three years later. Our home was taken. I lived as a refugee for eight years and my mother died as one. No one likes attacks and wars less than me, my friend."

"I'm sorry," said Chris. "And thank you for helping us."

Fareek nodded his acceptance. "Where are we going?" he asked.

"California. I was never supposed to have left."

"Will you be in trouble when you return?"

"That depends. Open up that laptop, I want to have a look at these videos you make." Chris tossed his phone to Fareek. "Call Igor Poskovich, he's in the contacts."

Fareek took the phone and saw the lock screen. "What's your password?" he asked Chris.

"I reset it. It's two. The number two."

CHAPTER 82

SAN FRANCISCO, CALIFORNIA
MONDAY, 10:42 p.m. PST

It was freezing on the street in front of Biz's apartment. Colder than it was when she stepped off the plane, and she thought that was bad. She was wearing a red Wowiecloth kimono that Chris found in the plane's closet, but it wasn't helping all that much. What it has in softness and stain-resistance, Wowiecloth lacks in insulation.

"I only know what you know," Biz was saying to Chris as they exited an Uber. "I haven't spoken to the FBI since we left. And I don't know why Jasper's phone never left Zazaristan. My guess is they took it as evidence." She looked up to her curtained window. "I'll call to find out about Jasper when we get upstairs. Get inside."

With Chris and Fareek trailing behind, she walked briskly through her building's deserted lobby and up one flight of stairs. She opened her apartment door and stepped inside. The first thing she saw was FBI Special Agent Sullivan standing on her white suede ottoman, attempting to remove the smoke detector from the ceiling. He turned to see who entered and quickly drew his pistol.

Dick Barry then stepped into her sightline from the kitchen on the right, followed by Murphy, who also had his pistol raised. Barry spoke first. "Good evening, Elizabeth. Chris. Drop your things, put your hands up, and step inside." They did as he asked.

"Who are you?" Barry said, looking to Fareek, who also put his hands in the air.

"My name is Fareek Wazaan. I'm a refugee from Zazaristan,"

"You're aiding and abetting a known fugitive, Fareek," said Barry. "You could be an enemy combatant. There's a lot going on right now, it's all in play." In Zazarish, he added, *"Beware of new friends."*

Sully quickly frisked the three of them, and he indicated they were all unarmed.

"Sit down, everyone," Barry invited. Biz, Chris, and Fareek all squeezed onto the sofa.

"Director Barry," Biz began.

"Shut up," said the Director. "Why were you there?"

"Where?" asked Biz.

"Don't pull that shit with me, Byner. Zazaristan. Nice kimono by the way. Is that Wowiecloth?"

He had her there. "Is Jasper Wiles OK?" Biz asked. "Your team should have picked him up hours ago. Did they confiscate his phone?"

Where'sWiles had shown Wiles's phone moving away from AJI headquarters shortly after they left. It had stopped moving at a remote location in southern Zazaristan.

"Why did you run, Dawkins?" Barry barked, turning his attention to Chris.

Biz also looked at Chris. He glanced at her, then said to Barry, "I'll tell you, but then you tell us what happened to Jasper." He took a deep breath. "I went to Zazaristan. Against my lawyer's advice, though. She told me to stay."

Barry didn't seem surprised. He said, "And what was it you needed to do in Zazaristan?"

"Look," Chris said, boiling over. "The case you have against me is bullshit." He gave Murph and Sully a hard look. "We went over there to prove it, since no one over here was interested in the truth that I was innocent. There's a laptop over there by the door. It has MILF's entire operation laid out. Financial records, strategy, locations, everything. It's all you need to take them down for good. When you do, remember it was me who helped you. And Fareek helped me. Now tell us where Jasper is."

Murph rooted through the pile of bags near the door and produced a thick, black laptop computer.

"Wiles was recovered by Air Force Colonel Clete Roy," said Barry. "They're still together in Zazaristan."

"I want to speak with him," Biz demanded.

Murph handed the computer to Barry, who turned it over in his hands, opened it, and studied the home screen. "What's the password?" he said, without looking up.

"I don't know," Chris said. "I didn't set it." He leaned his head toward Fareek. "He did."

"What's the password, Fareek?" Barry asked evenly, staring at the young Zazari. "This can be easy for you."

"Do you know where their friend is?" Fareek asked.

"Yes. But first, the password."

"The password is *Qoomah*."

"Zazarish spelling?" asked Barry.

"Hazimish dialect," Fareek said.

Barry tapped out the password. Without looking up he said, "Jasper Wiles is dead."

CHAPTER 83

Biz wept quietly in the otherwise silent room for several minutes. She gripped Chris's hand painfully hard. Barry ignored her as he examined Fareek's computer.

He clicked and tapped, tapped and clicked, and at one point pulled a pair of earbuds from his suit pocket and plugged them in to listen to something. His face was inscrutable as the minutes drew on.

Fareek's head was bowed and he mumbled a prayer. Chris was silent as a mouse.

Barry eventually removed his earbuds, closed the laptop, and looked up. "How did you get this computer?" he asked Chris.

Chris tilted his head toward Fareek. "It's his. He agreed to help me if we got him out of Zazaristan."

Barry spoke again to Fareek. "Have you seen these videos?"

"Yes, of course. I have seen some in person as they were being shot. I used to work for Wahiri Shwarma in the building your military raided."

Murph glanced over to Sully. Wahiri Shwarma!

"Fareek," Barry said, "can you confirm that the content of these videos is legitimate and authentic?"

392

"Yes," said Fareek. "The men in those videos will do exactly as they say."

"Who else has seen these?" Barry asked. "Ms. Byner... Ms. Byner... Have you seen them?"

Biz looked up. "No. We deserve to know about Jas—"

"We'll get to Jasper Wiles in a minute, Elizabeth. May I call you Elizabeth, by the way?"

"No," Biz said.

"Fareek," Barry said. "Why do you have all these videos? Did you shoot all of them?"

Fareek said, "No. The other leaders send me USBs of their videos twice a month for distribution. They keep no copies, for security. Only Wahiri Shwarma and I have seen all of them. And you won't be hearing from him anymore."

"Dead?" asked Barry. Murph and Sully glanced at each other.

"Just gone. You saw the video. It's over for him."

"Where is he now?" said Barry.

"I don't know. Just because a man surrenders doesn't mean he wants to leave a trail behind as he retreats."

Biz said, "What? Who surrendered?"

Barry took a deep breath. "Chris, can we speak privately?" he asked.

Chris said, "No. If I'm back in custody, I want my attorney present."

Barry only thought for a second before saying, "Ms. Byner, join me and your client in the other room. Murphy, open the door."

Murph, his Glock still drawn, quickly walked to the bedroom door and opened it to allow Biz and Chris to enter. Barry followed them, gestured for them to sit on the bed, then shut the door. The curtains allowed just a sliver of streetlight to sluice in.

Barry held up the laptop. "The video files on here show the leaders of over a dozen of the most well-known terror groups in the Middle East and Central Asia, including Wahiri Shwarma of MILF, all vowing to disband their operations and reconcile with the West.

They forswear future violence and they say they wish only to live in peace with their neighbors. All of them used slightly different terms, but each one repeated the phrase, 'immediate and unconditional surrender.' Some different languages, but all the same message."

Chris's mouth dropped open a little. Barry said, "The War on Terror appears to be over." He paused to measure the reaction of Biz and Chris. "Does that surprise you, Chris?"

Chris said, "I guess so, yes." Biz's eyes flicked over at him, and then back to Barry.

"Drop the charges against my client," Biz said. "You think you could still convict him now? Now that the group you claim he worked with no longer exists?"

Barry said, "You know, for someone who didn't know what was on this computer a minute ago, you're pretty quick in turning it to your advantage, Ms. Byner."

Sixth Grade: *When someone offers you a compliment, say thank you.*

"Thank you," Biz said.

Barry said, "But the videos are only partly what I wanted to talk about."

Chris said, "What happened to Jasper?"

Barry walked to the window and took a quick look outside. "You never should've run, Chris. All of this could have been avoided." He turned back around. "I wanted to bring you back in quietly. We knew Wiles was in Taboor City, but there was no time to run a full-scale operation into a sovereign nation up the chain, so I called in a favor from Colonel Roy to track him down and lead us to you. Roy's a good man, but... his decision making has been... questionable as of late. Especially concerning the warlord Bashir Hallazallah. They've... crossed paths before.

"There was no intelligence to suggest that Hallazallah would be anywhere near the location where Roy found Wiles. But when Roy ID'd him, he saw a target of opportunity. Against my orders, he engaged Hallazallah. His helicopter went down in the firefight."

Biz said, "How did Jasper die? In the crash? Did Hallazallah kill him? Did Roy?"

"I don't know," said Barry. "He was lying dead in front of the building by the time Roy was on the ground. Roy reported there wasn't a mark on him. Hallazallah was gone. Roy took possession of Wiles's body, commandeered a van from the building, and tried to pursue Hallazallah. He's still somewhere in southern Zazaristan."

"Is he coming back?" Biz asked sharply. "You sent a lunatic out there and got Jasper killed!"

"Roy acted against orders. He's now considered AWOL, Ms. Byner. If it makes you feel any better, once he returns, *if* he returns, he'll be court-martialed and imprisoned. There's even a scenario where we all join him."

Chris interjected, "But you just said—"

"There are several ways this could play out, Chris." Barry held up the laptop. "Does anyone else have copies of the video files on this computer?"

"No, you heard Fareek," Chris said. "Now, just you. You can probably show those to the public and be the one to take credit for winning the war."

Barry smiled. "Chris, I'd like to release these videos and give the American people a big victory, but there are two problems. One: in Wahiri Shwarma's last message, the one you liked on the internet last week, he says something about possessing what he called the 'power of the universe.' We believe what he's referring to could be a nuclear device. Roy didn't find any weapon at the scene in South Taboor, but I can't ignore that this weapon is still out there, even if the group who possesses it is claiming to embrace peace all of a sudden. Two: Bashir Hallazallah did not appear in any of these videos. He alone is responsible for eighty percent of the violence in that region. If we can't recover the weapon, we can't use Shwarma's video. The public would never feel safe knowing there was a loose nuke out there. And without Hallazallah's surrender, we can't use any of them, because these groups don't speak for him. These videos mean nothing. It's not a win. It's not even a forfeit." Barry patted the computer. "So, I'm going to sit on these for now and you're still going to be my win, Chris. We're bringing you back in tonight."

"I know where the nuclear weapon is," Chris said.

Let this be a lesson against littering.

Back in Zazaristan, as Chris and Wiles snuck around MILF's garage after being freed from Conference Room B, Chris spotted his kebab stick on the floor where Walid had tossed it the night before. He picked it up and slipped it in the pocket of his dust-, booze-, tea-, sweat-, and more dust-stained linen shirt.

Minutes later in the Vanagon, when Biz suggested returning the package to Shwarma, Chris was inspired to try to track the elusive man who had caused him all this trouble. Using the sharp kebab stick to puncture and slit the packing tape of The Weapon's box open a few inches, he slipped Wiles's dented but still functioning Model XXI into the box before Wiles carried it off. When Shwarma suddenly rode off without accepting the package, Chris had been disappointed, but now his action was paying off.

"And guess who has it?" he said to Barry.

"You know where Bashir Hallazallah is?" Barry asked, incredulous. He looked at his watch. "Roy is still in-country. *If* I can reach him, and *if* we can recover the weapon and capture or kill Bashir Hallazallah in the next"—he checked his watch again—"five hours, by seven a.m. Eastern, I'll drop your charges, Dawkins. But not because I believe any of this. Once the news about the nuke *and* Hallazallah gets reported, and only *if* they get reported, you'll be small potatoes to the press, and they'll move on from you. Your lawyer is right. We'd never get a conviction at that point, anyway. Tell me where the weapon is."

"Where'sWiles," said Chris.

"Roy recovered his body," replied Barry tersely. "Where's Hallazallah?"

Chris said, "Director Barry, do you know what the white stuff in bird shit is?"

Barry said, "That's the bird's urine. Tell me where the nuclear device is, Dawkins."

Chris turned to Biz. "Is that true? Urine?"

Biz shrugged. "Sounds right."

Barry raised his voice. "Hey! You think I don't know what you do for a living, Dawkins? You think I didn't notice the rhyming in those videos? How long do you think this surrender story will hold up? I need it up there in front of everybody, then gone just as fast. The sooner we get Hallazallah and the recovery of the nuclear weapon to push it off the front page the better. Tell me where they are. Now!"

Chris looked the Director of the FBI in the eye. "I told you. Where'sWiles. The GPS app on Biz's phone. I put Jasper's phone in the box with the nuclear bomb to try to track Shwarma. If the box was gone when Roy got there, the only one who could have taken it was Hallazallah."

Barry wheeled around and opened the bedroom door. Sully had been listening at the door of course and already held Biz's phone in his hand. Barry took it and passed it to Biz. "Open it," he said. Turning to Chris: "How much charge was on Wiles's phone battery when it went in the box?"

Chris said, "Maybe thirty percent."

Biz held her phone screen angled away from Barry as she tapped in the code.

She handed the phone over to Barry. "The Where'sWiles icon is on the home screen."

Barry snatched the phone as he said to Sully, "Get a call through to Roy's sat phone."

CHAPTER 84

ZAZARISTAN/QUUDIA BORDER REGION
TUESDAY, NOON ZST

When he had finally made it back to the safety of his headquarters in the foothills of the Pir Mountains Monday night, Hallazallah opened the hefty, heavily taped cardboard box. Inside, he found a loose XXI phone and a hard-sided suitcase. He opened the suitcase and saw its odd contents. He could only assume that the phone was used as some sort of controller for the vaguely threatening mechanism and he noticed the phone's charge was getting low, so he plugged it in using its ingeniously designed universal power port. There was also a thin sheaf of paper, which may have been an instruction manual, but Chinese-to-Zazarish translated technical writing was notoriously poor, and Hallazallah hadn't been able to make heads or tails of the information.

The phone had taken a full charge overnight. Hallazallah was now searching the internet for a downloadable manual or anything that might help explain what exactly he had acquired when, with a sudden crash, his door exploded inward and a quivering, red laser dot appeared on his chest. Colonel Clete Roy stepped into the room. In rudimentary Zazarish, he said, *"From hell's heart, I stab at thee, Bashir."*

Hallazallah looked up. *"Do you mean America or Quudia?"*

CHAPTER 85

SAN FRANCISCO, CALIFORNIA
MONDAY, 8:15 a.m. PST

Superhero movie, furniture, lawn care, car insurance, *Hugh Strapman: A Special Report* promo.

The face of *HawkNews Morning*, Lillian Morley, appeared on the TV in Biz's living room.

"Historic. Stunning. Unprecedented. These are the words being used to describe the mass surrender of virtually every violent Islamic extremist group early this morning. According to FBI Director Dick Barry, these groups have been responsible for ninety percent—"

Chris clicked over to BSNMC.

"—recovery and dismantling of the nuclear weapon, believed to have been Chinese in origin. Chinese officials have denied—"

He turned down the volume and said, "They said I was 'not a person of interest' a few minutes ago," as Biz entered the living room. Chris had been anxiously watching the news at Biz's apartment since they had returned from the courthouse. Barry had arranged for some sleepy officials to come into work on a holiday to sign and stamp a few documents granting Chris his freedom as well as a renewable one-year work visa for Fareek, who already had a job lined up at Sixdub.

400

Biz was too spent to make the joke about Chris being of any interest.

"That's good." She had been in the bedroom making arrangements to bring home Wiles's remains. Biz had redrafted his will several months earlier, and in accordance with his wishes, he had been cremated. It was done in the basement of a military hospital in Germany. Biz had been sent an image of his body beforehand. He died with that weird look on his face.

CHAPTER 86

The news of the surrender and apparent end to the decades-long War on Terror brought great joy to all parts of the world.

Wherever people carried cell phones or had computers, the tweets, likes, memes, and comments celebrated the day as one of peace and unity the likes of which few could remember.

In Taboor City, a fiery vehicle crash that claimed several (goat) lives went completely unreported and unclaimed.

In Cairo, a man threw an antique phone in the trash.

In San Anselmo, that guy Kyle said to a woman in Starbucks, "What a day, right? Hey, I live right around the corner. Do you want to come over and celebrate with me?"

On an offshore mineral rig he owned in the Molokai Fracture Zone, Belgian industrialist Heinz Gossler, who stopped there on his way home from Vegas (Gossler was now the 638th richest man in the world) so he could write off the entire trip as a business expense, pondered the long-term global consequences of the Terror Surrender and made a few advantageous transactions.

In Madrid, deep-cover MILF operative Awamiri Waliq watched the news on the TV above the bar of his kebab restaurant and said quietly to no one in particular, *"Well, that's that, I suppose."*

In New York, HawkNews News Director Jed Newton muted the largest of the televisions in his office. Needless to say, he and his staff had been covering the historic events nonstop (except for commercial breaks) for twenty-four hours now, and he had not left his desk.

"We just led with the same angle BSNMC led with!" he shouted at his gathered staff. He pounded a few keys on his laptop. "And the numbers say public sentiment is matching. Over ninety-nine percent. It's not news if everyone agrees, people! How many times do I have to say it?! Get me something new!"

Around the same time over at BSNMC, Gwen Kelley-Shipman muted her own television and grabbed the phone off her desk and punched a short number. Newly promoted Morning Couch Producer Issandra Bowman answered.

"Issandra!" Gwen seethed. "We just said the same thing Hawk said! Almost verbatim! Didn't you see my memo about that?"

Issandra said, "We're working on it, Gwen. We—"

"If the new position is too much for you, Issandra, please let me know."

Issandra had some truth she wanted to speak just then, but Gwen had already hung up.

CHAPTER 87

Cell phone, cat delivery service, electric car, *Not So Fast, Mister with Lisa McNally* promo.

"A BSNMC exclusive this morning: breaking news of the once-billionaire-now-broke Jasper Wiles. Software tycoon and bestselling author Jasper Wiles is reportedly broke and has fled the country ahead of creditors. A video has surfaced of the cowardly capitalist running aboard his private jet... "

CHAPTER 88

NEW YORK, NEW YORK
THURSDAY, 7:03 a.m. EST

Breakfast cereal, data protection, food delivery, denture adhesive, *HawkNews Tonight* promo.

"Sad news this morning, as we begin our hour on *HawkNews Morning*. Jasper Wiles, software tycoon and philanthropist, has died. Mr. Wiles has been in the news lately... "

CHAPTER 89

NEW YORK, NEW YORK
FRIDAY, 11:40 a.m. EST

Internet service, razors, parcel delivery, protein shake, insurance, *The Downlow* promo.

"After a day of questions and speculation, Jasper Wiles's attorney Elizabeth Byner has agreed to meet with the press this afternoon. We go now to BSNMC correspondent Michelle Burch in San Anselmo, California, with the latest... "

CHAPTER 90

SAN ANSELMO, CALIFORNIA
FRIDAY, 1:24 p.m. PST

The day was sunny but cool.

Biz had made a statement putting the suspicions over Jasper Wiles's solvency to rest, now that his estate had been opened. She explained that the video of Wiles "fleeing the country" was a practical joke of sorts perpetrated by his longtime frenemy Perry Mott. The FBI had interviewed Mott to confirm his story and he subsequently tweeted that the video was an inside joke between friends that was meant only for private circulation, putting the matter to rest. Biz then quoted from an official FBI statement that had ruled out foul play in Wiles's death.

Then Biz delivered a statement on behalf of the Wiles estate.

She had taken off her sweater to appear on camera, and she shivered in the cold gusts of autumn wind. The heat of Zazaristan seemed a long time ago. It really was hot as the Devil's taint over there.

She ended the statement with a few lines from the introduction of *Place Directly on Rack*. "The horizon cannot be reached in one great and mighty effort. Make your efforts many and small, but still mighty."

She paused a moment, thinking of her friend.

"As I said, Mr. Wiles's estate is in good order and considerably large. After making a lifetime endowment to the San Anselmo public library, his last will and testament calls for the remainder of his estate to be liquidated and evenly distributed among every American born from 1982 to 2000 who has ever used a Sixdub product, all eighty million of them. Checks for $695.22 will be sent out in the coming weeks... "

CHAPTER 91

NEW YORK, NEW YORK
FRIDAY, 1:21 p.m. EST

Millennial America's windfall caused something of a stir at the news stations, but aside from minor concussions suffered by two junior producers who conked heads in the hallway while both running at full speed, operating five electronic devices between them at HawkNews, and the guy at BSNMC who had a heart attack, they handled it pretty smoothly.

News of Wiles's final wishes had set off a storm of tweets and editorial opinions ranging from outrage over the obscene amount of wealth that had been hoarded by Wiles the evil capitalist robber baron to outrage over the cry-baby socialist redistribution of the same wealth that Wiles the intrepid capitalist earned fair and square.

Social media hummed with people posting about how they would make use of the cash, which all led to a fresh round of humble-bragging, virtue-signaling, consumer-shaming, and obviously, more outrage.

There were also those who loudly proclaimed that they would *reject* their checks in the name of... well, not so much in the name of anything, more like just to do the opposite of what people they didn't like were doing. Believe it or not, that created some outrage, too. After that it became pretty hard to keep track.

CHAPTER 92

SAN ANSELMO, CALIFORNIA
FRIDAY, 2:44 p.m. PST

When Biz drove through the gate at Sixdub headquarters, she noted the dozens of handmade signs people had posted outside commemorating Wiles and his bequest. Most of the signs said, "Thanks, Jasper," while some read, ""Thanks," Jasper." Sarcasm is hard to get across in print.

Inside the building, she found Chris and Fareek upstairs in Poskovich's office. Chris sat across from Igor at his desk, Fareek on a small sofa across the room. The three nerds appeared to be having a grand old time, but they quieted down when Biz entered.

"We saw you on TV, Biz," Chris said, turning around.

Poskovich said, "After you made announcement,"—he spun around his monitor and tapped it to show Biz some wiggling graphs and code data—"internet traffic spiked. Mentions of Chris Dawkins, San Francisco Mall Bomber, Terror Surrender, Shwarma, Hallazallah, all down and dropping fast. Trending up are 'Jasper Wiles will' and '$695.22.'"

Biz shook her head. She and Dick Barry had a long talk earlier about how things could go. How they *would* go. Barry had been right. Gross.

She said, "Hey, Fareek, how's your new office?"

Fareek said, "This is actually my first day here. The FBI just finished interviewing me this morning. Igor said he would show me some office choices, but I can make do with just about anything. I don't want trouble."

Igor then scooped the papers on his desk into a file and got to his feet. He waved Fareek toward the door. "Let's go look now. You like window or no window?" he asked as they left the room together.

Chris said to Biz, "On my way out, I was going to the break room for a tea. You want to come with me?"

"Sure," said Biz, turning to join him.

As they walked slowly down the sunny hallway, Chris said, "Do you really think nobody will ever find out that I used my work software to lip-sync the surrender videos on the plane?"

Biz had given more than one assurance over the past few days. "Remember what Jasper said? People stop looking if they find something better. Barry's not going to push it. Now that Shwarma's out of business, an accident's just an accident. Nobody's creating any more so-called attacks with false claims. Plus, there actually will be less violence now with Hallazallah gone. You did that, Chris."

"You're right, I guess. Are you still going to work for Jasper? His estate, I mean. You could come to work here, like Fareek."

Biz shook her head. "Jasper's estate will keep me busy for a few months, but then it'll be an hour or two a month, if that. But I don't want a job here. I'm thinking of moving into patent law full-time, helping young inventors. That was the best part of working with Jasper, the new ideas, the creating. I'll be happy with that. What are you going to do? Now that you've resigned officially?"

Chris had accepted a year's severance in return for his amicable resignation from Sixdub. All those concerned agreed it was for the best to go their separate ways, on paper, at least.

"I have some ideas," Chris said. "You looked good on TV, by the way. New dress?"

Biz had her sweater back on, over the sleeveless navy dress that was indeed out on its maiden voyage. "Yes, thank you."

Chris looked down. "New shoes, too?" he asked.

"Mm-hmm," said Biz.

"Nice." They walked in silence for a few steps. "Do they hurt your feet?"

EPILOGUE

DUBAI, UNITED ARAB EMIRATES
FIVE WEEKS LATER

Things had really fallen into place nicely for Shwarma.

Creemee Tyme Frozen Yogurt had filled a niche in Dubai. Word had spread around the city that the fro-yo peddled by the clean-shaven newcomer, known as Mohammad Mohammad, was the best anyone had ever tasted. From a business standpoint, the new shop had two full-time employees and was on track to show a tidy profit in the first quarter. The future looked bright. Shwarma had kicked out his roommate a week ago.

When the UAE emir's teenage daughter dropped into the shop one afternoon with her religious minders and security team in tow, Shwarma sensed an opportunity. The girl was known as something of a social media influencer, and her endorsement of Creemee Tyme would be invaluable. Shoving his young employee aside, he stepped forward and said, *"Hello, to what I serve you?"* His Arabic was getting better, but still not perfect.

The emir's daughter ordered a small cone, peach. Shwarma made a show of serving the young lady personally, but he didn't actually handle the dispenser all that much and he made the common mistake of overflowing the cone slightly at first. He balanced the uneven bottom as best he could, then as a show of generosity to his important young customer, added an extra dollop on top to make up for the slightly curved and imbalanced fro-yo structure.

The minders might have chalked up to unfortunate coincidence the fact that the dessert looked remarkably like male genitalia, but when Shwarma handed it to their young charge and said, *"I enjoy seeing this go in your mouth,"* that crossed the line. They signaled to the security team, who quickly dragged Shwarma from the shop and brought him to the Ministry of Justice, where he was executed later that evening.

BONUS CHAPTER

CHAPTER 53

Author's Note:
Didn't see that coming, did you? Take that, Dan Brown!

SOUTH TABOOR CITY, ZAZARISTAN
MONDAY, 12:59 a.m. ZST

Shwarma had "invited" Wiles and Chris to spend the night at his headquarters. Zebar was dismissed for the night (overtime loomed), then Shwarma and Walid marched their American guests across the garage, up one flight of stairs, and offered them supervised use of the bathroom. The supervision aspect was novel to Wiles, not so to Chris.

Wiles said, "Think about what my Security Architect said, Mr. Shwarma. It may sound risky to you, but the riskier path is almost always the best. You said yourself the one with the information is the one that comes out ahead. To get that information requires risk. Risk for you, risk for us."

Shwarma said, "Do you think I don't know about risk? I run a global conglomerate. Do not let my humble headquarters deceive you." He swiveled his rifle across Wiles's chest. "Stop there."

They had reached an unmarked door. Shwarma addressed Walid while pointing to Chris. *"Walid, take him into the restroom."* Walid ushered Chris into the bathroom. Now obviously, one cannot polish a turd, but the smell of MILF's restroom would be familiar to anyone who's ever attempted it.

416

Shwarma turned back to Wiles. Wiles said, "This global conglomerate. I assume it was easy to build? Completely risk-free?"

Shwarma snapped, "A thousand have tried. I succeeded. I crawl forward an inch a day, Mr. Wiles. Never more, never less. Discipline, patience. These build empires. Risk is a fool's errand."

"There is always risk," Wiles said. "And there are always fools." Shwarma scowled at him.

The scowl told Wiles that the time was right. He had worked his way to the center of the circle. Any direction would lead out from here.

He said, "As Mohammad Mohammad would say, 'Man must live by his convictions.'"

Shwarma cut him off. "Stop! You said 'Mohammad Mohammad.' Where did you hear this name?"

Was Wiles hinting that he knew of Shwarma's secret identity? Could he know of the exit plan to Dubai? The fro-yo operation? This complicated things for Shwarma. If Wiles could locate and identify him once his new life was established, he would never be safe.

Shwarma tried to recall if he had ever said, 'Man must live by his convictions.' Yes. Yes, he had. In last week's video, claiming the donut shop fire in England. Building a bridge with the strength of your convictions, he had said. Of course, Wiles had slightly misinterpreted it, but Shwarma didn't expect this grinning fool to understand anyway.

Nevertheless. Wiles must somehow know that Shwarma also went by the name Mohammad Mohammad. But how? Could this just be a coincidence? It's a very common name, after all. No. Shwarma couldn't take that chance. He would never be safe. Wiles and his friend could not leave Zazaristan alive.

Wiles saw that the mention of Mohammad's name clearly provoked a reaction from Shwarma. Of course, Wiles still believed that Mohammad Mohammad, the friendly rug merchant, was one of Shwarma's employees, an access point to MILF. Dropping his name in the course of his negotiations with Shwarma was basic networking strategy. The reaction itself was encouraging, but Wiles also felt a sense of responsibility to tread lightly around the subject of where exactly he and Mohammad had met. The poor fellow was clearly a problem gambler, and it seemed ungentlemanly to inform Shwarma that one of his employees spent his evenings indulging his vices. Shwarma was at the arena too, of course, but he had admitted arriving late, and Wiles hoped he hadn't spotted Mohammad amongst the crowd.

"I don't know the man very well," Wiles admitted. "But I know we both value discretion."

Yes, Shwarma thought. *Of course. These two Americans definitely have to go.*

Walid and Chris emerged from the bathroom and Shwarma motioned Wiles to step inside. As the door closed behind them, Wiles approached the short, trough-style urinal and took his ease. He zipped up, then turned and said, "Do you still have that plastic bag with you, Mr. Shwarma? I require some medication."

Shwarma had Wiles's cash in his right vest pocket and his bag of pills in the left. With his rifle still raised, he removed the cloudy, wrinkled bag. "What is this?"

Wiles gently laid his hat on the edge of the sink. There was no soap in the dispenser, but Wiles rinsed his hands under the faucet. He splashed some water on his face.

"Trizortrin," he said.

"For what?"

"I require it to treat a... serious condition."

Shwarma glanced at the bag. "Later. Go," he said, motioning Wiles toward the door.

"It's very important I take it, Mr. Shwarma," Wiles said. He extended his dripping hand.

Shwarma met it with his gun barrel. "No, I said! Later. Maybe. Go."

Shwarma pocketed the capsules. Wiles slowly walked to the door and rejoined Chris and Walid in the hallway. He looked to Chris and quietly said, "You asked what our chances would be earlier. I'm going to say excellent. Close to one hundred percent."

"Quiet! Move!" Shwarma snapped, stepping behind them.

Chris looked over at Wiles as they began walking back. Wiles's face was sweaty. He looked tired. He had forgotten his hat in the bathroom.

After passing a few doorways, they were herded into "Conference Room B," according to the sign on the door. They were told to sit where they could be seen from the doorway. Shwarma stepped forward, still holding his rifle. He turned and dismissed Walid with a short bit of Zazarish.

"Think about what I said, Shwarma," Wiles said. "We know something about your computers that you don't. Can you take that risk?"

Shwarma was about to close the door but stopped. "If it's risk you're after, Mr. Wiles, I would invite you to spend the night on the streets of Taboor City without money, phones, or weapons."

Wiles and Chris glanced at one another.

"In that case," said Shwarma, "make yourselves comfortable as my guests. We will continue our talks in the morning."

Without another word, Shwarma closed the door and checked to be sure it locked. He wrote on the whiteboard to reserve the conference room for the following day, then went downstairs to make sure Zebar had bolted the garage door before he left.

EPILOGUE II

GOSSLER INDUSTRIES DEEP WATER
DRILLING PLATFORM
MOLOKAI FRACTURE ZONE
NINE WEEKS LATER

Walid blacked out momentarily when he hit the water but came to quickly with a mouthful of Pacific Ocean.

He struggled, gasping, to push the wet, shining duffel bag into the inflatable Zodiac boat. He flopped in after it, rolling onto his back. Black, oily smoke billowed from the superstructure that loomed above him, blotting out the tropical sun. A distant, buzzing alarm could be heard.

Walid thumbed the starter and the small craft's electric motor whirred to life. He prayed its battery would last the four hours he had been promised it would.

It had been an extremely risky job, but it looked like he might just pull it off.

He wished Zeb were there to see it.

STUDY QUESTIONS

1. Who or what was the antagonist in this story?

2. At any point, were you rooting for Shwarma to get away clean?

3. What would you say is the smoking age in Zazaristan?

4. Why did Biz join Chris and Wiles? There was very little translating done, as it turned out.

5. What does Chris Dawkins look like?

6. Was Jasper Wiles all right? Physically? Mentally?

7. Were the "Author's Notes" really necessary?

Author's Note:
The end.

Thanks for reading!
Please take a minute to rate and review on
Amazon or Goodreads.

ACKNOWLEDGEMENTS

I should begin by acknowledging that the practice of spending quiet hours looking at words on a page, imagining people and places that don't exist is conspicuous temporal consumption of the highest order. Modern writers and readers don't need to draw water, gather firewood, and spend every minute of the day battling the entropic forces of the universe. We are among the most fortunate percentile of human beings who have ever walked the earth. Most who came before us would only be, and could only be, interested in titles like *How to Subsist*, and later on maybe *Girl, Stop Subsisting and Irrigate Your Crops!*

The point here is that I feel very grateful for the life I've been given and those who have helped me along the way.

My parents provided me a calm and happy home with all the books I could read, a basketball hoop and a bicycle. If there was anything else I needed, I've yet to figure out what it might be. Thanks Mom and Dad, you showed me the way.

There were daring early readers of this book who I would like to thank. The Three Toms: Tom Hartman, Tom Malone and Tom Propp. I would attend a goatfight with these gentlemen anytime.

Thanks Mike Rosenbush, who built me a Remote Detonation Module in his garage and had the sense to not send it to my house through the mail.

Thanks to Dan LeRoy and Alexis Behilo for making me look good. And to Marty Moran for the incredible job of making me sound good.

Special thanks to the wise and talented artist Maura McGurk.

Todd, Nate, Heath, Kraig, Kevin and all the cousins, you all gave me a hand when I needed it. Thanks.

ABOUT THE AUTHOR

Mark has a degree in communications from Central Connecticut State University, which he parlayed into a job producing local cable television commercials. From there, he took an eighteen-year paternity leave and is currently a part-time garbage truck driver. He is a distant relative of 1980's French-Canadian pop star Roc Voisine and a ten-time winner of *The Hartford Courant* cartoon caption contest. He lives a charmed life in New England with his wife and two daughters. This is his first novel.